THE O[...] [...]OT

KANDISHA PRESS

WOMEN OF HORROR ANTHOLOGY

VOLUME 3

Edited By Jill Girardi
With Foreword By Gwendolyn Kiste

FRIGHTGIRL SUMMER RECOMMENDED READING
Check out a roundtable with the authors of this book at
www.frightgirlsummer.com
#FRIGHTGIRLSUMMER

Dedication

This anthology is dedicated to all those who love horror fiction regardless of their gender, race, religion, orientation, identity, disability, physical appearance or any other such constructs. All are welcome.

This is a work of fiction. Names, characters, businesses, places, events, locales, and incidents are the products of the author's imagination or used in a fictitious manner. Any resemblance to actual persons, living, dead, or undead, or actual events is purely coincidental. This book contains adult situations and is not suitable for children.

COVER DESIGN by Ilusikanvas
KANDISHA PRESS LOGO by Lisa Kumek
INTERIOR FORMATTING by Eham

Copyright © 2021 Kandisha Press
All rights reserved.

Table of Contents

Foreword by Gwendolyn Kiste 1

1. Heavy Metal Coffin - Amira Krista Calvo 3
2. Bodiless - Faith Pierce 12
3. Minor Malfunction - KC Grifant 20
4. The Incident On Asteroid 4 Pandora - Stevie Kopas 32
5. The Lady Crow - Lucy Rose 51
6. The Recliner - Marsheila Rockwell 58
7. Call Of The Tide - Demi-Louise Blackburn 67
8. Date Night Ablaze - Rowan Hill 78
9. Shell - Barrington Smith-Seetachitt 87
10. From Scratch - Sonora Taylor 96
11. Invasive Species - Dawn DeBraal 106
12. Josephine - Michelle Renee Lane 113
13. Lure - Catherine McCarthy 135
14. The Thrill Of The Hunt - Villimey Mist 146
15. Simba Of The Suburbs - Ashley Burns 154
16. Rippers - Ellie Douglas 162
17. Liked - Mocha Pennington 186
18. The Lady Of The House - Yolanda Sfetsos 198
19. Should Have Gone To Vegas - Janine Pipe 213
20. Atla's Journey - Carmen Baca 229
21. Nightcrawler - Ushasi Sen Basu 241
22. Little Sally Ann - Shawnna Deresch 248

23. Bramblewood - Meg Hafdahl.. 265

24. Cold Comfort - Amy Grech.. 286

25. Kiss - R.A. Busby.. 304

26. The Last Thread - Paula R.C. Readman... 314

27. The Letter - Lydia Prime 329

28. Piano Keys And Sugar - Hadassah Shiradski 343

29. Dear Meat - J Snow... 351

30. The One That Got Away - Rebecca Rowland 372

Foreword
by Gwendolyn Kiste

I've said it before, and I'll say it again—Women in Horror Month is one of my very favorite times of year. Ranking right up there with Halloween, this wonderful annual celebration gives us a whole month to commemorate the incredible accomplishments of female horror creators from around the world. And now in its twelfth year, Women in Horror Month is going as strong as ever.

Growing up, I always lamented the lack of female characters, both in horror and literature at large. While there are certainly many memorable women in books, there still weren't nearly enough. That, in large part, was due to a dearth of female authors being accepted in largely insular literary communities. But times have fortunately changed for the better in this regard, and more than ever before, we're finally seeing female characters in horror that are written by women.

That brings us at last to the book you're currently holding in your hands. This anthology features some of the very best names in horror literature today. A few of these authors, including Michelle Renee Lane, Sonora Taylor, Meg Hafdahl, and Yolanda Sfetsos, have written fantastic works that I've been lucky enough to read in the past, which made me particularly eager to check out this anthology. Many of the authors in this book, however, are completely new to me, which is every bit as exciting. There's nothing quite as important as ensuring new voices are being heard in the genre, and editor Jill Girardi has put together a table of contents that combines award winning and nominated authors with those who are just debuting in their careers. But regardless of how many stories they've written, this anthology proves all of these women are making their own unique mark on the genre. This absolutely won't be the last we hear from these thirty authors. In fact, they're just getting started.

It's also thrilling to think that this very anthology series is now on its third volume with two additional volumes already underway. I truly can't wait to see what Kandisha Press releases next.

Happy Women in Horror Month, and enjoy reading this fabulous anthology. I have no doubt you'll discover a few new favorite authors along the way.

GWENDOLYN KISTE is the Bram Stoker Award-winning author of The Rust Maidens, from Trepidatio Publishing; And Her Smile Will Untether the Universe, from JournalStone; the dark fantasy novella, Pretty Marys All in a Row, from Broken Eye Books; and the occult horror novelette, The Invention of Ghosts, from Nightscape Press. Her short fiction and nonfiction have appeared in Nightmare Magazine, Tor's Nightfire, Vastarien, Black Static, Daily Science Fiction, Unnerving, Interzone, and LampLight, as well as Flame Tree Publishing's Gothic Fantasy series, among others.
Originally from Ohio, she now resides on an abandoned horse farm outside of Pittsburgh with her husband, two cats, and not nearly enough ghosts. You can also find her online at Facebook and Twitter.
https://www.facebook.com/gwendolynkiste
https://twitter.com/gwendolynkiste/
www.gwendolynkiste.com

Heavy Metal Coffin
Amira Krista Calvo

He played every day from sunrise to sunset, sometimes long into the night, until his nails chipped and his fingers bled. The blood blended into the scratched, black pick guard, giving it the shine it so badly needed. Dusk until dawn, the apartment shook with violent reverb. I was always surprised to find the photos of Ozzy and Richie Faulkner still hanging on the wall. Judas Priest covers crescendoed like smoke from a fire, licking at the beams of his deteriorating bedroom. His room was always unkempt, food containers piled in every corner, stacks of Decibel and Heavy Metal Magazine turning to dust. I would encourage him to clean, to have a shower, or call his mother, but all he wanted to do was play.

His 27th birthday was the beginning of the end.

I wasn't with him when the guitar arrived. My shift at the hospital morgue turned into a double, and we had to reschedule the birthday dinner I had been looking forward to for over a week. His birthday and our anniversary were on the same day, and I thought it would be a good time to tell him I was pregnant. I spun a fairytale about building a home together, one with clean white walls and paintings of floral arrangements instead of magazine cutouts of Alice Cooper and Witchfinder General. Maybe when he found out about the life growing inside of me, the life we had made together, he would turn the music down, or at least wear headphones.

I called him when I left the hospital. We had an agreement that I would never show up at his apartment unannounced, which was difficult for me as he only lived one floor up. No matter how hard I knocked on his door, it was never loud enough to be heard over the music, but the buzz of the phone in his pocket was enough to get his attention. Miguel always answered the phone, but that night I got his voicemail again and again until it just stopped ringing. I tried not to worry, hoping he had gone out on a binge with his friend Carlos. On Saturdays they would hop from metal bar to metal bar, crawling around Brooklyn in their ratty black denim jackets and combat boots. Or maybe he was trying out his new guitar.

It had shipped from Mexico, an eBay purchase from a washed-up metalhead in Teotihuacan. The guitar was a cherry red Ibanez 1985 Roadstar, the axe of Miguel's dreams. The seller, who was definitely *un loco*, said the guitar was inhabited by the spirit of Xochiquetzal, a Mayan goddess of sexual prowess and a patroness of childbirth. "*Cuidado guey*, she's pissed-off. If you don't treat her right, she will come for your firstborn." he wrote in his cryptic confirmation-of-purchase email. That tickled Miguel. He was thrilled it had come from his hometown. He had always been one to stay connected to our heritage, using metal as a way to communicate with the ancestors, or so he said. "Metal is about death, Tati, and connecting with the dead. Maybe if I shred hard enough, I can open a portal to hell or something." That was his favorite joke, and I had made the mistake of laughing the first time he told it. By what felt like the hundredth time, I caved and told him that he probably could.

I called Miguel six more times on the way home. It continued to go straight to voicemail. I had always tried to be a calm, relaxed partner. Latinas had an unfounded reputation for being wild and hot-headed, and I swore to myself to never fulfill that stereotype. I had the patience of a stone, but something was crawling under my skin. The feeling subsided slightly when I walked up the stairs to my apartment – I could hear the hum of his guitar growing louder with every step. I should have been comforted knowing that he was home, but my arms still itched, and my head began to hurt. From my sofa, I could make out the song. The number of times he had played Ozzy Osbourne's Mr. Crowley for me was obscene; there was no mistaking it. As I drifted off to sleep, I grew further and further away from the music, only to awake the next morning to its insistent droning once more. I called him again and the music stopped.

"*Hola, quien es?*" His voice was barely a whisper. He almost sounded pained. "It's Tati, you *bobo*. I tried calling you last night."

He breathed heavily into the receiver. The drawn-out pause made me wonder if he was doing mental gymnastics to figure out who I was.

"Miguel are you okay? You sound really hungover." The pause continued and I could almost feel the heat of his labored breath on my ear.

"Uh, yeah. I'm fine. Come up. I have someone I want you to meet."

I loved Miguel with all my heart, more than I should have. I wanted so badly to tell him about the baby, but today it wasn't in the cards. I hadn't fixed my hair or my makeup, but it didn't matter. I just wanted to hold him. Maybe if I held him tight enough, he would feel our baby growing inside me and I wouldn't have to work up the *cojones* to tell him. Maybe he would just know.

The building hummed once more. Whatever he was playing now was far more haunting than the previous song. It filled me with an unease I could not wrap my head around. I never understood why the neighbors hadn't complained. The volume of his amplifier was always maxed out, and I had considered anonymously calling the cops on him myself on nights before an early shift. I never followed through. Like I said, I loved Miguel more than I should have. I could never break that bond over something as silly as a noise complaint. I simply got used to being tired.

After several minutes of aggressive knocking, Miguel finally came to the door. He left the chain on and peered at me, a foul stench seeping through the sliver between the door and the frame. His eyes were sunken, his cheeks drawn and gray. The golden-brown warmth had left his face. He was the color of cold oatmeal. His skin clung listlessly to his body, as if it wanted nothing more than to slip to the floor and disappear into the peeling linoleum. I did not know this man. He squinted at me as if though we had never met, as if every memory we shared had been a strange dream that left him years before.

"Are you going to let me in?"

He tucked a bit of greasy hair behind his ear and unlatched the chain, walking aimlessly into the bedroom without saying hello.

I followed him, just as I always did, and touched my palm to my stomach. I hoped our baby would never see him like this. His bedroom was dark, and I realized that it was the beating heart of the smell. Mountains of laundry remained unwashed. A box of pizza sat open on his bed, maggots dancing like drunken teenagers on a thin layer of green fungus. Bile rose in my throat as he raised his arms to slide his head through the strap of his new guitar.

"Her name is *Dama Malvada* – Lady Evil"

So, this was who he wanted me to meet.

I crept closer to him, careful not to breathe through my nose. "Can I see it?" Miguel did not reply. His shoulders began to tremble, shaking more violently with every step I took toward him. I didn't know how much longer I would be able to stand the foulness of his bedroom. I placed my hand gently on his shoulder. Miguel's skin was feverish, hot to the touch, yet he shook as though he were freezing. I opened my mouth to say his name, to say anything to get him to look at me. As suddenly as it started, the shivering stopped. The room grew still, except for Lady Evil. She glowed, pulsating in the little bit of sunlight that found its way through the grimy window.

"*No la toques. No puedes tocarla!*"

Don't touch her. You can't touch her.

Miguel's voice was a low, unrecognizable growl. He clenched and unclenched his fists as if stopping himself from shoving me away or tearing out my throat. His hair hung limp around his shoulders. It was thinner than I remembered. He pulled away from me, grabbing his black marbled pick and turning the volume on his amp all the way up. He locked eyes with me, eyes I had never seen before. He slowly moved the guitar closer and closer to the amplifier, the shriek of the feedback piercing my eardrums. "Miguel please stop doing that!" I cupped my hands over my ears and turned to run. Could the baby hear what was happening to me? To us? Before I could reach the door, Miguel grabbed my wrist, leaving the guitar propped up against the amp. The screeching persisted. A searing pain radiated through my arm and I tried to tear myself away, clawing at him, at his sallow, dead eyes. I could hear the baby's heart thumping, slowly growing louder than the feedback from the cackling amplifier. Something warm dripped from my ear. I yelled for help, but I knew no one could hear me.

"Where do you think you are going, Tati?" He sneered, all love for me lost from his eyes. "I told you I wanted you to meet her. I want you to meet *Dama Malvada*, the love of my life. Have some respect."

His fingers tightened around my wrist. I could smell his breath. It reminded me of the morgue. Sometimes the bodies that came in had gone undiscovered for days or weeks, and the odor of decomposition could not be covered by the formaldehyde that stung the air. The plaque on his teeth brought back memories of the adipocere that clung to the skin of long-forgotten corpses, and the bile rose in my throat once more.

"Miguel, please let me go!" We were caught in a tug of war, a frenzied dance to the beat of the baby's heart. He pinned me to the wall, his free hand moving to my throat. When I had awoken that morning, I decided that today would not be the day I told him about the baby, but there was something about staring the patron saint of death in the face that made me change my mind. "Miguel I'm pregnant!"

He cocked his head and slowly released his grip on my neck, drawing his hand back, a puzzled look on his face. That was when I saw them. The tips of his fingers were ragged, bits of raw, red flesh dangling off the exposed bone. The room began to spin around me, the rancid smell, the wailing of the guitar, and the gore all closing in at once. The baby spun in my belly. I had to run. I begged the ancestors to quicken my pace. I bolted through the door and I could feel them carrying me into the hallway and down the stairwell, the speed bringing hot tears to my eyes.

I couldn't tell anyone, not my parents, my friends or the police. No one would believe me. Besides, the cops don't come to ungentrified areas unless it's to lock us up. Desperate to catch my breath, I slumped to the floor and held my baby in my arms. I could feel her swimming, swimming to the sound of Miguel's guitar. The wailing grew louder and louder and no one did anything. No one complained. I sat there and listened for hours. I lay in my bed and listened for days.

Miguel played for two months straight, twenty-four hours a day, seven days a week. Ozzy song after Ozzy song bled through the ceiling and into my apartment. Each warbled note slid down the wall and under my blankets, making me itch as if though my mattress was infested with bed bugs. Now and then, he would play Judas Priest, but it was mostly Black Sabbath's Dio-era *Lady Evil* that haunted me day in and day out. Sometimes I could hear laughter coming from his room, the sultry giggling of a mysterious woman. I convinced myself I was imagining this; who could stand to be in that place with him? At the end of the first week, I went back to work, having finally fessed up about my pregnancy if only to get the time off. Mostly it was to escape the music, to escape the proximity to Miguel. I carried with me a guilt I could not shake. I refused to check on him. I refused to put our baby in danger. No. I refused to put *my* baby in danger. Maybe the washed-up metalhead in Teotihuacan was right. Maybe Lady Evil was cursed. By the fourth week, I started looking at apartments. If I continued to live like this, I would end up childless. I would find myself at the end of a rope.

One night, the music stopped.

The silence was abnormal. The music had woven itself into my daily life until I couldn't hear it anymore than I could hear the overground trains that rattled the building throughout the night. The quiet had become louder than the noise. I waited for the sounds of an ambulance or a neighbor yelling for help, crying out that they had found Miguel dead in his bed. The silence persisted. I knew it would have to be me. After everything, after all of this, it would have to be me who saved him, whether to admit him to a hospital, or see him off to the morgue. What if it was me that had to assist on his autopsy? Having nearly reached the end of my first trimester, I had grown stronger, if only a little. I lit candles to the ancestors every night to keep the baby and me safe from the darkness radiating out of Miguel's apartment, to wash me clean of his grip. The bruise had never faded from my wrist and it became a constant reminder that the further away we stayed from him, the safer we were. Yet the longer the silence lingered, the clearer it became that I would have to return to the place where the end began.

I walked up the stairs and down the hall, running each scenario through my head, all of them ending with a call for help. The closer I got to his apartment, the harder I prayed that the music would start again. I don't know how long I stood in front of his door, or how long I tried to figure out whether the smell that slipped from beneath it was spoiled food or Miguel's wasted body laying in a pool of its own melting viscera.

Pleading for the chain to be off its hook, I picked the lock with my hairpin. It was the ugliest thing Miguel had ever given me, a grinning silver skull surrounded by flames made of red and yellow crystals. I wore it all the time to make him happy, but it never grew on me. Why I continued to wear it was beyond my own understanding, but every morning, it whispered to me, and I slid it into my hair if only to hold on to what Miguel and I once were. At least it was finally serving a purpose. The lock released with a sticky click, the door groaning slightly as it yawned open into the empty apartment. The dangling chain clinked against the moldy wood. "Miguel?" I whispered, praying that no one was home. It would be easier to deal with nothingness than to answer for my break-in, or to stumble across a corpse. At twelve weeks pregnant, I felt that I wouldn't be able to handle anything more than silence, but I needed to put my mind at ease. Stress-induced miscarriages were common in the early days of pregnancy. I would not allow myself to be a statistic.

The only thing that answered my hesitant call was the dust that danced in the moonlight. An unnatural heat radiated through the apartment. The sweat from my upper lip was salty on my tongue. I heard a crackling coming from his room that made my guts churn. The doorknob was hot to the touch. I pulled my sweater sleeve down over my hand and turned it, terrified of whatever was on the other side. I pushed it open and was engulfed by a thick cloud of smoke. Through the ash, I could make out yellow and red flames dancing to the heavy drumbeat of Sabbath's *Lady Evil*. My disdain for the song was swallowed by my fear. I couldn't scream, I couldn't cry, I couldn't even say his name. The smoke stung my eyes, my lungs constricting with every arduous breath. Incandescent pains pinballed inside of me, and I could feel the baby flailing desperately. Was she gasping for air too? I had to protect her, but the fire called to me. I floated toward the flames, a fiery phantasm returning to the world of the living to find its lost love.

As I drifted toward the center of the room, the floor began to fall away from beneath my feet revealing a gaping, endless hole from which no light emerged. A shape appeared behind the flames – it was Lady Evil, licked with fire but never burning. Something was different about her. It was only then that Miguel's name left my lips, a whimper even I could barely hear.

Lady Evil hovered above the gaping black mouth that replaced the floorboards, her cherry red body shining brighter than the fire itself. I rubbed the smoke from my eyes, seeing her in all her glory for the very first time.

Her strings, vibrating with each wail of the Black Sabbath tune were greasy and limp. The smell of burnt hair coiled in my nose, yet Lady Evil remained pristine. Each tuning key was a different tooth, yellowed from years of smoking and overindulging on rum and coke. I rubbed my eyes again in disbelief; her bridge was a row of split, bloody fingernails, Miguel's fingernails. It was then I realized where Lady Evil had gotten her hellish red shine. She was covered in blood that dripped from her neck, no longer slender and flat. The waxy vertebra that replaced her fretboards glimmered with blood, the spinal arteries still pulsating as though powered by a beating heart. I reached out to her. I needed to know this was real. The closer I got, the more the baby quivered. I slid my fingers down the cool, oily strings, past each boney fret until I reached Lady Evil's belly. The flames began to lap at my toes, crawling up my legs and toward my midsection. I felt invigorated. From the guitar erupted a shrill, blood-curdling laugh as I touched the soft brown velvet of her pick guard. I traced my finger around its edges, following the curling old English letters that adorned her, a small tattoo I knew so well - *Tatiana, Mi Amor*.

The flames continued to crawl up my torso, kissing my shoulders until it reached my neck. I whispered to my baby, to *our* baby, that I loved her with all my heart, and she began to dance inside me. Someday, I said, I will teach you to play the guitar.

AMIRA KRISTA CALVO is a Ph.D. student at Northumbria University researching child corporeal transgression and autonomy in 1980s American biological horror cinema. They are the founder and head editor of Horror Chromatic, a website dedicated to intersectionality and the representation of LGBTQIA, BIPOC, and Disabled artists in the horror community. Their work has been featured in Horrorbound Blog, Death and the Maiden, BUST Magazine, and The Huffington Post.

BODILESS
Faith Pierce

I was twelve when I saw it for the first time. It was lying motionless, covered with a blanket up to its shoulders.

"Do you see that, Grace?" Mother Jessica said with pride in her voice. "That's your body. Your gift. When you find your match, of course."

We were in a long hospital room with narrow beds lining the walls, curtains drawn tight around each bed except mine. Mother Jessica had glanced around to make sure we were alone, sharp eyes sweeping the room for the tenth time since we'd entered, before she finally moved aside the curtains of the bed that held my body.

I didn't know what to say. I offered a noncommittal half-smile up at her.

"Would you like me to uncover it?" Her expression was strange and unreadable as she looked down at me. Not discouraging, yet not inviting either.

"No." I shook my head as the blush crept up my neck.

She smiled then, like I had passed some invisible test, and began closing the curtains around my body.

"I understand," she said, turning to walk back down the corridor , her tapping heels echoing through the room while my feet moved silently beside her. "It's a bit embarrassing, isn't it? Don't worry. It won't be too bad once you have it, when you're with the right person."

I wondered what Mother Jessica's right person had been like. If he had been kind, if he made her laugh. If she missed him. He was dead now, of course, but it was hard to imagine her ever having been around a man, touching him, being touched by him. I'd only ever seen her with girls like me, her arms held so close to her own solid body it seemed impossible that even air could fit into the space between them.

I was sixteen when the courting started.

Groups of boys, laughing and putting hands over the sides of their mouths to whisper to each other as they were led through the school and seated in rows before us: the glimmer girls. They brought noise into our quiet world, rustling clothes and thudding boots, slamming doors, and scraping chairs. But they would all fall silent and subdued when the Mothers caught their eyes and glowered.

All except one, my first year. He would return the Mothers' meaningful gazes and he would smile, unabashed and sincere, until they had no choice but to offer a reluctant, tolerant twist of their lips in return.

This one was nothing special to look at, with freckles and a large nose, but it was that smile and the joy that radiated from him that made me love him. And so I waited, tolerating conversations with the other boys who showed up each year and patiently watching as the other girls were spoken for and left the school in droves.

I was nineteen when my freckled, big-nosed boy asked for another girl's hand. I stayed in the dorm room for a month after that, refusing to meet with other boys, too brokenhearted to think of the consequences. Another glimmer-girl tried to comfort me, told me the man who eventually chose me would be the right one because he chose me, and that my freckled boy couldn't have been because he didn't.

I was twenty when they said it was time to leave the school.

"It's not that there isn't still time for you," Mother Jessica said. "We will continue to arrange meetings with young men who might be late in making their choices. Or maybe a widower. But we don't keep young ladies at the school after twenty. There's nothing else for us to teach you, you see. And we have to focus on the younger girls."

"Where will I go?" There were stories about where unmatched shadow-women went. The nicer stories had a special school, sad and lonely, but safe.

Others claimed we would be put out on the street to fend for ourselves, or sold to collections for lewd men to leer at in dark mansions.

I thought up another possibility on my own, one I didn't mention to the other girls because I was too afraid it was true, and it crawled around my mind at night when there were no laughing girls or kindly Mothers to make it ridiculous. I thought I would be sent nowhere at all. Maybe the Mothers had a way of disposing of their unsuccessful students; my soul would be erased from existence, my empty body tossed into a hole.

"None of the stories are true," she said, as if my thoughts were as transparent as my shadowy form. "We have lovely homes for unmatched young ladies. You'll still have a Mother to help take care of you and keep you safe. There won't be so many of us, but you'll be more independent. Doesn't that sound nice?"

I tried to keep my lip from trembling. I had never been outside the school grounds; that was supposed to happen only when I had been given my body. It wasn't something to be faced as a helpless shadow.

I knew there was no use, but I couldn't keep from blurting out, "Why can't I just have it? Why can't I have it for myself?"

Mother Jessica looked abashed. "That is absolutely out of the question--"

"Not to go out into the world without a mate," I interrupted. "But I could stay here and learn to be a Mother like you. I could be useful."

She was shaking her head vehemently. "Ladies may not have bodies 'for themselves'; they are a gift for your mate. You do not have a mate and therefore have no one to give it to. Frankly, knowing you harbor ideas like this, I'm beginning to understand why."

"I'm not trying to be improper, but--"

"That is enough. I will not hear another word about this." Silence fell and she waited, making sure I would not continue arguing. I didn't. I stared at my hands, tears running down my face.

"Now," she continued, her voice calm again. "You are leaving for your new home tomorrow. As I said, we will continue trying to help you find a mate. If you behave and are agreeable, and trust the process, I'm sure you'll earn your body in no time."

The house was a two-room cottage outside of town, tucked away from the rest of the world with a high fence. One room for the shadow-women and one room for our bodies, laid out in bunk beds, no longer kept in sacred shrines.

There were more than a dozen of us staying there, with one harried Mother Adelaide to care for our bodies, to keep us supplied and entertained as well as she could, and to chaperone when the not-so-young men came to visit. These men had none of the bravado and good humor of the boys who visited our school. These men were sad, often angry about being sent to the house of castoffs for being too old or too poor or undesirable in other ways; they came into the house with an air of having been wronged, full of entitled righteousness. I had no patience to match their ill-temper with agreeableness, and so a dozen shadows rotated while I remained to haunt the sad little house.

I was twenty-three the first time I saw a solid person that wasn't either a Mother or someone accompanied by a Mother.

I was alone in the yard. I had heard groups of children in the houses next door many times before then, but I had never seen them. Now, the first time I stayed behind when Mother Adelaide and the others went to the monthly service held especially for shadow-women, it appeared, as if it had been waiting for an opportunity.

It peered at me over the high fence as I strolled through the yard, and I started. I wanted to demand, "Who are you?" but my voice caught in my throat. I gaped at the small face; it belonged to a boy of twelve or thirteen, and he grinned at me.

"You're a Nothing Girl," he declared. It wasn't a question, so I didn't answer. I heard other voices begin chattering excitedly through the fence, and gathered that they had manufactured some kind of platform to see over the fence.

He kept grinning. "We saw those others leave," he said. "You all by yourself, lady?"

I glanced back toward the house, wanting to lie, but knowing he wouldn't believe me. I shrugged.

Before I knew it, he had been given a boost, hopped over the fence, and stood in front of me. I gave a strangled cry and leapt back, but he was followed by three other boys in quick succession. They formed a semicircle before me.

I had never talked to boys like these. I had never talked to any solid human at all without a Mother around to supervise. Two of the boys were taller and looked a little older than the first boy, the leader; one was smaller. They stood staring at me, brazen. To my shock, the leader stuck his hand out and ran it through my waist, something no one had ever done to me in my entire life. I gasped and stumbled back as he chuckled.

"Ha, awesome," he said.

They can't hurt you, I reminded myself. That's the whole reason you don't have your body. You're safe.

My stomach flipped at his next words. "So, uh… Is it true?" he asked, inching closer to the house. "Is your real body in there?"

"No," I said, too fast. He gave a wicked grin and sprinted toward the house, his companions close behind, hooting and laughing as they went.

"No!" I cried, following them but helpless to shut the door or lock them out even if they hadn't gotten there first.

I found them in the room with the bodies, staring around in open wonder.

"Stop! You have to leave," I pleaded. "You have to, someone will come back. You're not supposed to be here. You can't do this. It's against the rules."

I was praying that they wouldn't notice my body, that looking at the dozen empty women lying there would be enough to satiate whatever mad desire brought them here, and they would leave. But the leader followed my gaze and lighted on my body, covered to the shoulders, and his lips curled.

"This you, huh?" he asked, and he jabbed his finger into its shoulder.

I cried out as though in pain, though I couldn't feel it. I had never seen anyone touch my body, ever. Only the Mothers were allowed, and they did it in privacy, with the utmost respect, we were told.

He laughed at my reaction, and the other three clustered around, mischievous energy coursing through them as they bounced on the balls of their feet and twisted their fingers in anticipation.

One of them pinched its cheeks and pushed them up into a ghoulish smile. "Look, she's happy to finally get a little attention," he said gleefully.

Another ran his fingers through its hair, then pulled it and watched my face for a reaction. He must have liked what he saw there, my frozen horror, because he yanked it again and laughed.

Then, in one sudden motion, the first boy ripped the cover from the body. I screamed and covered my face. How could the first time I saw it be like this?

"Please, this is against the rules!" I shrieked again, but I was drowned out by their laughs and howls of amusement.

None of the rules designed to protect me were working, and I knew then that I must have brought it on myself. My stubborn refusal to follow tradition and find a mate; my foolish whim to stay home alone that day. Mother Adelaide had given me a disapproving frown when I asked if it was allowed, but shrugged her shoulders and left without me.

Through the humiliation and terror, a harsh voice bit at me—you deserve this.

The children's' hands began to travel over the inert form, squeezing and prodding. Turning it over on its side and exploring every crease. One of them pulled a bright red marker out of his pocket and began scrawling words and images—names of sex acts alongside dollar signs, obscenities, badly drawn genitalia—over the stomach, arms, and breasts as I sobbed.

"What the hell is going on here?" A man's booming voice cut through the room and we all jumped, the marker clattering to the ground. I turned and saw through my wretched tears a man, tall and bearded, maybe forty. Maybe he came from the house on the other side of our cottage. The quiet side.

"What the hell are you kids doing?" he asked, his voice a low growl.

"We were just messing around," the leader mumbled.

"Shame on you," the man barked. "Get the hell out of here, now! Be glad I'm not calling the authorities."

The boys fled, leaving us alone in the room, the man standing awkwardly in the doorway while I collapsed, falling to my trembling knees and trying to comfort myself that at least it was over.

He waited several moments before asking, "Are you alright, miss?"

I rose shakily and tried to compose myself. "I think so," I said.

He stood watching me in awkward silence, and I remembered myself enough to whisper, "Thank you."

He nodded. "I always thought it was a shame how they treat women like you," he said. "Left with so little protection, no way to keep a body safe."

I couldn't find words to answer and my throat was thick, my shadow-body shaking, so I only nodded. I couldn't stop staring at the exposed flesh streaked in marker and dirt from the boys' hands, and I wanted to beg for him to cover it up but I was too embarrassed, as though acknowledging the naked body would make it real.

Then I lifted my eyes to his face and decided it would be better, much better, if he would just leave, please leave, because his eyes had begun darting from my shadowy figure to the solid body beside him and in those eyes was something hungry.

"Our Mother will be home soon," I said, and my voice was false and desperate.

"Such a shame," he said as though he hadn't heard me. His voice had shifted, a new note of falseness and greed. "These poor bodies just left here, no use at all…" His eyes lifted to meet mine then and I couldn't speak, could only stare back at him in terror.

"I could help you. I could keep it safe."

He moved toward my body and didn't seem to expect a response, didn't seem to care what the response would be.

I watched in stunned silence as he carefully wrapped it and lifted it into his arms.

"It would be far safer with me than here, with so many other bodies to care for." He moved slowly toward the door with my body, and now he was watching me, waiting to see if I would protest, and my mind screamed for something to say that could make him stop.

But the objection rose to my lips and died there. It wasn't really mine to fight for, had never been mine, and would never be mine. And maybe he was right. Maybe this was another way of being chosen, a terrible way that nobody had bothered to warn me about—the real story of what happens to unmatched shadow-women.

The neck rested securely in the crook of his arm and I watched the head loll back over his elbow, hair swaying down his side. He turned and the body's feet brushed the door frame with a harsh knock, concrete and substantial. They had never worn shoes; I had never held a pair in my hands and bent over to tuck feet into them, felt the tight security of limbs encased in tangible warmth.

My eyes stayed glued to those dangling feet as he left. I wondered if he would put shoes on them.

FAITH PIERCE writes horror, dark fantasy, and other forms of speculative fiction. She's written a handful of short stories, and her first novel will be published with Crystal Lake in 2022. She grew up in a small town in Texas and now lives in Missouri. Find her on Twitter @faithepierce

Minor Malfunction
KC Grifant

The best part about her arm was the jealous looks she received, Madeline thought to herself as the awning of the sushi restaurant came into view.

Before entering the restaurant, she paused to admire her new model, freshly implanted that morning. When the technician had unveiled the polished cherry red arm in the outpatient room, Madeline lost her breath. She couldn't recall ever seeing anything more beautiful, with black accents swirling along the muscular limbs like abstract calligraphy strokes ending in dark grooves along the tapered fingers. So much more interesting than her old purple piece.

A woman with a baby strapped to her chest popped out of the restaurant entrance and did a double-take.

"I've never seen one up close before. What does it feel like?" The mom was older, well past Madeline's generation, a large percentage of which had been born missing limbs due to a yet-to-be-identified environmental pollutant.

"Great. The physical design itself is under-*actuated*." Madeline rolled the word off her tongue like an exotic dish. "Making it lighter and smoother than other models. This one isn't even on the market yet." Her dad had gotten her on the shortlist of beta volunteers, letting Madeline test experimental models for a premiere leisure-brand line of prosthetics.

"What's it feel like to have a fake arm?" the woman asked and Madeline's lip curled. She never referred to her arm as "fake." It was as real, as functional, as her flesh hand.

"Just like this." Madeline raised her flesh hand. "Only it's stronger and doesn't get tired as fast."

After the woman passed by, Madeline checked her hair in the reflected glass and slid the edge of her fingernail into a notch under one of the prosthetic veins. A little door opened, revealing a compartment meant for a spare finger, and she tapped out a lipstick case. *BloodBlastBlam*, the shade she had worn on one of her first dates with Kev.

She'd had the worse luck when it came to dating before Kev. Lots of guys got creeped out by her prosthetic arm, even if they tried to hide it. Their eyes said it all: *different, diseased, freak.*

Madeline heard a sharp crack. Her prosthetic fist had balled up around the lipstick like a vise. *Relax*, she thought hastily, the mental attention prompting her fingers open. It always took a few weeks to "synch" with a new limb. She took off the cap, glad to find the lipstick was unharmed despite a split in its case. She thought: *apply,* and the prosthetic slowly pressed the lipstick to her mouth. When she was younger, her pediatrician had taught her that mentally saying an action to herself would help her focus the devices for a precise motion.

After applying her lipstick, Madeline strode into the restaurant, spotting Kev at a table in the back. His brown hair rose, perfectly coiffed, over a sliver of augmented glasses. A blue nanoharvesting shirt caught and absorbed the light, giving him the opaque look so coveted by high-end leisure-wear designers.

"Hey babe," Madeline said, kissing his cheek before sliding into the booth across from him. "Happy almost-4-month anniversary."

"I cannot even deal with this week, TGIF for real," he said as he tapped glowing icons on the table. "My client sent back like ten revisions this week. I ordered."

She cleared her throat and lay her arm on the table next to blinking pictures of sashimi and cocktails. "What do you think?"

The waitress breezed by, plopping down two bowls of edamame and glasses of ice water.

"Sushi'll be out in a sec. Anything else?" The waitress puckered her lips, as though Madeline had set a snake down on the table.

"No thanks," Madeline said as Kev glance up at the waitress's cupped chest bursting out from a black top, tickled by strands of hair flashing like sunlight.

"Isn't this new model arm hot?" Madeline asked, pushing her lips into a smile. "Not even on the market yet." With the fingers of her flesh hand, she worked the sleeve of her tunic up over her robotic elbow, exposing the deep red.

Kev pushed his glasses back into his hair. Eyes like cuts of faded turquoise rested on her, sending a trickle up her spine. "It's whatever. You always look hot."

He changed the subject back to his client and Madeline felt a pang of… *relief*, she decided. It was nice he didn't make her feel like a freak.

"Oh, babe? My parents are visiting next month," Madeline said as the food came. She stared down at her sushi rolls, her tongue clumsy all of a sudden. "You should meet them. You know, if you want."

He chewed, waving chopsticks over the next piece. She didn't tell him she had already picked out the perfect restaurant, had already imagined it happening ten different ways.

She looked down to see her new fingers had accidentally mashed the sushi roll into a pulp, pressing the wooden chopsticks together so firmly she was surprised they hadn't snapped. She thought, *relax*, and quickly put the remains in her mouth. Usually a new prosthetic took a month or so before the self-learning artificial intelligence system and her brain adapted to receiving each other's signals and made her intended motions seamless. But this model had a new chip, something the technician had gone on about as a breakthrough prototype, meant to quicken the synchronization. Already Madeline could feel this arm improving in tiny fits, responding to her commands.

She ventured a look at Kev again. "We'll probably go to that steak house you like in midtown," she added. "Their treat."

"Sure, why not," he said at last, grinning. "Parents love me."

A few hours later, sitting in his Swedish-inspired kitchen and sipping pulpy OJ with gin, Madeline drank just enough to feel buzzed, but not so much she'd get sloppy and unsexy.

"You're so lucky you live by yourself." Madeline imagined making breakfast there every morning, scrolling through her friends' feeds in his cotton bathrobe. "I hate having roomies."

She popped open her lipstick again, using the reflective surface of his glossy black kitchen counter as a mirror to reapply. The sensors in her artificial fingertips picked up the finely grained texture of the casing, the jaggedness of the crack. The sensations sent waves of pleasure through her, as if she were stroking silk. In the dark reflection of the counter, the fingers deftly swiped the lipstick on. She hadn't even needed to tell herself, *apply*.

"C'mere hottie," Kev said, refilling her glass.

She giggled and followed him into the bedroom. He passed a lighter over the handful of pillar candles on his nightstand. She loved that he lit candles, real ones, for her.

After they stripped each other, she used her flesh hand to caress him and her prosthetic arm to brace against the headboard as she climbed on top of him. Once in a while, her eyes drifted up to watch the candlelight flicker in the dark chrome of the arm, the heady scent of vanilla filling her nostrils.

* * * *

That morning, she woke up to Kev thrashing next to her.

"Let's sleep in," Madeline murmured. He kicked her in the leg and her eyes flew open. She had slung her robotic arm over his chest to cuddle him but something was wrong.

She lifted her prosthetic and he shot up with a strangled sound.

"Are you OK?" Madeline gasped, turning on the light.

"What the hell," Kev said, his voice still muffled as the light bloomed. Red spread across his face.

Madeline's heart dropped to her stomach. "Let me see."

He stumbled out of bed and she saw it wasn't too bad. Just a scrape across his cheek, probably from one of the tapered fingertips. He came back, clutching a wad of toilet paper to his face.

"I must have been dreaming," she said. "I am so sorry, babe." None of the other arms had acted out her dreams; they, like the rest of her body, became inhibited when she went into a deep sleep.

Kev perched on the end of the bed and didn't smile, didn't say it was OK.

"It was an accident. I guess the arm needs to be recalibrated. I'll call it in first thing tomorrow, OK? Let's go back to bed." Madeline didn't like the way he was looking at her robotic arm, as if it were a dog poised to spring. "Babe?"

Kev continued to dab at his face, not saying anything.

"It's a minor malfunction. I'll get it fixed," she said, trying to sound light. "Why are you freaking out?"

"Just the thought of lying next to that thing again, ugh."

"That *thing*?" Madeline stared at him, not sure if she heard him right. "It's not a *thing*. That's me you're talking about. Any*way*, I'm sure the technician will be able to fix it."

He sat on the edge of the bed, lowered the wad of bloodied tissue, and looked at it. "Why don't you get one of those flesh-imitation ones?"

"Gross. Only losers who are ashamed of themselves wear those. It was an accident, Kev. Are you going to crucify me for an accident?" She licked her lips. "It's not like you never elbowed me in your sleep."

"*Hardly* the same, Mad," he said and closed his eyes.

"I said I'd get it fixed."

He was silent for a long moment before settling back on the bed, as far from her as he could be.

"Well?" she demanded and her robotic fingers twitched. "Are we just forgetting about this then?"

He mumbled something.

"What?"

"I said I think we should take a little break. A hiatus."

24

"A hiatus?" She laughed. "Who uses that word?"

He kept his eyes closed.

"You seriously want to take a break because of an accident? That's ridiculous, but fine, whatever." She rolled over, away from him.

It'll be fine in the morning, she told herself. The distance between them felt infinite, his body heat dissipating in the handful of inches between them. Maybe she *should* get rid of it—the thought only crossed her mind for a second, and she shook her head imperceptibly. He was just freaked out.

Madeline woke early in the morning, the memory of the word *hiatus* crashing around her, turning what should have been a fun weekend bleak. He slept like a log, even though she stomped as she got dressed. She wanted to be understanding; she *did*. She should be happy. School was going well, she lived in one of the greatest cities in the world, had a fantastic arm, and good—*great*—looks.

She slammed the door on the way out and thumbed in a request for an urgent, non-emergency appointment.

* * * *

A technician from the Bionic Medicine and Amputee Institute got back to her the next day, his face appearing on her computer screen for a remote check-in.

"Any issues, concerns, changes?" The technician looked down at something in his office. "Daily auto report looks good."

"One thing. The arm—it's totally moving at night," Madeline said. "On its own."

"Not unusual. Most motor activity is suppressed during REM sleep, though it's still possible to twitch or move a little bit. In that sense, the device is acting like an organic limb, which is a good sign. I can kick up the override signal during sleep." His fingers flicked at the bottom of her screen. "There, that should take care of any excess night movement."

"So this sleep moving stuff won't happen anymore?"

The technician nodded and Madeline let out a long breath, feeling the first bit of happiness seep back into her. So, she wouldn't have to choose between Kev and her arm; she could have both.

"Another thing. What if I, like, thought about flipping someone off but didn't actually want to do it. The arm wouldn't just do whatever on its own, right?"

"You always have the ability to override." The technician looked amused. "It's no different from urges in your flesh limbs. You can stop those, can't you? Oh, interesting."

"What?" Madeline didn't like the way the technician's brow creased into a slight furrow as he read something off of his report.

"The artificial nerves are doing very well, forging new connections in the motor cortex. Synch is better than average in fact; it is already responding to your subconscious and unconscious signals." The technician nodded, pleased. "This model is really something special."

Madeline nodded. "One more question…" she hesitated, and decided to throw it out there. Not that she would really do it. "If I wanted to switch to the older model, that's easy to do right?"

"I suppose," the technician said, with a tone that suggested Madeline would be crazy to think of such a thing. "But you do know how much these will be when they're officially launched right? Customizable, made to order, out of reach for most. We have a long waiting list for beta testers if you aren't interested."

"I am," Madeline said hastily. "I am."

They disconnected and Madeline hurried out of her apartment.

I should call Kev, Madeline thought as she walked toward the subway, changed her mind, and started down the city blocks toward his place. It was still early but he might be awake. Both of her fists clenched simultaneously, and knew she needed to talk to him, face-to-face, to straighten everything out.

It was possible he was embarrassed at how he had acted, that he worried she was mad. But she was a forgiver, she was benevolent. She had some errands to do in his neighborhood, anyway. She might as well surprise him and see if he wanted to talk things over. On impulse, she stopped at the next corner and got two lattes. *I am such a good girlfriend*, she thought.

In front of his condo complex, she sipped on her drink and scanned her social streams until a guy in workout clothes ventured out. She slipped in behind him and hurried up the steps. She got ready to knock when it opened, revealing a girl in black leggings and a gray V-neck. Madeline sloshed a latte onto the hallway rug as she stepped back.

His cousin or coworker. His sister, Madeline thought.

The woman shot her a smile as her hair seemed to flash with stored sunlight. "Excuse me," she murmured.

"Who are you?" Madeline asked, trying to temper the harshness of her voice with an unconcerned smile as she stepped past her and into the glossy kitchen. The girl picked up her bag and strode out the door. Kev's voice said something from the bedroom and Madeline hurried forward.

He sat in bed, shirtless. He didn't look happy, she thought, her nostrils catching the smell of smoldering candle. Not at all. Something fluttered at her side. She looked down to see her flesh hand shaking.

Who was that, she wanted to say, but she thought it would come out badly. She tried to breathe and wiped her hand against her jeans. She would *not* be the crazy girlfriend.

"What's going on?" she said lightly instead, pressing her flesh hand against her leg to stop its shaking.

"Madeline, I told you I needed a break. You can't just come in here like that," Kev said, almost tiredly.

"Did you..." the words died in her throat. She thought about the flash of hair. She had to get it out, even though it would sound absurd. "Did you hook up with that girl?"

She had to be an old friend who was staying with him or a sister, maybe. "*Did* you?"

He shrugged, and something heavy inside her dropped. It must have been her lungs because she couldn't breathe, could hardly gather enough air to get out the next few words.

"*What is wrong with you*," she spoke low and hoarse. She was shaking all over, except for her robotic arm, which twitched once, and then remained steady.

"Chill," he said. "You're acting as if we're married or something."

Madeline squeezed her eyes shut. He was supposed to meet her parents, but how could he possibly meet them now? She thought of the first time they had met, and almost reeled back. How could she have been so wrong?

"*You bastard*," she screamed. His eyebrows darted up and his mouth fell open before he regained himself.

"Wait a second Mad," he objected, the lines all over his face hardening. "We never said we were exclusive. I'm sorry if you thought we were."

She grabbed the closest thing to her, a stray pillow at the bottom of the bed, and lunged forward to hit him with it as hard as she could across the head, her knees twisting in the satin.

"Hey! Calm *down*," he snapped, and grabbed her flesh wrist, jerking it until she dropped the pillow. The feel of his warm hand made her want to burst into tears, but only for a second. He was gripping it too tightly, but the pain felt good, grounding. She saw it clearly, suddenly. He was jealous, trying to make her feel bad so he could feel better about himself. She stared at him, into his ice cavern eyes.

"How could you do this to me?" she whispered.

"You're overreacting." He shook her wrist a little. "Just chill." He shook her arm again, so hard it felt like it would pop out of its socket, and she nearly fell off the bed.

"What are you doing?" she shrieked.

"Stop shouting—"

"*Let go!*"

She had to do it, she would say later to herself, every night for a while.

Her fists clenched and the robotic arm shot out, faster than she could see, a liquid blur of red streaked with black. The fingers pressed, hard and strong and sure into his neck, and his hand dropped her flesh one.

She breathed out, relieved that she could think for a second, now that he was quiet.

"Madeline," Kev gagged. His hair was askew, flattening against the headboard. What had she ever liked about him?

"Shut up."

The prosthetic hand squeezed harder, and she let it. Kev clawed at the glossy red, his own flesh hand a mark of his inferiority.

"Mad—" His eyes were wide, too wide. His soft vocal cords shifted like strips of sausage under the grooved finger pads. The heat from his blood rose as the fingers plunged, deeper.

"I said, *shut up*," Madeline snarled, her voice ringing out. "I should have known. You don't *deserve* my forgiveness, you jerk." His eyes closed and he slumped. She let go, the red fingers arching and then relaxing.

"I *loved* you," she said. It was the first time she had said it.

Madeline looked at her hand, which rested calmly by her side, gleaming darkly in the sunlight that slipped in between the shifting curtains.

Kev looked like he was breathing.

She wet her lips and thought she ought to call someone, maybe an ambulance, maybe the bemused technician.

She rubbed her sore flesh arm with the gentle red fingers. It wasn't her fault, really. The robotic arm had malfunctioned; it had acted more intensely than she meant it to. Some grease from Kev's fingers glinted along the red forearm, and she wiped it with the edge of the sheet.

She pictured him waking up, furious, streaming complaints to his networks, maybe even—the thought ran her blood cold—wanting to call the police.

But of course, she would tell them it was an accident. The technician could explain how it was an experimental model, a medical mishap.

Panic suddenly rolled into her and twisted her stomach so badly that she plopped down on the foot of the bed and almost cried out. What if they took the arm away? Or booted her from the beta program entirely?

She sat up straighter and rested the red hand in her lap. She couldn't help but admire it, despite herself—it really was a piece of artwork, a twisting sculpture of metal and plastic.

It was self-defense, she thought suddenly. The arm hadn't malfunctioned, really. It had saved her. She touched the red wrist with her flesh hand. Tiny force sensors in the material fired in response, sending the signals to her nerves so she could feel her flesh fingers, the microscopic folds of her skin, the warmth and pulse of blood beneath.

"I had to do it," Madeline whispered. "He was attacking me." No one would understand what an ass he had been. She rapped on her forehead with her flesh knuckles in frustration, eyes falling on a candle and her thoughts racing, presenting her with different scenarios.

The blonde's hair flashing over bare shoulders, straddling Kev, his eyes closed in concentration.

Madeline going to class without an arm, people glancing at the bare stump before looking away, pity flooding their faces.

The technician walking away with the detached red arm, its fingers outstretched toward Madeline as if pleading with her to save it.

"Bastard," Madeline said, and the panic rose again, a blackness that moved in like a storm and clenched her organs. She straightened as the robotic fingers fished in the drawer, rooting among the different sized candles. She wondered if he had lit any for other women. Had there been others?

We never said we were exclusive. I'm sorry if you thought we were.

The fingers wrapped around the cool smoothness of a lighter.

She lit the largest candle and pushed it toward the curtain's rustling edge. After a little while, the flame spread out, exploring the curtain.

It would be up to fate, Madeline reasoned. He might wake up and escape. He would forget about reporting her arm, since he'd have to deal with the fire damage of his place.

And if he didn't wake? It was his own fault.

Madeline's red fingers twitched and she stepped back, casting one last look at the crumpled figure in the crumpled sheets who had crumpled her heart. But she would recover. She and her arm would survive.

Madeline paused at the doorway, the heat rippling against her. Slowly the hand crept into her side pocket and took out the lipstick. It thumbed the case off and applied *BloodBlastBlam* perfectly on her lips; she didn't even need to look.

KC GRIFANT is a New England-to-SoCal transplant who writes internationally published horror, fantasy, science fiction, and weird western stories for collectible card games, podcasts, anthologies, and magazines. Her writings have appeared in Andromeda Spaceways Magazine, Aurealis Magazine, the Lovecraft eZine, Unnerving Magazine, Frozen Wavelets, Tales to Terrify, The Macabre Museum, and Colp Magazine. Her short stories have haunted dozens of collections, including We Shall Be Monsters, Beyond the Infinite: Tales from the Outer Reaches, Trembling With Fear, and the Stoker-nominated Fright Mare: Women Write Horror.

The Incident On Asteroid 4 Pandora

Stevie Kopas

The crew of The Tyche sat gathered in the mess area, liquor sloshing up and over the sides of each cup as they celebrated the day. Just that morning, the research team had been collecting possible alternative fuel source samples from Asteroid 4 Pandora near Titania, but they stumbled upon an unprecedented discovery instead: alien life.

Dr. Chadwick Schore first noticed the lifeform. Even in the freezing vacuum of space, the creature danced gracefully along the surface of the heavenly body, a free-flowing blob that resembled nothing short of a fat gingerbread man made of delicious jam. The creature had noticed Dr. Schore, too, albeit a few moments too late, as the man quickly scooped it into his sample kit before it could escape. Schore's excited cries crackled over the comms, startling the rest of the crew as he screamed about naming something after himself. The crew agreed that of all the people in the universe who deserved to discover an alien life form, Schore was the least worthy candidate, but he'd pleasantly surprised them all when he invited them to participate in his research and share in the credit of the discovery.

They'd hurried into one of the many labs on the ship and transferred the alien specimen into a research container. Unlike when it was discovered on the asteroid surface as a shimmering gelatin, the creature was still and solid.

"Remarkable," Dr. Kelvin Whitney whispered as he crouched before the container. "The creature can undergo phase transitions at will."

"It could be a means of defense," Dr. Amara Khatri chimed in.

Whitney nodded as Schore joined him at the sterile counter.

"Of course it's scared," he smirked, pulling on his gloves with a loud snap. "Intelligent life can clearly sense when it's in the presence of an alpha male, and I'm not talking about ol' Whitney here."

Schore clapped the older scientist on the back and chuckled, but was ignored. Khatri exchanged glances with the only other female crew member, Dr. Kat Glennon, and she rolled her eyes.

"Nothing? Really?" Schore looked around, arms out. "Not even a snicker?"

"Oh, you're a roaring hoot," Whitney assured him, his voice dripping with sarcasm.

"'Atta boy, old man."

Despite his mask, everyone in the room could picture his gleaming, bleached grin spread from ear to ear.

Whitney ignored Schore again and motioned for Khatri to join him in front of the container. As she slipped past Schore she felt the palm of his gloved hand rub purposefully against her rear end. She shot him a glare and he winked at her. Her nostrils flared and she took a deep breath. Now was not the time to give the man any unnecessary attention; he was like a child, she hoped, in that he would eventually stop if he was paid no mind.

"What do you think, should we introduce it to a new organism?" Whitney asked her, snapping her attention back to the tight, purple ball that was their alien specimen.

Her dark, thoughtful eyes narrowed as she pulled her thick, black hair up into a tight ponytail. "Yes, one of the rats would be safest."

Whitney gave the thumbs up to Glennon and she jumped on the comms to summon Dr. Williams from the animal bay.

* * * *

"Earth to Amara, come in Amara," Schore waved a drink in front of Khatri's face.

Khatri, snapped from her daydream of the day's events and looked up at him. He'd wandered from the others at the main table to the small, fixed booth in the corner where she sat quietly.

"Mind if I sit?"

"Uh, sure, if you'd like." She motioned for him to sit across from her and shook her head at the drink in his hand.

"Fine," he scoffed, "more for me."

He downed the drink in his left hand and slammed it on the table before plopping down into the booth. He grinned at her, expectantly, sipping from his second drink. She didn't understand the man. She thought she'd find someone like him on a football field, maybe in a frat house pounding brews, or even on the cover of a magazine, but definitely not an award-winning Biologist on a research mission in space.

"So," he started, "you never congratulated me. You know, for the alien."

So full of himself, she thought, cringing inside. Maybe she should have had that drink, after all.

"I mean, everybody's celebrating," she said, motioning to the others, "but should we be?"

He frowned. "Why would you say that?"

She leaned forward and narrowed her eyes. "Schore, the life form is a hostile parasite. Under no circumstances can we bring it back to Earth. What's there to celebrate?"

He rolled his eyes. "Man, with an ass like that who'd have thought you'd be such a drag, Khatri?" He laughed and leaned toward her, causing her to sit back in her seat.

She sighed, ignoring the reference to her body, and continued.

"Space Corps will be sending a proper team to investigate the life form and the asteroid. Our mission is over early and your discovery means nothing. They'll NDA us to death and keep it from the public just like everything else that happens out here."

"Hey, but you and me," he waved his hand back and forth between them, "we'll know. And those guys over there, they'll know. That's what matters right now, right? Besides, if it comes to it, I'll blow the whistle and sell the information to China or something, make more money that way, anyway."

She shook her head and sighed again. *Unbelievable.*

"Doesn't it bother you that we have a dangerous organism on board?" She asked, a crease forming in her brow.

Schore shrugged. "Doesn't bother me as much as this little game you keep playing with me."

Puzzled, the crease in her forehead deepened. "Game?"

How it was possible, she wasn't sure, but he leaned forward even further across the table. She could smell the cheap vodka on his breath and she grimaced, her whole body tensing up.

"Yeah, Amara, you know… this game. This whole *serious scientist work thing* you've got going on, yet, you wear these pants that…" he leaned back and closed his eyes for a moment. "Oh man, you're killin' me with those pants. You know what I'm talking about. Earlier in the lab, you got awfully close to me." He leaned back in his seat and she relaxed a bit now that he was further away.

"Schore," she said, trying to hide the nervous waver in her voice. "I'm wearing regulation pants. And if I get close to you it's only because—"

"Because you want my attention." He cut her off, smirking and crossing his arms over his chest. "I saw you staring at me earlier today."

Her face grew hot and flushed, red with frustration.

"Hey, don't be embarrassed," he continued, leaning forward again, "it's hot, but listen, doll, you don't need to explain yourself, I get it. I just want you to know that hard to get isn't really my thing. It gets old after a while. So, let's just get things out in the open, shall we?" His smirk gave way to a leering grin and it turned her stomach.

She swallowed hard, paralyzed by anxiety.

"I want you, Dr. Khatri, and I know you want me too."

She couldn't believe he was actually saying these things to her. As a woman in a male-dominated field, she'd had to work a hundred times as hard to be taken seriously and seen for what she was truly worth. Her fellow crew members were world-renowned leaders in their fields and she'd looked forward to this mission for nearly a year. Never having met Dr. Schore before the mission, his reputation for being a handsome prodigy preceded him, but she hadn't prepared for him to be quite so deviant and predatory. And yet here she was, on her long-awaited first mission to space and staring down the barrel of sexual harassment she could never tell anyone about; her career would be over. She glanced over at the others, desperately hoping she could get someone's attention, but they were all in their own drunken stupors. She forced her mind to a different place as she fought off the rising panic in her chest.

* * * *

Dr. Williams joined the others in the lab, toting a small, white rat.

"Do you think it'll hurt him?" Williams asked, a sensitive, concerned tone to his voice.

"Oh, I don't—" Khatri started, but was cut short.

"Who cares, Williams?" Schore asked with a laugh. "It's a gross rat! Plus, you have like, a hundred of them. It'll be fine, now, hurry," he held out both his hands, "give the vermin to me so we can get on with this."

Khatri sighed and gave Williams a reassuring nod. The quiet, spectacled man reluctantly held the small carrying case out and Schore snatched it from his hands.

Schore transferred the rat into the containment connector and it let out a few squeaks of protest as he shooed him down the tube. The moment the rat was clear of the tube, Schore slammed the connector closed and the purple creature suddenly came to life.

The group gasped as one, too nervous to exhale. They held their breaths and stared on with wide, nervous eyes as the creature took on a slender, gelatinous form and slithered around the container, scoping out the rodent before it. The rat squeaked and scurried away in the opposite direction. As if the creature sensed its discomfort, it suddenly changed shapes.

"Hoooooly shit," Schore said with a loud exhale.

The creature was now a flubbery, purple rat similar in stature to its new roommate. The rat seemed to relax, letting out a few curious squeaks, and inched closer to the alien. It gave the purple shape a few sniffs and as it began to sit back on its haunches, the creature suddenly reared back like a cobra and in a flash of shimmering purple, swept over the rat-like a tidal wave. The rodent squealed and Williams hollered his protests as the creature began to force its way into the rat's mouth.

"That thing is going to kill my rat!" Williams shrieked. "Stop it!"

"There's nothing we can do, Robert, it's too dangerous," Khatri said, placing a hand on his shoulder.

"Holy shit!" Schore repeated, but this time with an enthusiastic laugh and a shit-eating grin.

The crew watched, stunned, as the purple gel disappeared entirely inside the rat. The rodent twitched a few times before finally lying still. As they were about to assume the poor thing dead, purple liquid began to ooze from its mouth and the rat twitched once before blinking rapidly and hopping onto all fours as if nothing had happened.

"What the..." Whitney let his sentence trail, his mouth hanging open.

The purple puddle took a form more similar to when Schore had found it. It was now a stocky, little creature standing on two legs with four long tentacles and an odd, hammer-like head. The rat went to its side and sat like a faithful dog would with its master. To the crew's absolute disbelief, the creature began to pet the rat with one of its thin tendrils and the rodent looked from scientist to scientist as if it were studying them.

"Is it- is it looking at us?" Glennon asked, her eyes narrow.

"It would appear that way," Khatri replied, leaning forward and moving side to side. The rat's eyes followed hers. "The better question would be, who, though, is looking at us... the rat, or the creature?"

"What do you mean?" Whitney asked.

"Well, considering the way the creature entered the rat and now the rat's behavior would suggest a parasite."

"Only one way to know for sure." Whitney slammed his hand down on a red button to his left and gas hissed into the container.

The rat squealed in anguish as the asphyxiant gas quickly put it out of its misery, however, the creature, not needing oxygen, was unaffected and simply changed back into a tight, solid ball.

"No! What are you doing?" Schore hollered, shoving Whitney away from the button. "We were just getting started here!"

"The sensible god damn thing, that's what I'm doing. As Deputy Commander while Holt is in suspension, I want this thing off this ship first thing tomorrow. Khatri, Williams, carefully, and I mean *carefully*, retrieve the rat and cut it open, I want to know what that thing left inside it. Glennon, write up the report."

The crew nodded as Whitney issued his orders and made his way to the door, but Schore stepped in his path.

"This is our chance at something big here. We can study this thing. We have so much to learn here. Please, Whit, this could be huge." Schore implored.

"I want the creature returned to the asteroid and then I want Holt woken and debriefed before we return to Osiris Station."

"Return?" Khatri asked, shocked that he was ordering the mission cut short.

"Yes, return. This is a hostile lifeform we've encountered. Space Corps needs a full report. Now, I've got a suspension termination sequence to start. If you'll excuse me."

Whitney sidestepped Schore, not giving him any further attention. Khatri noticed that for the first time, the overly confident scientist seemed cut down, dejected, but as she stared at him from the corner of her eye, she noticed an odd look wash over his face. The thin line that was his mouth became a sinister smirk and his stare burned holes in the back of Whitney's uniform as he exited the lab. The door slid closed with a hiss and Schore turned to catch her looking at him. She quickly looked away and busied herself beside Williams and the dead rat before her arrogant colleague could presume anything about her curious observations.

* * * *

"You've had enough to drink." Glennon's voice tore Khatri from her thoughts.

The tall redhead placed both hands on the small table and stared down at Schore. "You hear me?" She snatched his drink up and held it out of his reach when he went for it. "Time to turn in."

"Ah, come on, what's with you broads? Nobody wants to have any fun tonight?" He rolled his eyes and looked over at the main table, secondary shift was starting to trickle in for coffee. Williams was the only one remaining from his shift whose name he'd bothered to learn. He sighed and stood up.

Khatri breathed a sigh of relief. "Thank you, Dr. Glennon."

"If you'd like, we can continue this conversation in my quarters." He turned to Khatri and placed his hands together, giving a slight bow.

"I'm declining on her behalf, now go, turn in." Glennon shooed him off.

He began to stagger away and Glennon slid into the booth in his place. "You alright?" She asked.

"I don't get it," Khatri said, ignoring the question. "All his accolades and accomplishments, and he behaves the way that he does."

"Hey, just because you're a genius doesn't mean you're not a douchebag."

"I heard that," Schore called back to them.

"Good!" Glennon shot back.

"I mean," Khatri lowered her voice, "how is he even here? How is he still in the Corps?"

"Oh, that's an easy one, newbie. You'll learn that men like him surround themselves with sycophants."

"Amara, doll, don't let her fill your head with that man-hating horseshit she likes to spew when she gets drunk," Schore called over from the main table. Williams seemed to sink into the seat beside him, growing more uncomfortable by the second.

"I don't hate men, *doll*," Glennon shot back, "I just hate you." She gave him her best angelic smile and fluttered her eyes.

"You know what your problem is, Glennon? You just haven't ever had the right kind of dick." He sucked his teeth and gave her a wink. "I can fix that for you real fast."

Khatri's eyes went wide and she thought her head might come off with how fast she turned to see Glennon's reaction, but her expression remained blank. Williams turned away and hid his face in his hands.

"Fuck off, Chad."

Schore threw his hands up and backed away. "Hey, I'm just saying… you think you like women until you don't."

He finally left the room and the tension left with him.

"How could you let him talk to you like that?" Khatri asked, shocked, and offended on the woman's behalf.

Glennon shrugged. "Look, you learn to let shit from shitheads like that roll off your shoulders or you become the problem. The "pot-stirrer" so to speak." She made quotations in the air and waved off the conversation. "You just live with it, Khatri. You can't let weaselly little fuckers like him know they're getting to you, you don't show them you're offended or scared or intimidated. And you *definitely* never sleep with them. I know that's not what you want to hear, but that's the best advice that I can give."

Khatri nodded, looking down at her hands. She didn't realize it but she'd been squeezing them together so hard they'd begun to grow numb. She stretched her fingers in and out, sending pins and needles up her forearms.

"Now, enough of that. What's up with our little purple friend? I've got a bitch of a report to finish in the morning."

"Well, it's as I suspected," Khatri started, taking a sip of water and relaxing back in her seat. "The organism is definitely a parasite, but it infects the host by fragmentation which is phenomenal. I don't think I've studied an organism that literally splits from itself in order to infect a host. I'm thinking regeneration probably occurs at a rapid rate as well. What we don't know, and probably never will now that Whitney's given the order, is what effect the parasite has on the host. Williams and I theorize that it's similar perhaps to toxoplasmosis or horsehair worms."

Glennon raised her eyebrows. "Like, are we talking parasitic mind control here?"

"Well, we don't know for sure, it's just a theory."

"Damn, good work newb. Too bad Whitney is so by the book. We could really learn a lot from this thing." The short redhead stood up and clapped her hands together. "Right, well I'm off to turn in. See you next shift."

Khatri nodded, noting that Williams had also retired to crew quarters and she was the only one left. Her mind raced though, and she didn't think sleeping would be an option. She kept going back to the creature. Maybe, if she got up early enough, she'd be able to observe some more in the lab before Whitney returned it to the asteroid surface.

She started for her quarters and as she rounded the final corner she was caught off guard as she was spun around and pinned; her face slammed hard against the wall. She cried out, but her assailant pushed down on her harder and covered her mouth.

"You know what separates me from the rest of the people that I know?" Schore asked.

A single tear escaped her eye despite her best efforts to control her fear.

"I'm a man that knows what he wants. I'm a man that *gets* what he wants. I show people like *you* what they want and I help them get it. I'm a nice guy, always looking out for others and how to make them better. I make people better just by being me." He slid one of his hands around and forced it inside her uniform. She felt his filthy hand crawl up her midsection and clumsy fingers grasp at her breasts. "Let me help you, Amara. Let me help make you better."

She felt his hot breath on her neck and let out a muffled cry, willing herself to be strong, forcing her eyes closed.

"Please, no," she begged through clenched teeth.

He snickered and pressed himself harder against her trembling frame. "Nobody tells Dr. Schore no."

His response finally struck the right nerve. His cocksure arrogance lit a fire inside of her and she let out a loud cry as she mustered up the strength to push herself from the wall. She had just enough leeway to thrust an elbow back with all her might and directly into his stomach. He let out a pained grunt and doubled over. She spun around and saw the rage in his expression as he caught his breath.

"You fucking bitch!" He yelled and lunged for her.

She sidestepped his attack and backhanded him. She gave him a quick shove and wasted no time rushing into her quarters. She didn't care to stop and have another look at him this time. She slapped the lock panel repeatedly, in a panic, until she heard a familiar chime and a female robotic voice confirm that the door was locked.

She slid down the wall until she was seated on the floor and she sobbed into her knees. She could hear him banging on the door outside her quarters, cursing her.

"Don't even think about waking anyone, Khatri. It's your word against mine. You're a nobody, you're a nothing! I'm Chadwick Fucking Schore! Remember that." And with those final stinging words, he finally left her alone.

She let out another sob and wiped the tears from her face. She tried to steady her breathing and sat up straight. She couldn't believe she'd just fought back, but she did. She stared at the panel on the wall and considered contacting one of the crew members, but as he said, it was her word against his. She was sure she would be discharged from Space Corps and would never find a respectable job anywhere. It would be her shame and secret to carry.

When she finally mustered up the energy to get up from the floor, she took a long, hot shower and collapsed onto her bed. She closed her eyes and let the wave of exhaustion wash over her. The purple blob in the lab no longer danced through her thoughts. She didn't even think of Schore or his attack as she began to drift off. Her mind was a welcome, blank.

She didn't even hear the override chirp at the door or the hiss as it slid open because she was so quickly and soundly asleep.

* * * *

Khatri's eyes fluttered open yet her vision was still a bit blurry. She tried to move, but quickly realized she was tied down on an exam table in one of the labs.

"What… what's going on?" She managed to ask, her tongue thick and dry in her mouth.

"Relax." Schore's voice drifted to her from across the room, but he sounded so much further away. "I administered a standard dose of Pentobarbital, you'll be fine soon enough."

"What?" She was so groggy and tired; it was hard to gather her thoughts. "Why? Why would you…"

He finally stepped into her line of sight and she could see he was in full lab gear; face mask, visor, gloves, the works.

"I told you, Amara, nobody tells me no, especially not when it's something I deserve. Do you know who even helped you to get on board this ship? Do you think Dr. Whitney or Commander Holt said 'oh, hey, you know who would be a big help? A twenty-eight-year-old nobody fresh off the boat.' No, they sure as hell didn't, but me, well, I happened to like what I saw in your Space Corps data file. I'm the good guy here, and you have the nerve to treat me the way you did. You *owe* me, Dr. Khatri."

"Owe you?" She asked, her voice still weak. "Owe you what?"

"Everything." He whispered, running a hand over her tethered body.

She grimaced and chills went running down her spine. She managed to squeak out a hoarse call for help, but that only elicited a chuckle from Schore.

"You think anyone's going to help you?" He shook his head. "No, I can't take any chances, not when I'm on the verge of the single most important discovery in human history. Whitney was going to try and take this from me."

"I don't understand, where… where are the rest of the crew?"

Schore returned to whatever he was doing across the room, ignoring her question.

"Chad!" Khatri yelled, fighting her restraints, finally able to muster some strength. "Where are the rest of the crew?"

"Whitney took a walk on the asteroid. He was so eager to get out there next shift I decided to help him out a little early."

Khatri gasped. "You… you spaced him? W-where are the others?"

"Suspension," he replied, "for now."

Tears were trying to force their way from her eyes, this man had become absolutely unhinged. She tugged at her restraints. She needed to figure out how to get off this exam table. She couldn't bear to think of what he might do to her after learning he'd murdered the Deputy Commander.

He walked slowly back to her exam table, something in a small container in his hands.

"What is… Schore, what is that?" She squinted, desperately trying to focus her still unclear eyes. Her heart raced and the blood seemed to drain from her head causing the room to spin as her vision focused and she realized what he was carrying. "No," the word barely escaped her lips. "No, please."

She fought harder against the restraints, grunting, and screaming as the panic set in. She felt the skin on her wrists and ankles tearing and bleeding as she pulled. Schore placed a hand on her shoulder and leaned down, his masked face brushed against her ear.

"I promise, it'll be over before you know it."

Dr. Schore had barely opened the containment tube and the purple creature had already launched itself onto Dr. Khatri's face. Before she realized it, her mouth was wide in a piercing scream of terror, the perfect open door for the alien. She gagged and choked, the blood vessels in her eyes bursting as she tried to fight it from crawling down her esophagus. She felt fingernails pop off as she clawed at the exam table, her back arching and cracking. Her entire throat, and now midsection, were on fire. She thought for a moment she might be burning alive from the inside out, but, just as Schore had told her, it was suddenly over and Amara Khatri fell still and silent, unfeeling, simply unbeing.

* * * *

Khatri, for the briefest of moments, had lost consciousness. When she returned to the waking world, she felt as if she was floating in a thick, inky darkness, yet she felt no worry, no fear, and no pain. She felt slightly euphoric, strangely free. Her thoughts were scattered and somehow, she felt, not entirely her own. There was something else there, a distant, unfamiliar voice calling out to her in the thick, black nothing.

Find me. Follow me. Focus on me.

She drifted further out of the darkness toward the voice and felt a warm, comforting light spread through her body.

I am you. You are me. We are us.

The voice, assuring and peaceful, wrapped itself around every fiber of her being.

It sounded like her own, but she knew better. She knew whose voice it was.

It's you, isn't it? She asked, and without having to hear its answer, she already knew.

It was the creature.

I am you. You are me. We are us.

Somehow, she felt like she trusted the voice, but she knew the real reason why. Schore had infected her with a hostile, alien parasite, of course it *seemed* like she could trust this thing; that was its only means of survival. She had to figure out a way to regain control.

You can't. I am you. You are—

I get it! She quickly shut the voice up. She couldn't take the droning repetition. *What do you want from me? Why did Schore do this?*

He thinks he can control us because he thinks he traps the Origin. But the Origin is of the Origin. We are infinite. We are control. He cannot control.

I don't understand any of this. Please, how do I fix this? What do you want from me? She felt like she wanted to cry, yet the creature wouldn't let her, and suddenly the small, mounting anxiety that had begun to build melted away as if it had never been there at all. The creature was eating her fear.

You began to steal pieces of the Origin and we had to stop you.

She couldn't believe she hadn't thought of it sooner. The alternative fuel source they were sent to research, it was the creature, just in a different form. The Origin.

Amara Khatri, you are correct. You call us an asteroid, but we are the Origin. We are anything, we are everything.

Khatri didn't know what to think or what to say on her own as the creature continued to fill her mind with thoughts of its own. She rapidly learned its history and discovered that the creature was nearly as old as the universe itself. The Origin. It was part of the infinite life cycle of all the universe, of space, of time. It ate away weakness, it kept things balanced, it kept things pure.

Suddenly, a sharp, white-hot pain spread through her face and she was sucked from the tranquil darkness.

As her vision focused and the harsh laboratory lights brought everything into view, she realized Schore had slapped her clear across her face.

"There you are," he said, grabbing her face by the chin and staring down at her. "Thought I'd lost you for a minute there."

She could only manage to stare up at him, she tried to speak, tried to move, but found that she couldn't. The creature wouldn't allow it.

He held up the small transport container that held the purple creature that had undoubtedly oozed from her mouth as it had from the rat's. He tapped on the container and his eyes creased in the corners, a big smile spreading under his masked face.

Khatri twitched slightly in response.

"That's right," he cooed, "I've got the rest of your buddy in here, and I'm prepared to do all sorts of wrong to it if you don't cooperate."

Her body involuntarily twitched again.

What do you want from me? Khatri asked the creature inside of her.

To save your species.

From what? She asked, her own voice desperate and wild in her head.

Yourselves.

"Alright, now I'm going to untie you, but you're not going to stand up until I'm clear across the room. Understood?" Schore stood and waited a moment, but Khatri's expressionless face just stared up at him. "Good enough for me."

He undid her tethers and then bolted, transport container in hand, to the far side of the room. Khatri remained on her back until suddenly she flew up into a sitting position and slowly, her torso turned toward Schore.

"Christ, that's fucking freaky," he said, a sick pleasure in his voice.

Will you help us, Amara Khatri?

Help you what? She asked.

Save your species.

"Stand up and turn toward me," Schore ordered Khatri, and, unable to control her own body, the creature within her obliged.

He pulled his mask and safety visor away and she could now see the sick, twisted smile on the man's face.

"Remove your uniform."

No, please, why are you doing this to me? She implored, she wanted to scream and cry, yet her fingers were making their way to the clasps on her uniform, preparing to remove it.

You are doing this, Amara Khatri. You are playing the passenger.

Its answer puzzled her. *I don't understand, please, how could I be doing this? It is safe, it is easy. But it is wrong.*

She felt her shoulder and right arm slide out and soon the left followed.

Please, make it stop! She begged the creature.

You can stop it. Make it stop like you did before.

She thought back to how she stopped his attack outside her quarters.

Help us save your species from itself.

She felt a strange sensation in her head, a burning fire again like she'd felt in her throat earlier. She slipped her uniform off and felt herself stepping out of it. She wasn't in control, yet she was. Were these thoughts her own, or the creature's? It all blended together and she could no longer differentiate between the two. Who was in control? Who was helping who?

Her head swam and burned and buzzed all at once and she begged for it all to stop and found herself answering her own pleas.

So, then make it stop.

She froze, staring straight ahead at Dr. Schore. She suddenly felt the chill of the room on her skin and felt the gooseflesh spreading on her extremities. Schore ordered her to cross the room and come to him. She knew she didn't have to, but she did it anyway, ensuring that she could get just close enough.

She could see the bulge in his white lab pants and though she was disgusted by it, she no longer felt any impending dread or discomfort because of him. Her nerves were calm, and as she approached him in her underwear, she'd never felt more in control.

They stared at one another for a moment before he placed his hand on his erection and ordered her to kiss him.

Will you help us, Amara Khatri?

Yes.

As she pressed her open mouth onto his, the awful, wretched burning was there again, the horrendous acid creeping up her throat. Without warning, it was bursting from her mouth into his. The purple creature was purging itself from her body. She screamed uncontrollably as it left her, the pain nearly unbearable, but it was a healing pain, like no other she'd ever felt before, and soon it was soothing and welcome as the last of the creature emptied itself from her vessel.

Chadwick Schore's body fell in a heap to the floor, convulsing. His white lab pants were soon filthy with his own excrement and his face swelled like a balloon, eyes bulging from their sockets, blood trickling from every orifice she could see. He could barely manage a squeak as the creature grew in his throat, stretching and cracking his windpipe and esophagus. His skin turned a strange, reddish-purple hue before beginning to crack and bleed as the creature continued to expand within him. He gurgled and his eyes rolled into the back of his head, his arms flopping lifelessly at his sides as his torso exploded, sending viscera and gore in every direction; the laboratory painted with Dr. Schore.

Khatri stood staring down at the ghastly mess at her feet, but she felt nothing. Of all the people she knew who deserved such a fate, he was the worthiest candidate.

A shimmering, purple puddle gathered outside Schore's lifeless body and slid over to the container with the rest of the creature. Khatri crouched down and opened it, allowing the fragmented gelatin to reunite. She could feel them throughout her as they rejoined and realized, though small, a piece of the creature remained.

"You aren't a parasite," she said, looking down at her piece of the Origin.

The purple blob bobbed and danced in response.

"You're a symbiote."

From the moment it had entered her, the creature sensed the immense strength in Khatri that had been buried by a world so keen on weakening her. The creature knew a deep, unwavering strength like that could help them with their objective. Khatri knew that the creature would never hurt her; it would continue to eat her weakness and feed her strength, it would aid her, help her overcome her shortcomings, and be the woman she was meant to be. Together they would become the perfect host to lead the better world that they would create.

* * * *

Khatri made her way to the central computer, stopping briefly along the way to check on the suspension pods. Satisfied that the crew was safe and sound, she injected some of the creature into each pod's nutrient filter. Now that she knew the true intent of the creature, it wasn't such a sinister act at all, was it?

She was sure it was her idea and her idea alone.

She logged on to the flight planner and overrode Whitney's flight path, instead ordering the computer to bypass Osiris Station and head straight for Earth. They'd extracted enough of the Origin for their initial fuel research that she could begin her work immediately.

And there was much work to be done.

STEVIE KOPAS was born and raised in New Jersey. She is a gamer, a writer, reviewer, and an apocalypse enthusiast. Stevie will never turn down a good cup of coffee and might even be a bit of a caffeine addict. She is the author of bestselling dystopian series The Breadwinner Trilogy, Never Say Die, Slashvivor, and other bodies of work. You can follow her on Twitter @apacotaco, Instagram @theapacotaco, facebook.com/thebreadwinnertrilogy.

Her official website is http://someonereadthis.com. She currently resides in East Tennessee with her husband, son, and stinky old dog.

The Lady Crow

Lucy Rose

Cumberland, England. 1950's.

It was a normal day when the Crow came to visit Meriwether Woodrow at her window. It had been watching her for a while, mornings and evenings, to learn about her routine. Today was no different than any other.

Meriwether was cleaning the kitchen, cleaning away, washing up, and polishing every surface until it shone like marble. Not one speck of dust would remain by the time her husband returned from his trip.

The kitchen sparkled and she'd prepared a tray of canapés and a bottle of whisky ready for his arrival. All she needed to do was lay them out for him in the living room – on the table beside his favourite armchair. It was a place he sank in to enjoy a cigarette and the cricket tournament commentaries from the radio. Despite the clean and presentable disposition of the house, the wallpaper was cluttered with kitsch floral patterns. It was over-decorated, and each room had one too many pieces of furniture inside it. Cigarette smoke had buried itself into all the fibres of the soft furnishings. It seemed the house had a gift for remembering all the smells that had floundered on the air inside of it. Namely, it was the smell of smoke, because much like her husband, Meriwether loved the relief a single cigarette could give her. It was a medicine for her solitude.

Though she missed her husband, she did not miss his cruel words and hands. The trip, and the space it had given them both, made Meriwether realise how she had become repulsed by her marriage and how their distance was dry instead of longing. Their passions had become misplaced.

She'd never seen the marble floors shine the way they did now and yet she continued to clean. Any tarnish or stain had been wiped away. Meriwether had a talent for forgiveness. Forgiving stubborn stains and mould and forgiving her husband. Despite her good, she still had wicked thoughts of closing her eyes, pressing her finger down onto a map, and driving to that new place, no matter how many counties she had to cross to get there.

All that was left to do was to make herself look beautiful and wash a few more plates and then everything would be perfect. Perhaps then, her husband would love her again the way he did when they had met. His eyes would sparkle again at the sight of her in rouge, the way they had in their youth.

Meriwether, taking off her apron, hurried upstairs and opened her wardrobe. Her husband always liked her in the red dress, with the red lipstick. It is how she had looked the night they met. He was ten years older than she was, and when their eyes met, all at once the world stopped turning. All the lights around them went out and all the people disappeared. It was everything you hear about in stories of great love and Meriwether prided herself and her marriage on that story. It was in part the reason she stayed. Juliet would not leave Romeo. She would die one day but she would have died loving greatly, like Jane and Mr. Rochester, whom she read of every few months in private.

Meriwether loved books, but her husband hated them.

They clutter the house and gather dust and, by God, the smell. I can't abide them, they will have to go, he once said and so the next day, they were gone. She and her husband took them to a charity shop in the nearest town and she grieved for them over the coming weeks.

There was one book that escaped with its life – pages, spine, and body intact. Jane Eyre. She loved the line about being a bird being ensnared by a net. It became a hymn through the dark days. While they were at church and they sang the lord's hymns, she would think of that book, and of how thankful she was she could still have its words.

She kept the book hidden and when her husband wasn't around, she'd put her nose between the pages and take a heaving breath. It relaxed her, more so than holidays or a nice cup of tea. Sometimes, when she had more time, for instance, while the husband had been on the trip, she could manage a few chapters, or if she had time, the whole book.

Meriwether took the red dress and pulled it over her body. It was a little bit tight. She wasn't fifteen anymore, but he loved the dress, and so she would wear it, no matter if it hurt or looked foolish. Sitting by the mirror, she brushed her hair and tied it into a conservative bun before dragging a rouge lipstick across her lips and puckering them in the mirror.

'Oh George, I'm so happy to have you home, dear,' she feigned joy in the mirror, practicing a seamless wifely routine. She had always wanted an all-American housewife smile but all she could muster was a tired sense of northern charm. 'You must be so tired, why don't you sit? I'll get you a whiskey,' she said and then touched her cheek with her hand as if it was his.

Meriwether longed for intimacy, but it wasn't the thing she needed the most. It was a temporary rush, a short-term fix, and she knew that. 'I love you,' she said, tracing the contour of her mouth with her fingers. 'I love you,' she breathed again. She held onto those words in the same way she treasured postcards from her husband's trips away. He had had six now – each organised after a savage argument about work or money or children, though they argued mostly about reputation. Her husband reminded her she needed to make more of an effort so as not to tarnish the way his peers saw him. She kept all the postcards in a box and when she was alone in her solitude, she would take them out and one by one, trace each letter with her fingertips and press a kiss on her husband's sign-off at the end.

All the postcards were short and to the point. They were all the same.

Dear Meriwether, I hope all is well in Cumberland. I will hopefully be home soon. I am enjoying the sun and golf very much. I am teeing off soon. I will write again.

Loving Regards,
Your husband

When she read *Loving Regards*, her throat filled with bile and her breath caught on her gullet because none of his words had held loving regard since the day of their wedding.

It was the happiest day of her life but had grown into a bittersweet memory.

Meriwether took one last glance at her reflection and made a silent promise to pretend she was a happy wife, which is a very specific kind of happiness. Through all the years of her marriage, she'd never encountered the feeling of euphoric happiness that some of the other wives discuss, perhaps they too lied about their matrimony.

* * * *

Meriwether was back in the kitchen, taking plates from the cupboard and placing them on the table when she heard a tap at her window. At first, she ignored the tap, but it became a nuisance as she straightened out cutlery and plates. The tapping noise cut through the quiet once again until Meriwether, losing her nerve, went to the window and thrust it open.

Pushing her head out into the cold air, she couldn't source whatever creature was responsible for making the noise until, in a flurry and blur of midnight feathers, a crow flew past her and into the house.

Meriwether shrieked, pulling back from the window and grabbing a broomstick in her grasp. Wielding the broomstick close, she looked up into the high ceilings of the kitchen and glared at the crow hovering above.

'Get out!' she shrieked. 'Get out, get out, get out you vexing creature!'

Thank god that at least there wasn't a murder of them, for Meriwether would be outnumbered. The crow parted its beak and spoke.

'Can I stay? Only for a while.' From the beak of the feathery beast, came the voice of a woman trapped inside. Caught in complete bewilderment, Meriweather stared. The broomstick fell to her side and she listened to the voice of the crow as it hovered closer. A familiar voice she was sure she had heard before. Her forehead produced pearls of sweat as she took deep inhalations in and out, staring up the crow.

It flapped its wings and landed on the table.

'Stay away! That is our wedding china,' Meriwether said, holding the brush end of the broom towards the crow. It hopped from surface to surface until it sat upon the kitchen counter. Its beady eyes looked deep into hers.

'How can you speak?' Meriwether asked, lost for words. 'Ungodly foe.'

'Why would God make me so if I were ungodly?' it said, staring at her. The bird cocked its head to one side.

'I am mad. I have lost my mind. Or perhaps I am dreaming?' Meriwether pressed her hand to her forehead and glared at the crow. It offended her knowledge of science. 'A temperature. That's right! I must be having a fever dream.'

'Dreaming Lady, I have watched you from the outside and you are always alone,' it said.

'I am not alone,' Meriwether protested, but was well aware of her solitude. She hovered away from the crow, reaching for the table to straighten plates but her hands trembled, and her lips quaked as she tried to perform each movement. Her nerve was troubled.

'I think that you are,' it said. Meriwether, with her fingers resting on the plate, turned to face the crow. A clatter shattered through the room as the plate fell to the floor and cracked into a hundred broken shards. Meriwether's eyes began to water as she fell to the ground. She gazed upon the broken wedding china.

'This is your fault, Crow. You did this. How will I fix our wedding plates before he comes home?'

The crow did not answer. It felt as though her insides were melting and toiling, but she decided it was the heartbreak making her feel this way. Her lovely garnet lips made way for sobbing as her lipstick smudged on her chin. Meriwether stared at the mess for a good long time before she hurried up to her feet with shards of pottery in her hands and opened the utility drawer. 'You seem quite scattered, Dreaming Lady,' spoke the crow.

'Where is the glue? For goodness sake, where is it?' she muttered. How could a simple corvid have set such ruin upon the night she and her husband would mend their hearts once again.

As her fingers scurried through the drawer, her hand began to throb, warm and sweating. Without warning, her bones started to crack and splinter from within her skin. Pulling her hand close, she looked down in horror as blood spurted out from the broken grooves carved from the inside of her palm. Meriwether screamed and fell to her knees, transfixed by her twisting fingers. A china plate fell from the table and shattered around her as she wept.

The crow pottered down to the floor and looked at Meriwether, a measured, but innocent look across its face.

'Are you not happy, Dreaming Lady? I thought you were not happy,' the crow said as Meriwether writhed on the floor, holding her rotting hands close to her chest. Pools of blood gathered on the floor. It smeared across what remained of the skin left on her bones, but soon, that skin too began to eat away at itself like a thousand feasting ants.

'What are you doing to me?' she shrieked, but her breath caught, and her words morphed into the hideous caw of a bird. 'Argh,' she cawed, and the crow watched over her with gentle regard. Her body began to shrink, and her bones crushed into splinters. Black feathers sprouted from what was left of her skin and muscle of her trembling arms as they shuddered into wings. The sound of her bones chipping and shifting and splintering reverberated through her as she cried out in pain. *Please*, she wished she could say. *Please stop this*. But Meriwether couldn't say a word as her skull contracted and her eyes compressed. Her lips would not let her speak, and as she parted them for one last shriek, they hardened and stretched out into a beak. Teeth dropped to the ground like raindrops as they came loose in their sockets.

It was a pity the kitchen was a mess and covered in blood and sinew, but at least her husband loved the colour red.

In front of her, the crow's bones cracked and shifted too. Black feathers fell out of its skin and left behind large holes that formed into perfect human flesh. Not a blemish in sight. Its beak, while cawing out, opened but the cry of the crow finished in a crescendo. It was the moan of a woman as lips and teeth formed around the sound. The crow, now almost a fully formed human, smiled and Meriwether watched the creature as it lingered close to her. It hadn't shifted into the form of a stranger, no, it had stolen Meriwether's own face.

The creature took its clumsy, trembling fingers and clasped them around Meriwether. It clutched her close to its naked breast as it limped to the window on its newfound legs. The creature was like a doe learning to walk but the movement came naturally. It didn't seem like the creature had never taken a step before, but that it was just weary from a dormant rest.

'Little bird. You are free now,' the creature said as it let Meriwether go into the air.

Little Meriwether couldn't remember a thing about her husband or her marriage, only that she needed to fly. She had the strongest feeling that all of this had happened before.

LUCY ROSE (INFP/T) is an award-winning horror screenwriter/director and a published writer. Lucy has a BA (Hons) in Film and Television production and is currently studying for a Masters Degree in creative writing. In 2019, she received funding from the BFI Network for her horror short film 'She Lives Alone', which is currently visiting festivals. She is currently doing lots of writing and working towards publishing a novel and writing a feature script. Most recently, her prose was featured in The Same Havoc Anthology from The Selkie. Lucy is proudly LGBTQ+ & Working Class. @LucyRoseCreates

The Recliner
Marsheila Rockwell

Familiar dread tingled across Luka's scalp and down his spine as his mother fumbled with the house key. He had to be quick once the front door was open; if he took any more than five seconds to cross the living room, the recliner would get him.

The key clicked in the lock, and Luka took a deep breath. As the door creaked open and late afternoon sun spilled across the worn carpet, he brushed past his mother with a mumbled apology and raced for the hallway, not daring to look in the far corner, shrouded as it always was in darkness in the long moments before his mother flipped on the overhead light.

A small noise from the corner sent fear coursing through him and he hit the wooden floor of the hallway going much too fast. His feet slid out from under him, his small arms pin-wheeled for precious seconds, and then he was falling, his head coming down hard on the living room floor. Dazed by the impact, he twisted his neck, trying to see the recliner, to make sure it hadn't moved.

Luka often had nightmares about the recliner chasing him through the house, its footrest opening and closing like a hungry maw, eager to devour him, just like it had his grandpa. Mama said that was nonsense, that Grandpa had suffered a heart attack while watching wrestling, but Luka had seen the expression on the old man's face before the paramedics covered him with their cold, white sheet—the look in Grandpa's staring eyes had been one of fear, not pain. Luka understood the truth, even if his mother couldn't—or wouldn't. The chair got his grandpa. Just like it would get him, if he ever let his guard down.

His view of the corner was blocked by two skinny legs and a pair of dirty canvas sneakers. He followed the legs up to his mother's pink waitress uniform, and higher, to her frowning face.

"How many times do I have to tell you not to run in the house like that? One of these days you're going to kill yourself, and then what will I do?"

She reached out a hand and hauled Luka to his feet, then gave him a quick once-over. When she was satisfied he wasn't hurt, she tousled his mop of thick brown hair and pecked him on the cheek.

"Go play in your room for a while. Mama needs to rest."

Luka obediently trotted down the hall to his room. Once there, he hurried over to the little table he used for drawing and upended his backpack. Arts and crafts supplies he had been pilfering from his kindergarten classroom for the past few weeks cascaded onto the tabletop—uncooked macaroni, a handful of buttons, three popsicle sticks, and a tangle of multi-colored yarn. He ran his hands across his plunder reverently, picking up the popsicle sticks and clutching them to his chest. With these, he might just be able to save Mama from the chair before it swallowed her up, too.

Miss Gina had given him the idea when she told the class how pictures could sometimes say what words couldn't—that they were worth a thousand words. Luka knew thousands were a lot—Mama often said if she just had a few more of them, they could move to a nicer place. So, if his few words couldn't convince her of the danger, maybe a thousand of them could.

He pulled out construction paper from the bins his mother had arranged against the wall, found his glue stick in the toy box and the scissors with the rounded tips under his bed. Then he set to work.

Soon he had an orange gingerbread man with two mismatched buttons for eyes, and a larger pink one behind it. He used crayons to draw noses and mouths on them both. Then he painstakingly glued pieces of macaroni all over the orange body, imagining it was armor made of the purest gold. The popsicle sticks completed his construction paper knight, glued together to form a mighty sword.

He cut bits of yellow yarn from the variegated tangle and pasted them all about the pink figure's head. He used scraps of white paper to make shoes for the figure and a nametag that read 'Mama.'

Finally, he started on the recliner. With brown, black, and purple crayons grasped in his fist, he scribbled a dark, angry vortex on the paper, as far away from the pink figure as it was possible to get. He used two red buttons for eyes and tried to separate darker strands of yarn to fashion shadowy tentacles. When that proved too difficult, he glued the whole tangle on top of the crayon blob, stretching out several of the longer pieces past the macaroni warrior to reach for the damsel he protected.

The finishing touch was his grandpa's head, cut from the only photograph Luka had of the two of them together. Luka treasured the photo, and when Mama saw he'd been willing to sacrifice it to craft his glue and paper warning, she was sure to understand the danger. With trembling fingers, he placed the cut-out head into the mass of yarn, then quickly snatched his hand back, lest the mock tentacles prove all too real.

He didn't know how many words his picture was worth, but Miss Gina said he was the best artist in his class, and this was easily his finest piece of work. It would do the trick.

It had to.

He crept down the hallway, prize in hand, and paused at the living room threshold. His mother was dozing in the recliner, her legs covered by an old afghan, and the TV set to some silly game show where adults tried to win letters. As he tiptoed nearer, the recliner let out a warning creak. Fear washed over Luka and he stood frozen in place for what seemed like hours, his heart crashing against his ribs like a fly against a window. Then his mother stirred and blinked at him blearily, and the recliner's spell was broken.

"Not now, Boo. Mama's tired."

The game show people cheered as his mother closed her eyes again, and Luka could almost feel the recliner gloating. Turning away swiftly, so the chair wouldn't see his tears and know it had won, Luka let the picture slip from his hand.

He knew what Mama's words meant. His dinner would be PB&J, and he'd be tucking himself in tonight. If he was lucky, she'd sleep the night away in the chair… but he was very rarely lucky. No, she'd wake up as the summer sky finally darkened to indigo and head for the kitchen, where the sharp knives and hidden bottles would call to her as they did before, just after Grandpa died. Luka had had to go stay with the Fosters for a while after that, and he knew that the only reason the recliner hadn't gotten Mama yet was that it thought she'd go back to the drinking and cutting and save it the trouble of killing her.

And as Luka walked dejectedly back to his room, he thought the recliner was probably right.

* * * *

Luka lay in his bed, the blankets pulled up to his chin, listening. He'd eaten his sandwich (tearing the crusts off and tossing them in the trash, something Mama would never have let him get away with if she'd been awake.) He brushed his teeth, and said his prayers, then, too afraid to hazard the recliner's grasp, he'd blown Mama a kiss from the safety of the hallway before retreating to his room to wait.

His room was lit by the soft glow of a Superman night light, and the customary shadows assured him that everything was in its proper place. The bat rested by the foot of his bed, and the toy box where he'd shoved it, partially blocking the doorway, leaving just enough room for him or his mother to squeeze through, but ensuring that nothing bigger could enter while he was at his most vulnerable.

But he couldn't let the comfort of his safe-hole lull him to sleep. He had to stay awake and listen for the sound of his mother's footsteps on the kitchen tile. If she headed that way, he'd have to stop her somehow, distract her, even if it meant braving the living room—and the recliner—in the middle of the night.

The warmth of his blanket-nest and the fuzzy-round-the-edges light coaxed him to drowsiness, and Luka could feel his eyelids closing against his will. Had to stay awake…had to….

Ring-ring. Ring-ring.

The shrill, insistent cry of the telephone snatched Luka out of the dream realm, and he was abruptly wide awake, heartbeat thumping hard and fast in his throat.

Mama!

He heard the squeak of the recliner's footrest and tensed, but the sound was followed by his mother fumbling for the phone she kept on the little table beside the over-stuffed chair.

"Hello?" Mama's voice was thick with sleep. "What? What time is it? No, I can't come in now! Who would take care of my kid?" Her voice grew thinner and higher. "Are you crazy? I can't leave him here by himself! He's only five years old!" There was a short silence, while Luka contemplated the thought of being alone in the house with the recliner and nearly wet his pants. Then Mama spoke again, and her words were cold and brittle. "Fine. Fire me. God knows I'd make more on unemployment than you pay me, anyway." A crashing sound, followed by one of the words Mama only used when she hurt herself or when somebody did something stupid while she was driving. Or when she was about to go get one of those half-full bottles she kept in the cupboard above the fridge, 'just in case.'

As he threw the blankets back and reached for the bat, prepared to race to her rescue, Luka's keen ears caught another sound…the crunch of dry pasta breaking underfoot.

His picture!

In the ensuing silence, he imagined his mother bending down to pick the construction paper hero up off of the floor. He wondered if she'd be angry that he had left it there. Or would she be proud, and want to display it on the fridge with his other masterpieces? On the fridge, next to the drawer full of knives he wasn't allowed to touch, beneath that hated cabinet?

The moments dragged out forever as Luka wavered on the edge of his bed, unsure what he should do. Then he heard her move, the pad-pad of her feet on the carpet becoming the shuffling of dry skin across tile. Then the scrape of wood on linoleum as she dragged a chair over to the fridge.

In a flash, Luka was out of his bed and running. If she started drinking again, he'd have to go back to the Fosters, and then who would protect her?

"Mama, no!" He slipped and staggered toward the living room, his sock-clad feet finding little purchase as he raced across the wooden hallway floor. He didn't pause when he reached the threshold, rushing heedlessly into the recliner's domain, determined to save his mother. The chair was between him and the kitchen, but he didn't stop. In his haste, he didn't give his enemy quite a wide enough berth. As he passed by the recliner, the footrest shot out, catching him mid-shin and pitching him headlong into the corner of the television set.

As Luka lay there, stunned and bleeding from a nasty gash at his temple, the bat rolled out of his numb fingers. His mother appeared in the kitchen doorway, but to his blurry eyes, she was little more than a shadow with a shiny, full glass in her hand.

"What the... *Luka!*"

Then she was rushing towards him, but her movements seemed slow and exaggerated, like that old show about the expensive robot woman that his mother always liked to watch. He could only look on as she stumbled over the bat that was supposed to have protected her, and then she was falling, falling, dropping the glass and bringing her hands out in front of her—too slow—crashing into the side table, landing beside the hungry recliner in a heap of blood, broken glass, and cheap wood.

The blackness was closing in, dimming the edges of Luka's vision, but still, he saw the tentacles rise from within the recliner, long strips of upholstery ripping themselves away from arms and back in their frenzy to get to his mother.

"Mama!" he cried, trying to rise, but dizziness engulfed him and he couldn't move. Luka knew then that his mother was going to die, just like his grandpa, doomed by his very attempt to save her. As darkness and despair claimed him, his cries softened, became whimpers, then faded off at last to silence. "Mama...gotta save...Mama...."

Luka dreamt.

Long, leather tentacles wound themselves about his mother's neck, and her hands scrabbled ineffectually against the upholstery noose, while other tentacles grew appendages like tongues to lap up the blood that dripped from her wounds. Behind them, a wind rose, a miniature tornado that whipped the fringed edges of Mama's afghan into a colored froth. Unnoticed by all save Luka's dreaming self, the whirlwind picked up his discarded picture and spun it about, round and round, faster and faster, until it began to spread and glow. Luka watched as his macaroni knight grew and changed within the heart of the maelstrom. No longer a paper gingerbread man in pasta armor, but a real warrior, in golden mail, bright like the sun, except for a tiny spot on his left leg where Mama's foot had broken off a piece of macaroni. And best of all, the shining knight carried a long, equally shiny sword.

The wind quieted and Luka's hero stepped in front of the recliner.

"Release the woman, foul creature!" he ordered, his voice like the church bells on Easter morning.

The recliner roared, an angry sound of metal on metal. Then it began defiantly to draw Luka's mother into the dark space beneath its footrest.

The knight wasted no more time; with several quick, decisive blows, the recliner's tentacles were severed, spewing ichor like furniture polish, and Luka's mother was free. As he dragged the now-unconscious woman out of harm's way, the recliner shot a barrage of sharpened metal springs at his back. At Luka's warning cry, the knight spun, easily deflecting the projectiles with the flat of his blade. Then, with a lion's roar of his own, the warrior took his sword in both hands and buried the blade to the hilt in the recliner's wretched, writhing heart. As the blade sank deep, an unearthly scream blistered the very air and Dream Luka's world exploded into a million nightmare fragments.

* * * *

"Luka, honey, are you okay?" He woke sometime later to the sound of his mother's worried voice and the feel of a cool cloth upon his forehead. He'd had the most amazing dream; he couldn't wait to tell Mama all about it....

Mama!

Luka's eyes snapped open and he jolted upright, sending a wave of sick through his tummy and making his throat burn.

"Whoa! Slow down there, partner," his mother cautioned, but Luka wasn't listening. He slewed around in her arms, searching for the recliner.

There, in its accustomed place in front of the television. Looking perfectly normal, except for the wooden bat that now protruded from its back, skewering it like a spear.

Or a sword.

Following his gaze, Luka's mother gave a tiny laugh. "Crazy, huh? Must've happened when you tripped." She hugged him then, too tight. "It's okay, sweetie. I never really liked that old chair, anyway."

Luka's mother bandaged them both up, then brought him into the kitchen while she made some hot cocoa. As the water boiled, she pulled every last bottle from the high cupboard and emptied them into the sink. That night they slept cuddled together in Luka's bed, with the Superman night light standing guard over their slumber.

The next morning, Luka helped her clean the mess in the living room. As he picked up bits of fluffy white stuffing and scraps of leather, he looked for his picture. It was nowhere to be found, not even under the recliner's broken footrest.

He turned to ask his mother about it and felt a small breeze caress his cheek. Something fluttered by his face, then floated gently to the floor. He bent to retrieve it.

And there, in his trembling palm, his grandfather's picture smiled up at him, knowing and proud.

* * * *

Later, at the landfill, two sanitation workers struggled to lift the old recliner off the flatbed full of used mattresses, broken toys and other Goodwill rejects.

"What do you suppose happened to it?" one of the men—the name 'Dave' was stenciled on his orange jumpsuit—asked, sticking a gloved finger into the gaping hole in the chair's back.

"I dunno. Bar fight?"

Dave chuckled.

"You know, it's really not in that bad of shape. No structural damage. I bet it wouldn't take much to reupholster it…."

"You want it?"

"Yeah, help me get it into my truck. Fixing it up'll give Lucy something to do… besides nagging me, that is."

The men hefted the recliner between them and half-carried, half-pushed it into the bed of Dave's old Chevy. Dave slammed the tailgate shut and they walked off, laughing about Lucy's latest tirade.

And in the back of the truck, the old recliner creaked once, as if in anticipation, then settled down again to wait.

MARSHEILA ROCKWELL - I am the author of twelve SF/F/H books, dozens of poems and short stories, several articles on writing and the writing process, and a handful of comic book scripts. I am an active member of SFWA, HWA, IAMTW, and SFPA. I am also a disabled pediatric cancer and mental health awareness advocate and a reconnecting Chippewa/Métis. I live in the Valley of the Sun with my husband, three of our five children, three rescues, and far too many books. You can find out more here: www.marsheilarockwell.com.

CALL OF THE TIDE
Demi-Louise Blackburn

Sleep finds Maya easily on the day of the move, but never again.

She cannot see the ocean from their bedroom, but she can hear it, and its whisper drags her into a dreamless landscape. When she wakes, it's to the smell of salt on the air and Cecil pressed, warm and persistent, against her back.

His hand brushes her waist, and she wonders how it might have looked on another woman's skin, how yellowed her complexion might have been against white sheets and the dim lights inside a hotel room. With that, Maya enters their fresh start with a chill that hangs, remains, and grows stale.

Nothing will change, she thinks. The lack of surprise in that distant voice cuts into her mind, and scars.

Furniture fills the seafront house over sluggish weeks.

Maya loses herself to paint swatches, floor plans, catalogues of decorations that she will allow to collect dust. All the while, Cecil's presence lingers. The brush of fingers against Maya's neck while she opens boxes smelling of damp. She unearths trinkets which tug in sore, familiar places – infected wounds. Distantly, she hopes Cecil won't notice if she condemns their wedding pictures to the attic. In the end, the warmth in her husband's eyes as he flips through years of memories thaws her somewhat, and she commits herself to ordering new frames for them, instead.

He's trying, she reminds herself, and offers a silent gesture with squares of walnut wood and Perspex. When they arrive, she secures them above the fireplace, in the hallway, cupped in the shadows of their bedroom—and they always hang crooked.

By the time the hollow echo of the home is muted by curtains and clutter, Maya is lost to her work.

The cramped spare room is whitewashed and bare floored, converted to an art studio standing a fraction of the size it was in their old home. It doesn't deter her. The narrow space and its bland walls morph with every passing night, and freshly painted pictures line the lower wall with every turn of the clock. She hangs few of them. Most lay like the slab of a skirting board, jutting out as though she's trying to thicken the walls.

Maya positions an easel so it faces the window, turning away from the sound of Cecil wandering through the building as though to haunt it. She watches the distant ebb and flow of the tide, until she can imagine the murky water rising directly under the sill. Sometimes, in the early hours, the horizon cracks open from distant storms, and the shadows that spill into the space are long and twisted.

Months pass, and the echo in the house has been entirely consumed.

A pristine white sofa dominates the bulk of the living area, and the dining room table has two chairs too many. Cecil's footsteps up the stairs are muffled beneath the beige carpet. Their mattress has been replaced; the frame swapped for some monstrous four-poster - trapping them together in the dark.

Cecil soon makes a tradition out of walking onto the seafront after dinner. Stomachs swollen with food, he laces sweaty fingers between his wife's and talks for them both. His words are smothered by the scream of gulls, and Maya's own thoughts drift to the waves, wishing the water would swallow her up.

In the quiet hours of twilight, Maya often thinks their love is out there on the beach with them. Crushed to a grain of sand or tucked into the stinking carcass of a shore crab. At times, she wriggles out of Cecil's grasp to stoop down and flip an empty shell belly up, hoping the birds haven't picked it clean. All she finds are scraps.

When she rises, Cecil winces before grasping her salt-slick hand, and Maya wonders what they can make of the remains, of that sun-bleached carcass half-entombed by the coastline. The rusted cogs in her brain begin to move. Cecil's voice returns to drown out the noise of the tide creeping in.

It is then her work begins to shift.

Cecil squeezes into the studio one gloomy morning, and a greeting fades on his lips. He looks around the room, crouches to ease canvases from the wall as though sifting through old records.

Maya's paintings have changed.

First, he finds carbon copies of landscapes, her old things, the flourish of a brush their only defining feature. But, painting by painting, they melt into jagged cuts of the shoreline outside their home. The lifeless forms of sea birds and crustaceans, warped and out of proportion, brooding between a portfolio of open fields.

Brushstrokes transition to cuts from a palette knife. Green melts to blue. The paint so thick it flakes at the touch of a finger. Cecil frowns at them, nervous, and Maya watches his features, willing them to change. When he doesn't speak, she turns towards her latest project. The peachy underbelly of a crab, gutted, the sand surrounding it as messy and uncoordinated as static.

"Trying something new?" Cecil asks, and his voice dies in the claustrophobic air of the place.

Maya hums, mulling the question over, and tucks a strand of dark hair behind her ear. "I suppose I am. What do you think?"

The quiet of the studio thickens.

Cecil looks anywhere but at his wife until he catches sight of a naked bulb hanging from the ceiling. "We should order a lampshade for this room."

Maya mumbles a half-hearted response, and her husband slips from her workshop as though his body was nothing but smoke. She stays awake late into the night and obsesses over the painted creature before her. Irritated, she cuts through the image with a wash of black oil, and Cecil is dead to the world when she retires to bed.

A few days later, Cecil returns to the city, and the singing begins.

Maya scrubs dishes with an intensity that betrays the calm surface of her face. Her thoughts thrum with suspicion and she tries, in vain, to dismiss them. When the first note flutters into the kitchen, her mind clears.

There are no words to the song.

Her ears prickle to catch the intricate melody and they evade her skilfully. Maya drops the sponge to push open the kitchen window, but the sound doesn't become any clearer. It churns with distant waves and the incessant call of seabirds. The breeze pushes it nearer. Pulls it away. Pushes it.

Maya abandons the dishes and rushes to the front door. She listens out, feels the warm breeze, hears the whisper of the ocean—and nothing more. The ballad disappears as soon as it arrives, and only then does the house feel truly suffocating.

She returns to the foamy water of the sink, now cold, swirls her finger through it, and doesn't touch another dish. Abandoning her chores, she scurries to the studio and locks herself inside. By the time she emerges, fingers are stained dusky blue and Cecil's car is in the driveway.

Night comes, morning rises, and with it, Cecil's guilt is illuminated.

He wanders through the home and picks up after his wife's mess, washes counters flecked with food and oil paint, finishes the dishes, dusts the pictures, and chatters loud enough that even the gulls circling the house can't drown him out.

All the while, Maya trains her ears on the currents, waiting for the whisper of a lyric. Cecil's incessant questions can't drag her away, and the silence dyes his cheeks red. He locks himself inside his office, and Maya, in turn, retreats to the studio and waits for the day to subside.

She works deep into the dark hours. The sound of Cecil tapping at a keyboard carries through the halls. From the window, the moon bobs above the oil slick of the sea. In her tired vision, Maya can see a woman's features within it. A new canvas is retrieved from the clutter and Maya works until her fingers grow tight and hot.

When she stops, steps back, and looks, she cannot see the moon or the face within the painting. There is a sheet of black, the gnarled shape of something stillborn resting in the centre. Frustration rises and fills her eyes. She blinks back the tears, feeling foolish, and so incredibly lost.

The bed is empty when she slips into the sheets. Sleep is evasive and, when caught, fitful. Cecil doesn't stay with her that night, simply creeps into the bedroom to grab some clothes before returning to his office. Maya breathes deeply, smells salt and perfume, and rest doesn't come.

Not a week later, the call returns when Cecil leaves again.

His car pulls away, trundling down the narrow road until the purr of the engine catches on the wind, and is replaced by song. She dithers at the entrance, *stay safe* still resting in her mouth before her head snaps towards the ocean. It's clearer. Still only the trickle of a foreign melody, but the pitch of it has become shrill. Pleading.

Maya slips inside to grab a cardigan and makes her way to the waves. The wind rises, whipping clothing around her, and the tide slinks close. Seaweed hangs in the gale, crisp and sour. Gulls circle. Maya can taste the spray of salt on her tongue.

At the trembling lip of the water the melody swells, but words evade her. There's no language to the noise, no form or composition, but she can feel the notes. They wrap across her chest and squeeze, clutch her hair at the root and pull, demand she draw nearer - to listen. Escape.

Cold liquid seeps into her shoes. The shock draws her back with a gasp and the tide races to greet her, ocean frothing. When Maya gazes up, she can see a storm marching inland. Water laps at her feet. She turns, running towards the house as though the sea is chasing her. Maya's heart flutters like a panicked bird.

On the front steps, she turns to find the waves have retreated. The storm is nowhere to be found. Music lingers on the air like pollen, a trace, and Maya must stop herself from going to the shore again. There is a thread being tugged inside of her. A longing. She feels like time itself has grown distended, waiting to rupture. Maya closes the door in a bid to block it out.

For the rest of the day, she feels at a loose end.

There's no solace within the house. It's as though she's returned to find every piece of furniture replaced with a prop. The frames are empty. Seats look as frail as cardboard cut-outs. The marbled counters in the kitchen appear to peel at the corners like cheap acrylic coating. Doors might as well have been painted walls.

Dusk drifts in.

When she walks into the studio that evening, the atmosphere is off-kilter. Out of balance. Vertigo slithers into the cracks of her skull and she moves through the room like a phantom, neither here nor there, tripping over stray canvases and cobalt-stained brushes. She fingers through her portfolio.

All manner of portraits, of far-reaching landscapes and lush gardens, are picked up, pressed tight against her chest. She stumbles over to the window and opens it wide, feels the flicker of a note on her cheek, and throws the old paintings through it. They clatter to the ground.

What is left is a shell of her work. Muted imaginings of crustacean corpses line the walls, broken by ever-reaching swathes of ocean, sand dunes rocketing into the horizon and off the page. Sea birds struck in the cold flight of death; wings glued in black-red tar. And crowned by the sill of the window is one more visage, a half-formed grimace in the clutch of the moon. A woman's scaled features. Screaming. Perhaps singing.

Then, as though summoned, the music reveals itself, a hypnotic wailing that chokes Maya as it drifts towards her ears. Beyond the frame, the sea swirls into rabid froth, the sun a rotten plum rising amid the gloom, and she can sense more than see the electricity cutting through the sky. Gulls rise, scream, and scatter. Maya's fingers turn pale as she grips the ledge.

It is only the sound of the front door opening, closing, and muffled footsteps creeping upstairs that stops Maya from throwing herself from the window. Instead, she rushes to the door, locks it, and clumsily reaches for a new canvas. She pushes the easel closer to the glass and secures the blank slate. Paint slips and splatters on the floor.

Her hand, slick with inky oil, touches the canvas as Cecil calls from the hallway.

"Maya? We need to talk."

She swipes her palm across the white and blackens it. Blots out every sliver of light. Catches the murmur of a word. Maya wipes a hand on her skirt, dips an index finger to blue, middle to green, ring to purple, and colours the sky. Cecil knocks. Tries the handle.

"For heaven's sake, Maya. Stop hiding and just listen to me for a minute."

Words grow to a sentence. Maya wipes her hands, uses a cracked nail to cut images into the bleak foundation she's created. Eyes form in the sky like narrowed stars. Her own flicker to the window, back again, and she sculpts hollow features, carves out a gaping mouth. Within it, the teeth of sharks; around it, hair as oily as seaweed.

Cecil's shouts fade as Maya's hands retract from the canvas. A moment of suspension follows. Only the howling wind through the studio brings movement. It elbows through the curtains, curls in Maya's hair and twists, seeps under the door to cool Cecil's feet.

Maya stares at the monstrosity she's created, and squeezes her eyes shut in a bid to hold off angered tears. She wipes dirtied hands against her face, colours her cheeks black and blue, and turns to open the door.

Cecil traces her form. Looks through her to the mutated canvas, beyond to the windowpane where a storm writhes, stills, then blooms into fury in quick succession. A restless creature.

"We need to get you some help," Cecil says, quiet and sincere.

Maya winces before huffing out a disbelieving laugh. "It's *you* that needs help, Cecil. You're worried about me being holed up in here when you're out of town doing God knows what again?"

"It was for *work*."

"Don't you dare try lying to me," Maya scoffs, and the wind carries her past Cecil, down the hall, and to the bathroom. She scrubs at the paint on her hands, the colour under her nails, rakes a hand across her cheek to try and persuade the stains to leave. Cecil follows and hovers in the doorway. Maya is struck again by how ghost-like he is. Haunting the house.

"What did you expect me to do?" he asks, and it's as though something uncorks in Maya's throat. The words come as easy and graceful as lyrics.

"Be a decent husband. Keep your word to this being a new start, a fresh beginning for us."

"What was I supposed to do? You hardly speak to me, Maya. You can't even stand me *touching* you."

"Are you surprised?" Maya says, looking at Cecil through the bathroom mirror. "You think I can forget her so easily? Every time you come near me, all I can imagine is what you did. What *I* did to deserve any of this."

"Then why are you here?" Cecil shouts. "I'm trying, Maya. But if you can't do the same…"

The words fizzle away to the buzz of wasps in Maya's ears. *Why are you here?* skitters around her head, echoing… *singing*. She turns to her unfaithful husband and stares at him. His mouth shuts with a clack of teeth. Maya searches his expression for any sign of recognition. To see if he, too, hears the song.

He does not.

She catches a glimpse of Cecil's confused expression before she barges past him. Her feet hardly touch the ground as she races along the hallway, slanted wedding photos and holiday snapshots blurring in her periphery. Maya knocks her hip against the white couch. Cecil's voice comes high and shrill as she bursts through the front door.

The wind aids her descent. Her legs burn as she sprints down the path towards the seafront. Rain falls in cold sheets and threatens to blind Maya, but a reedy voice guides her towards the dunes, rotting brambles catching on her ankles, sand seeping into the gaps in her shoes until the water greets her.

Frothing like spit, the shore trembles in Maya's presence and rushes inland like a tongue slipping over grainy lips. The moon peers out and winks at her. Somewhere between the waves, the sky, and the stars hanging like freckles, Maya can see the face. No longer an aborted thing, unfinished and curled in on itself, but an expression of longing. A beautiful woman carved of steel, painted in ebony, highlighted in bleached coral reefs long forgotten in the bowels of the ocean.

Maya steps into the flood.

An orchestra erupts. Maya's skin prickles from the freezing water but her blood is alight with flames. Her ears fill with silt and salt and weeds. The music burrows deeper. Whispers of words are etched into her bones and when she opens her mouth to sing them back, she gulps the voice down, litre by litre. Someone grabs at the hem of her dress. Cecil. But his fingers cannot battle the tide.

It sucks her in. Away. And the embrace of her drowning is sweeter than any love she'd had before.

* * * *

Maya feels little after her walk into the folds of the ocean. There is only the music. No longer pleading but subdued, akin to an ancient lullaby, and it holds her. Suspends her like a baby in the womb.

With time, she is birthed onto the shores of an island she doesn't recognize. Her skin is pale and wrinkled. Hair matted into tendrils of seaweed. She expels water for minutes unending and blinks fruitlessly to wash away the sting of salt. All the while, there is a crooning around her. Not song, but just as sweet. Clicks and chittering. Calls of birds. The splash of fish darting across the surface of the sea behind her.

Eventually, Maya takes in the sight of the island, wrapped in mist and cupping her in a cove of gleaming green. The mountains tower above her in dizzying spires. Sunlight is muted, hidden by clouds, but no less warm.

On her back, a hand rubbing circles into her skin.

Maya chokes out her last drink and cranes her head around. The woman is there. Hair falling down her shoulders in emerald clusters, braided with sea grapes, her eyes as milky as the moon itself, and when she grins – her lips reveal the razor edges of shark teeth. Scales as black as night peer out from her hairline, outline her translucent skin as though waiting to be painted.

Maya's mouth trembles. She scoots further inland and the creature's eyes grow wide. Concerned. Behind, the screeching of a bird rockets between the ridges and echoes across the land. Maya snaps her head up, and watches as an enormous gull cuts past the sun and settles on the rocky shoreline.

The bird looks at Maya with the gaze of a long-forgotten human. Changed. Talons protrude where feet should be, skin painfully pink where feathers sprout, but her hands are delicate, and so very elegant. Gull screams erupt and when Maya turns and turns and turns, more of the flock burst out from their mountain nests. Some with the face of women. Others display beaks where lips should be. Their half-formed bodies twitch relentlessly.

A scaled hand lands on Maya's leg. Gentle and frightening. Her attention snaps to the shore's edge where a hundred faces emerge from the dark water. Fish eyes plunged into human skulls. Bristled jaws of prehistoric whales. The whiskered snout of a malformed sealion open and screaming. And others so very like Maya—if the sea did not hide their transgressions.

At a loss, Maya stares at the creature closest to her, settled with the water lapping over a forked tail, the crimson, fleshy gills on her neck and chest fluttering with half-breaths. Around her nothing but misshapen things. Half-breeds. Suspended between one and the other. A lost colony of those both trapped and free.

The creature unhinges her jaw and Maya watches the white, bloated tongue inside of it writhe and click. Then, song. Elegant and moving. Beyond all rational thought and structure—a symphony of off-key notes that erupt so sweetly, and sound so untethered.

Maya's erratic breathing slows.

The trembles in her body fade, but a terrible fire begins to rip its way through her. At the base of her neck, the muscles flex and bulge and Maya's lips fall into a silent shout of pain. When her fingers reach for the spot, they come back bloody, and she can feel something hard and spiny beginning to blossom in the open wound.

All the while, the Siren watches and her blank eyes flash, then film over—a predator's keen glare. Maya falls and writhes against the beach, and the hushed tune surges into a wail of delight. Clouded sky greets her as she changes. Skin peels like it is boiling away and, beneath it, sandpaper scales greet the light. Maya's legs snap together as though possessed, knit themselves with ribbons of flesh, and she doesn't have to see to know what she is becoming.

Maya opens a mouth lined with a hundred teeth – and sings.

DEMI-LOUISE BLACKBURN is a horror and speculative fiction author from West Yorkshire, England.

Most of her childhood was spent reading. As such, she went on to study English Literature at college and wrote short horror pieces in her free time. After this, she applied for a Sociology degree at Leeds University. In her final year before graduating, Demi signed on for a Creative Writing module to improve her work, and it was then she began to see writing as more than a hobby.

With encouragement from friends and family, she began submitting her work for publication. Since then, some of her short stories have found homes with *Kandisha Press* and *All Worlds Wayfarer.*

When not wrapped up in her next writing venture, you can most likely find Demi settled down with a nature documentary, listening to true crime podcasts, or dabbling in a new art project. In the summer, she likes to attend music festivals and take trips out to the coast.

You can keep up to date with Demi's work on the following platforms:
Website: demi-louise.com
Twitter: @DemiLWrites
Facebook: demilouisewrites
Instagram: demilouisewrites

Date Night Ablaze

Rowan Hill

Fire raged through the Australian bush and set the night sky aglow with angry oranges and reds. Kate's land, however, was still quiet in the midnight hour. The acrid smell of bushfire, still some five kilometers away and on an adjoining cattle station, was rife as she brought her open-topped Jeep to a stop on a wide part of the trail bordering her fence.

Giving an unconcerned but cursory glance to the glow, confident there were at least another two hours before desert winds brought the flames to her land, Kate stood in the driver's seat and flipped on the Jeep's large spotlight on the crossbar behind her head. Immediately aiming it into the scrub, a goanna was caught unaware by the high beam. It rustled through the brush and away from the invasive light.

She huffed a frustrated breath up to the delicately coiffed hair sticking to her forehead and it obliged by shifting to the side. Another deep breath and she let out a long whistle, the pitch loud enough that she was sure it would reach far into the bush for her dog to hear it.

"Buck!" She shouted to the darkness, pierced only by the high beam and warm glow of the flames. Her voice cracked the second time she whistled for her dog to come and find her. It had been raw for the last few hours after much crying, and when she had finished, her body felt drained from the ordeal of the entire night.

Kate caught a glimpse of herself in the rearview mirror and leaned forward to study her face. Lipstick worn off, eyeliner smudged, mascara running, even the new miracle foundation to cover her burn mark looked caked and not at all flattering. No wonder tonight's date was literally the worst she had ever experienced in her short life. She looked grotesque, and doubted the sight would change once she was out of the fluorescent light's glare.

A twig cracked in the bush. Her attention stolen, the sound stilled her breath. Nothing followed the sound for another minute and she quickly hopped out of the Jeep, red dust stirring beneath the dainty heels she had recently purchased. She strode away from the car and its light, down the dark bush track, and stood still, her ears perked for any noises. After a few minutes of silence, she let out another call to her herding dog.

Swearing at the silence, Kate kicked her toe into the ground, forgetting she was not wearing her everyday work boots, and was rewarded with a foot full of dry, abrasive dirt. She swore again, this time at Buck. He leapt out of the car as soon as she pulled up to the house, spooked. When she ran after him, the long and awkward pencil skirt she had also bought for the date nearly made her topple over in the front yard.

She trod back to the Jeep, deeply frustrated with the turn of events of the night; one she'd been looking forward to for a week. There were few eligible men in the sparsely populated outback, where Kate could drive for an hour and still be on her family's land. It felt like divine intervention in her lonely life when her friend mentioned there was a new ranch hand on a neighboring farm. The sneaky picture she sent Kate nearly made her jaw drop. He was gorgeous, beyond anything normally available in the bush. He was like a gold nugget in a dry creek bed full of river rocks.

Kate turned the engine over again but kept the spotlight on. He couldn't have run farther than here, surely? She was at least five kilometers from the house. There was no way he would be able to escape through her boundary fence that was a man's height with razor wire lining its top and bottom.

She drove slowly down the track, occasionally whistling, hoping it would carry on the hot wind that stoked the raging fires now parallel to her fence. In the spotlight, the occasional thick cloud of smoke wafted across, highlighted in the beam, and served as a reminder she did not have much time. Abruptly, a large male red kangaroo, a boomer, launched itself over the boundary fence and onto her track, not bothering to pause for the Jeep only meters away from hitting it.

The dainty shoe hit the brakes for it and she watched as she began to notice other signs of animals running from the fire. Rabbits, wombats, snakes; if they couldn't smell the fire in the air, the palpable fear on the land would have hit their animal instincts long ago. *Run.* Kate glanced aside to her passenger seat, at her father's old hunting rifle, sitting and waiting patiently for her to need it. The fire would be making all the animals run for their lives but occasionally one might mistake her as a threat. A kangaroo could kick in your chest while an emu's big claw would slice it open.

Kate caught sight of her sleeve as she looked at the gun, a long red stain marking the new white puffy blouse. Not two minutes after he had stumbled into the empty outdoor seating of the pub, already hammered by what smelt like rum, her blind date had knocked over her red wine. Anger at the man and the offending stain bubbled in her chest, tears spilling out once more. Gripping the top of the shoulder in her hand she violently ripped off the sleeve, "For fuck's sake!" she cried as the threads shredded with force.

Using the offending material as a hanky, she wiped some new tears away. He had been so mean. Not just rude—*mean.* Even as he arrived, he eyed her face, lingering over the side that was deformed and scarred, and she knew. Someone had told him what monstrosity he was about to meet for drinks, and he felt he needed some liquid courage to face it. As Kate had experienced before, rum brought out a man's real thoughts. It whispered to them to tell the truth as they saw it.

He made jokes. She had heard them all before. Then he asked questions. Undoubtedly, no one wanted to tell him the story of how her father died in the annual bushfire when she was seventeen, and how she herself had barely escaped as they tried to save the paddock horses. She had been about to leave the pub quietly. No one had seen them together, no one would know her shame of yet another dismissive suitor, when he finally made *the* joke.

The one about her money, her vast fortune, the land she inherited. And how maybe, even with her scars, he could overlook them if the lights were off. It wasn't just mean, it was malicious. And it stirred her vengeful side.

She sniffed her running nose again and started the Jeep back up, turning away from the boundary fence and heading towards the creek, now low with the summer heat. The tilt of the land meant everything lost eventually found its way to the creek that coiled itself throughout her thousand acres like a wandering serpent. If anything was missing on her land, it would end up somewhere on the creek.

She let out another long whistle for her dog, a slight panic swelling in her chest at the thought of him wandering about with the fire approaching. That dog knew this bush, and had explored every cranny on it as he herded up many a lost cow. But he could easily get himself trapped within a ring of fire if he was chasing something and was distracted.

A sound in the console drew her attention and she slowed the car to a roll while she read a text from her friend.

??? How did it go??? Any luck with this one???

She replied immediately, using one hand to drive while the other texted.

He was a no show. It's okay tho, I had to get back with the new fire coming on the South ridge. It won't get past the river to the house, but just in case.

She eyed the glow in the rearview mirror, confident of the assessment. After the fire that took her father, she calculated well and built the new house and cattle station in a crook of the river, clear of brush or anything that could catch alight. The fire would go right past her house and she would never feel its heat. The friend responded immediately,

HE WHAT!? I'm so sorry. Don't worry tho, dad says he is pretty lazy for a ranch hand, probably won't last the week. Good luck with the fire, EVACUATE IF THEY TELL YOU!

Kate read the text and pulled up near a well-worn part of the riverbed—a large, flat clearing, with a small amount of water still flowing through it. She turned off the Jeep's lights and left the car with the rifle crooked in her arm. The moon was half full and perched high, providing enough light for her to walk away from the car and along the creek, reveling in the semi-darkness and the sounds of the bush in chaos.

Evacuate?

Kate snorted. She hadn't evacuated once since she inherited the place. She was shaped by the yearly fires, literally and metaphorically. She expected them and planned on them to accompany her through the new year. They were as expected as Christmas. Fire was an old friend.

An old landmark boulder served as a seat and she leaned against it as she gave her dog another whistle. Kate surveyed the wide moonlit scene, calculating where he would run to, the direction she had seen him sprint off. He definitely wouldn't try to backtrack to the house. Not with her stony silence in the car as he was finally coming around, finding his hands bound behind him with a half-hog tie securing his neck.

Multiple twigs snapped in succession and Kate's head whipped up, searching in the direction of the faint noise. She quieted her breath and tilted her head towards the bush, listening to the pattern of breaking branches and undergrowth. Something was running. Running towards the creek. Fast and heavy.

Silently and with years of practice, she hoisted the hunting rifle and tucked it into her arm, aiming in the dark, using the half-moon and morbid bushfire glow to see her prey. The crash and upheaval of sound grew closer to the dark creek bed and Kate held the breath in her lungs in anticipation.

A flash of grey streaked across a white eucalyptus, highlighted by moonlight and shadows.

Kate shot.

The echo reverberated in the heavy air and shocked her bones. A groan came from the base of the tree and Kate sighed with relief at the sound. She took her time with deep calming breaths and wandered back to the Jeep, flipping the spotlight on and directing it into the bush where she had shot.

With a smile and a sense of great satisfaction, she laid the rifle over her forearm in a casual manner and strode over to the man lying prostrate on the ground.

"Hello, Buck."

His breathing was labored from exercise and pain and she looked away from the grimy, sweaty face down to his lean body. A few fragments of the rifle shot had clipped him in the hip and pelvis. He would survive but was incapacitated at the moment.

She crouched a few feet away, silhouetted by the Jeep's light, her face and smile hidden in shadow while a halo of light surrounded her.

"I really thought you got away from me there. We are at least seven kilometers from the house. Pretty fast for such a big guy, huh?" Kate confessed to her bad date with a chuckle that relieved her stress. She studied his face and large form. Buck, young and handsome, and a similar age to herself, groaned in reply and picked his head up from the dust to look at his wound. Blood was seeping into his jeans from underneath, the stain growing with each pump of his heart.

Another beast, snapping the branches of the bush undergrowth, could be heard approaching and the blue-heeler herding dog Kate had never bothered to name emerged. It uttered a low, feral growl aimed at the wounded man in the dirt as it crouched closer to him, unaware if it still needed to continue rounding up and shepherding him to his master. Kate let out a sharp and short whistle through her teeth for it to heel. The dog flinched at the harsh, reprimanding sound and quickly lost the growl, trotting towards her legs and laying on the red dust behind her.

"You... you roofied me," Buck accused, a cough escaping his dry cracked lips.

Kate frowned, anger starting to rise in her chest, "You obviously didn't finish all of your drink, otherwise I wouldn't be here in the middle of the bush, waiting FOR A GODDAMN FIRE!" Her voice rose to a shout, displaying the ire she felt at the man, forcing her to extremes she hadn't taken in so long.

She stood up with the gun, towering over him, and took a calming breath while their eyes locked. With her anger back under control, she stated,

"You didn't have to be such a dickhead, you know? I know I'm... different. I'm not an idiot," she commented, unconsciously shielding her scarred cheek with her shoulder.

Her face was still hidden in shadow and it made him more nervous to not see it, instead hearing only the finality in her voice. Buck swallowed hard, trying to wince away the pain in his hip as the knot in his throat swelled further with panic. Kate carried the large hunting rifle confidently; it almost looked like an extension of her arm as she let it hang carelessly.

He had woken up in the car, bound. Kate, refusing to acknowledge him or his questions, told him she was not what she seemed and he was either about to get laid or shot. Not taking the chance, he ran as soon as she stopped the car. Now with the shot she had taken at him, the time for apologies had definitely passed, but he still had to try.

"I know, I'm sorry."

Kate sniffed the remnants of her tears away and wiped it on her remaining sleeve. He studied her for a moment with fear. The calm she exuded was unnerving. She was so tranquil in this dark, bloody scene, in comparison to his racing heart.

"Well, it's done now," she solemnly commented and looked away from him to the glow of the bushfire. It was so close she imagined she could almost see the flames lick the sky as they swallowed oil from the eucalyptus trees and fed on the dry tinder. He watched her from the ground, a chill shivering his bones.

"What were you going to do?" he asked.

Looking down at him, she shrugged with a slight grin, "A single woman living alone on a cattle station has needs, Buck… but luckily, this is also one of them." She casually tilted the hanging shotgun a little to her left and fired it again without warning, hitting him right in the upper thigh. At the intimate distance, his soft flesh and hard muscle ripped apart and looked like spare ribs caught in a tenderizer.

A scream tore through his body and the night air that was slowly starting to fill with the crackle of fire eating its way across the land. His body convulsed with the impact and she watched him indifferently now. The panic she had experienced at thinking he had escaped her, and then the relief that he hadn't actually thwarted justice had long gone. Now she just wanted to get back to her farm and watch from afar as the world burned once more.

A possum ran across the light of the Jeep and the bloody scene, a refugee on the run. The inferno was definitely near her land, if it hadn't hopped the fence yet.

Buck regained some consciousness after a minute while the young woman unloaded the shotgun shells and stowed them in her pocket.

He began to whimper with pain and the realization of his fate, and resorted to the last course of men about to die; leverage, revenge, comeuppance. Kate wouldn't get away with this, she couldn't. Even if no one had seen them together, seen her drive away with him in the car, they would find him, he had a job, someone would notice he was gone, a few people knew they were supposed to meet tonight. He gritted out to her through the pain of the new shotgun wound.

"They'll come looking for me. You can't think of getting away with this. They'll find me!"

Kate erected her posture at the threat, and swiveled around where she stood, as if she was looking for the audience he was speaking of. She then held her hands out from her, gesturing to the thousands of acres of bushland in central Australia where animals barely came, let alone people. Where fire would soon consume and destroy anything in its way. It was doubtful his bones would even survive. She finally let out something close to a maniacal laugh with her dramatic gestures, and leaned down to him like a lover with a secret.

"Oh Buck, they didn't find the others," she whispered conspiratorially.

He clutched his wounded leg, now just rags of flesh hanging onto each other. Blood pooled onto the dirt below, a perverse caricature of mud forming between the two. Kate, feeling satisfaction in her bones as she left another cruel, ugly man who had hurt her dying in the dirt, studied him one last time. Fire was a well-suited death. It would strip him of that beautiful face, would take away his youth and everything that made him attractive, and show what was really inside.

She strode away from him and to the car, noticing smoke was well and truly hanging on the ground, a harbinger of fire. Buck, immobilized and feeding the creek with the blood from his femoral artery, screamed out for her as she drove away with her dog. Whether it was for her to save him or kill him before the firestorm did, she wasn't sure, and she certainly didn't care.

ROWAN HILL is the pen name for Shannon Hillman, Ph.D. I am a dual national (Australian/Yank) ESL Professor on hiatus while my family lives in Southern Italy. I have been writing for the last few years and can be found sharing my writing on several writing platforms in addition to my website.

Website: writerrowanhill.com
Twitter: @writerrowanhill
Instagram: writer.rowan.hill

Shell
Barrington Smith-Seetachitt

<hr />

Grace takes a cab to the treatment center because patients aren't supposed to drive after the procedure. The entrance area seems at first unpopulated, but as soon as Grace's taxi pulls up, two young women emerge from the salmon-colored building and skitter up the walkway, giggling and knocking into each other like teenagers. Grace is barely out of the car before they slide into the back seat and the cab pulls away. It makes sense that they'd been waiting, what with the no-driving edict and the facility's discreet location so far from the city—but Grace feels somehow stung at having her spot filled so quickly. Not to mention that in order to leave now, she would have to call and ask the company to send another car to pick her up, like some kid backing out of a slumber party.

Not that Grace wants to leave. She just needs a minute before she goes in. She sits on a stone bench looking out on the side lawn where gardeners wearing gloves and hats with loose-fitting scrubs tend the flowerbeds. She considers calling her husband. This morning, Joe had decided at the last moment not to drop her off in order to hit the gym before his busy workday. She'd like to think he'd have chosen differently if he'd understood what this place was. He assumes she's just indulging in some over-priced spa, and the way things are between them lately she hasn't had the opportunity to correct that assumption. She'd thought that on the drive today she might tell him—and half-hoped he might be shocked and say, No, you don't need to do that! But he'd fled to the gym, she'd taken a cab, and now she's here. Still... she dials. Voicemail, of course.

"I'm going in," she tells his recording, "I left you the address. If you'd like to pick me up tomorrow that would be nice. If not—well, I'm sure I'll figure something out." She hates the way the words sound coming from her mouth – there is no right tone to strike between nonchalance and neediness. She hangs up quickly then stands, awkwardly tugs her skirt down over the suffocating shapewear tasked with taming the bulges her daily workouts no longer banish, and strides to the entrance.

Inside, the lobby is cavernous, the lighting soft, and every surface a tasteful, pinkish-beige. The clacking of her heels on the tile floor is partly masked by burbling water features and bell-like pings of Asian-inspired music. She signs in and—probably due to the time she spent loitering outside—sits for barely a minute before she's approached by a droopy-faced nurse in raspberry-colored scrubs.

The nurse, whose nametag says Bethany, leads Grace to a small consultation room. She gives Grace a glass of water and makes a show of placing a box of tissues on the side table by Grace's chair. Grace has no intention of shedding tears or losing control. This is not therapy. This is the step one takes when therapy isn't enough.

Nurse Bethany recites the risks and possible side effects associated with the procedure. They are daunting but Grace has done her research and knows they affect less than a tenth of a percent of patients, mostly those with compromised immune systems. Grace lets Bethany's words slide over and around her as she watches the nurse's lips—or more specifically, the small vertical "smokers" lines around her lips. Lately, whenever Grace is with another woman, she finds herself guessing the woman's age, speculating as to what attempts she's made to hide it, and judging whether those attempts have been successful. Nurse Bethany has done surprisingly little—especially considering her workplace—to disguise the fact that she's probably in her mid-fifties. Her hair is peppered with grey. There are hollows under her eyes and the marionette lines around her nose and mouth are pronounced. A dye job and a few targeted fillers could easily take five to ten years off, but apparently Nurse Bethany is a woman who doesn't feel she needs to bother.

Grace is jarred from her analysis by a change in Nurse Bethany's cadence. The litany of risks and disclaimers has ended and Nurse Bethany is speaking with more intensity now, "You know, of course, that it is no small matter to discard a living being."

This is the last place Grace should have to defend her choice, and she's annoyed to find herself reciting justifications, "Professionally, I should be at the top of my game. I am—skills-wise, but this," she pauses, grasping for the right word, "this…situation robs me of the opportunities I should have."

"You understand there are laws that protect—"

"From discrimination. I know," Grace rolls her eyes. "It's admirable how good everyone has become at avoiding the legal tripwires." She thinks back to her last job interview. She'd sat across a desk from a svelte young man in a cornflower blue suit with striped socks, feeling unkempt under his gaze, knowing he was not failing to notice the few wiry hairs escaping her keratined coif, or the ignominious trace of a turkey's gobble under her chin. It's only a small excess of skin affected by gravity – much smaller than Nurse Bethany's – but that job had been destined for someone with a firmer jawline and smoother skin. Yes, she and the young man had smiled through the formalities of an interview, but she had been eliminated before she answered the first question.

"So you're making this choice for your career?" Nurse Bethany's voice is carefully neutral, but Grace can sense her judgment.

"Do you know what the training costs for what I do? I'm still paying the debt. It took me years of sacrifice to get to this level—is it so bad to want some time getting to do the job I love?"

"Of course not… But work isn't everything."

"Fine. Let's talk about my personal life. My husband is fucking someone else." It's the first time she's said it out loud. And as she hears it, she knows it's true. Amy is the trainer assigned to Joe by his gym when his last trainer moved away. Joe talked about Amy at first, then quit mentioning her… around the same time he began leaving his phone in his gym locker during his workouts.

"But that's not even the real problem. Last year he decided—after a decade of not being sure about children—that he's reconsidered." Grace cannot recount this without tasting bile. He'd said the words so ingenuously, as if oblivious to statistics that anyone who'd ever picked up a magazine would know. As if he had no recollection of the ten years of discussions where she'd quoted these statistics.

Damn it. She reaches for the box of tissues. "What's infuriating is that it will never occur to him to blame himself, even a little. Each month when I tell him, he talks about the importance of having a positive attitude. He actually believes I'm sabotaging his new project by not being positive enough to transcend biology. And when he finds somebody else—and he will—he'll be entirely sincere when he explains to her how I wasn't really on board with having children. And she's going to feel sorry for him for having had such a shrew of a wife."

She blows her nose—twice—and tries to breathe deep. Outside the window, two workers in jewel-toned scrubs rake the gravel in the Zen garden. Grace does not feel Zen. She feels betrayed. She feels angry. "I understand it would be more convenient for the world if I would politely relinquish my professional goals and my husband, if I'd just curl up and disappear, but I'm not doing that. I refuse." She tosses the wet, sodden tissues into the trash bin. "So give me whatever I need to sign and let's get on with this."

Nurse Bethany pushes a sheaf of papers toward her. "Please make sure you've read it all." God, that tinge of judgment—or whatever it is—in her voice. You'd think they'd hire people who could sound more encouraging. Grace flips through the pages and signs at every highlighted X, ignoring the trembling of her hand.

No amount of water elements and pinging music can make the next part feel anything but hospital-like. Scrub-attired attendants measure Grace's vital signs and draw blood. She has to pee in a cup and answer the question, "Is there any chance you could be pregnant?"

She puts on the piece of cotton uselessness they call a gown, lies on a gurney, and allows more nurses in more brightly-colored scrubs to insert needles, tape them down and test the flow of dripping chemicals. The sedative begins taking effect as her body is wheeled like luggage down a series of hallways. At first, she looks at the ceiling attempting to track the turns, but then allows her eyes to flutter closed, opening them just in time to see a rubber cone descend over her nose and mouth. Everything goes black.

* * * *

Grace wakes in a dimly lit room. The needles and drips are gone. The bed is soft. The hospital has receded and once again, she's at a luxury spa. She wriggles her fingers and toes, gingerly stretches, notes the absence of any aches, and stretches again. She runs a hand over the back of her opposite arm and finds skin pulled smooth and tight over firm muscle.

She jumps from the bed and rushes to the mirror. Fearing that what she sees could be a trick of the light, she yanks the curtains open to let the sunshine confirm there is no trick: The woman in the mirror is a version of herself she hasn't seen since she was what—twenty-seven? Twenty-five maybe. Any age in her twenties where one year seemed indistinguishable from the next. She runs her hand from cheek to chin. Not even a hint of jowl.

Tears spring to her eyes. She hadn't expected this feeling of ... relief. Of a burden dropped away. She's crying. But even crying, she can't help but admire her skin as the glistening droplets roll down her cheeks. Jesus, she's gorgeous—she didn't realize it the first time around, but she does now. She's going to take advantage of everything. She lets her gown drop to the floor and looks—her body is taut and slender, the stubborn pad of fat over her belly, evaporated. She opens the wardrobe and finds her suit on a hanger, the shapewear folded on a shelf. She flings the elasticized undergarments into the trashcan and slides the blouse and skirt directly over her skin.

There's a knock at the door.

"Come." Even her voice sounds younger and smoother.

Nurse Bethany pops her head in the door. "Are you doing okay?"

Grace looks at the nurse in the mirror, "I knew," she says, "but I didn't really understand how much weight it was. I was wearing a stranger's body and trying to convince myself it was still me, but it wasn't—this is me!" She laughs and twirls. Her nipples rub against the satiny fabric of her blouse. She feels electric. She sees Nurse Bethany's eyes follow her and remembers what it's like to have another women look at her in this way, acknowledging her power. Nurse Bethany looks even older today, Grace notices. She's only slightly ashamed of the thought that crosses her mind next: It's what she deserves. Nurse Bethany is old because she is unwilling to do what Grace has done, unwilling to make bold choices. Grace was willing, and now she will reap the rewards.

She steps barefoot into her high-heeled shoes and is surprised by the sight of her slim ankles and high calves. Apparently, she'd spent so much time worrying her hips and belly and neck she hadn't noticed the gradual thickening of her legs.

Grace feels the pleasurable glow of knowing – with more certainty than she's felt in a long time – that she has just made the best decision of her life. She flips her hair over a shoulder and addresses Nurse Bethany. "I have a job interview tomorrow, and you know what? They're going to offer it to me in the room. And my husband? He can do what he wants. I'm going to have options." She strides into the hallway.

"I'm ready to check out."

* * * *

Grace opens her eyes, not sure at first where she is. She looks around at what seems to be a hotel room and remembers. The spa. The procedure. The tubes and wires are gone, but she is still wearing an institutional cotton gown, which has become a wrinkled mass beneath her. As she wriggles to adjust it, her back creaks in protest.

She feels a stab of anxiety. The testimonials all gushed about the absence of stiff joints. She extends her arm, letting the beam of sunlight sneaking through the curtains illuminate the back of her hand. The skin is still thin with fine wrinkles and pocked with the beginning of an age spot she has tried to convince herself is a freckle. No. Please, no. It had to have worked.

She swings her legs over the side of the bed and stands. Her heart sinks as she feels the familiar, mysterious pain at the back of her right heel that greets her each morning, and the tight muscle on the left side of her neck.

With a growing sense of dread, she jerks open the curtains, inviting the sun's brutal honesty, then takes inventory of her disappointments in the mirror. The deep vertical crease in her cheek, the little droop of her right eyelid, the infuriating wattle under her chin—all intact. Joe will laugh at her…if she's lucky. She hasn't prepared him for the expense, and the paperwork was very clear that nothing is refundable.

A rap at the door, and Nurse Bethany pokes in her salt-and-pepper head. She looks at Grace directly, not making excuses or trying to put a good face on it. "I brought you these." She holds out a pair of emerald-green scrubs.

"I don't need an extra day. I'll just take my suit."

Nurse Bethany's eyes flutter with some emotion Grace can't quite read, "Your clothes are gone."

"I paid for a very expensive procedure that hasn't worked in the slightest. I understand I signed a waiver so I won't make a fuss, but I'll be damned if I walk away from a twelve-hundred dollar outfit.

"I'm very sorry. I'd hoped you understood. It was in the contract – about the shell?"

"Of course. We discussed it. There's a shell that's discarded after the procedure. How does this pertain to my clothes?"

"Ms. Ayers… Grace. You are the shell."

The area around Grace's heart constricts so tightly she can barely breathe. "I don't understand."

Nurse Bethany crosses to the window and points, "The procedure worked."

Outside, a woman wearing Grace's suit walks across the lawn. Grace blinks, disoriented. Watching the woman, Grace feels the memory of a slender waist. She recalls a vitality that flowed through her and lent a bounce to her every step. And when the woman bends to pick a flower from the garden, Grace gasps, seeing her own profile, her smooth skin, the flush of her own cheek.

Involuntarily, Grace presses her hand to the window. Beneath the shock, there is an odd surge of joy—as if she has given birth to a beautiful daughter. Grace thinks the young woman might turn and see her, too. She wants that.

But now a late-model Tesla is rolling into the circle driveway. Joe is at the wheel, his posture somehow managing to convey annoyed resentment even as he drives. He pulls to a stop, lifts his phone, and impatiently texts a single word: Here. Reprimand implied.

The young woman raises her phone—Grace's phone—in a careless wave. Grace can't help but grin as Joe freezes in surprise, and then, as she had dreamed of, his demeanor changes. He jumps from the car and moves toward her, walking briskly, and then, as he sees her in more detail, running. Through the window, Grace cannot hear his exclamations as he embraces her youthful version, but she can see his look of approval as he runs his thumb tenderly—and assessingly—across her cheek.

She is happy to see that her younger self is unimpressed by the paternal gesture and does not duck her head under his caress. She holds herself with the bearing of a queen. She stands strong and indifferent, allowing Joe all the time he needs for understanding to sink in—that the power between them has shifted. It is satisfying to see the play of emotions cross Joe's face – his renewed desire for her followed quickly by a look of fear as he recalls his recent behavior and realizes he is in danger of losing her. His earlier sulkiness is gone, replaced by an almost-obsequience as he carries her bag, opens the car door, and waits with infinite patience while she lowers herself and swings her stiletto-clad feet inside. For a moment, Grace feels victorious.

But as the car carries her husband and the young woman out to the road and disappears, she feels a sharp emptiness. Grief blows through her like a cold wind.

Becoming aware again of Nurse Bethany standing at her shoulder, Grace takes a moment to steady her voice. "What now? When I read the word discarded, I didn't realize I would still be… that I would be."

"At another facility, you might not be. There's some debate as to how to interpret the laws. But here, you should be fine as long as you never try to access your old life. We're lucky, I suppose."

We're lucky… It takes Grace a moment to digest the implication of Nurse Bethany's words. She looks out the window at a worker in blue scrubs tending to a rose bush, another in aqua, trimming a hedge. All the workers she's seen here have been women. All of a certain age. Grace looks at Nurse Bethany—she has good bone structure under her sags. Her twenty-five-year-old version must have been beautiful, as she strode away into her future.

"You tried to tell me, but I didn't understand."

Nurse Bethany's smile is wistful as she sets the emerald scrubs on the bed, "We never do."

BARRINGTON SMITH-SEETACHITT is a former Midwesterner who city-hopped around the globe before landing in Los Angeles, where she writes for page and screen while doing typical Los Angeles things like working day jobs and trying to eat less carbs. Her work – which is often but not always speculative fiction – has been published in journals that include *Colorado Review, Sycamore Review, Chariton Review,* and *The Drum.* She recently co-wrote a segment for Season 3 of AMC Shudder's anthology series *CREEPSHOW.* You can sample her short fiction on her podcast, *Words to Drive By,* or read random thoughts about her life and projects on her blog at BarringtonSmith.net.

From Scratch
Sonora Taylor

The ooze was Heather's least favorite part. The skin on her palms she could deal with, as well as the mottled red and orange pulp that seeped under her nails when she peeled the skin away after boiling it. She didn't even mind the ooze that much. It was simply her least favorite part because it was the messiest to clean up. She had to wash her hands after every slice, or else the knife would stick to her fingers and make the cutting all the more difficult.

Heather washed her hands and lifted another peach from a bowl of ice water. It was soft and ripe in her hand, ready to go into her famous cobbler. She set the peach on the cutting board and stuck her knife into it. Slowly, not too fast — she didn't want it to turn into mush. Peeling the skin and cutting the peach slice-by-slice was what made it worthwhile. It was what made cooking an outlet to scratch the itch, one she'd felt since she was young.

The softened pulp oozed through the slit in the skin. It smeared on Heather's wrist. She paused and watched it bleed, then closed her eyes and licked the ooze away.

* * * *

Heather brought a plate of roasted brussels sprouts to the dining room table, where Brad was waiting with a knife in hand. The brussels sprouts were lightly charred, folded and black beneath a darkened glaze of balsamic and ashen flecks of pepper. It was one of her best dishes.

"Oof," Brad said as she set the plate down. "Brussel sprouts always smell like broccoli died in a diaper."

Heather pursed her lips as she sat down, and Brad took her wrist. "Come on, baby, you know I'm kidding," he said.

"That doesn't mean it's funny. I worked hard on this meal."

"And I'm grateful for it." He grabbed a brussels sprout and grinned.

Brad popped the sprout in his mouth, and the change from a smirk to delight in his face was enough to quiet Heather's temper. "They're delicious," he said as he reached for another.

Heather batted his hand away. "Use the serving spoon," she said. The spread was too good to be handled by greasy fingers. Next to the plate of brussels sprouts were mashed red potatoes with flecks of rosemary, roasted chicken breasts dripping with peach-bourbon barbecue sauce, and glasses of iced tea mixed with fresh-squeezed lemonade.

"You got it, boss." Brad began to serve himself, and Heather closed her eyes. Most of the time, she could handle his jokes. It helped that she enjoyed handling his body in the bedroom once dinner was over. But he could be especially irritating when they weren't having sex — especially when he joked about her cooking. Cooking was her passion, a hobby that kept her sane.

The sound of Brad scraping the food she prepared onto his plate rang in her ears. She saw his snarky grin, heard his jokes above the din of crackling sprouts and the thump of potatoes onto his plate. She imagined him cutting himself on a knife, or gagging on a stray chicken bone that hadn't made it out of the breast.

Her thoughts instead turned to the chicken breasts, raw and pink on her cutting board. They'd wobbled as she cut them, left their juices behind in the wood. They seemed to bleed as she brushed them with her homemade sauce, sizzling in the hellfire of her oven. It was almost as satisfying as every lemon half she'd squeezed dry into the pitcher.

Heather opened her eyes and smiled as she took the serving spoon from Brad. "Hope you like it," she said.

* * * *

Heather had felt the itch of inflicting pain for years. She went to school and watched the other kids at recess instead of playing with them. She imagined them falling off the monkey bars, or leaping off the swings and landing head first on the ground below. *Crack, crunch,* like the sound of her father eating chicken wings. She giggled at the thought.

It soon became old to imagine them being harmed by chance. Heather imagined pushing them from the swings, pulling them from the monkey bars, and driving a rusted bar through their skulls. Every day became a challenge for her to imagine some new way of hurting someone. She'd get so lost in thought that she'd sit for minutes on end without saying a word, staring at the wall and thinking only of the harm she wished she could inflict.

"What happened to your arm?"

Her fourth-grade teacher, Ms. McMillan, looked at Heather with concern one day after recess. Heather looked down and saw a large red splotch on her arm.

"Do you have eczema?" Ms. McMillan asked.

Heather vaguely remembered scratching her arm as she thought of clawing Stacy Turner's eyeballs from her sockets. "I just scratch when I daydream," Heather said.

"Well, maybe try playing with the other kids instead," Ms. McMillan offered. "You don't want to scratch yourself until you bleed."

No, she didn't — she wanted other people to bleed. But she knew from watching other kids get in trouble for hitting, biting, or other lesser offenses that doing so would just get more unwanted attention from her teacher.

As she grew, her daydreams grew stronger. Heather imagined scratching through flesh, absorbing other people's blood and pus as if they were her own. She hadn't started out wanting to kill, and even as the urge grew stronger, she knew deep down she couldn't. That didn't mean she didn't want to, though. She wanted to very, very much.

* * *

"Today, we're going to prepare pork tenderloin."

Heather stood in a cubicle designed to look like a kitchen. She'd signed up for Cooking and Nutrition as an elective to pad her senior year of high school. They'd spent the first six months learning about nutrition, and now, at last, they were going to cook.

"You'll see the pork in your refrigerators," Mr. Dale said as he walked by the students. "Cut it into two pieces. We're going to roast one half, and sear the other."

"No deep frying?" Stacy cracked. Stacy's friend Pamela laughed, but Heather didn't say a word. Their laughter surrounded her like flies as she pulled the tenderloin from the fridge. It sat pink and glistening beneath the saran wrap, with globules of fat swimming through the meat. Heather studied it. It looked like a skinned thigh, freshly shorn from the leg of a cackling girl.

Heather shook her head and brought her focus back to cooking. She unwrapped the tenderloin and saw a bit of ooze from the meat stick to the plastic.

"That is so gross."

Heather turned and saw Stacy staring in disgust at the pork. "It looks like a giant, dead mole rat," Stacy said.

"What mole rat?" Pamela said. "It doesn't even have a face."

"It's purple and wrinkly and nasty!"

"Yeah, like your boyfriend's dick!"

"Ladies!" Mr. Dale strode over to their section while Stacy and Pamela laughed. "Do I need to separate you?"

Heather could separate them — she just needed the right knife. Heather picked up the chef's knife and turned to the pork loin, the flesh she was supposed to slice. She carved into the meat and felt immense relief at being able to slice through something. She made the next slice more carefully, slowly. She watched as the flesh jiggled beneath the blade, as if the pork was nervous for its fate. She smiled a little as she carved.

The third slice to fall wasn't pink. Inside a ring of the standard purple flesh, Heather saw a white and grey ooze that poured onto the cutting board. She took a step back, but it was Stacy who cried out. "What the hell is that?" she screamed as she pointed at the loin.

Mr. Dale walked over, then yelped when he saw the loin. "Oh my God," he said as he grabbed a trash can from under the sink. "That's a tumor."

"Gross!" Stacy wretched a little. Heather stood silent and watched as Mr. Dale scraped the meat into the trash. A trail of slime with bits of pieces of the tumor remained on the cutting board, an image Heather burned into her memory before Mr. Dale shoved the cutting board into the sink.

"I'm never eating meat again," Stacy declared as Mr. Dale went to retrieve a spare loin of pork. Heather, though, had found a better way to scratch her itch.

* * * *

Heather hadn't had much interest in cooking before the incident with the pork loin. She took the class as an elective, and figured it'd be good to learn the basics for when she was finally able to move out on her own. But the memory of the loin on the cutting board stayed in her mind with a persistence only matched by her imagined kills. She felt a familiar itching in her fingertips, one she thought could only be sated by blood — blood that could only be imaginary.

Heather didn't have to imagine the blood of meat, though. She could cook it — and that's what she began to do. Heather could bloody her fingers without needing to hide any evidence. She watched cooking shows with fascination, studied their techniques with knives, and learned about the best ingredients. Her only complaint was that their kitchens were too clean, the mess of yolks, bloody meat, and pulpy fruits and vegetables scrubbed clean from pristine white countertops before filming began.

But that was what her kitchen was for.

Heather delighted in the mess that cooking made. For every head she couldn't bash, she could smash a head of garlic beneath the blade of her knife. For every limb she couldn't cut, she could sever a cut of meat. The fattier, the better. The meat didn't even need to be sick, like the pork loin had been. Meat's normal state was enough to satisfy her cravings.

Heather began offering to make dinner multiple nights per week. She excelled in her cooking class, and earned consistent praise from Mr. Dale. "This soufflé is amazing," he said on the last day of class. "You have a gift."

Heather smiled, but more at the memory of pulverizing the eggs into yellow muck, the mucus of their whites becoming foamed and fluffy through the whir. It sizzled and foamed like pus. Heather already had plans to make meringue for Jessica's graduation party next weekend.

Heather's talents had the residual effect of drawing people closer to her. Her classmates in cooking class told their friends about her food. Her parents told her relatives and their friends, offering up her snacks, desserts, and entrees for company or a church potluck.

Normally, Heather would've glowered at the thought of being around so many people, especially so many people she couldn't harm. But cooking for them was a different story. It gave her an excuse to spend more time in the kitchen, more time with her recipes and all the visceral ingredients she could find. Heather didn't mind having others around her when she could scratch her itch through cooking. She didn't mind that her cooking brought them close to her, so long as she had the kitchen to retreat to when the desires she'd held since she was a girl grew too intense to bear.

Heather trusted that cooking would always be a way to lessen the intensity. But there were days when the intensity rose like dough.

* * * *

"This is delicious, babe."

Brad chewed on a mouthful of hot peach cobbler fresh out of the oven. He opened his mouth and fanned his tongue as the heat caught up with him. Heather imagined his tongue boiling and sizzling. She tried not to cross her legs in response to the rush of tingles that swirled between her thighs.

"I'm glad you like it," she said as she licked a bit of filling from her spoon.

"Of course I do. It's why I'm dating you." Brad smiled at his stupid joke. "Well, that and your mind, of course."

"Of course." Heather rolled her eyes and faked a smile as Brad leaned forward and kissed her cheek. She didn't mind his humor. She had to force a smile so he wouldn't see her brow furrowed in thought; thoughts of Brad's skin being sliced and his blood pooling on her palms like the juice of the peaches.

"You want some more ice cream?" she asked as she stood up.

"Nah, I've got plenty," he said as he held up his bowl.

"A drink or something, then?" Heather had to get to the kitchen, her refuge for when her thoughts went from a swirl to a maelstrom. "Maybe some berries, or —"

"Get me some more cobbler if you want." Brad grinned as he ate another large mouthful. Heather saw filling and caramelized crust seep through his teeth. She imagined blood in their place, pouring out as he bled from inside out after she ran a knife through his lungs. She pivoted and sped into the kitchen.

* * * *

Heather kept cooking into her early twenties, but she felt the satisfaction dissipate with each passing year. It grew boring to see pulp and slime on her cutting board. She'd serve meals to her guests and on her worst days, imagine their heads and hands on the platters instead. Heather would retreat to the kitchen, but it would only do so much.

"Honey, what's wrong with your arm?" Her mother looked at her with wide eyes as she followed her into the kitchen after a sudden departure at Thanksgiving. Thanksgiving was a particular time for Heather to shine, with an array of dishes to make, meats to carve, and vegetables to mash and sear. Even the pumpkin pie made Heather smile as it trembled with the firmness of a perfect bake.

But Thanksgiving also brought a surge of people into the dining room — aunts, uncles, grandparents, and cousins; all ready for food and all talking and laughing loudly over multiple glasses of red wine. Heather's Aunt Margaret spilled a glass over her mashed potatoes, and all Heather could see was everyone's blood pouring over the plates. Heather had to get away — but her mother hadn't let her.

Heather was about to say nothing was wrong, when her fingers began to move up and down her forearm in clear view. "Just itchy, I guess," she said.

"You getting a food allergy from all that cooking?"

"That's not how it works." It'd be so much easier for Heather if everyone around her weren't so damn irritating. She scratched harder, but stopped when her mother yelped. Heather looked down and saw three beads of blood coming from an open scratch in her skin.

"You're working too hard," her mother said as she grabbed a paper towel and moistened it in the sink. "You do all this cooking and you need to take a break —"

"Stop!" Heather pulled back her arm before her mother could blot away the blood. "I've got it, Mom. I just have an itch."

"Well, let me handle the pie then, or —"

"No!"

Her mother stepped back as Heather grabbed the knife. Heather caught herself, and set it back on the countertop. She grabbed the pie and pulled it towards her before lifting the knife again.

"I'll get it," she said, adding a softness to her voice that she knew would bring out her mother's sympathy the way a bit of instant coffee brought out the flavor in banana bread. "It's fine."

* * * *

Heather told herself it was fine, told herself that whenever she cooked and fantasized. She didn't want her fantasies to spill over into her life — it would be far too risky, not to mention messy — but with each new dish, the quelling of her urges became harder to come by.

Heather responded by challenging herself. She made more items from scratch. She expanded from cooking and baking to pickling (the way the vegetables shriveled in the brine was especially delicious to watch), curing (a salty end for scraps of fat and flesh — her mouth watered just thinking of it), and any method she could find. When the cooking itself dulled for her, she looked for new tools to inflict torture on her ingredients. Tenderizers, fruit and vegetable cutters of various shapes and sizes — it seemed the store in the mall had some new cooking innovation every month, one that Heather was all too delighted to try.

Her urges led to experimentation. The experimentation led to more people asking for her food. More people led to her urges growing. It was a cycle that once was freeing for Heather, but became its own oppressive trap. She wondered how much longer she could cook in the kitchen before she took her skills and her urges to the people she fed.

* * * *

How bad would it really be? Heather ran her fingertip over the blade of her chef's knife. It was far too sharp to cut another square of cobbler. She hadn't pulled it out for dessert.

How much trouble would it be to hide Brad's body? Her parents didn't know they were dating. They didn't have any mutual friends.

How satisfying would it be to watch him bleed onto the empty plates? To hear him scream like steaming potatoes whistling from the microwave, then gurgle like a thick stew in the middle of a simmer? Would it be worth all the trouble it would take to clean up her mess — not to mention cover her tracks?

"Baby?"

Heather looked to her right and saw Brad leaning in the doorway to the kitchen. He smiled, but she saw a concerned glint in his eyes when his gaze landed on the knife. "Did the cobbler solidify or something?"

Heather smiled back — one that was cool, confident, and gave off an essence of just what she could do with that knife. "No," she said sweetly. "I just wanted to see if it needed sharpening."

"I've got a tool that needs sharpening." Brad thrust his hips out, and Heather widened her grin.

"Sounds good," she said. "Go wait for me in the bedroom. I'll bring dessert."

Brad scampered off, and Heather hummed to herself as she put the chef's knife away. Before closing the drawer, she took out a tiny, but sharp, dicing knife. It would be easier to conceal. She then grabbed a bowl and a serving spoon, and looked at the cobbler. The cobbler lay cool, waiting. Oozing into its glass dish.

Heather plunged a spoon into another square, and sighed with relief as filling pooled around the ladle. Dessert was going to be heavenly.

SONORA TAYLOR is the award-winning author of Little Paranoias: Stories, Without Condition, The Crow's Gift and Other Tales, Please Give, and Wither and Other Stories. Her short stories have appeared in multiple publications, including Camden Park Press's Quoth the Raven, Kandisha Press's Women of Horror Vol. 2: Graveyard Smash, The Sirens Call, Frozen Wavelets, Mercurial Stories, Tales to Terrify, and the Ladies of Horror fiction podcast. Her latest book, Seeing Things, is now available on Amazon. She lives in Arlington, Virginia, with her husband.

facebook.com/sonorawrites/
https://twitter.com/sonorawrites
https://www.goodreads.com/sonorawrites
https://www.instagram.com/sonorataylor/
Sonorawrites.com

INVASIVE SPECIES
Dawn DeBraal

~~~

Dottie Latham opened the mailbox and found a little plastic envelope. The outside of the package said it contained stud earrings. She pondered when she had ordered earrings.

She looked across the street. Patsy Nelson was working in her front yard garden. It was looking glorious. She was going to give Dottie a run for her money in the neighborhood "Best of Blooms" landscape competition. The winner was entitled to two-thousand dollars toward an outdoor makeover. Dottie wanted to win so bad she could taste it. All-day long, she weeded, shaped, fed, and watered her gardens. She wanted her display to be the envy of the neighborhood, but most of all, Dottie wanted to put her neighbor Patsy in her place.

Patsy waved. Dottie called out. "Looking good!" but on the inside, she said a few choice words about her neighbor that Patsy would never hear. Patsy was not numb to Dottie's feelings. This had been an ongoing feud for many years. On the surface, they kept it cordial.

Dottie cut open the package when she got into the house. It was a package of seeds. She hadn't ordered seeds from anyone. She turned the gray plastic bag over in her hand. Everything was written in a foreign language. She couldn't read it.

Dottie wondered what the seeds were and then decided, what could it hurt? She took the package behind her house and sprinkled them in her garden. There was only one way to find out. She watered the garden, dousing the new seeds while she dreamed of what exotic plant would come up.

A couple of weeks later, Dottie found a few strange seedlings in the garden. Excited, she studied them carefully. She knew these strange plants were the result of the package she received in the mail. By now, she had convinced herself that it was a gift from one of her gardening friends who undoubtedly wanted her to beat Patsy Nelson. Patsy had already won the "Best of Blooms" a few years ago. The beautiful fountain in her front yard was what she bought with her winnings. Despite getting first place, Patsy entered the competition every year, much to the chagrin of her fellow gardening club members.

The seedlings were three inches high with a very unique shaped leaf. While lost in thought, her neighbor Lorraine came into her yard to admire Dottie's garden. She spied the strange plants.

"What are those? I've never seen them before."

"Oh, those. I don't really know. The seeds came in the mail. A gift, I think. They are interesting though, aren't they?" Dottie said offhandedly.

"Dottie, are you daft? Haven't you heard that people are receiving invasive seeds from foreign countries? You aren't supposed to plant them. You are supposed to save the container and the seeds and send them to the Department of Agriculture. You might have planted something that can hurt our whole city garden horticulture!"

Dottie pooh-poohed Lorraine but found herself still bothered by the accusation after her neighbor went home. She thought it sounded like a wild conspiracy theory. There was so much of that going on nowadays.

Dottie hadn't ordered the seeds, and she didn't know what they were, and they came from outside the United States. Just in case, she pulled every seedling out. She didn't toss them in the garbage. She put them in the firepit and started them on fire. A good dousing of charcoal lighter fluid and a farmer match gave her the satisfactory *whoosh* of destruction. Dottie watched the seedlings shrivel up and die in the heat of the flames. She felt much better when she saw they were destroyed.

Her garden flourished as she continued to work on it. She ordered magazines and studied their displays. Dottie took pictures and put them on her home page, delighted when people told her how lovely her gardens were. She could taste victory.

A week away from the "Best of Blooms" competition, Dottie noticed a dead spot in the garden. She shrieked as she ran to the area where the dead flowers lay. Just yesterday, everything was robust and healthy. What was going on? She studied the area intensely and surmised she probably had a cutworm living in the ground. Dottie rooted around the dead plants looking to find the cause of their sudden failure.

"Ouch!" She observed the cut on her finger which was dripping blood. The cut was deep. She wondered if there was a piece of broken glass she had grabbed. The blood was coming out profusely. Dottie trotted to the bathroom turning the water on to sluice down her burning cut. It was painful, and it was deep. She needed to get it cleaned out. She allowed the cut to bleed freely by hanging her hand over the sink for a bit, making sure all the dirt and germs drained out of the wound. When she felt it was clean, she applied pressure and then a bandage.

Her hand hurt. There would be no more gardening today. She lay on the couch, keenly aware of her throbbing hand. She kept it above her heart, something she remembered reading somewhere. Dottie flicked on the remote control to watch the nightly news on the television. She was horrified at the top story.

"Seedgate. That is what they are calling it, folks. Mysterious mailings of packages containing unidentified seeds have been received by residents across the United States. The Department of Agriculture is cautioning those receiving the seeds in the mail not to throw them out or plant them, for they could contain an invasive species. Recipients of the seeds should mail the shipping bag and its sealed contents to the State Department of Agriculture for further identification. Again, the Department of Agriculture cautions those who have received the gray mailing bags in the mail not to plant the seeds, and not to throw them away, for they could take hold and grow in the landfill."

Dottie sat up quickly. She was a fool to have planted those seeds and needed to make sure that every last plant was gone from her garden. Could that be the reason she had the bald patch—had the invasive species taken hold in her garden? She decided to take another look. As she stood, she felt woozy and flopped back down on the couch. Dottie raised her hand. It had turned purple and swelled to twice its normal size.

Dottie called her doctor and was amazed when they told her to call an ambulance immediately. She was having an allergic reaction to something that entered her bloodstream most likely through the cut she received in the garden. There were some fatal diseases like leptospirosis that came from contaminated soils. They told her to keep her hand above her heart. She knew that. She wasn't an idiot. She called for an ambulance.

Clancy meowed signaling he was hungry. Dottie couldn't get up to feed him and she was told not to move as it could circulate the poison through her body. She called Lorraine to let her know she was on the way to the hospital by ambulance. Could she check on Clancy?

"Of course, I will. I'm on my way." Lorraine burst through the door. "Good Lord, Dottie, your hand!" A short time later, the ambulance came and hustled Dottie out the door. Lorraine assured her friend that she would take care of the cat, finish watering her garden, and lock up the house before she left. *It must be bad,* Lorraine thought. The ambulance had the siren going when they left Dottie's house.

Lorraine tidied up as she promised her friend. She washed the blood down the sink. Dottie really did a number on her finger judging by the mess. She filled Clancy's water dish and took out a can of food, plopping the smelly mess into his crystal bowl. After locking up the house, Lorraine went to check on Dottie's flowers. She knew her friend took pride in them and was a fierce competitor in the "Best of Blooms" competition coming up in a few days. Her flowers looked a little dry.

Lorraine turned on the hose and put the nozzle setting on a gentle spray. She started at the back of the garden, giving it generous amounts of water.

Patsy came from across the street.

"Lorraine, what's happened to Dottie? I saw the ambulance." Her eyes scanned the new landscaping Dottie had created; it was quite extensive.

Dottie had not allowed Patsy to see the backyard all summer. Patsy supposed it was because Dottie was afraid of the competition.

"She cut her finger and had an allergic reaction, her hand swelled up like a balloon. I tell you it was horrific. The doctor told her to take an ambulance. I just fed Clancy and told her I'd take care of the garden."

"That's terrible. Please let me know how she is doing. My goodness, Dottie has outdone herself this year." Patsy left Lorraine to her watering.

The vine moved subtly. Lorraine continued to douse the garden as the small tendril wrapped around her ankle. Lorraine didn't notice until she moved a step ahead.

In a rude awakening, Lorraine fell flat on her face. She looked at her foot to see the slender vine around her ankle.

"What a fool I am." Relieved she hadn't broken anything, Lorraine used her hands to pull the vine from her leg. Another vine whipped up and wrapped itself around Lorraine's arms.

"What?" Lorraine tried to pull her arms away when a third vine came around her neck. She started to protest. The tendril snaked into her mouth and down her throat. The vine with strange leaves encapsulated Lorraine in a few short minutes. At first, she struggled but then surrendered to her fate. As Lorraine shrunk, the bud on the new plant grew.

Patsy snuck over to Dottie's house bright and early the next morning. She had heard through the grapevine that Dottie didn't make it, that she died of some sort of sepsis last night. Patsy tried calling Lorraine, but the woman didn't answer her phone. Patsy found the hidden key and let Clancy out. She didn't want Clancy to starve in the house, but she was also not a cat lover and refused to take the animal home.

The water was running. Lorraine, watering again? The woman knew nothing about gardening. She was going to cause root rot if she didn't let the plants dry out in between.

Patsy indignantly stomped to the back of the house. There was no Lorraine, only a wet soppy patch in the garden and an unusually large plant with a huge bud. Patsy's mouth fell open at the impressive plant. She turned off the hose and scoped out Dottie's garden. The woman had some beautiful plants. Just what Patsy needed to win the "Best of Blooms" this year.

Patsy grabbed a shovel and dug out several of her favorites. The most impressive was the giant plant looking as if it were ready to burst. She put all the plants she took in Dottie's wheelbarrow to take them back home.

Patsy felt a little guilty. She had sent Dottie some invasive seeds. She hoped that Dottie's flowers would choke out before the big show. Obviously, Dottie was smarter than she gave her credit for. She must not have taken the bait because her garden looked beautiful.

Patsy lifted the handles of the wheelbarrow. The wet plants were heavy. She ran down the driveway to her back yard before any of the neighbors saw her. She dug a new area to plant the massive budding plant beside the other showy plants she'd stolen from her dead neighbor.

Patsy was breathing hard as she backfilled around the plant, tamping the dirt down, and watering deeply. Then, satisfied the new plants would survive the transplant, Patsy brushed off her hands. She had better get dinner going before her husband Ed came home.

Patsy turned to head for the house falling to the ground. She looked down seeing a small tendril of a vine with strange leaves had curled around her ankle.

"What a klutz," she laughed as she reached to unwind the plant from her foot. The vine grabbed her arms; another went around her neck and ran down Patsy's throat before she could even get out a scream.

The invasive plant's ballistochory reaction to Patsy's sustenance spewed thousands of seeds that quickly worked their way into the ground of the freshly watered garden.

"Patsy? Where are you?" Ed Nelson stepped off his back porch admiring the new plants his wife had planted. He wondered how much money she'd spent today on this ridiculous garden show but admired the giant bud on the exotic looking plant with strange leaves. The bud looked as if it were ready to burst. He called his wife again; there was no answer.

"Meow." Ed jerked around, startled. It was only Clancy, the neighbor's cat, who came up to him rubbing himself on Ed's legs.

"Good kitty," he said, patting its head. He'd heard that Dottie died in the hospital last night from sepsis. Patsy, being the good neighbor she was, probably took Clancy in. He reached down to catch the cat who ran from him. Ed hurried to grab Clancy, falling to the ground. He had tripped over a vine that wrapped around his foot.

DAWN DeBRAAL lives in rural Wisconsin with her husband Red, a slightly overweight rat terrier, and a cat. She has discovered that her love of telling a good story can be written. Published stories with Palm-sized press, Spillwords Author of the month 2019, Mercurial Stories, Potato Soup Journal, Edify Fiction, Zimbell House Publishing, Clarendon House Publishing, Blood Song Books, Black Hare Press, Fantasia Divinity, Cafelit, Reanimated Writers, Guilty Pleasures, Unholy Trinity, The World of Myth, Dastaan World, Vamp Cat, Runcible Spoon, E. Merry Publishing, Siren's Call, Iron Horse Publishing, Setu Magazine, Literary Yard, Falling Star Magazine 2019 Pushcart Nominee.

Amazon.com/Dawn-DeBraal/e/B07STL8DLX?
Facebook.com/All-The-Clever-Names-Were-Taken-114783950248991/
Twitter: @dawndebraal

JOSEPHINE
Michelle Renee Lane

Luna entered the small warehouse in the Mitte neighborhood of Berlin that had recently been renovated into office space, an art gallery, and the small film production company that had hired her for a series of shoots. Luna was a free agent in the adult film industry and was invited to locales all over the world to star in high and low-production pornographic films. Born in Brazil, Luna spent most of her time traveling and working in Europe. An adult magazine had recently dubbed her the "Josephine Baker of Porn." It was a strange moniker that smacked of racist fantasies about women of color, which wasn't surprising given the fact that she worked within an industry that encouraged voyeurism and catered to the white male gaze. She was a beautiful, young black woman who loved sex and wanted to earn a living while traveling the world and fucking strangers. There was only one career path that allowed her to live that life: porn star.

At twenty-five, Luna had been working in the industry for nearly six years and she had built an impressive following among not only the people who subscribed to various porn channels, but also among filmmakers and other porn stars. She had worked with some of the most famous male porn stars in Europe, young and old, and had developed a taste for some of the older men who were hitting their peak performances over the age of forty. While the younger men were athletic and full of energy, the older men had developed better techniques with years of practice, and fucking them was like taking a master class on sex. There was a guy in Czechia who had made her cum four times before he even penetrated her with his cock. She often thought about him when she was having trouble getting off with someone else.

Inside the modern metal and glass structure, there was a large freight elevator. A sign on the wall listed the different businesses and floor numbers next to them. The building had six floors, and she wondered if she'd be able to catch a glimpse of the *Weltzeituhr* from the top floor, where the film studio was located. She pressed the up button to call the elevator and while she waited, someone entered the building behind her. The only reason she knew someone came in was that the outer door rattled slightly when it closed. The footfalls of the person who entered the building were completely silent. When he suddenly appeared next to her, she covered a gasp with her hand and then laughed at the fact he had startled her.

The older man had salt and pepper hair closely cropped in a fashionable cut that made her think of aging punks she'd seen in London. This man wasn't as old as them, and she guessed that he was somewhere between forty and forty-five. The smile he flashed her reached his sparkling crystal blue eyes. He had a handsome face with good bone structure, full lips, and a hint of dimples that would allow him to flirt without ever speaking a word. But when he said 'hello,' in French-accented English, the hairs at the back of her neck stood on end. Before she could respond, the elevator arrived.

He opened the metal gate and held it for her to step inside, and then he closed the gate before pushing the button for the top floor.

"Are you going to the film studio?" Luna spoke to the man's back.

He glanced at her over his shoulder. "Yes."

"Me too. I'm Luna Kohl."

He chuckled with his back to her. "I know."

"You look familiar to me. Would I have seen you in any films?"

He turned to face her, and his eyes roved over her body from her toes to the top of her head. "Perhaps. I've been working in adult films for fifteen years." He extended his hand to her. "I'm Nicholas Blue."

Luna recognized the name but had never seen his films. Still, she couldn't help feeling like she knew him from somewhere. Gazing into his impossibly blue eyes, she understood where his name had come from.

A smile played at the corner of his mouth, and he licked his bottom lip. "I'm very excited to be working with the Josephine Baker of Porn."

Luna was no shrinking violet, but the timbre of his voice and the raw need in his eyes made her cheeks flush. She laughed nervously. "You read that article? What does that even mean?"

Nicholas took a step closer to Luna and continued to caress her with his gaze, but he didn't try to touch her. "I think they mean, that like Josephine you work almost exclusively in Europe as an expat, and you are a beautiful black woman who knows how to use her body to tell a story and entice audiences."

She was suddenly very aware of how fast her heart was beating. The space inside the elevator seemed to be getting smaller, and she was relieved when it stopped on their floor. Nicholas opened and held the gate for her again.

The open floor plan of the studio allowed for a variety of films to be shot at once, with different themed rooms separated by moveable privacy screens. In the center was a lounge of sorts. The director, a woman Luna had spoken to three weeks ago during a Zoom meeting, was on the phone and motioned for them to have a seat.

Luna set her overnight bag on a chair and then made herself comfortable on the leather couch. Nicholas placed his duffle bag on the floor and sat at the opposite end of the couch, unbuttoning his suit jacket before straightening his tie.

"Have you been in Berlin long?" He asked.

"My train arrived at noon, so I've only been here about seven hours. Have you worked with this company before?"

"No, have you?"

She shook her head. "I wonder if they usually do shoots at night. Typically, I'd be ending my day at this hour."

"I'm afraid that's my fault. I prefer to shoot at night."

Luna wasn't sure how to respond, and since he didn't seem to be offering any further explanation, she just smiled and shrugged.

Luna had a knack for reading people, but she couldn't quite figure Nicholas out. He hadn't done or said anything inappropriate, but something about him made her nervous. The kind of nervousness you feel when you're watching a scary movie and the anticipation of the next fright is building and you know at any moment something bad is going to happen. You're afraid, but excited about it at the same time.

"How long do you think we'll have to wait?" Luna said.

"I hope it won't be too much longer. I really want to kiss you."

Luna shifted in her seat.

"Am I making you uncomfortable?"

"No," she lied, and pretended to be interested in a potted plant on the coffee table instead of looking at him.

Nicholas moved closer to Luna and took her hand to kiss it. "I'm not going to hurt you," he said, pausing to make eye contact. "Not unless you ask me to."

Luna pulled her hand out of his. "Are you usually this friendly with co-stars before a shoot?"

He laughed. "No."

"Then why are you flirting with me?"

"Because you are beautiful, and I can't wait to fuck you."

Something about the way a Frenchman said the word 'fuck' always turned her on, but there was an almost hypnotic quality to Nicholas' voice. Before she could decide if his words concealed a threat, he pulled her closer for a kiss. He tasted like strong French cigarettes, cold night air, and something she couldn't quite place, a metallic tang that reminded her of pennies. She wasn't sure how long they'd been kissing when the director came to talk to them, because Luna didn't hear her approach.

"Should I just set up the camera here?"

Embarrassed, Luna ended the kiss, and stood on shaky legs. "Sorry, I never behave like that at a job when I'm not on camera."

"Don't apologize. It seems you two already have great chemistry."

Nicholas stood and shook the director's hand. "It's my fault. I've been coming on to her since we met in the elevator."

"I'm waiting for my lighting guy to show up. He's running late. Can I get you both something to drink? There's wine, and beer in the fridge. We also have water and since it's going to be a late shoot, I can make coffee or tea."

"I'd love some coffee," Luna said.

"Nothing for me, thanks," Nicholas said.

The director went to the small kitchenette across the room and started a pot of coffee.

Nicholas took Luna's hand again. "I don't mean to be unprofessional, but I am drawn to you. I'll stop if I'm making you uncomfortable."

She laughed.

"What's so funny?"

"It's just that, we have sex with people for a living. We're supposed to be turned on for the camera, but we feel strange about being attracted to each other behind the scenes, so to speak. I'm not ashamed of being attracted to you. It's a rare pleasure to feel this way about a co-star and not have to act for the camera."

"This is going to sound like a really lame pick-up line, but do you think we could have a drink after the shoot? I'd really like to talk to you about your films."

She didn't answer right away, choosing her words carefully. "I don't date people I work with. It's one of my rules. Let's do the shoot and see what happens later."

He leaned close to her ear. "Well, at least we know we're both getting laid tonight."

She giggled like a schoolgirl and playfully pushed him away, surprising herself. Luna took pride in her professionalism and rarely behaved in such a childish manner.

"Hello, I'm here." A man's voice announced from near the elevator.

Luna welcomed the distraction.

"Finally," the director said, and brought Luna her coffee.

A young man with spiky black hair joined them in the lounge area. He smiled at Luna, but quickly looked away when she made eye contact. "Where should I set up the lights?"

The director stared at Luna and Nicholas for a few moments without saying a word. Then she seemed to come to a conclusion. "Nicholas, you've been working in this industry longer than any of us in this room. And, you obviously like Luna. What fantasy would you like to live out with her tonight?"

He turned to Luna and his gaze locked on hers. "My fantasy is a bit racist, and I apologize for suggesting this, but I would like to see Luna in a banana skirt with beaded necklaces draped between her breasts. And, I want to fuck her in a jungle setting. I want to press her against a tree and take her from behind."

When he stopped speaking, the room was so quiet you could have heard a pin drop. Goosebumps covered Luna's arms.

The director took a deep breath, turning to Luna. "Well, that's oddly specific. Sadly, I don't think we have a banana skirt in wardrobe."

Nicholas bent over to pick up his duffle bag and set it on the coffee table. He unzipped it and withdrew a banana skirt. "It's a replica of the one worn by Josephine Baker in Paris in 1926 at *La Revue Nègre*."

The director's confusion was palpable. "Again, weirdly specific. How long have you been thinking about this scenario?"

Nicholas handed the skirt to Luna. "After I read the article about you a few months ago, I began watching your films. When I found out we would be working together, I got a little overzealous about meeting you. If this is too much, I'll understand if you say no."

Luna fondled the rhinestone-encrusted bananas while enjoying the look of unabashed lust on Nicholas' face. She didn't know what to say. Did his behavior qualify as stalking? Should she reject his idea and call off the whole shoot? The thrill of possible danger coursed through her blood, making her pulse thump between her thighs.

The director looked back and forth between the two actors. "Any objections, Luna?"

Luna's eyes were still fixed on Nicholas when she answered. "No."

Nicholas' only response was to smile and slowly lick his bottom lip as if he had just tasted something delicious.

"Banana skirt it is," the director said. "Otto, set up the lights in the jungle room."

The lighting guy just stood there staring at the actors.

"Otto. Lights. Jungle room," the director said.

Otto snapped out of it and went to set up the room.

"Nicholas, would you like to start getting ready?" The director asked.

He turned his gaze to her as if it was painful to look away from Luna. "Where can I get undressed?"

"There's a dressing area behind those screens where we keep male costumes. Or, you're welcome to just get naked. Will you need any enhancement drugs?"

He smiled and shook his head. "Thank you for offering, but I prefer to work without the drugs."

"There's no shame in accepting some help. I've never worked with anyone who didn't use drugs to stay hard during a shoot," Luna said.

"I agree. There's no shame in using male enhancement drugs if you need them. But I don't like the side effects. I was on set once, and saw an actor fall through the glass wall of a shower in the middle of a scene. He stood up with shards of glass sticking out of him and his cock was still hard."

The imagery made Luna shiver. "That's terrible."

"It felt more like a horror film after that. Besides, I'm not going to need any help staying aroused tonight," he said, kissing her hand.

"Ooh-kay," the director said. "Luna, I'll help you find what you need in the women's wardrobe."

Luna followed the director. When she looked over her shoulder, Nicholas was watching her walk away. He winked and blew her a kiss.

Once Luna and the director were behind the privacy screens that functioned as the women's dressing room, the director lowered her voice so only Luna could hear. "Are you comfortable with this scenario? I mean, our heteronormative white male audience will love it, but I'm trying to create films that appeal to women and I want to be as inclusive as possible without being blatantly racist or sexist."

"Well, it's the colonizer's fantasy, isn't it?"

"Yeah, and apparently Nicholas'."

Luna shrugged. "I had a lot of mixed emotions when *Club International* called me the "Josephine Baker of Porn." I still have mixed feelings about it, but the way Nicholas talked about it made me feel a bit less upset. Like I'm part of some legacy of how Black women are portrayed in film. There's always an undercurrent of racism in adult films featuring black and brown bodies. You're the first director who's even given that a second thought, and I appreciate it."

"My mission is to make films that aren't offensive to women, and especially women of color. I respect your work, and you were made for the camera. I'm not sure how, but you bring a certain dignity to an art form that traditionally debases women. So, I want to make sure that *you* are comfortable working with me."

"Nicholas' fantasy is problematic, but I get the sense he wants to worship me, not dominate or humiliate me. I've walked out of shoots because the director fetishized violence against women of color, or co-stars spoke to me as if I was subhuman. By comparison, Nicholas' kink is harmless. I want to fulfill it for him."

"Why?"

"He knew I might find his fantasy offensive, but he took a risk and asked. Besides," she laughed, "he's hot, and if he wants me to be Josephine tonight, then why not?"

The director smiled. "Okay. Let's see if we can find some beaded necklaces."

Twenty minutes later, Luna was dressed. The skirt was a perfect fit. She felt weirdly empowered and couldn't wait to see the look on Nicholas' face when he saw her.

She wasn't sure what she'd expected, but the set was beautiful. It vaguely reminded her of the jungles in South America, and there was ambient music playing that had rainforest sounds sampled into it. The lighting created a nighttime scene, and they had somehow managed to turn the set into the forest floor, with plants, dirt, and a large tree trunk near the center of the back wall. She was impressed.

She turned around, and Nicholas was standing beside the director looking at the set, examining camera angles, and asking questions. But when he saw Luna, he stopped what he was doing and made a beeline for her.

He stroked her bare arm. "You look good enough to eat."

His choice of words brought that feeling of unease back, and it took her a moment to notice what he was wearing. Again, not knowing what to expect, she was a bit confused by the fact that he was wearing a tuxedo that was reminiscent of Bela Lugosi's in *Dracula*. What was this guy's fascination with the early twentieth century? The outfit would have looked ridiculous on almost anyone else, but he oozed confidence which was one of the sexiest things about him. Who the hell was this man?

"How does the tux fit with your idea for the jungle scene?"

"Let's talk about the scene," he said, taking her hand and escorting her to the tree. "I've been thinking about how to make you the more powerful person in this scenario. I want you to seduce me and have your way with me. Whatever you want to do. You're in control."

Luna was confused. "But this is your fantasy."

"Exactly, and right now, you're the most powerful person in this room. You tell... no—show me what to do."

She still had no idea why he was wearing a tuxedo but decided she didn't care and just wanted to get through the shoot so she could find her hotel and get some sleep. It had already been a long day and the shoot would probably take a few hours.

The director asked Luna to stand in a circle created by lanterns that gave off a soft glow. Small white twinkle lights hung over the black fabric covering the walls, giving the illusion of the night sky between the foliage that covered every square inch of the set. Then, the director clicked a button on a remote and the dark rhythms of Afro-Caribbean drums filled the air. Nicholas went to stand near the director, and Luna began dancing. That was the director's cue to start filming. Luna's hips and torso swayed seductively as the music lulled her into a meditative state and her muscles released all the tension she'd felt throughout the day. Dancing always made her feel at ease. Even though she was performing for an audience, including her co-star, dancing was something she did for herself as often as possible. It brought her joy.

Luna was aware of Nicholas watching her, which made her feel more aware of her body and she made sure to make eye contact with him to gauge his arousal. Because he was still standing near the director and camera, looking at him gave the illusion of her looking at the viewer. She continued to dance for about ten minutes, and then the director said, "cut."

Luna stopped dancing, and the director came over to tell her what she wanted her to do next. Luna was to continue dancing and undulating her hips, while lying on the forest floor. Once Luna was in place, Otto moved some of the lighting and another camera was used to shoot this different angle. Again, Luna moved to the music for a few minutes and Nicholas watched from the sidelines.

Luna remained on the forest floor for the next shot, but she was to pretend to be asleep. The director asked Nicholas to come through the foliage and look as if he were lost. When he stepped out of the plant cover, he would "discover" Luna. Trying not to wake her, he would watch her sleep for a little while and Otto would use a Steadicam to film close-ups of her body as if it were seeing her from Nicholas' POV. Then he would "accidentally" step on a fallen branch, waking her.

After Otto captured the close-ups of Luna's body, Nicholas followed the directions he was given, and when he woke Luna, she pretended to be frightened. Which wasn't that difficult for her to do. She was suddenly aware of how pale his skin looked against the fabric of the black tux, and he had used a kohl pencil under his eyes to make them appear even bluer. Once again, his appearance reminded her of the actors in black and white movies.

They didn't speak, which gave the illusion of a language barrier, but he tried to make her understand that he was lost. She was fascinated by his bowtie, so he took it off to show her. Her interest in his clothing made him laugh, but his smile slipped when she tossed his tie on the ground and started unbuttoning his shirt. He watched her and kept his hands at his sides.

She knew he wanted to touch her but was waiting for her permission. Once his shirt was unbuttoned, she slid it and his jacket off his shoulders and let them fall to the floor. She explored his body, first caressing his muscular shoulders and arms, and then she dragged her nails down his chest, eliciting a soft moan from him. Her hands slid around the back of his neck to pull him toward her and his strong hands pressed her bare skin to his chest as he kissed her deeply.

Luna lost all sense of time. His kisses were like a powerful drug and she wanted more with each taste of him. His hands became more urgent, almost possessive as he tried to touch every inch of her body. As his kisses became more aggressive, his hand slid under the banana skirt, seeking more sensitive flesh.

A mix of emotions ranging from confusion to joy flitted across his face in rapid succession. "You're wet," he said. "You want me."

Confirming his statement, she unfastened his trousers, freeing him from the fabric that was becoming tighter and tighter at his crotch. When she grasped his cock in a tight fist, she met his gaze, and couldn't help giggling. "It's so big," she said.

He laughed with her. "I guess you really haven't seen my films."

"If I had, I would have asked to work with you sooner."

Realizing that they were no longer in character, they turned to the director to see if she wanted to stop shooting. She said nothing, and the camera kept filming.

Nicholas was still smiling, but there was carnal darkness to his smile now and he let his trousers fall to the floor around his ankles. Luna was still holding his cock. He kissed behind her ear, and whispered, "Stroke it."

She didn't need to be told twice. While she stroked his cock, he fondled her breasts, pinching her nipples until they turned a darker hue. Her mouth hung open slightly as she teetered on the edge between pleasure and pain. His lips replaced his fingers and he drew each breast into his mouth alternating between them. She was so turned on that she almost didn't notice when he bit into the flesh of one of her breasts and began drinking her blood.

His back was slightly turned to the camera, so no one was able to see what Luna was experiencing. The only clue they'd have that Nicholas was drinking her blood, was the expression on her face which bordered between lust and fear. Nicholas' tongue flicked out, cleaning up all traces of blood from her breast, and the flesh seemed to heal itself when he was finished.

He looked deep into her eyes trying to determine what she was thinking. "You didn't scream. Are you not frightened?"

She still held his cock in her hand and gave it a squeeze, making him moan. "You said you wouldn't hurt me. I believed you."

He kissed her deeply. "I hope you don't mind that I tasted you."

She pressed her lips to his ear. "What are you?"

His lips brushed her neck and he whispered, "I think you already know."

"Let's talk after the shoot," she said.

Pleased by her suggestion, he said, "I'm glad you trust me. There's so much I want to talk to you about."

She wasn't sure if she trusted him, but she had plenty of questions. Remembering they were still shooting a film, she slowly lowered herself down in front of him until she was kneeling. She enjoyed performing fellatio, but the trend of deep throating made the experience less pleasurable in her opinion. It was an expectation, so she usually endured having cocks shoved down her throat, but she didn't like it. She found the practice of slobbering, spitting, and choking while giving head disgusting. To her surprise, Nicholas wasn't encouraging her to do it. She wasn't sure if he was just being polite, or if he had some other reason for not forcing her to choke on his cock, but she was relieved given his size.

The director didn't seem to have any objections to her giving sensual, old-fashioned fellatio as opposed to the graphic thrusting of a cock down her throat that she saw as an act of violence. Regardless of her profession, she still deserved to be treated with respect and there were times that certain sexual acts made her uncomfortable. Slowly, things were changing in the industry and people were starting to listen to women who felt they'd been violated during shoots. Just because you had sex for a living, didn't mean that people could do whatever they wanted to you. She believed you could have sex on camera without being humiliated.

Nicholas' moans dragged her from her thoughts. "Luna, if you don't stop, I'm not going to last much longer."

Although she didn't want to stop, she couldn't fight that strange quality in his voice. Aside from his admission of being a bit obsessed with her and drinking her blood, the influence his voice had over her was the scariest thing about him.

He helped her stand up. "I'm a gentleman. I believe that ladies should come first."

Luna's cheeks flushed and she was again surprised by how this man made her feel almost shy. She couldn't remember the last time a lover had made her feel so vulnerable, let alone a co-star. Or was it that she never allowed her guard down enough to feel that way with anyone?

The director spoke up. "I'm getting some great shots, but I feel like we've gotten away from some of the basics. I hate to make formulaic films, but there are some shots that most viewers expect."

Nicholas and Luna listened. They both knew the shots she was referring to. She had performed fellatio, but there was no disgusting gagging. Next, he would be expected to perform oral sex on her, which would lead to him entering her from behind, or fucking her on her side, or some variation of that. She hadn't agreed to do anal for this shoot, thankfully, or she wouldn't have been able to walk for a week. There wouldn't be any BDSM in this film, so there was really no need for him to spank her. Although, she wondered if he would do that to her later after they had a few drinks. Something told her he wouldn't say no.

"Anna," Nicholas said, addressing the director, "I understand the expectations most viewers have when watching porn, but there are ways of getting around some of that by getting creative or making things more sensual than just having a basic fuck fest."

Each time Nicholas said the word 'fuck', it felt like every muscle inside her womb tightened. Whatever he was, and she wasn't going to admit to herself what she thought he was, because that was insane, he had some kind of power that he was wielding over her. She knew she should be more afraid, but she wanted him so badly that she didn't care how dangerous he was.

"What do you suggest?" Anna said with a hint of impatience.

"When you became a filmmaker, was this the industry you wanted to work in?"

Confusion creased Anna's forehead. "Well, no. I wanted to make movies that would be shown at Cannes, but in order to make a living and save up money to film other projects, this was the easiest path to follow."

Nicholas nodded. "We often find ourselves on paths we didn't expect to walk. Have you given up on your dream?"

Anna smirked at him. "No, but...."

"How would you like to set up cameras in multiple locations around the set, and rather than follow the formula, why don't we make something a little more erotic? A little more artistic."

Anna nodded. "I'm willing to experiment. What do you think, Luna?"

Luna considered the expression on Nicholas' face. It wasn't exactly lust, but there was hunger there. "I'm willing to try something different."

"Once the cameras are set up," Nicholas explained, "Luna and I will simply make love. We'll do whatever comes naturally in the moment rather than staging specific shots."

Otto spoke up for the first time. "How is that different from what you normally do?"

Nicholas regarded the young man with a smile. "The difference is that even though the sex is real in pornographic films, the staging and expected formula of shots or sexual acts create a simulacrum of sex rather than what normal people do with each other. There are no breaks between scenes. No imagined audience to please. I do not wish to perform for an audience. I want to have sex with this beautiful woman and maybe, if I'm lucky, I'll convince her to see me another night."

"Oh," Otto said.

Luna giggled at Otto's response to Nicholas' rather academic critique of adult films.

"Have you ever thought of directing these films?" Anna said.

Nicholas sighed. "Perhaps, someday. When I grow tired of performing for the camera."

It didn't escape Luna's notice that he hadn't said anything about growing too old for the camera. If he really was a, well, she couldn't even allow the word to form in her mind, then maybe he was much older than he appeared. What if his fascination with Josephine Baker was rooted in memory as opposed to just fantasy?

Otto and Anna set up cameras around the set as Nicholas had suggested. He hadn't bothered to put any of his clothes back on, but once the cameras were where he wanted them, he excused himself and disappeared behind the privacy screens that acted as the men's dressing room.

"Would you like more coffee, Luna?" Anna offered.

"How late is it? I've lost track of time," Luna said.

Otto glanced at his phone. "Almost 10:00. I could use some coffee, too. How do you take yours, Luna?"

"Black is fine, thanks."

Otto headed across the studio to grab coffee, and Luna and Anna found seats near the set.

"How do you feel about Nicholas usurping your power?" Luna joked.

Anna laughed. "Honestly, it's refreshing to work with someone who has an artistic eye and a sense of adventure when it comes to filming live sex. He's right, the formula is boring. How are you feeling about the shoot?"

Luna took a deep breath before answering. "Do you notice anything strange about Nicholas?"

Anna shrugged. "Now that you mention it, even though his suggestions are great, when I wanted to contradict him, I felt like I couldn't."

"Right? I'm attracted to him and he's a pleasure to work with, but I feel compelled to please him. He insists that I'm in control, but it doesn't feel that way."

Anna nodded and made a noise of agreement.

Otto returned with the coffee, and Luna drank hers eagerly. She was usually in bed at this hour and she had been traveling for days. Her exhaustion was catching up with her. The coffee would help, and regardless of how tired she was, she fully intended to have a drink with Nicholas later that night.

No sooner had she thought his name, when he appeared next to her dressed in his tuxedo again.

"That was fast," Luna said, gesturing toward his outfit. "Should I change into something a bit more formal?"

He knelt before her, caressing her thighs and fondling the bananas around her waist. "Don't you dare. You look just like Josephine in this costume."

"What's that all about, anyway?" Anna asked.

"What do you mean?" Nicholas said.

Anna chuckled. "Your obsession with Josephine Baker, and apparently Luna?"

He titled his head and considered her more closely. "Is it a crime to find a woman beautiful and wish to worship at her feet for all eternity?"

"Eternity? I don't know what your schedule is like, but I'm hoping to be out of here by midnight," Otto said, making Anna and Luna laugh.

"Make all the jokes you like, young man. You won't be laughing when you meet a woman who occupies your every waking thought and makes your body burn with desire."

Once again, Nicholas' words hung in the eerie silence created when he stopped speaking and no one knew what to say next.

Finally, Anna cleared her throat. "Shall we get back to work?"

Nicholas stood in one fluid motion and extended a hand to Luna. She took it and followed him back to the make-believe jungle. As they stood among the foliage set against a black felt star-filled sky, it was easy to imagine they were really in the wild.

"What should I...?" Luna's words were cut off when Nicholas gently placed a finger against her lips.

"Pretend that we are alone in the jungle and do what comes naturally," he said. "I'll follow your lead."

Again, Luna questioned who was leading who. Clearly, Nicholas was running this shoot even if he was giving her license to do whatever she wanted with his body. With her own body. She turned to Anna and Otto. "Play the music you had on before."

Without waiting for Anna to confirm this direction, Otto turned the music back on.

Luna's hips began to sway. She allowed herself to relax into the sounds. As she danced, Nicholas watched her with that hunger in his eyes that excited and frightened her. More than anything, she wanted him to devour her, but before that happened, she wanted to play with him and enjoy herself. He reached for her, and she slapped his hand away playfully, shaking her head. She continued to dance, circling him, just out of reach. He stood completely still, allowing only his head to move as she traced a path around him in her bare feet on the dirt floor again and again.

This time, when she continued her suggestive dance moves on the jungle floor, she upped her game and made Otto blush while he filmed her with the Steadicam. When he finished capturing the close-up shots of Luna's gyrating hips, the languid motion of her hands caressing her skin, and the unspoken invitations to touch her body, he backed out of the wider shot and Nicholas took his place. He gazed down at her, not making any move toward touching her. He simply watched her as a ravenous desire sparked in his eyes that seemed to get darker as his excitement increased.

The shoot ended an hour and a half later, but once again, Luna had no real sense of how much time had passed. Nicholas had done exactly what he said he wanted to do: make love to Luna. And, he did so all over the set in one continual shot without interruption or direction from Anna or Otto. Aside from the sound of their moans, gasps, and cries of pleasure, there wasn't another sound on set. When Nicholas finished making love to Luna after bringing them both to climax countless times, Anna said, "cut," breaking the spell of dark magic her co-star had woven around them.

Luna was on her back, still wearing the banana skirt. Nicholas gazed down at her lazily, completely satiated. What had transpired between was too sacred to simply call sex or fucking. And Luna suddenly felt more exposed and vulnerable than she had in a very long time. She suppressed the urge to cover herself, and smiled when he asked, "How about that drink?"

"Sure. I need a shower and have some paperwork to sign for Anna, and then I'll be ready to go."

He kissed her gently before standing and offering her a hand up.

* * *

Later, when they were sitting at the bar in her hotel, knees comfortably touching as they perched on barstools, she began asking the questions that forced her to accept the truth of what he was. Since they left the film set, he hadn't stopped making casual contact with her body. Nothing overly invasive like the sex they'd had, but there was something very possessive about the way he kept touching her. Her shadow self enjoyed his attention and even the strange possessive behavior. Vampires were supposed to be territorial, right? At least, that's how they were described in all the novels she'd read about them. And this vampire was more than a little obsessed with her. Now that they'd had sex, did he think of her as belonging to him? Again, the thought frightened and excited her at the same time.

"Did you know Josephine Baker?"

"We were lovers," he said, setting down his highball glass of expensive whiskey.

She laughed. It was more of a nervous impulse than an expression of joy. "What happened between you?"

"I loved her and offered her eternity, but she didn't feel the same way about me. At least, not after she found out what I am."

Luna almost felt sorry for him. "What did she do when you told her the truth?"

"She rejected me. Called me a demon and told me she never wanted to see me again."

"I'm...sorry."

He laughed. "That was a long time ago."

Luna took a sip of her wine. "Did you find love again?"

His gaze captured her, and its intensity made her uneasy. "Not until tonight."

Another nervous laugh threatened to escape her throat, but she took a deep breath instead. "Nicholas, I'm leaving Berlin in a few days. My calendar is packed with travel and shoots between now and Spring. I'm flattered, but we just met. How can you possibly love me?"

"You're so much like her. I want to make the same offer to you that I made to her so many years ago. I want you to accept the gift of my blood and spend eternity with me."

This time Luna did laugh. "It's late. I need to go to bed. You are a fascinating man and I had a wonderful time working with you tonight. But like I said, I don't date the people I work with." Luna finished her drink and stood.

Nicholas' hand became a vice on her arm. "I'm not interested in dating you. I want to make you a vampire like me and spend the rest of our lives together."

She tried to pull away from him, but his grip was too strong. "As appealing as eternal youth sounds, I don't know you well enough to make that kind of commitment. We just met."

He shook his head. "No, I believe you are her reborn. Deep inside you somewhere you felt as if we already knew each other. I felt it the first time I kissed you tonight. That skirt isn't a replica. It's the original banana skirt that belonged to Josephine and it fits you perfectly."

She wanted him to let go of her arm. His fingers were digging into her flesh. "So, we're the same size. So what? Lots of women would fit into that skirt."

His sensual mouth hardened into a straight line. "It was custom made for her. No one else could wear it."

Her unease was quickly becoming anger. "I'm not her. Just because some stupid porn magazine compares me to her doesn't mean anything. She died a long time ago. I'm sorry things didn't work out the way you wanted them to, but I can't help you recapture what you lost."

As her voice got louder with her irritation, she drew the attention of the bartender. "Is everything okay over here, miss?"

Nicholas' head snapped in the direction of the bartender and practically hissed at him. "Mind your own fucking business."

The man stepped in front of Nicholas in a threatening stance. "The safety of my patrons is my business and I get the feeling that this young lady doesn't feel safe around you."

Nicholas' eyes darkened. "She seemed to feel safe when she was sucking my cock two hours ago."

"Okay, that's it. Is there somewhere I can escort you, miss? Can I get you a taxi?"

"I'm a guest here in the hotel," Luna said with a quaver in her voice.

"Fine, then I'll walk you to your room." The man stepped from behind the bar and offered his arm to her.

Nicholas was off his barstool and next to the man before Luna could register the movement. "If you touch her, I will break that arm."

Not wishing to find out if what she'd read in books was true about vampires, like inhuman strength and a lack of impulse control when it came to violence, Luna held up her hands. "Thank you for the offer, but my friend is a little emotional right now. He lost someone and is still grieving. He isn't going to hurt me. Right, Nicholas?"

Nicholas straightened his tie and seemed to regain his composure in an instant. "I'm not going to hurt her."

"Miss, are you sure?"

"I'm sure." The words were a lie. She wasn't sure of anything at that moment, but she didn't want to put anyone else in danger.

Nicholas stepped close enough to press his nose behind Luna's ear. "Your fear and rage smell delicious. I want to taste you again."

Hours ago, his voice had made her shiver with desire and now she was quaking with fear and revulsion. "Stop. I'm not Josephine, but I'm not interested in spending eternity with you either."

"Why? I thought you wanted me. Your lust was so pure tonight."

"I don't feel the same way you feel about me. Just because I find you sexually attractive doesn't mean I want to build a life with you. I know nothing about you except that you're suffering from heartbreak."

"You don't have to decide tonight. I have all the time in the world to wait."

"No, you don't." Luna reached behind him to the plate of potstickers she'd eaten after the shoot since she hadn't had time for dinner and grabbed one of the wooden chopsticks off the bar. Without overthinking it, she simply plunged the thin piece of wood into his chest, hoping she hit his heart.

His eyes went wide, and his mouth opened in surprise. Then pain replaced the shock on his face. Clutching the tiny improvised stake protruding from his chest, he coughed up blood that splattered the front on Luna's shirt.

"Josephine only rejected me, but you have killed me. Why? Is it because I am a monster?"

He coughed again and another gout of blood poured out of his mouth, staining his tie. Not sure if she was more surprised by her actions or by how easy it was to hurt him, she stared at the vampire with pity in her eyes.

"I'm not rejecting you because you're a monster. You can't change what you are. It wouldn't be fair to hold that against you."

"Then why?"

"Because you're too needy."

As he clung to his last moments of life, he stared at Luna in horror. He had been a vampire for over three-hundred years. He'd witnessed war, famine, plagues, and death. So much death. But he'd never experienced anything as cruel as the words she had spoken. The last words he would ever hear.

MICHELLE RENEE LANE writes dark speculative fiction about identity politics and women of color battling their inner demons while falling in love with monsters. Her work includes elements of fantasy, horror, romance, and erotica. Her short fiction appears in the anthologies Terror Politico: A Screaming World in Chaos, The Monstrous Feminine: Dark Tales of Dangerous Women, The Dystopian States of America, Graveyard Smash, Dead Awake, and Midnight &

Indigo: Twenty-Two Speculative Stories by Black Women Writers. Her Bram Stoker Award-nominated debut novel, Invisible Chains (2019), is available from Haverhill House Publishing.

Follow Michelle's blog, Girl Meets Monster, at michellerlane.com/

LURE
Catherine McCarthy

~~~~~~~~~~~~~~~~

"Catch anything?" the fisherman asks, as he draws close. He's packed up. Given up. Off home. Tackle box heavy as his disappointment.

You attempt to suppress the grin that quivers, but can't help yourself. You were here at the crack of dawn. Got the best spot in a concealed bay among the reeds. "Take a look," you say, pointing to the loaded keep net. He squats low, green waders to match his jealousy. Then a bite, and you're up, ready to do battle. By the time you turn around, he's gone, couldn't stomach your success.

This lake is ancient. Secret. Birthed by a glacier twenty thousand years ago right in the heart of Wales. Mother Mynydd Epynt wraps her arms around it, possessively. Eight acres of amniotic fluid, warm and writhing, and she won't let go.

Since childhood, you've been coming here, like your father before you. He taught you how to fish, the art of patience. *Be still, and you shall be amply rewarded, son.* And you did... and you are. His word was your command.

The sky has blackened, the surface of the water ripples as the wind whips up. Just one more cast, then call it a day. Within seconds, there's a tug on the line. Mother is watching. She knows you need to leave before the storm hits, so she's offering a last-minute gift. Wind the reel, torso bending and swaying with your prey; a sensuous dance.

But it's not a fish. It's just a tail fin. A predator's leftovers, spat out. Then how did it take the bait? The tail fin twists and sways, hypnotic. Hand reaches out, grabs it, and then you realize. It's not a tail at all, at least in the real sense of the word. It's the tail end of a crankbait lure. You can tell by its weight.

Unhook the loop, hold it in the palm of your hand, enjoying its slick density. Mud-caked. It's been sitting on the lake bottom since god knows when. What are the odds of the hook snagging that tiny loop? You laugh and shake your head. *Jesus Christ!* Bending low, you rinse off the worst of the mud in the water before slipping it into the front pocket of your gilet.

* * * *

What did your father always say? Never look a gift horse in the mouth. And you've lived by his word all your life. Over the kitchen sink, you scrub at the lump of weighted wood. Nail-brush. Baking soda. Vinegar. Nothing too abrasive because... that shine! It's coming through, now. Charming you with its wares, like that young girl did. The one by the lake that time. Don't want to think about that. Your irksome misdemeanour. Why is that stain ingrained more deeply than the dirt on this lump of wood?

Or is it wood? You squint in the dimness. Flick on the light, and hold it up to the window. Iridescent blue, purple, green, depending on the angle. Rain lashes against the pane in teary streaks. Remorseful, and for a moment you imagine the tail fin flicks between your fingers, trying to escape. But your grip is strong, like it was on her, and it can't break free.

* * * *

The lake's a mile from the road and you're sweating by the time you reach it. Legs like lead, and heavy-headed. The dreams didn't help. Nightmares. About this place—back then. Why have they resurfaced now, after all this time? You overslept, and the sun's already risen. By the time your gear's sorted, the fish are lethargic because of the heat. But you know the best spot: among the rocks, in the shade of the overhanging alder. The fish will already have eaten their breakfast, unlike you, who couldn't stomach a mouthful. But you know how to bait. Had plenty of practise at snagging them. Carp float rod, centrepin reel. A four-pound mainline to a three-pound hook-link, baited with a single grain of corn.

Sometimes that's all it takes—one little nibble, and she's yours.

The lulling lap of water calms, and you drink in the meditative atmosphere, drifting. A violent tug on the line jolts you awake, and you spring into action, reeling in, teasing. Give a little, then pull back. A battle of wits and strength. A pair of red kites circle overhead, wanting in, their haunting cry impatient.

After a lot of coaxing, your prize slips over the rim of the landing net: a pristine, perfectly formed wild carp. Lateral scales in copper-gold, translucent tail fin forked like the devil's tongue. Her lower lip pouts, sulking. She's a beauty, but spent. The wind snatched from her sails.

You lay her down on the hooking mat, caressing her damp curves, and she calms. She's stopped fighting, her gill slits pulsate: open, close, open, close. Left hand firm on her flesh and with the index finger of your right hand reach inside her mouth, prodding, poking until you manage to release the hook. And all the time her saffron eye watches, pupil dilated in fear. "You're free to go," you say, slipping her into the water. Then, under your breath, "Not a word to anyone, mind." Perhaps, you think, perhaps you can make up for it. And in that instant, make a solemn vow. Set them free—every single one. Redeem yourself.

And the sheep on the mountain bleat their approval.

* * * *

The sky is gloomy today. Sullen, like your mood. There's hardly any wind, so the surface of the lake is a mirror of grey stratus. Been busy all week with the day job. Couldn't wait for the weekend to come around, regardless of the weather. Need the solace of this place. No one else is here, which is a bonus, but then there rarely is. That guy the other week, the one that disappeared when you turned around. The fact that he was here at all was unusual. Can count on one hand the number of times you've had to share the place. Most folk are either too lazy to carry their equipment such a distance, or they're unaware of the lake's existence.

By the time you reach the shore, it's already raining. A persistent drizzle that soaks your face and steams your glasses, so the first thing you do is put up the bivouac. Rod next. It's been dry and warm for days so the rain should oxygenate and cool the water. The fish will be energized into feeding in the prime foraging area right where you've set up. "Come to Daddy," you say, grinning. They'll play right into your hands, won't they?

An hour later and nothing. You know they're there because the water is murky where they've stirred up the silt. Been using 20mm boilies and a pretty big hook because of the weeds, so switch to something more subtle—a tiger nut on a smaller hook. Irresistibly sweet. Sugar for the ladies. A handful of loose feed adds to the temptation, halibut pellets, and hemp. Could use a spliff yourself—calm the mind, so you roll a quick one and wait for the hit before casting.

That's better. Calmer now. The drizzle has stopped and the mass of clouds have parted company, revealing the odd patch or two of blue sky. Are your thoughts more lucid, or is it just the weed? Can't answer, and don't really care. It feels better, is all. Less angsty. Hands have stopped shaking. The rod's steadier, and you take a deep breath and cast beyond the reeds. Good aim. You're right where you want to be, and soon you sense the bite, and reel it in with masterful precision, judging the resistance, the struggle at the tip of your rod. This'll be a beaut. Her muscles ripple and sway beneath the surface of the water, and every now and then you catch a glimpse of her shimmering scales.

She breaks through the surface—but it's not a fish. About two inches in length, a circumference no bigger than your thumb. But you saw her move, so how is this possible? Heart racing. It's the weed—has to be. Mind's playing tricks on you. Don't know whether to laugh or cry as you release the hook from the tiny metal loop and dip it in the shallows to rinse off the mud. It's the mid-section of the lure you found the other week. You're certain. Fucking unbelievable! You're not even in the same spot.

* * * *

Back home, scrub up, clean up, then look for the tailpiece. But where the hell did you put it? Can't remember. Haven't a clue. You turn the place upside down, inside out, determined. Won't rest until it's found. No way.

Half an hour later and the contents of your fishing tackle box lie strewn on the kitchen worktop. And you usually keep it so neat, but you're a man possessed. Obsessed. Why? What's so important? You've plenty of lures, in all shapes and sizes. Ah... but they're not like this one. This one's special. It found you—not the other way around.

And then you remember. The day you found the tail-piece. It was sunny and you wore your gilet. Perhaps it's in one of the pockets. Scrabble about in the cupboard under the stairs—the one with far too many coats and shoes—the one you keep intending to sort, but, you know...time.

Not much light under there, so you feel about in the dark. The faint scent of fish and dried mud, and the brush of canvas against your fingertips, and you snatch the gilet up in haste, thrilled as something drops to the floor. *Thank Christ for that!*

Out to the shed, and spend the next few minutes re-uniting the sections, hook to hole. No easy task as the calming effect of the joint you smoked wore off ages ago and the panic over being unable to remember where the tailpiece was has made your hands unsteady, like you have bloody Parkinson's or something. Don't think about that. Your father had it. Is it hereditary? You never asked. Didn't want to. Typical! Go on, bury your head in the sand.

* * * *

It's Sunday. You never go fishing on Sundays, and you went yesterday, didn't you? But you have to. Can't resist. What are the chances of finding the head-piece of that lure? A million to one? Lower? You're buzzing. Hardly slept a wink. If the lake was easier to access, you'd have gone night-fishing.

One rod, one reel, one type of bait—fake corn since that's what you used the first time round. No interest in catching fish now.

All you want is the head of that lure.

Haven't felt this *up* since you did crack, and that was years ago. Another life. Packed it in after what happened with the girl because deep down you blame the crack for having altered your mental state. Weren't in your right mind. Wouldn't have happened otherwise. Not a hundred percent your responsibility. Your father hadn't long died—a horrible death—and it was your way of coping, the crack that is … and the girl? Well, you were angry about the way he suffered. Full of pent-up aggression.

You're twitchy. The serenity of the place hasn't spun its magic yet, and that's because your mind's on one thing and one thing only—the head of that lure. You know you don't do your best fishing when you're wound like this, so you lie back, face to the heavens, and try to calm down. Didn't bring the stash today. Need to stay focused. Wish you had now, though. Might have helped.

Great clumps of cumulus race past, combining and parting, making all sorts of shapes as they journey onward. It's as if they don't want to stick around for long. Elbowing each other out of the way. People have all sorts of theories about the shapes clouds make. See all kinds of images: faces, animals, you name it. Load of bollocks. People see what they want to see.

This lake's taunting you today. Messing with your head because you've never had so many bites. One after another they keep coming: carp, bream, gudgeon. You reel them in, hoping, but time and time again you're left disappointed because there's no sign of the one thing you want. *Come on. Please!* But at the same time, there remains an element of logic and you know how crazy this obsession is because it's just a fucking lure, for Christ's sake!

Morning drifts into afternoon; afternoon seeps into evening, and you've lost count of the number of fish you've caught. Didn't bother to bring a keep-net. Just set them free, like you promised.

So many sheep on this mountain. They're laughing at your failure. Some of the brazen ones come close—look you straight in the eye before bleating a snigger and wandering off. Rubbing your nose in it.

Anger is mounting. Night's drawing in and soon you'll have to give up the ghost and go home. Daren't stay until it's dark or you'll never find your way back to the road. One last attempt, blow on your fingers for good luck. This one feels promising. Like watching the lotto numbers drawn. That moment of anticipation, but your heart sinks because it's just another gudgeon. Another desperate, dull eye staring into yours, begging for release. Angry now, so you pick up a stone and bash its head in with one swift thud.

That's done the trick. Its eye is a leaky mess of slime that slides down its face and your stomach churns with guilt.

What have you done? You made a promise. Your father would clip you across the ear for that. Shake out the plastic bag that earlier in the day held your sandwich and toss in the gudgeon, refusing to look at the mess you made of it because you don't want to see the unnecessary suffering you've caused. You'll feed it to next door's cat, even though you can't stand the thing. Then you won't feel so guilty. Waste not, want not, and all that bullshit.

* * * *

By the time you reach home, it's dark and you're knackered. Worn out. Drained. Don't even bother unpacking your stuff—just sling it in the shed. You crack open a six-pack and the first one goes down without coming up for air. Feet up on the sofa with a rollie, taking long drags, deep in the lungs.

What happened with the girl ruined you for a proper relationship. Couldn't forgive yourself, and you still don't know to this day how you got away with it. That's why you can't rest, see. Always that nagging doubt in the back of the mind. But the evidence would have disappeared a long time ago, wouldn't it? They couldn't possibly hang it on you now, could they?

The image of her face has never left. All matey you were at first; all nicey, nicey, though you knew what you intended to do the minute you saw her. It was fucking good, though, that sense of power, while it lasted, which wasn't long. But the shame afterwards. My God! Why? You weren't brought up to behave like that, for Christ's sake.

It's not been easy to live with the guilt. The way you rammed your fist in her mouth to stifle her screams and worse. Much worse. That's the last thing you remember—her spitting blood, whimpering.

The next thing you know, you wake up on the sofa. Empty beer cans strewn across the floor, and the pungent stink of stale cannabis in the air. It's Monday morning and you should be at work. Will have to ring in sick—again. Then you remember the gudgeon, still in the tackle box. Christ, it'll be rank by now. Not even suitable for the cat to eat, and you laugh. Perhaps you'll give it a go. Sick of cat shit in the garden. Best get rid of it, but you doubt a cat would die from eating day-old fish.

The stench of decay hits as you open the tackle box, acrid, like stale semen, so you try to pick up the bag using only your finger and thumb, but the bloody thing drops to the floor and you end up having to use your whole hand. It's then you feel the lump—in the fish's guts—something hard. Heart races. What if? The thought's insane, but you have to be certain. After all, look at the way the other two sections fell into your lap.

Drop the fish into a sink full of water and add a squirt of bleach in the hope that it will help counteract the smell. Best use a fishing knife, not a kitchen knife for this job. She's a slippery bastard—dead as a doornail, but still trying to get away, and you make one long incision, anus to throat. Entrails spew out, claggy, slick, and something else. A fish inside a fish, or the top third at least. It slips from the gudgeon like a birth. A tiny fish inside its mother. A freak of nature because fish don't do that, dickhead! That's not how it works. It's on its side in the bleached water, one beady eye watching, and you're ecstatic.

She's a cracker. Unlike any other crank-bait you've seen, and you've spent enough time trawling the internet to know. There's something special about this one. Her eyes are alive. You've read about this type, where the manufacturer uses photographs of real fish eyes and imprints them onto the lure. This is the first time you've seen one in the flesh, though. She'll mimic the swim pattern of a real fish to perfection.

The rest of the day is spent in the shed, cleaning her up and renewing her joints and hooks because you want her to be strong enough to withstand the extreme pressure of catching a monster.

The design and engineering that's gone into making this head-piece are second to none. You test the lure out in the sink, grinning like a Cheshire cat as water enters its open mouth and exits through the gills. Tied to a bit of line and a chopstick, it gurgles and bubbles when you jerk on the make-shift rod. Prime bait! You're like a kid in a candy shop, playing in the water like you did back in nursery.

Five days to wait before you can try her out because you'll have to go to work tomorrow. They've stopped paying sick leave. Stingy bastards. Then again, anticipation makes the final act all the sweeter.

* * *

The mist hunkers low on the mountain, so you don't get a view of the lake until you drop down from the ridge. It's 6:00 a.m. so unlikely anyone else will have gotten here before you. The last thing you want today is to have to share the experience of using the virgin lure with another fisherman. But as you approach, you notice that someone is there. Heart sinks like a lead weight. It's a child, a girl. You squint into the mist. She's still a couple of hundred yards in the distance, squatting among the reeds, dressed in pale blue just like *she* was. Her hair's wet, clinging to her shoulders, as if she's been swimming. Bile rises in your throat. It can't be. She'd not be that age now, prick. You blink and she's gone, but it's unnerved you. Thrown you off guard. Spoiled the moment, and it takes a while for you to calm down. A figment of the imagination is all, that and the mist.

But it's put you on edge, and you keep glancing back towards the mountain, expecting her to appear again. But there's only the sheep, with their incessant bleating. Sounds like they're choking today. Gagging.

It's cold. Fog clings to the surface of the lake so that you can't see any sign of life. Ah, well. Stick to your favourite spot and hope for the best. The fog will likely burn off as the sun rises. But it doesn't. It hangs around like an uninvited guest making it impossible to see where you're casting. This must be what it's like to fish blind. You fear going blind. Eyesight's been shit since childhood. Always back and forth from the hospital with one thing and another.

Time ticks by and you've not even had a nibble. Shoulder's aching from repetitive movement, but you're determined not to change to a different lure. This one will prove worthy. It's the weather that's causing it. Then the line snags, and instead of going with it, you pull up sharp. The worst thing you could do, and you know it. Should know better than that. In a panic, you grab the line as it feeds through the reel, splicing your palm in doing so.

Christ, only a newbie would make that mistake. Searing pain, ten times worse than a paper cut, but still you won't let go. You fight against the drag, jerking and yanking at the rod in temper, doing all the things you shouldn't, but you're not going to lose this lure. You're determined. Then snap! And the rod's in half.

With your left hand, you fumble for the knife and cut the line, wrapping it round your wrist a few times so as not to lose it. You're not wearing waders, but in you go, thigh deep, cursing the air blue as you fumble among the reeds and rocks, slick with algae.

The line bites into your wrist, garrotting the blood supply, and it hurts like hell but you're determined not to let go. Inch by inch, you feel your way down the line. The tail section is snagged between two rocks. Fingertips frozen, but you can just about feel the head jutting out. There's the eye. Half expecting it to blink as you run your fingertip over it—reflex, but of course, it doesn't. Pinch its mouth between forefinger and thumb and with the other hand reach down to try and free the tail. But the rocks are slippery and in you go, head first, gulping great mouthfuls of water as you struggle to get a grip.

To your immense joy, you now hold the lure in the palm of your hand—the one with the cut—and blood runs free as you raise it above the water, leaving an anaemic trail behind. Gasping, spitting, but delirious with relief.

It's as you straighten again that it happens. Out of the mist it comes, icy breath stagnant, putrid. The stench makes you gag. It drifts closer and you grip the lure tight, ignoring the pain from the cut because you won't give it up. No matter what. Fight to the death if need be. And you might have to, because its intention is clear in its watery gaze.

Its tentacles reach out, suck you in, like some kind of enormous, silver-grey jellyfish with a gelatinous body. Transparent on top so that you can see its innards, and even how it thinks. Electric cogs that pulse and glow in a rippling pattern, like mating fireflies.

Then it grins, and stings, and a shot of venom, an electric shock, travels shoulder to fingertip, forcing your palm open. The pain is horrendous. Unbearable.

And the precious lure slips from your grasp and into the welcoming arms of its mother.

You're sinking now, like a scrap of meat, bleached of all colour. Water floods your mouth, nose, ears, and you can't even fight it. Immobile. Paralysed, but not yet blind.

The last thing you see is the face of the lure. Pale blue, iridescent, in the prime of its life, and safe in mother's arms.

CATHERINE McCARTHY is a spinner of dark tales, often set in her native Wales, U.K. She has published two novels and a collection of stories, and is soon to publish her new novel, The Wolf and the Favor. Her short stories and flash fiction have been published both online and in several anthologies including those by Flame Tree Press, Crystal Lake Publishing, and The British Fantasy Society. In 2020 she won the Aberystwyth University Imagining Utopias prize for creative writing for her magical realism story, The Queen's Attendant.

Catherine lives in an old farmhouse with her illustrator husband and its ghosts, and when she is not writing she may be found hiking the rugged coast-path or photographing ancient churchyards for story inspiration.
https://www.catherine-mccarthy-author.com/
https://twitter.com/serialsemantic

THE THRILL OF THE HUNT
Villimey Mist

~~~

That supple skin.

    Smooth, beautiful.

I love how it feels against my big, callous fingers. How it tenses when I put more pressure on it.

Her eyes are widening. With shock. With fear.

Yes. Struggle more. Let me feel that despair.

Her nails don't hurt me. They only spur me on, urging me to squeeze harder. Her feeble strength is nothing compared to mine.

Those short bursts of breath that escape her lips are like a sweet serenade to my ears.

When she lets go of her last breath, I moan with pleasure.

The ecstasy is always so short, though.

I hate that.

I look down at the body. It's useless to me now. I need to feel the blood pumping in the veins as I squeeze the life out of her.

I drive to the nearest deserted highway and dump the body there. I don't bother laying it down gently. It's just a heavy marionette. Absolutely useless.

Well, not quite. I have her necklace. It still feels warm to the touch.

It should quench my thirst for a couple of days.

* * *

The itch is back.

It's time for another prowl in the night.

I take my car and cruise downtown Portland.

I can't say there's slim pickings in Old Town. It's more like a smorgasbord, waiting for me to select the best of the best.

The women give me sensual looks, turning in circles to allow me to see the whole package.

None of them excite me, though.

I don't feel that rush bubbling beneath the surface.

I'm about to turn the car around, irritated that I can't scratch my itch tonight, when I spot her.

Sharp cheekbones, tanned skin, braids on the side of her head, pulled into a thick ponytail. My fingers yearn to pull it.

She sees me. My heart gives a little jump.

Her eyes are big, almost doe-like.

So delicious.

I pull over next to her.

She gives me a coy smile while running her eyes up and down my body. Funny. It's as if she's appraising me.

"Good evening, stranger," she says when I let the window slide down and she leans over it. "What brings you here?"

I lightly lick my lips with the tip of my tongue. Her voice is like honey. I bet her gasps are like Turkish delights.

"I was hoping for a good time with someone special." I dip my chin and give her my best smile.

She giggles. Her laugh is like a tinkling bell. "And I'm the lucky gal?"

I nod, gripping the steering wheel. "You bet. Hop in."

A tremor of pleasure runs through me as she jumps into the car with a triumphant smile. She waves to her "coworkers" while I take us to a more secluded place.

What a Godsend.

* * *

"What's your name?" I've never asked them their names. It never mattered to me, but I feel like I must burn that girl's name to memory. She doesn't seem to have anything on her that I can keep for later, anyway.

"Cynthia."

I glance from the road to her. She's got her eyes straight on the asphalt, a stoic calm about her. Something tingles within me. I've never felt that before. I shake it off by chuckling. "That's a pretty name."

She shrugs. "It's nothing special."

"You'd prefer something different?"

"I'd prefer a name that goes places. That people will remember."

Don't worry, baby. I won't forget yours. For some reason, I feel compelled to take her further up into the mountains, where I did my first kill. That girl had been unremarkable. I barely remember what she looked like, but she had satisfied my urges and that's a good enough memory. The place I killed her is secluded and quiet. I doubt even the animals there will bother us.

"Are we going hiking?" Cynthia giggles.

"I like a little privacy."

Cynthia's eyes glint. "So do I."

Once more, something creeps up at the back of my mind. It's like a tick, biting into my skin. Never felt that way before. I shake my head. It's probably nothing. It could be a new form of excitement. Besides, I have to be focused. My itch needs scratching.

Not long now.

"What are you expecting for tonight?" Cynthia asks as she twirls one of her tiny braids between her fingers.

I smirk. "Something of a thrill, perhaps?"

Cynthia nods, smiling. "I can give you that."

A surge of excitement courses through me. *I'll bet you can. You'll be my best kill yet.*

The road has become dark, with the moon the only beacon of light above us. Fir trees as tall as skyscrapers flank the car as we climb higher up the mountain. I couldn't be happier with the spot. I have to hurry.

I park the car near a small rest area with a lonely bench almost shrouded by the trees. I better not dump the body there when I'm done. It'd be too easy to see.

"Well, we're here." I turn to Cynthia and graze her cheek with the back of my hand.

It's so warm, as if the whole sun radiated from her. I can't wait to squeeze it out of her, so nothing remains but the cold terror in her eyes.

"You really picked a great spot," Cynthia purrs as she sidles closer to me. Her hand snakes towards my thigh and caresses it. A greedy gleam in her doe eyes.

Not as greedy as mine.

My fingers drift down from her cheek and I wrap them around her throat.

If she senses something, she's being coy about it. From what I feel, she's allowing me to take the reins.

The perfect victim.

Part 2

I squeeze around the windpipe. My heart is jumping in my ribcage. I look up to watch the terror unfold on her face.

Irritation clouds my excitement. Cynthia doesn't seem frightened. Her eyes aren't bulging. Her breath is stable. In fact, she seems mildly bored. Her hand has retreated to her side.

I throw pretense out the window. No more playing "Mr. Nice Guy".

I push her against the door, with such force that she bangs her head against the window. I clamp my other hand on her breast and dig my fingers deep into the flesh, as if ready to tear it from her body. That could be her memento.

She gasps, her eyes widening.

I smirk. There's the look I've been waiting for. The thrill rushes from within, giving strength to my arms.

Cynthia thrashes in the seat. She claws against my chest. The pain is bearable. It only makes me want to savor the moment longer.

However, my irritation remains. She's not giving me eyes of terror.

She's narrowed them. They shine with malice. I've never seen it on my victims before.

"Did you do this to Helena as well?"

Her question momentarily stuns me. My fingers freeze. How is she talking? I'm squeezing as hard as I possibly can.

Her smile is rueful. "Did you know that was her name? The woman you killed and left here in the woods?"

My own breath lodges in my throat. Cold sweat glides down my back. How does she know? Is she a cop? Are they already onto me?

Panic grips me. I clamp both hands once more on her throat and squeeze.

"Enough with the foreplay, I guess." She speaks calmly, even though I'm so close to crushing her windpipe.

She grabs my wrist and bends it. It hurts slightly. I grit my teeth. She smirks and bends it back more. My stomach drops. What is she doing? The ligament has begun burning. Her eyes glint with a dark purpose. She bends it back even further.

The crack of my bone penetrates my ears like a drill. I stare at the crooked shape. Then blinding pain shoots up my brain, like venom. I scream.

"Did that hurt? I bet Helena was hurting more when you killed her." Cynthia cocks her head to the side, as if actually oblivious of her own action.

"Who the fuck are you?" I scream, clutching my broken hand.

She ignores me, instead opening the glove compartment and picking up the necklace that I had put there for safekeeping. "Another victim? Where's Helena's memento?"

"How do you know about her?" I spit angrily.

"Her sister, Lydia, prayed to me when Helena hadn't been found within a week. Given her line of work, Lydia knew she was dead. And Lydia wanted revenge."

Prayed? Is she a priest? She certainly doesn't look one with those ripped jeans and leather jacket.

A wolf howls in the distance. Cynthia smiles as she gently pockets the necklace.

"I thought I wouldn't find you. Portland's a big city. Lots of people. But I'm patient. As a hunter, you have to be."

My brow furrows. Hunter? What is she talking about?

She laughs. "You still haven't figured it out? Nah, you killers don't seem to have either the intellect or the patience. I go by many names. Cynthia after my birthplace on Mount Cynthus. Diana in Rome. I, however, prefer my true name. Artemis."

She slowly turns her head to me. Markings appear on her face and body, like stars popping up in the sky outside. They look ancient, pagan even. Like Egyptian hieroglyphs and Greek letters melted into one. Black soot covers her eyes, yet they sparkle like diamonds.

I almost forget about the pain in my broken wrist.

"I promised you a thrill. You have twenty seconds to run. I wouldn't waste them. You saw what I did with your pathetic human hand."

I can't explain how she changed like that. Is she an illusionist? How can a girl her size be stronger than me? She said her name was Artemis. If I remember my high school mythology class correctly, she's said to be the Goddess of the Hunt. How is that possible? How can she even exist and inflict pain on someone like me? I want to stay and fight her, but my dominant hand is useless. I can't trust my own strength.

I scramble out of the car and rush into the woods. I haven't run like that in ages, the searing pain in my side reminding me of that fact.

The moon is the only light in this maze of a forest. Trees everywhere. Nowhere to hide. Why can't I hear her running after me?

A wolf howls again. This time, it feels closer.

I don't like this. How my heart is almost exploding. Not with exhilaration, but with a fear that digs deep.

Something whistles in the air.

It plunges into my shoulder, nailing me to a Douglas fir. I scream. Wincing through the pain, I look down at the wound. Nothing. So, why do I feel like there's an arrow stuck in my bone? I grope for it in the dark. Again, nothing.

Another whistle.

I scream again. My other shoulder has been hit. I wheeze through the pain as it sends flames up and down my body.

A laugh echoes through the forest.

It sends chills down my spine. I've never felt fear like that.

She struts towards me, carrying a primitive bow. Her smirk is victorious. "Nothing beats the thrill of the hunt."

"All right, all right. You've got me. You've got your hunt. Now let me go." I demand.

She shakes her head, chuckling. "You're right that I've got my hunt. But I haven't avenged Helena's death yet."

Light footsteps pitter-patter on the soft ground. Too limber for a person.

A wolf strolls towards Artemis, its amber eyes gleaming in the dark.

Sweat beads down my temple. "Your pet?"

Artemis scratches the wolf behind its ear. "A companion. He usually gets what I hunt."

I struggle against the invisible arrows. The wolf growls as it approaches. I kick frantically, sweeping dirt into the air.

"Are you really feeding me to the wolf?" My voice comes out high-pitched in disbelief.

"Not just the wolf." Artemis' smile is sinister.

Heavier footsteps crush the ground. I feel slight tremors behind me.

I swivel my head. My breathing has become erratic, fearful. Not at all what I'm used to. What could she possibly have summoned from the dark?

A giant bear comes lumbering to my side. The scent of rotten leaves on its fur tickles my nose.

My legs go numb. Blood drains from my face.

"Please."

"Too late for please. You gave that up when you squeezed the life out of Helena. I'd wish you a good journey to the underworld, but I hear your kind isn't received well there."

She gives her head a jerk forward.

The bear stands up on its hind legs. It raises its clawed paw and strikes down in one, swift motion.

For a moment, I think it missed.

Something slithers with a squelch on the ground. My middle feels cold. I look down. My stomach has been ripped open. Innards leak in a mess down my pants. The grass below is painted in crimson.

Blood trickles down my mouth. My eyes shoot up when I sense movement.

The wolf's open maw is the last thing I see.

But it's not the last thing I feel.

I'm still alive as those beasts feast on my open stomach.

The last thing I hear is a girl's tinkling laugh.

VILLIMEY MIST has always been fascinated by vampires and horror, ever since she watched Bram Stoker's Dracula when she was a little, curious girl. She loves to read and create stories that pop into her head unannounced. She lives in Iceland with her husband and two cats, Skuggi and RoboCop, and is often busy drawing or watching the latest shows on Netflix. She has written two books, Nocturnal Blood and Nocturnal Farm in her vampire horror series. She is currently writing the third book in the series.
Twitter: VillimeyS
Instagram: fangs.and.light

Simba Of The Suburbs
Ashley Burns

~~~~~~~~

My little girl is... different. Yeah, let's go with that. She has all her fingers and toes, an adorable button nose, long, curly blonde hair, and bright blue eyes. It isn't a physical or mental difference, if that's what you're thinking. She is clever and sweet and really, I feel quite blessed to be her Daddy. The "different" part is she has a unique proclivity with animals, and I don't mean with just your average domesticated variety either; think animal whisperer with a splash of Carrie and you might start to form a solid idea.

It started innocuously—a squirrel in our suburban backyard would come to nestle in her lap, as docile and tame as your average house cat. When my wife and I realized they were sitting together, we took the obligatory pictures because in my wife, Amy's words, it was "just so dang cute." To Lucy, it seemed as normal as breathing, so we remained casual observers, happy that she was happy.

One squirrel became two, and two became three. The changes were so gradual we scarcely noticed. That is, until the day I came home from work and the whole neighborhood was in chaos, men and women in varying degrees of concern and panic, standing outside their houses, calling for Fluffy or Mr. Whiskers. My mind began coalescing into a broader, more complete picture and I had a sinking feeling I knew where they were. Sure enough, as I rounded the corner of our normally quiet street, I realized I couldn't even pull into my driveway because every forest critter, bird (domestic and wild), and personal pet alike was taking up every square inch of my front lawn. Several deer pawed at the ground while others casually nipped at the grass. I did one of those slow-motion panoramic turns like my head was on a swivel and noted skunks, rats, mice, badgers, loudly quacking ducks, and softly growling wolves with their litter of pups. Owls hooted, crows cawed, and hummingbirds flitted around at the speed of light, always hovering in the trajectory of the centerpiece. And who was smack dab in the middle of this jungle? The Queen upon her throne. My little Lucy, smiling ear-to-ear, having the time of her life.

I felt like my voice attempted to make words, but nothing came out. I was too shocked to form a coherent sentence. All I felt capable of at that exact moment was constrained awe. I thought it was a little cool—my daughter was like the Simba of the Suburbs. The neighbors, unfamiliar with Lucy's ability, panicked and called animal control. I suspect it wasn't just one of them either. I could hear, on the fringe of my consciousness, concerned mutterings and several people talking in agitated and frightened tones. I don't think I will ever forget those screams, like glass shattering, and the subsequent deluge of tears when the men with nets came and captured all of Lucy's new friends. Two large white vans with black block letters came to a screeching halt in front of my house and jumped out, yelling for people to "stay back" as if all the animals were feral monsters.

The poor animals panicked, and their cries might have been worse than the human ones. It felt like it happened in slow motion, but in reality, the animals that couldn't flee were rounded up and tossed harshly into cages; rattling loudly as they strained against their metal prisons. Some neighbors had the decency to look guilty, while others simply drifted away now that they had their own pets in tow. When everyone was gone—animal and person alike—I stood rooted to the lawn, watching my little girl curl into a fetal position. When I tried to pick her up, she screamed, anguish vibrating her vocal cords. On unsteady feet, she rose and walked listlessly back inside the house. Amy reached a tentative hand out only to jerk it back like she touched a scalding pot. Lucy shut her bedroom door and cried herself to sleep.

* * * *

Lucy was inconsolable for days. Her eyes had a never-ending flow of tears with purplish bags underneath, revealing her lack of sleep. Food and water sat untouched. She was too young to understand why the neighbors reacted the way they did, and equally upset with us for not interfering to save her friends. Whenever we attempted to comfort her, she would rebuff the affection and swipe our hands away angrily. My wife took it the hardest, crying herself to sleep each night. Pleading glances in bed begged me to somehow fix it.

On the third night of the cold treatment, I had an epiphany. Once Lucy was in bed and asleep, I brokered my idea to Amy.

"I think I have an idea to fix this," I said triumphantly.

"How?" Amy was still teary; our daughter's distress was killing her.

"How about we take her to the Zoo. Maybe she'll feel better after seeing all the different kinds of animals." What I didn't say was that maybe it would defrost her love for us in the process.

Amy brightened, pushing a lank strand of unwashed hair behind her ear. "You really think that will work?" Hope shined in her wet, red-rimmed eyes.

"Only way to know is to try, hun." It was a gamble, but it was the only idea I'd had so far. I also didn't have the foresight to know how many ways my great idea could go south. We kissed each other goodnight and went to sleep. I tossed and turned for a bit until finally, I got my brain to power down.

We decided to surprise Lucy and not tell her where we were going the next day. The weather was short of perfect, balmy, and early 70's, with pastel blue skies and clouds that looked like cotton candy. Lucy was silent in the backseat. Amy shot me a nervous look. I simply reached out and held her hand, giving it a little squeeze for support. The highway held little traffic and within a little over 20 minutes, I turned off Exit 29 and followed the winding road toward signs for the Nashville Zoo at Grassmere. When we crossed under a painted sign depicting a cartoon family with an elephant and giraffe, Lucy began paying attention. I couldn't read her expression, but decided to just let roll with it. I crossed my fingers and said a short Hail Mary.

We got out of the car and Lucy looked from the Zoo's entrance, to us, and back again. I realized she was asking if her friends had been taken to the

Zoo. Shit. I bent down and said what any Father would—that her friends were in the nursery where they take extra special care of them before letting them go. It felt terrible to lie to her, but at the same time, I knew the truth simply would not do. Lucy smiled, her first in days, and I swear it was brighter than the sun; filling me with a warmth I felt down to my toes. She let us take her hands and Amy mouthed *thank you* as we walked as a unit to the reception counter to buy tickets.

It was so nice to be a family again, I didn't stop to think that Lucy's gift *might* be telepathy with animals. The reality was, we did not fully understand her gift, and rather than probe her about it and make her feel like it was a bad thing, we just speculated. None of our speculations were close to right.

The first exhibit was the Meercats and Lemurs. Cute little bastards. There was a safety glass separating spectators from the animals, and Lucy made a beeline toward it. She pressed her tiny hands to the glass, and I watched as all the furballs mimicked her gesture with their little paws. It was surreal. When I turned around, I realized we had an audience on our side of the glass as well. People were snapping photos and filming. I ran to our daughter and stood protectively behind her, baring my teeth. With my glare just short of murderous, people took the hint and moved on. I tried to relax my shoulders, which so tense they were practically crammed into my ears. Again, I had one of those moments where I realized my daughters' gift would also affect her on the human side of things. People would try and exploit her, and that was a frightening rabbit hole to drop down. I knew, then, that the animals weren't what we needed to be wary of.

We stayed at the Meercat and Lemur exhibit for another twenty minutes, hoping the other families and visitors would be well ahead of us by then. Amy kneaded her hands anxiously, twisting and wringing them out like an old dish towel, as unnerved as I was about the whole episode. I tapped Lucy on the shoulder, gesturing towards the next exhibit on our flimsy maps, and she nodded with a grin. She turned back to her fan club and after some parting words, we left. I protectively engulfed her petite hand in my large, callused one as we walked further into the Zoo.

Checking my map, I knew the apes were up next. Lucy has always loved them; her bedroom wall has several posters of chimpanzees, so I was excited for her to see them in real life. Thankfully, we were alone. This enclosure was just a thick metal railing, no glass, with a manmade moat standing between us and the towering trees and massive boulders. The animals swung from the branches with loud grunts and belly laughs. When my daughter walked up to the railing, every single one of them stopped and turned their heads.

When a Silverback Gorilla is looking your little girl in the eye, it's natural to be afraid. From my limited knowledge of primates, eye contact was a big no-no, as it meant you were challenging them for dominance, or something along those lines. Lucy laughed, and the animals did the same, as if they had just shared a hilarious inside joke. Amy and I shared a look, both of us wondering if my great idea was really a terrible one. The Gorilla swam across the moat and climbed up the railing with a grace you wouldn't expect from such a large, swarthy creature. When its massive girth—God knows how many hundreds of pounds—was balanced on the railing, I was stuck in flight or fight. Lucy reached out and held hands with the animal, the Gorilla being extra careful not to crush Lucy's diminutive one. I was transfixed, staring as this Alpha animal treated my daughter like a Princess, doting on her every laugh and gesture.

All of a sudden, the Gorilla turned to face me, and it looked anything BUT happy. Lucy looked over her shoulder at me and said, in the most plaintive voice. "Daddy, Hantu doesn't like you staring, can you please stop. Pretty please."

I might have mumbled an apology, but I can't really remember. I turned around completely so my eyes wouldn't betray me, and instead held my wife's hand while trying not to soil myself. What happened next was a team of Zoo employees came running towards the enclosure like an animal Black Ops Team, two of them carrying tranquilizer guns that looked like AK-47S. I ran to cut them off, yelling that everything was fine—the animal wasn't hurting her. The commotion got Lucy's attention and she turned to face them, anger etched across her cherubic face. She scrunched her face up as if she was concentrating really hard, and everyone froze. Lions roared, giraffes screamed, and every other manner of beast or creature let out what sounded like a blood-curdling war cry. The ground trembled as each of the Zoo personnel shared terrified glances for what turned out to be exceptionally good reason. Every single animal that could escape their cage *did*. They all stood protectively in front of Lucy, baring their teeth in vicious animalistic snarls. An elephant wrapped his trunk around Lucy and gently raised her to his back. She looked so small in comparison, it would have been funny if not for the situation. I realized I had to do *something*, or this was going to escalate into something truly terrible.

"Stop! Lucy, I know you're worried they're going to hurt your friends, but they are simply scared for you, ok, honey? Can you ask all your friends to go back to their homes, so no one gets hurt, please? Please!" I begged her with my words and pleaded with my eyes for her to trust me, and thank God above, she did. She simply nodded, scrunched up her face again, and slowly but surely all the animals started walking back to their respective areas. They shoved the humans forcefully out of their paths, a deadly threat reminding them who was predator and who was prey. The elephant trumpeted one final declaration that if any harm came to Lucy, it would have to deal with him. Threat heard- *LOUD AND CLEAR.*

The Zoo personnel looked shocked. When all the animals were gone except for the Gorilla, I gave Lucy the *look*. The one meant to convey the words: *now, or you'll be in trouble, little missy.* She turned back around and hugged Hantu, kissing him on the cheek, and then he, too, turned to climb back down. As soon as he was no longer in sight, I ran to Lucy and scooped her into my arms. She hugged me fiercely, tears already forming in her eyes. We walked right past the guards and left the zoo. We'd had a big enough adventure for the day as far as I was concerned.

We stopped to get ice cream on the way home and that is when I decided to finally have *the talk*. We took a seat on a park bench with our treats as I worked out my speech on the fly.

"Lucy loo, I hope you know Mommy and me, we love you and your extra special gift. But other people don't understand, and sometimes that makes them afraid. Your gift is special, something you and only you know in your heart of hearts. Because I love you, I want you to heed my warning, ok? Be careful who you show your gift to. Not all people are good, right? Stranger danger for example. Some people might try and use your gift, to hurt your friends. I want all your friends to stay safe too. Does this make sense baby?"

Lucy looked thoughtful, as if she was weighing my words and deciphering their meaning.

"No." Barely above a whisper.

I thought I misheard her; I even rubbed my ear. "What honey?" I asked.

"NO." This time she said it with such conviction, I was taken back. Amy too. Lucy looked incensed, livid. Her cheeks blossomed a crimson red and she spoke with a voice that sounded as ancient as the Earth.

"People are the problem. Not me. And not the animals. They have done nothing wrong and yet people put them in cages and hurt them. No. No more."

Before I could utter another word, she stood tall, spine erect as a true Queen would. Regal and cold. This time she didn't even have to contort her face—her eyes just glossed over, hazy, as if she had glaucoma. A thin trickle of blood came out of her nose and I realized what she was doing. The ground rumbled so fiercely I thought it was an earthquake. Amy's face drained of color, a mirror of my own, I was certain.

Then I heard them.

Birds cawed triumphantly, dogs barked, cats hissed. They came in droves, blocking out the sky with their feathered wings until the entire scope of my vision went dark in every direction. Thousands upon thousands swirled and roiled above us. And then they dove. Human screams mixed with the animals' fever-pitched shrieks, building pressure inside my skull until I felt like I was on the verge of hemorrhaging. Everywhere I looked people were ducking for cover or trying to fend off their assailants. There were simply too many of them though, and as the screams died out and only the animals remained, I fell to my knees. There was a scream gaining traction, filling me up completely to the point of bursting. I looked at my daughter with a mixture of fear and horror. When I saw all the mangled corpses and people crawling on hands and knees, some minus half of their faces or with no eyes at all, I retched and retched until dry heaves rattled my ribcage like a pinball machine.

"Don't worry Mommy and Daddy, it will be over soon." And with that, she cast her arms out wide in mock crucifixion as a funnel of darkness—birds and bats and eagles and crows, hundreds of others I couldn't name or identify, surrounded her like the eye of a hurricane. When they exploded back up into the sky, I could find no trace of Lucy.

She was gone.

There one minute and simply gone the next.

A man with blood pooling out of a mouth full of jagged broken teeth reached out a desperate hand, grabbing Amy's arm as she rent the air with a blood-curdling scream. When the man choked on his own gore, eyes rolling back inside his damaged skull, I heard a ringing in my ears, and I realized I was screaming too.

ASHLEY BURNS : Mother, artist, and writer. My love for horror creates wonderful little worlds in my mind that I like to write and tinker with, pushing the boundaries of what terror means on any given Sunday. Some days it's as simple as a sponge. You can read more of my stories on Wattpad @AshleyBurns524 or my other social media.
Instagram: @ashmuaythai
Reddit: u/BufferCat
Facebook: Ashley Burns

Rippers

Ellie Douglas

~~~

PASSING THROUGH
THE DRIVER
MOMMY, MONSTERS ARE REAL...
REALITY BITES
DEATH... BLOW BY BLOW
HOME RUN

PASSING THROUGH

Darren was alone in the fifth passenger coach. He'd moved from the sixth when a couple of teenagers had gotten on at the Cambridge stop. The two young boys had filled the coach with enough loud music and colorful language that Darren decided to get up and take stock of the next coach. To his surprise, it was empty.

He sat in the middle row, propped his legs on the seat in front of him, and pulled out his book. He'd only turned the first page of Blood Brothers by Larry Grey when the lights went out. Then they came back on for a minute before going out again and throwing the coach into complete darkness. He left the book face down on the empty seat next to him and slid across the seats until he was facing the window.

Darren pressed his face against the cool glass to look out the window, only to find a sea of blackness devoid of any discernable landmarks. He assumed it was a citywide outage. He figured he'd find out more once they arrived at Bramble, the next station. He tried phoning his wife, but he wasn't getting any bars on his phone so he gave up and put it back in his pocket. He just sat there with his face pressed against the glass, wondering when the power would come back on.

He was startled out of his thoughts when he heard the doors opening from coach four. He tried to see who it was that was entering, but in the inky darkness he could only discern a faint dark figure moving against the lighter wall. It appeared to be the tall slender frame of a woman. Darren kept watching, hoping for the lights to turn on so he could catch a glimpse of who he'd have to share the coach with. Then he remembered his cell phone. He dug into his pocket and pulled it out. He turned its flashlight app on and lit up a narrow part of the aisle. The figure was indeed a woman, dressed in a sharp business suit.

"Thanks for the light. I nearly wet myself when it went dark. I don't know what caused the power outage, do you?" the lady said as she sat next to Darren. She stared at him as if she was studying a fancy restaurant menu.

"No idea. I think the entire city is out. Well, at least what I can see from here. What made you come in here in the dark?"

"There wasn't anyone left in the fourth coach. The ones that had been there got off at the last station. I didn't want to be alone. I hope you don't mind."

"No, of course I don't mind. Where are you heading?" Darren asked, changing the subject after noting how nervous the woman seemed.

"Home," she said. Her words came out in quickened breaths.

"Where is home?" Darren said, encouraging her to continue talking.

"Phoenix Station," she practically whispered.

"I see. You have seven more stops to go."

"How on earth do you know that?"

"Look above the seat near the exit door on the right. Do you see the map? That's how."

"Oh!" she said. Then she added, "But it's dark. How can you read that from here?"

"Oh no! It's dark? Really? Why didn't anyone tell me?" He was trying to get a giggle from her, but she was far too nervous and scared.

"Please, tell me how you did that. I'm not in the mood for jokes. Please."

"I've been traveling on this train for the last five years, so I've memorized every stop. You shouldn't worry so much. It's just a power outage, it'll be back on soon. My name's Darren. What's yours?"

"Melissa, and I have my reasons for being scared in the dark. Just please don't leave me, okay?"

Darren found it odd that a grown woman would be that terrified of the dark. He presumed she'd had something horrific happen to her. But if so, he found it more peculiar that she'd trust him. After all, he was just a stranger to her. How can one be scared of the dark but not of strangers? He did his best to keep her calm while his mind flicked to his wife. He grew anxious, knowing how jealous his wife was. If she knew he was even talking to another woman, his head would be on the chopping block. He looked at his cell phone and rolled his eyes at the absence of bars.

They both jolted at the sound of the doors opening from coach six. Darren watched as two lights darted in every direction as if a Parkinson patient was handling a flashlight. He swallowed hard and hoped it wasn't the two wayward teenagers. His hopes were dashed when the two fully entered the coach and headed right for them.

Darren felt Melissa move a little closer to him. He sensed the tenseness in her and could almost feel the tingles growing across her arms as the two rowdy boys got closer. He leaned toward Melissa and whispered, "It'll be fine. They're just a couple of drunk kids."

"Either of you got any smokes?" the lankier of the two asked.

"I don't smoke," Darren answered.

"How about you, hot stuff?" the taller boy asked while shining his cell light in her face.

"I don't smoke, either," Melissa said while she scooted even closer to Darren. Darren's thoughts drifted to his wife again. If she saw him now, she'd come to her own conclusions and presume he was cheating on her. He instinctively pulled back a little.

The taller of the two boys loomed over the seat and hovered before opening his mouth to speak. His breath reeked of alcohol. Suddenly the train pitched forward and began racing toward Bramble Station without slowing down. Darren seemed to be the only one that noticed.

The tall guy turned awkwardly to face his buddy, Tom. "Let's go to the other coaches. There's bound to be someone that smokes." Tom didn't reply, and Darren could only assume that he'd nodded to his friend in the dark. It was hard to see anything, even with the cell flashlight.

The lights suddenly came flickering on and Melissa nearly jumped right onto Darren's lap. He moved back some more, but soon found himself against the partition. Melissa eyeballed the two drunken teens and watched them walk unsteadily toward the doors to the coach they'd come from. She then cast her eyes toward Darren.

Darren stared back at Melissa. He noticed her dark eyes and found himself agreeing with his inner voice that she was a pretty woman, one that would earn him a knock on the head if his wife Suzy caught him looking. He diverted his eyes toward the outside. Looking through the window was pointless now that the train lights were back on. All he could see was himself. Through the reflection, he could see Melissa studying him, which made him very uncomfortable. She looked at him with cold fearful eyes, like she was going to suffer a nervous breakdown.

He turned sharply and spoke a little too loudly. "They're gone now."

Before Melissa could answer Darren, the train's lights went out again and her ears picked up a scream, followed by another that was much closer and louder. She tried to pinpoint the direction of the scream and immediately her mind went to the drunken louts.

"Do you think they just attacked someone?" She moved closer to Darren. He shone the flashlight toward her face, and he could see in the glow that she was on the verge of tears. He didn't feel like there was anything to be crying over.

"I don't think those two drunks are capable of attacking anyone," Darren said, trying to reassure her.

"Well, what was the screaming for then?" Melissa squeezed herself even closer to him as she spoke, and he didn't enjoy it. All he could visualize was his wife berating him.

"I dunno. I guess I'll go find out," Darren offered as a means to get away from the distressed woman.

"No!" Melissa howled, and Darren could feel her body trembling. He instantly felt guilty for wanting to bolt away from her. At the same time, he did feel a sense of urgency to find what the screaming was about.

"No? But don't you want to know?" Darren quizzed her as gently as he could.

"Well, yes, of course. But I don't want to be alone, and I don't want to go with you because someone in that next coach could be waiting with a knife to kill us."

Darren almost rolled his eyes. He wondered what this woman had endured in her life to be so terrified. He was pretty sure she'd be scared of her own shadow. It made him laugh to himself as he remembered a scene from Lost in Space when Dr. Zachary Smith thought he'd seen a monster and screamed, only to realize it was his own shadow.

Darren wanted to burst out laughing, but he didn't. He felt powerless with guilt over wanting to help. He knew then and there that his wife was sitting on his shoulder. She was the stern uptight devil of his conscience watching over him, ogling his every move, his every thought. He felt frustrated. Then, out of nowhere, a loud male voice shrieked from coach six. The lights flickered for a few seconds, before once more turning off and throwing them back into complete darkness.

"What was that?" Melissa asked while grabbing a fistful of Darren's white shirt.

"Without going to see, I won't be able to tell you, so I have to go have a look. You'll be fine right here. Do you have a cell phone?"

"Yes, but the battery died before I even got on the damn train. Please don't leave me." Darren felt Melissa's grip tighten on his shirt.

"Look, I need to make sure no one's seriously hurt. How about you lock yourself in the bathroom?"

"Yes. Sure, that's a good idea."

"Melissa, you'll have to let go of my arm and let me out."

"Sorry," she cooed in an embarrassed tone.

Darren stood up and took the lead. He shone his cell out front and took Melissa's eager hand. It was sweaty and hot, and he felt very uncomfortable holding hands with another woman. He quickly made his way to the bathroom, pulled open the door, and gently pushed her inside. "Lock the door, and I'll come back for you soon." As he made to walk away, she grabbed his arm roughly and pulled him back.

"Don't be long. I really hate the dark." Darren pulled himself free and turned to face her. When he did, the lights flashed on again and he was able to see her. She had the door almost fully closed, and only her head was poking out.

"I promise you, I'll come back as soon as I can."

He watched her close the door and heard her lock it as the lights went out. Then he made his way to the doors leading into coach six. He opened them and peered into the darkness, trying to adjust his eyes to the stygian blackness of the coach.

THE DRIVER

Myer McKenzie stood up from his seat, leaned over the control panel, and peered out the driver's window. His mouth gaped wide open and his cigarette started to slip out of his mouth as he became transfixed by the falling bright blue lights. He assumed they'd crashed when they went out of sight. He hadn't seen the ones that had already landed several hours earlier.

He was fixated on where the lights had vanished when suddenly his headset started to emit loud static. He raised his shoulders, pulled his head down, and tried to squeeze the sound away. Before his hands had the chance to pull off the headset, something came out of it that had pulsed through miles of wires like lightning and crawled into his left ear. It quickly transformed from soundwaves. to a spark of light, to a living organism. He felt a strange sensation, like thick cream had been poured into his ear, as it started to slither around his eardrum. He lost his balance and his cigarette dropped from his mouth. It hit his boot with a small spark of orange glow before it bounced off onto the metal floor. He glanced down and stomped on it. At the same time, he shook his head as if trying to expel trapped water.

The static from his headset disappeared completely. It was what he could hear inside his head that freaked him out now. He could hear a horrific whooshing sound that grew in intensity. To make it stop, he pushed off the headset and slapped at his ear with an open palm. The thing was on the move. Myer's eyes moved rapidly left and right, trying to spot something he could shove into his ear. He spied a screwdriver, but before he could pick it up his body began writhing in pain. His mind screamed at him as the thing in his ear moved toward his brain. He felt it wriggling around just before it penetrated the lower part of his brain. He let out a primal scream while whipping his head around in frantic jerks.

He clasped both hands to his head and violently shook all over, trying to force the thing out. At first, he felt woozy, and then a severe headache took him hostage and forced him to his knees. He gritted his teeth and squeezed his eyes shut. Blood vessels burst across his face and inside his head.

He started to bleed out of his eyes, nose, and ears. He opened his eyes and couldn't see anything, but he managed to stumble to his feet. Clawing at his face, he screamed, "I can't see! I can't see!" Then the inside of his head felt as though he was taking an acid bath. It burned like the crematorium at a funeral parlor. He started to thrash around, banging his head into the walls of the cab and smashing it repeatedly. Then he stopped. The thing had taken him over. He was dead, and now his body was a vessel for the alien invader. It opened its mouth and birthed several slug-like creatures that were ready to find a new host.

With no one at the controls, the runaway train barreled ahead. The only working lights on the train were the instruments from the control panel and the glow of the train's headlight. His blood caught in the lights. It dripped down his front and made him look like a sacrificial being. His entire body morphed into something out of this world as his limbs cracked and his bones broke, reshaping themselves into new positions.

The door to the engineer's cab was locked from the inside. The thing started to hit the door with a closed fist, and then it turned and squished its face against the round glass window in the door. Then it stopped and turned and beat at the control panel before circling and hitting the door and its window again. It had no idea how to open the door. It could smell fresh blood five coaches away, but it couldn't get out of the cab to satisfy its hunger. It grew angrier and sped up its circular pacing, alternately pounding on the door and the control panel repeatedly like a gorilla having a tantrum. As it became more and more agitated, it smashed at the panel that controlled the passenger coach lights, turning them on and off.

MOMMY, MONSTERS ARE REAL...

Someone was rattling the door of coach eight. It wasn't just the train's movement. Something was trying to get through the door to feast on the living that sat terrified in their seats. Those who had been sitting peacefully in coach seven with earphones on had now been taken over, and they were hungry for new blood. No one knew what was going on except for one little five-year-old boy.

He'd tried to tell his mother about the monsters outside, but she wouldn't listen. Now, half an hour after he'd first seen the monsters attacking people on the platform of Temple Station, he sat on his mother's lap clinging to her for dear life. It wasn't until the lights kept going off and on that his mother started to listen. She was questioning him when all hell broke loose.

There were nine passengers spread out in different seats in their coach. One old man grew tired of the bashing on the door. He got up and opened it, and seven disfigured, bleeding monstrosities stampeded through the door. The old man was knocked to the ground and trampled by four of them. Two others stayed behind and tore him apart like a school of piranhas. They skinned his entire body in less than a minute. Several blackish slug-like things crawled out of the bodies of those already infected and into those that were being attacked.

The little boy, Jake, with help from his petrified mother, managed to crawl up into the overhead luggage compartment. It had a busted latch, but it still closed tightly. She prayed that he'd not fall out. "Stay out of sight my love, and be quiet. I'll get you soon," she promised. She'd barely gotten him secured when she felt something gnawing on her right calf. Tears stung her eyes as pain radiated up her leg. She kicked out like an angry donkey, tearing her leg from the creature's mouth. The sharpness of its teeth scraping away her flesh crippled her. She managed to move only two feet before she felt her body jerked violently to the ground. Two of the things pinned her down. One feasted viciously on her stomach, and she watched paralyzed with fear as it tore open her abdomen and ripped out her insides. Instantly, darkness flooded her vision. Her last living thought was of Jake.

He stayed inside the luggage compartment, quiet as a mouse and shivering with fear while silently crying for his now-dead mother. But it didn't matter how quiet he was. The things navigated by vibrations and smell. They honed in on him quickly, but they couldn't get the compartment open. Several of them hit it repeatedly. Each time they did, little Jake screamed for help.

Light suddenly flooded the train, illuminating the gore, guts, body parts, and organs splattered in all directions. The seats were soaked with bodily fluids, and the walls were bathed in bright crimson. The floor was slick like olive oil with blood, bile, and partially digested gunk. Jake couldn't stay quiet. He could be heard screeching as far away as coach four. It drove the things mad. They pounded on the luggage compartment and growled loudly like a pack of hyenas.

Jake stopped screaming when the things stopped pounding on the compartment. He waited a few more minutes, then slowly and carefully, he began to push open the compartment's lid. When there was enough room to see out, he peered through the opening. His eyes grew wide and his mouth opened into a series of howls. Multiple arms reached up for him, clawing and grabbing for his flesh. Jake could hear them as they hissed and growled like rabid animals. He leaned forward by accident and was grabbed roughly. He could feel their nails digging into his skin and ripping his flesh clean off as they pulled him out of the luggage hold. He felt numb and his body quickly went limp. He didn't even hit the floor—the monsters tugged and ripped him apart on his way down. In a matter of seconds, he'd been torn apart as if Freddy Krueger had carved him up himself.

With no more live bodies remaining in that coach, the monsters circled back and forth in a wild frenzy like a group of drugged pigs rooting for truffles. They moved toward the coach's doors and slammed into them with their bloodied bodies, then rushed forward to the center and circled each other again before heading back to the doors. The smell of fresh blood had them feverishly sniffing, eager and desperate to get into the other coaches. It wasn't long before those they had infected reanimated and joined them.

REALITY BITES

The lights flashed on, startling Darren. He hadn't expected the sudden brightness and it caused him to blink rapidly. His heart fluttered faster than it ever had before, but it wasn't from the unexpectedness of the lights blinking on. It was what the lights showed him.

The entire coach was covered in gore. He looked long and hard. He didn't want to see, yet he felt compelled to look. His eyes took in images that he knew his mind could never erase—bits of body matted with hair, teeth, intestines, arms, legs, pinkish liver remains, brain jelly, blood, and other liquids, all splattered about as if a lunatic painter had a massive outburst and turned over all of his paint containers.

He almost slipped on the spilled sanguine mess as he took a step inward. Without warning, the lights went out again and he found himself having a panic attack and fighting for air. His hands reached to his throat and he gripped tightly at his collar while trying to get air into his lungs. He panted and heaved, and his eyes bugged outward. A blood vessel burst, causing a spider-like pattern to spread across the whites of his eyes. He stumbled backward when he heard something slithering around at the far end of the coach. As he moved his arms and reached for the door behind him, his feet slipped out from under him and he fell. He could feel the sticky substances beneath him saturating his suit. He gripped onto a seat and pulled himself up. The sound grew closer and Darren panicked more.

"Get the fuck away from me!" he yelled, barely recognizing his own voice.

The lights flooded the coach again just as he grabbed the door handle. He pulled the door open and caught a glimpse of the thing charging at him. To him, it looked like a giant dark-colored slug, but with purpose, and behind it was a disfigured man whose limbs looked to be on backwards. Darren's heart pounded in his chest as he jumped through the door to escape the monstrosity. He caught his arm on the frame, scratching it deeply. He yelped in pain but managed to slam the door. Then he quickly turned around to face the window.

He braced himself against the door when the thing charged at it. The door rattled fiercely, and he worried for a moment that the monster would break through. He watched in horror as the slug creature slithered up the door and across the window, and wondered if it could squeeze itself under the door. His eyes looked down, and he let out a sigh of relief when he saw no gaps. The lights flicked off again and all fell silent. The only noise Darren could hear was his own labored breathing. He leaned against the door for what seemed like an hour, but it was really only a few minutes.

He took out his cell phone to try his wife again. Still no bars. He then used the cell's light and made his way through the next door and then to the bathroom. He frightened Melissa into a scream when she heard him knocking. Darren waited for her to unlock the door and come out.

"Well, what did you find out?" Melissa asked while she held tightly to his shoulder.

"Nothing. I didn't find out a damn thing. There's nothing but empty seats on the other side of those doors."

"Do you think it was just those drunken teenagers then?"

"I would say so. Come on, let's go sit. I need to get off my feet. The train is jerking around a little too much. It's making me feel dizzy."

Darren took Melissa's hand and again he felt the dampness from her excessive sweating. He led her to the first row of seats and sat her down, and then he flopped into the empty seat next to hers. His heart was still pounding and he felt woozy, though it wasn't from the train's movements. He shone the cell toward the window and saw nothing but his own reflection.

"What do you do, Melissa?" Darren asked her, fishing for a distraction. He didn't want to think about what was inside the adjoining coach or what was now tattooed in his memory forever. He just wanted to catch his breath and make it off the train alive. He thought about ways to do that while he chatted with Melissa.

"I'm a telecommunications operator for an insurance company. What about you, Darren?"

Darren looked at his stained suit and wondered if she'd noticed.

"I'm a branch manager at City Bank."

"What does your wife do?" she asked.

"She's a high school teacher. Are you married?"

"Me, married? That's a joke, right? I'm only twenty-four. I don't plan to get married for a while. Besides, you'd need a really stable partner for such a long commitment, and right now I'm…"

The lights unexpectedly came back on. Darren immediately tried to hide his clothing, but it was no use. Melissa's reaction showed that she'd seen the stains. She jumped up out of her seat and moved back away from him, bumping into other seats while tears streamed down her face.

"Melissa, I can explain…"

"No! You lied to me. I knew what I heard meant something. Damn you! Why did you lie?"

"I just didn't want you to panic like you are now. The thing responsible for what happened in that coach is still in there. I've never seen anything like it before in my entire life. It was grotesque. If monsters are real, then that thing is a monster. I'm naming it a 'Ripper' because, from the remains I saw in there, it was clear that it ripped those people completely apart. Honestly, I don't know what the fuck it was."

"Whoa, what? What did it look like, and what did it do? What do you mean it ripped someone apart? Jesus, your suit! Your damn suit is drenched in blood. Oh my God, Darren, what happened back there?" Melissa's eyes darted to the coach's door. She moved toward it a little before changing her mind and taking a step back. Darren grabbed her shoulder and put her back into a seat.

"The whole room was coated in human remains. The thing I saw used to be a man. It's now something else. Its limbs were on backward and it crab-walked fast at me. Then… Jesus… On the floor was this enormous slug-looking thing that came after me. One thing's for sure, at least, they can't open the doors."

"So, how are we going to get out of here?"

"We have to wait for the train to stop at a station."

"This entire thing is so screwed up! I feel like we're in a nightmare," she said as she stood.

"Come on, Melissa, sit back down. You need to calm down and be quiet."

"No!"

"Melissa?"

"I want to go home now!"

Darren's brain felt like it was on fire. His throat was as dry as the Sahara Desert, and he stank. He couldn't believe the rotten-smelling stench that was drifting to his nostrils. He wrinkled up his face and thought deeply about what to do. Then he realized there was the other coach. He stood up fast, rushed over to the door, and peered through its circular window.

"Wait, Darren. Where are you going?"

Darren mutely held up his hand. Melissa bit her tongue to keep from talking. She was shaking like a leaf caught in an autumn breeze. She moved toward Darren until she was pressed up against his back. Darren's eyes grew wide. He felt uncomfortable about her body touching his. If his wife caught him like this, she'd cut off his dick. He inched to the left a little and she followed like an unwanted shadow. He gave up and continued to look through the circular window. He couldn't see any movement. It didn't seem like anyone was in there. It was the coach that Melissa had come from, so he felt reasonably certain that those things weren't in there. The lights went out again, and he felt Melissa grip him tighter than a vice. She pressed her face against his back and squealed as she held on for dear life.

"For fuck's sake, Melissa, what the hell happened to you?" Darren asked as he moved away from the window and toward the middle of the coach. It was like walking with a sack of potatoes attached to his ankles. The dead weight of her frightened body acted like an anchor. "I didn't hear what you said. Why are you so afraid of the dark?"

"I was assaulted in the dark!" she cried. Then she became hysterical when, out of nowhere, something pounded loudly on the door of coach six. Darren took her into his arms even as his mind protested doing so. Flashes of his wife came at him like a speeding bullet and he had to push the images away. If Melissa lost it completely, they would both surely die. He had to keep her quiet, even if it meant embracing her. He had no idea that those creatures sensed aromas and vibrations.

"What are we going to do?" she asked.

"We're gonna get out of here."

"How?" she sobbed.

"First, we start by getting you calm. Then we can walk through the coaches, starting with coach four, okay?"

"Then what? I mean, that won't help us get off the train."

"Well, if we can get closer to the engineer's cab, we can go straight there and make the driver stop the damn train."

Melissa snorted up some mucus and nodded her head mutely. Darren waited for her to compose herself before leading her to the door. Together they hovered at the door, waiting in the dark.

"What we are waiting for?" Melissa shakily questioned him.

"I want the lights on first," Darren said quickly.

Melissa didn't reply. Instead, she looked into the darkness of the window and waited for the lights to come back on.

DEATH... BLOW BY BLOW

Farther back on the train, in coach twenty-two, seven people sat in the dark wondering why the lights were out. Some had heard distant screams, but none had gone to investigate until one bored twenty-something decided he needed to stretch his legs in the adjoining coach. The lights came on and caught his bright, pink-tipped, bleached hair. It was spikey at the top, almost like a Mohawk but shorter. He wore tattered black clothes and a huge safety pin swung from his waist, clipped to his holey shirt.

He pulled open the doors and moved forward, but he didn't get far. He was struck by something and pushed backward. When he fell, his legs and arms caught in the doorways, effectively keeping them open. Looming over his fallen body was a disgusting figure that crouched on top of him. His screams were quickly silenced as the thing tore into his body. It happened so quickly that the onlookers could barely respond. It was like watching a time-lapse film where something dissolves into nothing in the blink of an eye. A middle-aged woman was the first to react. She jumped up and rushed to the door leading to coach twenty-three. But she didn't get very far, either, as that coach was filled with ten of the things. As soon as she had the door open, they were on her like buzzards on a dead snake.

With both coach doorways wide open, the room was overrun in seconds. Suddenly, a thing lunged at a man, grabbing his ankle and dragging him into the middle of the aisle. A younger lady tried to yank the thing away from him, but her efforts only intensified the attack. The man pounded on the mutated nose of the thing, pulverizing it into a mushy rhubarb crumble, while the lady kicked at it. But then a hand grabbed at her shoulders and pulled her down fast. Before she could fend off whoever or whatever it was, two of the monstrous things were on her and biting her everywhere.

Her flesh was ripped up and torn from her like stringy melted cheese from a pizza. Blood spouted upward and sideways, covering the back of the seats, the walls, and the floor. Her mouth was split as another monster chewed hungrily at her nose and ravenously took the bloody nub into its greedy mouth.

Her face was now unrecognizable. With disfigured fingers, the things poked right into her eye sockets, digging in and pulling out her eyeballs and then bringing them directly to their bloodied mouths. They bit and shredded every part of her, and after they'd feasted they let the slugs enter her. Completely drenched in her own claret, she twisted, kicked, and violently convulsed as she died. The slugs entered her brain and took over, and her body jerked spasmodically as her bones reshaped themselves into odd formations. Abruptly, she stood up, fully awake, and searching for living blood.

The man could only gasp as he watched a slug slink across his bloodied torso. It was fast, too fast for him to stop it from entering his mouth. He felt it go to the back of his throat and up into his skull. He slammed his head on the floor hard, trying to beat it out of himself, to no avail. It penetrated his brain and took him over as well. He yowled out one final breath, and then he was dead.

Parts of his neck bones and spine could be heard snapping into different forms. His arms turned backward and his knees turned inward. When he got up and walked, he looked like an orangutan. He used his backward-facing arms to support himself as he searched for new blood.

HOME RUN

Darren felt like it had been hours since the lights were on last. He could feel the wild vibrations from Melissa's nervous twitching. "Soon," he whispered. In truth, he hoped it was soon. Another ten minutes passed, and the lights came back on. Darren opened the doors.

"Wait here," he ordered her as he stepped into the next coach and looked around. He stayed close to the doorway and purposefully made some noise by clicking the back of his cell phone on the frame of the closest seat. When nothing showed up, he opened the door and pulled Melissa in.

Together they carefully walked down the middle of the coach toward the next door. Melissa couldn't help but notice the speed of the train. The hoarse clickety-clack underneath her felt like roaring thunder and matched the rhythm of her fast-beating heart. Darren held onto the door handle while his eyes searched wildly for what might be in the next coach. He couldn't see anything. "Stay here," he muttered. He opened the doors and closed them swiftly behind him. His heart throbbed, and he felt like he was being hit in the chest with a baseball bat. Sweat was dripping down his temples and plastering his shirt to his back. He swiped at his forehead with the back of his arm and looked around the coach. It was empty and had no signs of blood in it. He made some noise, just to be certain. When nothing came at him, he opened the door and let Melissa in.

The lights went out again and Melissa pounced on him, almost knocking him over. Darren wanted to push her off him, but he knew she'd only clamber back on. He took a deep breath and moved forward. When he reached the middle of the coach, he abruptly stopped, causing Melissa to collide with him and freak out.

"Why'd you stop?" Her voice sounded muffled, and Darren realized it was because she was speaking into his back again.

"Move back some. I can't hear you."

She stepped back an inch, but held on to Darren's jacket with a forceful grip.

"I asked why you stopped."

He didn't answer for a few moments, which only intensified her panic.

"Darren?"

"Please be quiet, Melissa. I hear something."

He listened for more sounds. When none came, he caught his breath. He waited for his heartbeat to return to normal before he carried on, silently praying for the lights to come back on. He'd tried to calculate the time between lights on and lights off, but it happened too erratically to formulate any kind of pattern. There was no discernible link between the events, which frustrated him. He continued toward the door. When he reached it, he pressed his face against the window and looked into the blackness. He took a step back and accidentally stepped on Melissa's feet.

"Sorry," he apologized.

"It's okay. It didn't hurt much." Her voice was tight and sounded strained. Darren was feeling a bunch of mixed emotions. His wife's words kept penetrating his mind, reminding him that he shouldn't be around this woman. He didn't know what was scarier, the things on the train or the fact that his wife could scold him like a petulant child even when she wasn't there.

"Darren, do you think we'll get out of this alive?" Melissa said out of the blue. It surprised him and disrupted his thoughts.

"That's exactly what we're going to do. We're getting off this damn train and notifying the authorities. I promise." When Darren heard his own words, even he thought he sounded skeptical. No matter how much he tried to sugarcoat it, he knew he was trying to persuade himself as much as her. He couldn't believe his luck! The coaches so far had been empty of travelers, and this both shocked and pleased him. They went through another set of doors and entered coach two. It was void of Rippers, which again delighted him. He could only pray his luck would continue. The lights came flickering back on, and Darren launched into action. He opened the door, and this time he didn't tell Melissa to stay. But she stayed behind with the last door separating them. She looked through its circular window and watched with thunderous heartbeats pounding inside her ears. When Darren pulled the door open again, she practically fell into his chest. She righted herself, but made no excuses. They walked quickly down the middle together and came to the final door. Darren peered through the window. He could see the engineer's cab, and there was nothing between them and it but open space and wind. He opened the door and took a step forward.

Darren's mind sped like a rollercoaster as the wind slapped him hard and caused his eyes to water. The train was moving too fast, and this worried him. He already knew they hadn't made any stops, and now he was seeing for himself just how fast the train was going.

"Stay here, Melissa."

"Okay," she said, wincing.

Darren stood on the platform, not really sure what he was doing. He could see the circular window of the engineer's cab, but he couldn't see past that and into the cab. He took a precarious step forward and stopped quickly to regain his balance, looking like a poised ballerina. He glanced down and couldn't see anything but blackness. He hoped he wouldn't fall. He reached over to the guardrail and steadied himself before taking two larger steps. With his hands on the engineer's door, he peered through the window. He could see the gray overalls of the driver, whose back was to him.

As he pulled on the handle to open the door, the driver turned quickly and revealed his disfigurement. Darren almost fell off the platform. His hand involuntarily pulled down on the handle and he instantly panicked, thinking to himself he'd just let the thing out. But the door was locked. His left foot slipped to the side, and he quickly grabbed the railing and pulled his foot back up. He took a long deep breath before looking back through the window.

When he did, he was staring into the face of what used to be the driver. Deep black eyes stared back at him and a bloody hand pounded on the window, threatening to smash it with the force of its hits. Darren was so taken aback he felt like he was having an out-of-body experience. Everything around him turned to gray, and a dizzy feeling washed over him. He backed up, retracing his steps carefully, but he couldn't later remember doing any of it. He just remembered being back inside the coach and hearing Melissa yelling at him.

"Damn it, Darren! Snap out of it. Please, Darren. Wake up!"

Melissa slapped him across the face, then swiftly withdrew her hand and held it behind her back.

"Come on, Darren. Please snap out of it!"

Darren stood on shaky legs. He knew their fate was sealed. They weren't starring in some big-budget movie, and this wasn't just a nightmare. This was real, and he knew what would happen. With no one driving the train, they'd crash. If they were lucky enough to survive the crash, they'd have to avoid the things that wanted to eat them. He knew this, and all he could do was stand there frozen. Eventually, he came around, and when he did Melissa took in several gulps of air and punched him across the shoulder in anger at him for leaving her like that.

"I'm sorry, Melissa. It isn't good news. We're gonna crash, and we're probably going to die." He spoke coldly and without emotion.

"Why are you being so pessimistic? You said you'd save me. So save me!"

"What the hell do you expect me to do? It isn't like I can gain access to the controls. Not with that thing in there." He pointed at the engineer's cab.

"There has to be something. What about the emergency brakes?"

Darren wanted to bash his own brains in right there and then. He couldn't believe he hadn't remembered that. He cursed himself while looking around for the emergency brakes. He spotted the bright red handle with a placard stuck to the wall above it. In big bold letters, it read 'Emergency Brake'.

"You'd better sit down and hold on tight." Darren watched Melissa get into a seat and hold onto the frame. Then he grabbed hold of the handle and pulled. A loud hissing and scraping sound vibrated through the floor and into the coach, like fingernails down a chalkboard. The train jerked some, but then carried on at the speed it was going. The emergency brake had failed. Darren didn't know if he'd done something wrong, so he pulled the handle back and forth three more times. It still didn't stop the train.

He slumped to the floor in a crumpled heap. He didn't know what to do. Melissa looked blankly at him with tears washing down her cheeks. He got up and walked to the wall on the right side of the train and shone his cell light at the map, though he knew it would prove useless since he couldn't know what stations they'd passed. He had no idea when the train would crash. He pulled himself into a window seat and stared out into the darkness. Defeated, he started to pound the wall next to the window with a closed fist. He didn't stop until his knuckles split and blood dribbled from them.

"What are we going to do, Darren?"

"Pray for a miracle, and brace yourself for the crash. It'll happen. I just can't tell you when."

"What about jumping from there?" Melissa pointed to the door that led to the engineer's cab. Darren stood up and rushed to the door, then yanked it open and looked out. He couldn't see anything but darkness. He shone his light below him and couldn't see much of anything. He couldn't even make out where they were with the speed at which they were traveling. Everything underneath was too blurry to discern.

He rushed back to the wall map and studied it. He did a quick estimation of their speed, and then of the time they'd been riding. Double-checking his figures in his head, he came up with a reasonable ballpark for their location. If his calculations were correct, they were heading toward the second to last station, which was Nile Station. He reached deeply into his mind and tried to picture that station. When he did, his eyes lit up, and he grabbed Melissa's hand roughly and dragged her to the door.

"What is it?" she squealed.

"We're gonna jump. It's not going to be easy and we may break a few bones, but at least we'll survive this fucking train crashing. We have to do it now."

"I don't think I can do it!"

"Yes, you can. You want to survive, right?"

"Yes, but I'm scared."

"So am I." Darren grabbed Melissa around the waist, dragged her out the door with him, and jumped, taking her with him. It was so unexpected, she had no chance to prepare herself. They went flying out of the train, hit the stony ground, and rolled into a ditch. Darren felt something warm running down his forehead and reached up to touch it. He brought his bloody fingers to his face. He knew he'd hit his head, although he didn't feel any pain. He looked over to Melissa and noticed that her body was curled in the fetal position and she was moaning.

"Are you okay?" he asked her.

"I… I think so. I think I twisted my wrist, but nothing feels broken. Are you okay?"

"Just a head wound. But otherwise, yeah, I think I'm fine."

Darren took out his cell and turned the light on just in time to see Melissa's fisted hand as she punched him in his chest.

"What the fuck was that for?"

"I didn't want to jump. You pushed me out of the fucking train, and now I'm all cut up!"

Darren burst into laughter. It was contagious, and both of them laughed for a minute. Then Darren heard a strange noise. He shone the light toward the sound and saw creatures moving up the slope toward them. He didn't speak. Instead, he got up, yanked Melissa to her feet, and took off running.

"What are you doing?"

"Monsters! More of those damn Rippers, like the ones from the train. They're down there. We have to keep moving."

He ran with Melissa and came to the parking lot for Nile Station. He rushed into it and up the ramp, dragging Melissa without stopping for a breath. A few cars were still parked there, which gave him an idea. He stopped and motioned toward one of the cars. He managed to break into it and hotwire it just as a group of those things was about to catch up with them.

"Get in the fucking car!" he yelled to her.

Melissa got in and Darren took off. He drove right into and through the clutch of Rippers and kept going. He didn't know where he was headed at first, but an urgency grew, and then he had a destination in mind. As he drove through the little municipality of Nile, both he and Melissa discovered that the things were everywhere.

"Where are we going to go?"

"I'm going to get my wife," he said, and resolutely drove on. When he finally reached his house and rushed inside, he discovered that his wife was no longer his wife. He fell to his knees and hit the floor hard with his knuckles. Tears ran down his cheeks and he screamed out, "Why?" over and over. He looked up and watched his wife. She was stuck outside on the patio, pacing between poolside and the large living room windows. She could smell Darren and Melissa, but she had no idea how to get back inside her own house to get at them. Melissa tried to drag Darren back up, but she had no strength to pull him to his feet. She knelt beside him and just let him sob for a while.

"We really must go, Darren. Please."

"Why?"

"Because we'll die here."

"What's the point?"

Melissa didn't know what to do. She stood up and rubbed her aching knees. She looked at Darren's dead wife walking aimlessly but aggressively into the window, and she wondered how long that window would hold. She raced into the kitchen and grabbed a glass of cold water and took it to Darren. She wanted to throw it in his face, but she couldn't bring herself to do it.

"Drink this, and then let's get the hell out of here. I don't want to end up like them! Please, Darren."

Darren looked up and watched his wife hitting the window, and something flipped inside his head. He snatched the glass of water from Melissa and angrily tossed it hard toward the window. It hit a tall dark-stained oak cabinet, smashing the glass and spilling the water. Melissa jumped at the suddenness of the glass shattering and turned to see Darren's wife viciously throwing her body against the window.

"What the hell, Darren? She's gonna break through. Let's go, now!"

Darren was torn between his loss and the reality of the situation. He knew he had to leave, but something was holding him back. There was something about the way his wife was bashing her head into the thick glass window, and the way she was looking at him with her black eyes. She was judging him— even as a dead monster she was still judging him. He was in their house with another woman! Unexpectedly, he snapped and escaped from his frozen state.

He grabbed Melissa and dragged her to the living room window. Then he slid open the patio doors and pushed her toward his wife. The guilt of being with another woman, even as innocent as it was, caused him to sacrifice her. He didn't watch his wife tear Melissa apart, and his ears couldn't hear it. His brain had shut it all out. He didn't even slide the door closed. Instead, he casually walked back down the long hallway to the foyer. Then he grabbed his car keys, exited the house, and got into his car.

He gave one more fleeting look at his house and then drove away with purpose, but without direction. He didn't know where he was going. Out of nowhere, he felt a weight lift from his shoulders. He'd gotten away! Away from his obsessive, controlling, jealous wife, away from the clinging woman, and away from the Rippers. His lips turned upward into a half-smile as he drove off.

ELLIE DOUGLAS is an author who currently resides in New Zealand with her husband and four children. As a child, Enid Blyton and Stephen King inspired her love of writing and reading. When she is not writing, she can be found designing one-of-a-kind pre-made book covers. Her passion for creative art led her to become a talented sought-after freelance cover artist. In her free time, she enjoys the cinema, spending time with her children, music and dancing, and anything and everything to do with Horror, especially zombies. Feel free to explore her social media sites.

http://www.authorellie.com/
https://twitter.com/AuthorEllie

LIKED

Mocha Pennington

She held her breath, too frightened to move, knowing the slightest disturbance in the air would betray her.

She didn't breathe for three seconds... four... five... six...

Beyond the tiny fissure between the dilapidated cupboard doors where she hid, she could just make out his figure moving stealthily through a room of gathering shadows and shapes made ominous by dusk. It was a tall and bulky figure, the grace that it moved with menacing, ghostlike with its fluidity. He had a body made to be uncoordinated, a body that could easily leave shattered glass and upturned chairs in its wake.

She would have thought those quick, poised movements of his comical compared to his slovenly girth, had his clandestine footfalls not been what landed her here: in a lone cabin held hostage by the skeletal arms of an endless woodland. It was a small, crude cabin haphazardly erected from decaying wood, decorated in mounds of dust and black despair.

It began with an "I love you," commented on every one of her Instagram posts dating three years back, from a blonde-headed, rosy-cheeked man. As if he had an aversion to creativity, he went by the simple username, RP. She wasn't too perturbed by the sentiment, however, as she had accumulated a following close to a million, many of whom expressed their gratitude using those three words.

"I love you" turned into a lecherous "I want you," which still hadn't given her pause. Men, in her experience, especially those riding the rocky wave of solitary passion, often bestowed such written endearments below the post that stirred their desire. She had read much worse from men in an attempt to captivate her with their graphic, one-handed poetry.

He began to write long comments describing his need for her, how life was a simple, joyless act of motions without her to give it meaning. This enveloped her in creeping vines of unease. Her unease descended into cold fear after reading his declarations that the two of them would, indeed, be together. "I'll have you," he wrote to her. "You cannot deny yourself of my love."

After she blocked him, her DMs were swiftly flooded by anonymous accounts, their messages seething with a rage only a broken mind could summon. The private email she had never made public soon received the same treatment: long messages crafted by delusional hands, sinister threats woven with proclamations of a love born from madness.

A month passed without finding a dreaded email from him in her inbox. She had thought in that blissful recession he had come to terms with her rejection, perhaps sought help from a professional. A dark part of her, a part she kept tucked away in the deepest recess of her mind, wished that the hands used to type out his torments were the very hands that took his own life.

Poetic justice, she reasoned.

It was wishful thinking. She had come home, still elated from a business meeting with her manager, to find an envelope addressed to her taped on her apartment door. She knew it was from him even before the frayed letter torn from a spiral notebook was in her quaking hands. She read his words written in a near scribble, forgiving her for her lapse in judgment, for not seeing how they were truly made for each other, how he will have to prove his devotion to her.

Days later, while leaving the gym, she found herself mustering the courage to go to the police when, without warning, she was seized from behind by a pair of strong, savage arms. She felt herself pulled into a plush, sweaty body, its heat and soured stench an assault of its own. A rough hand clasped over her mouth before she conjured a scream.

"Gotcha, my love," a thick, guttural of a voice whispered in her ear.

She held her breath for forty-seven seconds... forty-eight... forty-nine... fifty...

Her lungs began to speak of their discomfort, of their growing need for the oxygen she denied them. She wondered how long a person could hold their breath. Didn't she read somewhere a person could go three minutes without taking a single breath? She couldn't remember.

She held her breath for one minute and ten seconds... eleven... twelve... thirt—

"Cassan*dra*!" he called out, his voice both slurred and singsong, sounding like a drunkard reciting a cheerless lullaby. Her body tensed at his voice; a startled gasp bloomed in her chest but was quickly murdered. "Come out Cassandra. Where are you, my love?"

She was trembling, fear and adrenaline twisting and gnawing through her. She was going to scream, she knew it; she felt that traitorous lump clawing up her throat, ready to explode from her mouth in a shrilling toll that would end only by his hands.

And that was what he intended to do. End her. He no longer groomed and dressed her, treating her like a treasured doll. She couldn't recall the last time he bathed her. Her legs were now carpeted in itchy brown hair, her clothing dingy and amorphous. The small, damp underground room where he kept her prisoner was perfumed with the thick, noxious smell from the metal bucket that had served as her toilet. The understanding that her days were numbered urged her to plan an escape.

It will all be for nothing if you scream, she scolded herself. *Don't you dare scream!* She balled her hands into fists. Her nails dug crescent moons into her palms as she watched that immense figure stalk silently through the living room.

There was another figure in the room with him, though she couldn't remember how long it'd been since that figure had spoken. Buried under a thickening gloom, it remained slumped on the couch with an expression of surprise forever engraved on its stiff, wizened face.

Cassandra had met the woman on her first day as a prisoner. After a long drive stored away in a shallow trunk that smelt of oil and gasoline, he lifted her from the cramped space and half-carried, half-dragged her to a deteriorating cabin in the heart of a dense wood, her body too exhausted and sore to protest.

"Your new home," he told her, swelling with pride. The scent of putrefied meat, mildew, and earth sat so heavy in that shadowy cabin, she could taste it at the back of her throat, could almost see it oscillating around her. A film of colorless grime was ingrained in the floorboards, the wooden walls and ceiling housed an accumulation of sagging cobwebs. The furniture appeared to have been collected from various yard sales and dumpsters. Each item spoke of a different decade, their verbose stories of neglect and abuse told in the scars on their dust-cloaked exteriors.

"Ya get 'er?" A gravelly, sexless voice had called out somewhere from the depths of the dimly-lighted cabin.

He gleefully confirmed his capture, and then that harsh voice instructed him to bring her to "the room."

They descended concrete stairs to a cold, dark room beneath the cabin, furnished with a tattered mattress garnished in questionable stains, an old metal bucket, and shackles complete with a long, rusted chain sprouting from the center of the cracked concrete floor.

He told her she'd be staying in that concrete cave until she "learned how to behave," and then she'd share a room with him. She had never wished for a learning disability so bad.

She sat on the soiled mattress in that dark room for hours, wrapped in a filthy blanket to ward off a penetrating chill as moist as it was cold. The erratic flow of muffled voices and the creaking floorboards above served as her only entertainment.

She had barely heard his approach, just the delicate whine of floorboards aloft and then nothingness for a minute or two before the door swung open.

"It's supper time!" He announced, his thin, chapped lips pulling into a smile better suited for a child. With her slender arm clutched firmly by his clammy, rough hand, he guided her upstairs and through a kitchen of cluttered dishes and stained surfaces.

A large woman sat at a rounded dining table. She had donned a Muumuu for the occasion. The garment hung shapelessly from her body, adorned in faded blobs of murky color that might have once been a bright and detailed floral design a decade or two ago.

Before her was a plate of slightly burnt fried chicken and a mountain of lumpy mashed potatoes drowned in gravy. She trained her eyes on Cassandra as she was guided to the table. Any thought swimming inside her head was absent from a face made droopy by time and deeply lined by a life of hardships.

Cassandra's captor gestured for her to sit. She did so wearily, searching the woman's face with hopes of gaining an ally. She felt a cold grip around her ankle, followed by the clunk of a chain hitting the floor.

"Until you get used to us," her captor said, bashfulness in his voice. Cassandra had the urge to hit him, to grab a fork from the table and stab him in the eye with it, watching as he fell to the ground, convulsing in pain.

"You're lighter in pitchers," The woman spoke. It was the same gravelly voice from earlier. Confused, Cassandra turned to her. "My Robby said you were a mutt, but I thought your skin was a bit lighter." A bushy eyebrow rose to an arch, as though trying to find a way to forgive her but was unsure if she could.

Normally, Cassandra would have explained that studio lights tended to brighten one's complexion, but given the circumstances, she hadn't been in a conversational mood.

"Fuck you!" Cassandra spat instead.

For a moment, an assortment of emotions contorted the woman's face, bulging and abating beneath her skin, fighting to be carried to term. Finally, she tossed her head back in a grating wheeze of laughter, showcasing dark gums lined sporadically with rotting teeth. "She's a pistol, *I like 'er!*"

Any plea to be let go on that first dinner had been handled with a patronizing gentleness, as if Cassandra were a senile old woman, her memories shattered glass with no chance of being pieced back together.

"Please, let me go. I won't tell anyone about this. I swear," Cassandra beseeched after the woman ordered Robby to clear the table. There might have been truth in her words. The woman met her frantic gaze, her expression soft with a pity Cassandra wanted to claw off her face.

"It must be nice to have a man who cares so much about you," the woman said. "I envy you; I really do. You see, my Robby has a big heart. When he loves, he loves hard. His old girlfriends never understood his love. Ungrateful bitches, all of 'em. But *you'll* be different, won't you?" A threat boiled beneath the surface of her sickly-sweet tone, a threat like the barrel of a gun pressed against her temple.

She was an enabler, that horrible woman, her sanity a labyrinth of meandering cracks just like her son's. How long had it been since that woman had met her fate? Days? Weeks? Cassandra was unsure. Time inside that dreary cabin was a long stretch of blackness, an endless horde of buzzing flies that slowly began to feast on her own decaying sanity.

She remembered Robby yanking her from her room on that woman's final day. He hadn't made his usual announcement about supper being ready, his words encompassed in that gross, childlike excitement she had grown accustomed to. His mood was gloomy, storm clouds pregnant with calamity.

Cassandra had heard them arguing earlier, the venom in their voices unmistakable, their words inarticulate sounds hidden in the mold seeping from the cracks in the walls.

The woman was in the living room, sitting on the picture-patterned velour couch. As Cassandra was shoved into her seat at the dining table, her heart sunk when seeing a fleeting image of herself on the television. She had only seen it for a second before the woman turned the television off, but she recognized that picture instantly. It was her Instagram profile image, taken during a photoshoot for her first brand deal six months ago.

"We're gonna have to lay 'er down with the others," the woman had said matter-of-factly, as though commenting on the change in weather.

Robby abruptly rose from securing Cassandra's shackle. "No!" He roared, a sob caught in his throat.

"It's what's best, my sweet boy. They're lookin' for 'er. We'll get you a *real* girlfriend soon."

They exchanged no more words. Robby paced the length of space behind the couch, his visage a blank canvas for an artist to project nightmares upon.

Cassandra sat at the dining table, consumed in a terror so strong it was nearly physical. She couldn't accept that her life would end here, that her legacy would be an unsolved missing person's case fading in a filing cabinet somewhere.

Cassandra shifted her gaze to Robby. He stood behind the couch, staring at her with a haunting smile. Just when she registered an object held tightly in his hand, the smile fell from his face, and his eyes became a vacant void, as if someone had switched him off.

In a blur of movement, he sent something crashing down onto the woman's head. The wet crack of her skull shattering filled the room like a blast from a shotgun. Cassandra watched in silent horror as scarlet ribbons sprayed into the air, throbbing in time with the woman's heartbeat.

He turned to Cassandra then, his face splattered in a roadmap of red, and grinned. It was a secret grin, as though the two had just shared a private joke.

She couldn't think about that enabling woman who had once inhabited that withering shell now. She first needed to direct her attention on escaping the cupboard she'd blundered into, and then leaving this crumpling place as a living being instead of a resentful spirit.

He stood beside that awful corpse and stroked its head, as if praising an obedient dog. His voice fractured the ominous silence, weaving through the scent of soured decay suspended in the air. What was it he said? An apology? A curse? Cassandra couldn't hear.

For one minute and twenty seconds, she held her breath; twenty-one... twenty-two... twenty-three...

Her lungs were on fire. She could nearly feel their panic, their desperation for just one intake of breath, like a drug fiend turned away from a dealer. A wave of dizziness passed through her. She couldn't allow herself to move. He was a man of little talent, though his hearing was sharp as a bat's. The faintest creak in the space she found herself sequestered in would alert him.

She could imagine him now, snatching the rickety doors off their hinges and dragging her from the cupboard by her hair. He would place his filthy, calloused hands around her throat and squeeze. Those beady, witless eyes of his that had once stared dreamily at her with delusions of love would be hard and deranged. That would probably be the last thing she'd see before collapsing into death: The dazed eyes of a madman.

One minute and thirty-three seconds... thirty-four... thirty-five... thirty-six.

He moved from her field of vision, his soundless footfalls keeping his location a secret. She didn't want to risk releasing her captured breath just yet. He could be standing next to the cupboard for all she knew. Her heart thumped a distraught Morse code against her chest, her lungs begged for air, and her tangled limbs, which had been silent until now, began to sing a gentle tune of discomfort.

A pregnant silence claimed the room. It was as if the decrepit house were her enemy too, and it was now taunting her, amplifying its silence to show her just how stealthy her abductor was, and how vulnerable to noise she truly was.

From what she could remember, there was a shadowy hall past the cupboard. Could he be making his way down it now, searching one of its rooms? Her burning lungs and aching limbs prayed for her to believe that he was. They urged her to flee the cupboard and shred the binding chains of the house. But they couldn't be wholly trusted now. Their misery made them reckless.

One minute and forty-six seconds... forty-seven... forty-eight.

Careful not to adopt her body's urgency for air, she released her breath as slowly as she could, feeling as though an age-long burden had been lifted from her shoulders. Immediately, she sucked in a swallow of the death-scented air and quickly released it. She continued that pattern for just a moment before a crippling dread settled over her.

She was panting!

Could he hear? Was I too loud? She panicked inwardly.

Cassandra closed her eyes and imprisoned a breath, listening for the faintest of movement. She heard nothing but a silence as deep and foreboding as a tomb. She pushed out a soundless sigh and opened her eyes.

The cupboard doors pulled outward. A vapid gaze bore into her. "There you are, my love!" He said with a child's mirth, his words slurred, as if he were talking around a mouthful of marbles. A smirk both childlike and demented snaked across his shadowed face as he reached for her.

Something inside her, dark and primal, fought its way toward emancipation. Her body became a slave to an animalistic need for survival. Cassandra heard herself emit an inhuman shrill and then felt her limbs come alive with delirious panic.

Her hands took the shape of talons and clawed at the fleshy impasse before her. His dry, porous skin tore beneath her nails, weeping ruby tears. Her legs then unraveled from beneath her and took on the motions of a bicyclist in haste to get home.

He belched a breathy grunt, his body deflating from the blows, yet he still stubbornly blocked her exit. She kicked at his protruding, dough-like stomach harder, determination a red beast flinging itself at its iron cage. The cupboard rocked from the commotion, shrieking its complaints as it tossed its contents from its shelves to the ground in clumsy heaps of glass.

Finally, he fell on his back. His face, webbed with blood, twisted in pain; his large chest, in an inharmonious rise and fall, tried to reclaim the breath that had been pillaged from him.

Cassandra lunged from the cupboard, crawling over his heaving body, hating how the dank fabric of his clothes felt against her exposed skin. She heard his broken voice as she rose on shaky feet. She wasn't concerned with what he had said, for the front door to this decaying madhouse stared at her from across the room.

She was quick but not quick enough. Just as she darted toward the delicious taste of freedom, she felt the clammy grip of her tormentor's hand firmly detain her ankle. She fell to the floor in a cloud of dust. Sharp white pain lanced through her.

"Can't you see I love you, you stupid bitch?" He roared, his fury sweeping through the room like the winds of a deadly hurricane. "Don't you get it yet?" He raged on. "You're mine! You'll always be mine!"

He began to reel her toward him. *This is it!* She thought. She knew the moment he had her wrapped in his arms he was going to kill her. Perhaps he'd snap her neck or use a shard of glass to slice a second mouth across her throat. A nameless trepidation cast a cold shadow over her. Her life was a few breaths away from nonexistence, she realized.

Glimpses of memories flashed through her mind like the fast flicker of a camera:

His sweaty body atop her, those hands—those terrible instruments of horrors—unapologetically roaming her flesh, his desperate voice lying next to her, his rough, lipless mouth pressing against hers; the precise moment she realized he forgot to secure her bedroom shackles.

"No," she whimpered, defeated and hopeless, her body inching closer to a horrible fate. "No," she said with more conviction. She couldn't surrender herself to the black tentacles of Death; she couldn't allow herself to be prey to this monstrous impression of a man.

She stretched her arms out to take hold of something—*anything*—to derail her journey into death. A flood of relief warmed her belly upon finding the stubby leg of the couch. She latched onto its leg with both hands. "Get the hell off me!" she screamed, kicking to rid herself of his grip.

Her defiance only angered him. He yanked her so hard her body lifted from the floor, her leg feeling as though it was going to pop from its socket in a shower of blood. With a beastly growl, he gave another hard yank, succeeding in bringing her just a bit closer.

The couch came with her. It moved along the dust-coated floor, protesting against its excursion in a high-pitched screech. The movement disturbed its silent occupant. As if trying to rise but not sure how to use its legs, the corpse jerked upward, then, seemingly abandoning the thought of walking, slid to the floor in a muffled thump.

The stench of decay filled Cassandra's nostrils and made a home in her mouth. The wounds beat into the corpse's head looked like tiny mouths depicting various degrees of sadness. Coagulated blood and brain matter contoured those awful mouths in a wine-colored crust that oddly provoked a childhood memory of a cherry pie her mother had accidentally let burn in the oven.

"Mommy!" She heard Robby gasp. "You knocked over mommy, you bitch!"

She had also heard something else, didn't she? Wasn't there a heavy metallic clink intertwined with the shrilling scrape of the couch just seconds ago? She tossed a desperate glance to her right and saw the shape of the weapon that had presumably murdered that terrible woman. It peeked coyly from under the couch's moth-eaten skirt.

Just as she snatched the soiled implement, she sensed Robby's wrathful presence looming over her. She didn't give herself time to think of her actions, to devise a vague idea of a plan. She rolled over on her back and blindly swung the hammer. She didn't know where she hit but knew contact had been made by his startled yelp.

Quickly, not wanting to give him a moment to recover, she sat up on her rear and swung the hammer again, this time watching through wild eyes as the hammer struck his fleshy thigh. Through the hammer's handle, she could nearly feel his soft muscle and the fracture of his bone.

He threw his head back and howled to the ceiling like a mournful wolf in a horror film. She clambered to her knees and brought the hammer down on his shoulder blade in a sickening whisper of a crack. The impact of the blow knocked her off balance and gravity called her to the floor.

Something like electricity surged through her, turning any trace of fear she had into ash. What she felt now was a fiery rage, and she let that rage possess her, sink into the marrow of her bones, to become her.

He lay before her, his voice inarticulate and gurgling like an injured animal. His limbs writhed slothfully in pain, the bloody mask he wore streaked with tears. Cassandra knew she could leave this deranged man-child here to suffer in a chaotic haze of agony. Once she'd called the police, they'd haul him off and commit him to Claudefield Medical, a mental ward known for hosting the criminally insane. But she elected herself his judge and jury, and she deemed life as a luxury this sick man was unfit for.

Hesitation did not present itself to her, and if it had, she would have regarded it as a nameless stranger in a throng of many. She bellowed a cry of victory as she brought the hammer down. There was a moist shatter of his skull, and then a burst of blood warming her face. She wasn't perturbed by this, barely noticed it. She sent the hammer down a second time... a third... fourth... fifth.

How many times had she struck the man who had kept her prisoner for a dark block of countless, terror-filled days, the man who had once spent his days hunting and harassing her? She didn't know. What she did know was that she bludgeoned him until her arms felt like rubber, until she no longer heard the wet squelch and sharp crack of his skull, only the solid clunk of the wood beneath him.

And as she lay amid bloody debris of flesh and bone, too exhausted to move, she didn't feel a thread of remorse, just liberation.

She was free.

MOCHA PENNINGTON lives in Kansas City, Missouri. She studied journalism with a minor in creative writing at UCM. Her short story, "Cedar Road," was featured in Secret Stairs, which saw #1 on Amazon in the horror anthology category. She is the co-host of Tea Time, a YouTube channel that currently sits at over 6,000 subscribers.

The Lady Of The House
Yolanda Sfetsos

When Spencer Mori first came into Ophelia's life, she thought he was a real boy. A breathing, heart-beating child made of flesh and blood. He even had a face back then. It wasn't until much later that she learned about the mask. About how easy it was for his kind to blend in by covering their true features, so they didn't scare others.

But he didn't scare her. He was the pesky boy who lived on the other side of the abandoned property between them. She would sneak away from her parent's estate to play with him whenever she could.

Spencer was the friend who pulled her braid and laughed about it. Played hide and seek in the old rundown mansion and found her in every hiding spot she thought might finally stump him. He was good at games because he could weave in and out of reality so well. He had the kind of access between worlds she always coveted. How many times did she throw herself against a wall hoping to come out somewhere else? She never went through, instead ending up with bruises and scratches, even a series of lumps on her forehead. But she didn't care, and never stopped trying.

She didn't wonder why Spencer could do such strange and wonderful things, or why he looked different. There were no other kids to point this out, and the adults didn't preach about appearances. No mirrors were around to reveal their differences.

Those childhood moments were the happiest time of her life. Her days were full of Spencer, and her nights filled with dreams of a sunny meadow.

The rainy morning her father left on business and never returned, her somewhat comfortable life changed. She overheard her mother saying he had stolen all their money and relocated to new pastures, to explore a new continent of souls. Her mother's wealth eventually dried out, so their home became a husk of its former self. Ophelia often heard her mother cry at night, the pitying sound echoing through the empty corridors as their possessions slowly disappeared.

That's when the meadow dreams shifted from joy to gloom.

When Mother died shortly after, she wasn't surprised or shocked, or even sad. She'd secretly waited for the woman to wither away. One day she was there sobbing, the next Ophelia couldn't find her anywhere. No one ever told her what really happened, but she still heard her weeping in the shadowy corners of her room.

Ophelia Memento left the crumbling dwelling and went to Mori House, where she was lucky enough to have Spencer's family adopt her.

The Mori clan was kind and supportive, but they were odd. Sometimes she felt like the only one in their big house. The hallways as empty as her mother's crumbling residence, the spaces dusty and the silence deafening. Other times, every room was occupied, excited conversation was everywhere, cheer reached every corner of the place, and the parties happened every night.

Yet, Ophelia had never felt more alone.

Something was happening to her and she didn't know what. Just that she would wake up hollow-eyed and even more exhausted than when she went to bed.

At least Spencer was there; he stuck by her side and encouraged her to open her heart and mind. To keep learning until she eventually found her own way in the world.

"But I don't have a place anywhere," she would say with a pout. Not so much for effect, but because she'd felt this was true.

"That's nonsense." He always took her hand, his skeletal fingers weaving around hers. "Your place in this world is the most important of all. So many depend on you for their eternal happiness."

Ophelia didn't agree because she felt so useless around such a talented and popular family. Still, Spencer encouraged her to write her thoughts in a leather-bound book he gave her for her thirteenth birthday. Whenever she asked him to read what she'd written, he told her to keep working on her craft.

By the age of sixteen, she'd forgotten her own birthday, and instead shared his. No one in her adoptive family thought this strange; they simply lavished her with as many gifts as they did their own son.

On that clear night, as they sat under their favourite oak tree with a white owl hooting in a branch above their heads, she told Spencer she loved him.

"I know you do," he said. "I feel the same way."

Her heart pounded so fast she thought her ribs might crack. She let the serene silence of the night fill the space of further words. Wanted to wrap his admission around her like a comforting coat she would never remove.

"But we can't be together."

The magic spell dissipated into the air. "Why not?"

"Because I'm not who you think I am, and you're not who you think you aren't."

"I know you're the best person I've ever known," she whispered, refusing to focus on herself.

"But what if I'm not a person at all?"

"I don't know what you mean…"

"Yes, you do." His bony hands engulfed hers, and the warmth of love spread within her.

She didn't care about his skeletal fingers or skull face; she loved him for who he was—bones and all.

"You're a wonderful girl, Ophelia, and I don't deserve you."

"Don't say that."

His dark, hollow sockets glowed under the moonlight and seemed to pierce right into her soul. When he kissed her, she didn't wonder about the mechanics and responded modestly. Even though she wanted to give in to the passion brewing between them.

After drawing back he said, "I'm leaving tomorrow."

"No." Her heart thundered for a very different reason.

"Please don't be upset." He gripped her fingers when she tried to pull away. "I've been accepted into a university in England."

"But that's so far away."

"Which is why I set sail first thing tomorrow morning."

"What will become of me?" She hated the automatic selfishness, but what would she do in this vast residence without him? His family weren't unkind, but they were distant and self-involved.

"This is your home. You will continue to grow." His face softened into a smile. "You'll learn all about the world and how to help those who need you most. You'll share your thoughts and stories with the page."

"I can't do those things without you." Even through the sadness, she marvelled at how his bony features softened into expressions as easily as hers did.

"You can, you're so much stronger than you think." He reached into his pocket. "This is for you. A new one."

She took the beautiful book and ran her fingertips over the skull etched into the cover, traced the rising sun behind it. "It's beautiful."

"Not as beautiful as you." He pushed a strand of hair behind her ear.

She wanted to respond, tell him she thought *his* heart and soul were beautiful, but only tears spilled from her eyes. He wiped them away with such tenderness it broke her heart.

"We must get indoors." Spencer scrutinised the empty landscape with foreboding eyes. As if he could see threats in the darkness of the prairies beyond.

"I want to stay out here forever." She tilted her head to seek out the owl, but found a black raven glaring at her.

"Let's go." She let him take her hand and lead her back into the house, up the grand staircase, and to her bedroom door. "Good night, my love."

"Stay with me." The words felt right, made her heart swell.

"I mustn't, I need to rest." He kissed her cheek. "We'll meet again one day soon. I promise."

"I'll be counting down the days."

"Don't do that—live and breathe, *thrive*." Spencer leaned closer and whispered near her ear, "And whatever you do, don't leave your room tonight."

She stepped inside, hugging the book he'd given her.

Ophelia never felt comfortable in these barren quarters. None of the furniture was hers, the paltry dresses she owned had been mended so many times they were threadbare. This wasn't her home. She'd never really had one.

Spencer was the only one who made her feel as if she belonged somewhere. But as much as she wanted to pursue him before he left, he'd cautioned her not to. She bumped the back of her head against the door, closed her eyes when the ghostly light lit up across the opposite wall.

"Get some sleep."

No.

"Lie down in your comfortable bed."

No.

"Rest in peace."

Never.

Ophelia ignored the calls and the shivers they roused. She clutched Spencer's gift so tightly the edges poked into her ribs.

"You can't ignore us forever."

Her breath misted in front of her as the restless spirits swirled into her line of vision in their nightly way. She ducked outside, closed the door, and the warmer temperature instantly thawed her prickling skin.

She tiptoed across the wooden floorboards, avoiding the squeaky ones.

When she reached Spencer's quarters, the door lay open and the space was empty. She was about to return to her disquiet place when excited mumbling caught her attention.

Should she risk spying on the family?

She nibbled on her lip and decided to investigate. Her childhood curiosity never subsided, so she continued along the hallway, took the stairs down to the foyer, and paused.

The mumbling was coming from the parlour. Were the Mori clan hosting a secret party for Spencer's farewell? But why would they leave her out of such a celebration? The fact she hadn't known about his departure until tonight only confirmed what her heart suspected earlier. Her beloved didn't want to hurt her, so he'd waited to reveal his plans until it was too late for her to change his mind.

Maybe it wasn't too late.

Every step weighed on her legs and the bottoms of her feet caught like sludge on the floor. She pushed on, kept lumbering until she reached the parlour and could peek around the doorway. A fire crackled in the chimney, the orange glow projecting long shadows all over the room.

"Are you ready, son?" She recognised the scratchy voice of Grim, the patriarch.

"Yes, father," replied Spencer.

"The face you'll wear for the next four years will be a stranger's," the old man said. "The old country wouldn't accept us showing our real faces as we do in this desolate new land."

Silence, followed by a sigh.

Ophelia didn't fully understand the exchange, so she focused on the sliver of the room she could see. A multitude of candles lined the hearth, every piece of furniture had been pushed against the other side, and the shadows revealed father and son weren't alone.

Grim was cloaked in black and stood in front of his kneeled heir.

Spencer was wearing the same clothes, but had put on his human mask.

"We must remove the old and welcome the new."

"We must welcome the new," several voices repeated Grim's words.

The patriarch removed the cowl, revealing his shiny pate. He reached within his cloak and slid something out.

Ophelia gasped, covered her mouth with both hands when she spotted the knife in her adoptive father's hand. Her body trembled when he raised the short blade above his son's head and started chanting in a language she didn't understand. Was it Latin, Greek? She was having trouble thinking straight.

Grim pressed the blade against Spencer's face mask and started carving into his hairline, tracing a curved line down his temples, cheek, and jawline.

Continued along the underside of his jaw and followed the same carnage up the other side of his son's face. Blood dribbled from the open cut and when each drop hit the floor, it sounded like a thump in her ears.

By the time Grim's blade cut all the way around, the droplets turned into a gush. Spencer's face slid off and into the patriarch's skeletal hand like a loose sheet of paper, revealing his bloody skull.

None of this made any sense. Spencer wasn't wearing a face when they were outside. So why had he donned the mask for this? And why did his father have to cut it away? A blast of memories flashed inside her mind, slicing into her brain until she couldn't tell which were truth or delusions.

"We say goodbye to the old." Grim held the bloody, flappy skin and when someone appeared at his side with an open book, he sandwiched the face between the pages.

The assistant slammed the book shut and stepped back into the shadows. Another two shrouded figures took his place, dragging a handsome young man between them.

"No," the boy protested, trying to pull away from his captors. "I'm not ready."

The robed men proved too strong and forced him to his knees beside Spencer.

Ophelia caught sight of the boy's terrified eyes.

"Help me." His voice reached her ears, as clear as if they stood together.

She lowered her gaze because she didn't want him to alert the others. Instead, focused on Spencer's stained skull. The face she loved the most, the *only* one she would ever love.

The boy's screams continued, but no one seemed concerned.

"We will take this new face so our child can experience the cruel world without prejudice," Grim said.

The others repeated his words.

The patriarch raised the bloody knife. This time he dipped the tip into the boy's supple flesh.

She watched as he removed the victim's face while lovingly cradling his chin. The anguished moans echoed throughout the house, making her shake like a leaf. She felt the cries sweep inside her very soul the same way her mother's wailing used to, but couldn't look away.

"We thank you for your sacrifice," Grim said.

The screaming sounded painful, tortured.

"Hush. You don't need this where you're going."

The cloaked couple clutching the boy raised him to his feet.

"Your body is useless in death." The patriarch stabbed the boy in the heart, and held him close until the screams, breath, and life slid from him. "Only your spirit will remain."

Silence filled the beats between her pulse, and she feared someone might hear her.

"Feed this expired shell to the hounds."

The cloaked dragged the boy out of sight and she caught a glimpse of their skeletal features.

Grim tucked the blade between the folds of his garment and glanced in her direction. He seemed to be looking right at her when he said, "It's your turn. Show him the way."

She held her breath, positive he'd addressed her.

Grim turned his attention back to Spencer. "Are you ready, my son?"

"I am."

His father placed the stranger's flappy skin over Spencer's skull.

"Why did he do this to me?"

Ophelia jumped when the whisper tickled her ear. The faceless boy's shell might be gone, but his ghost stood beside her.

"Am I dead?"

She couldn't bring herself to speak. Sawdust filled her mouth, hardened the lump inside her throat. She turned back to the doorway, hoping to see Spencer's new face, but the parlour was dark. Empty.

Her heart raced, smacking into her ribcage like a caged bird.

"What am I?"

She ignored the question and made her way towards the open doorway on unsteady feet. Every step made sickness gurgle up her esophagus, the acid burning her throat.

When she reached the parlour, she found all the furniture perfectly positioned. The candles were gone. The fireplace wasn't burning, stood cold and dusty. As she made her way across the bare floorboards, she spotted a line of smoke billowing from the smouldering wood. She wasn't sure if it confirmed or betrayed what she thought she'd seen.

Ophelia tried to calm her breath and left the desolate, frigid room.

When she reached the bottom of the stairs, the ghost returned to her side.

"What will become of me?"

She stared at him for several quiet moments, before noticing the bloody prints she'd left from the parlour to the staircase.

"Please, help me," the sad boy said.

"Follow me." She wasn't sure why she'd instructed him and, as she ascended the stairs, didn't bother to check if he was following.

Ophelia stepped into her bedroom, closed the door, and sat on her bed. She hugged the notebook against her chest.

"What am I to do now?"

The boy was persistent, so she pointed at the wall.

His ghostly light swept over her as she lay back against the mattress. By the time her head hit the pillow, her eyes were closed but she refused to dream.

II

After that strange night, everything was drained of colour. Ophelia's life turned a sickly shade of blurred obscurity. She shuffled through the days like a woman who'd surrendered her soul during her pretend sixteenth birthday so long ago.

Her body wandered through the hallways and rooms like a lost soul, but she didn't stop writing or reading or learning. She spent most of her waking hours in the library, trying to discover the language she'd heard the patriarch speak.

Grim was mostly away on business now, so she was alone a lot. The only bright sparks in her wasteful existence were Spencer's letters. He wrote often, and she received bundles of envelopes at a time, weeks apart.

He was enjoying his new life, discovering new places and people while studying. Claimed he was well on his way to becoming an expert in the thanatology field, and would teach her everything he'd learned when he returned. He said they were meant to work together one day, but not as rivals.

The words confused her. They also warmed her heart.

Her room still filled her with dread. She'd tried to stay in different quarters, but would wake up in the same god-forsaken bed after another dreamless sleep. The yellow wallpaper opposite where she lay quivered, and the whispering voices never stopped calling out.

"You need to help us."

No.

"We have to move on."

No.

"Rest in peace."

Never.

The demands had somehow multiplied so much, her brain seemed too small for her skull.

"You can't keep ignoring them like you've done to me," a familiar voice drawled.

"I didn't ignore you, *Mother*."

"You've left me in this wilderness longer than all the others."

She turned her back on her nagging parent and continued to write to Spencer. He hadn't provided a return address, but she wrote to him regardless. In her notebook, the special one he'd given her for her birthday. The one with the seemingly endless spool of pages.

As the years lapsed, and she stopped keeping track of time, she also forgot how old she was. Barely took notice of the hounds howling outside all night, every night. Chose to pretend she didn't see or hear the raven tapping on her window. Or the black cats watching her wherever she went, the stones constantly tripping her. She didn't even care about the dwindling food supply, or that the patriarch hadn't been back for years. Maybe decades.

Only one thing kept her going.

In his latest letter, Spencer told her he would be returning home. So, she waited and waited, her will to live diminishing by the second.

On the day he finally came back, she barely registered he was there.

"Ophelia, sweetheart, I'm home." The touch of his cold fingers felt like a feather against her wrinkly skin. "I've returned with the knowledge I needed most."

"Spencer." The name was a sweet whisper, but tore at the corners of her dry mouth.

"Yes, it's me. What happened to Memento Mori House?"

She forced her eyelids to open, and behold his handsome face through the gauzy fabric over her eyes. He still wore the boy's face, and hadn't aged like the mirror showed she had.

"Everyone's gone."

"I can see that," he said with a sad sigh. "Father was called away on business he couldn't avoid, relocated elsewhere. But he said you had company."

She pointed at the far wall, the one with the bright wallpaper. "*They're here.*"

He glanced over his shoulder. "How long have they been here?"

"Since... I don't know." She hardly recognised most of them. Her mother and the faceless boy were the loudest, the only two she remembered. But she knew many more had stopped by. They had no choice. It was the cycle of life.

They all ended up at the same destination.

"You were supposed to let them go, not keep them," Spencer said, but there was no judgment in his voice.

"I didn't..."

He touched her cheek and she startled. "They're killing you."

"No, I'm still here." *Barely.*

"You need to sit up, push away the lethargy."

"How?" She closed her eyes because even that drained her energy, but his strong hands lifted her. Propped her up like a living doll on the horrid bed that had become her prison.

"Open your eyes."

She wanted to. "I can't."

"You can, and you will." When his lips met hers, the cold kiss from Death awoke her. "You must."

Her eyes snapped open.

"Spencer." She stared at the pretty face his father had gifted him, fingertips chasing down the line she remembered Grim cutting along his temple and jaw. "I missed you. The *real you*."

"I missed you too." He pressed bony fingers against his temple and the mask faded, revealing his shiny and beautiful skull. "I came back with the intention of making you my wife, but…"

"You have?" She allowed both hands to caress his cheekbones and jaw.

"Yes, but I see that's not to be," he said, sadly. "Because you have to do something for me. Something that will take you away."

The words pained her, but she managed to ask, "What is it, my love?"

"You have to remember."

"Remember what?"

He sighed. "Why you came to live here."

"Because my mother died, because we lost everything—"

"No, it's because of the wall," Spencer said.

"The wall is part of the building's foundations. It has nothing to do with me."

"It's part of *you*. You've always lived in this house."

"But my parents—"

"Lived here too. Just like me, you were born here," Spencer said. "We are both part of this house."

She shook her head. "But there was a mansion between us."

"There are no other homes here. We live in the middle of a prairie."

"That can't be."

"Please remember." He touched her cheek, her lips, her temple. "If you don't remember they'll continue to feed on your energy."

His face blurred behind the tears captured in her blindfold.

"Ophelia, the restless spirits need to move on."

The restless spirits... The faceless boy. Her mother. The babies. The children. The discarded carcasses the hounds left behind. Dogs. Cats. Women. Men. As the many faces swept through her mind, their ghostly lights lit up her shabby lodgings.

Something sparkled inside her head. "I was supposed to help them."

"Yes."

She pulled off the blindfold she'd worn during her suffering loneliness. The sheer fabric that kept her from seeing the world for what it really was. Dying.

"Help us."

Yes.

"Let us move on."

Yes.

"Show us the way."

Always.

She used to believe *they* wanted *her* to die, to rest in peace but it was *their* wish.

Tears blurred her vision. "I've been neglecting them for so long."

"Change that," Spencer said.

Ophelia rushed to her feet, all the lethargy and years of self-neglect slid away like a decrepit dress. The closer she got to the wall, the younger she became. By the time she stood with the crowd of shiny spirits, she glowed as radiant as she had on her sixteenth birthday.

"I'm sorry," she whispered. She really was.

"We didn't mean to suck on your energy."

Ophelia didn't feel an ounce of malice towards the hoard. *She* was the one who'd failed *them*. She pressed both hands against the yellow wallpaper and the wall vanished before her eyes, to become a beaming meadow with a glowing sun shining down from a brilliant sky.

"I'll show you the way." She hadn't understood then what the patriarch meant, but now accepted that it was her turn to take the lead.

"Embrace your destiny, my love."

She met Spencer's dark, hollow eyes and felt his love flow through her. A connection deeper than life itself, but one that would lead them to different places and would ensure they never ended up together.

"I'll never forget you," she said.

"It's not possible to forget what we have."

Ophelia smiled at him before facing the glowing paradise. The one she used to dream about after taking over her father's obligation. She stepped into the meadow, dragging the restless spirits with her and finally fulfilling her deepest childhood wish of walking through walls. Finally accepting who she'd forgotten she was.

The hostess of dead spirits.

YOLANDA SFETSOS lives in Sydney, Australia with her awesome, supportive gamer husband and neurotic, photogenic kitty.

When she's not writing or reading, she's either out walking, watching a movie or TV show, or thinking about the new dark ideas fighting for attention. Pre-pandemic, she used to enjoy going to thrift stores to search for bargain books. Now, she does her book bargain hunting online.

Her novelette, BREAKING THE HABIT, was released by Demain Publishing as part of the Short Sharp Shocks! horror series, and her novella THE BONE FACTORY as part of the Murder! Mystery! Mayhem! series. She also has short stories in the UNDER HER BLACK WINGS and the GRAVEYARD

SMASH: 2020 Women of Horror anthologies released by Kandisha Press.

You can visit her website: www.yolandasfetsos.com, find her on Twitter:

https://twitter.com/yolandasfetsos, and check out her reading habits on Goodreads:

https://www.goodreads.com/yolandasfetsos

SHOULD HAVE GONE TO VEGAS

Janine Pipe

"You do realise, I would literally rather be anywhere on earth than here right now."

Jack looked over at Adam and smirked. His friend was huffing and puffing, displaying all-too-telling signs of too many beers and cigarettes and not enough fresh air and exercise.

"It'll do you good. Hell, it'll do us both some good."

Bitching and moaning about how he'd recently watched The Ritual and didn't Jack know what kind of sick shit went on during camping trips, Adam had tried his best to change Jack's mind about the trip. However, Jack won him over as usual and before they knew it, they were on their way to some ramshackle old cabin that Jack's uncle owned in the middle of the Maine woodland.

Uncle Smokey hadn't been out there for years, but there was the promise of yet more beer and hopefully shooting a coyote or two. Despite his reticence, being a hotshot lawyer meant many days chained to a courtroom, and Adam really needed to get away for a bit after a high-profile case had ended horribly for his defendant. Jack was a full-time writer, and was planning his next thriller, which he'd steeped with supernatural undertones. A night or two in an old spooky cabin coupled with Adam's snoring should be more than enough material to feed his imagination.

"If this was purely for research purposes," grumbled Adam, "there are plenty of very quaint and comfortable inns we could have booked."

Swatting some winged mini-beast in disgust, he winced.

"You know I like my creature comforts."

Sniggering at his city-loving buddy, Jack replied, "well, there will be plenty of creatures out here, man. And most of those so-called haunted inns are just tourist traps anyway."

Stomping through the overgrown bush and fighting back wayward branches, they finally reached the cabin Uncle Smokey had been so God-damn proud of.

"That's it?" Adam looked over at Jack, thinking if it wasn't for the fact his buddy was carrying most of the beers, he would have shot him with the rifle instead of some coyote.

"When exactly was the last time anyone in your family—hell—*anyone alive* came out here, huh?"

Pushing the door, if you could call it that, an incredulous expression upon his face, Adam wandered inside the wooden structure.

"Fucking stinks in here!" He remarked, throwing open the windows at the back.

Rolling his eyes, Jack joined him and opened the back 'door' to the cabin.

"Okay," he conceded. "It sure as hell ain't the Hilton."

"But," he added, taking in a deep lungful of fresh air from the back porch area, "we are all alone in the open air and it's a fuck-load less expensive."

There wasn't much to explore, but the guys poked around for a bit, checking out what they had to play with for the duration of the weekend.

Grumbling, Adam pulled back curtains separating various designated areas such as a kitchen and sleeping area, while coughing and sputtering, and moaning about the odour.

Finally having enough, Jack turned to his oldest friend.

"Look. If it's that bad, go home. Take your supplies and leave. Okay, we gotta shit in a bucket and sleep on the floor, but so fucking what? It's meant to be an adventure, two dudes living off the radar for a couple of days."

Chastised, Adam had the decency to look apologetic and before they knew it, they had aired out a couple of old lounge chairs and were sitting outside the cabin, drinking IPA and smoking cigars. Tomorrow, they'd hunt, but for this evening's meal, they'd brought along wieners and chili which they cooked on an open fire pit they had made with pride.

"Take that, Mom," Adam announced when the kindling caught. "And you said I sucked at Boy-Scouts."

Darkness fell all too soon and before long, all they could hear was the crackling flames and as Jack predicted, Adam's snores. He'd dozed off after the third beer, the fresh air and a full belly of beans the perfect antidote to stressful city life.

Jack looked up at the stars, feeling contented. Tomorrow, they'd look for coyotes and maybe a bobcat. Drink more IPA and likely move on to the Jim Beam he had stored away in the bottom of his bag. Chat about their Fantasy Football League and how the Pats needed to up their game this season …

"What? No, Your Honour, I didn't, call for recess!"

Chuckling at his buddy's sleep-chatter, Jack gave Adam a gentle shove to wake him.

"Huh? What? No, I didn't!"

"Hmm, guilty conscience, dude?"

He could just about make out a puzzled frown on Adam's face, the kind of 'half-awake where the fuck am I?' look you get when you forget your location for a moment.

Laughing, Jack added, "let's move inside or you'll wake up tomorrow with a stiff neck covered in insect bites."

That was enough to get his old friend moving. He might have been 6'2 and around 200lbs, but the guy hated bugs.

"Sleep well. G'night, John-boy."

"Fuck you …"

* * * *

"Wake up, Sleeping Beauty!"

Waving a mug of hot, black coffee under Adam's nose, Jack carefully roused his buddy. He'd spent enough nights with the native Bostonian to know he could be like a bear with a sore head in the morning.

Readying themselves for the day, they good-naturedly joked how the Red Sox wiped the floor with the Mets but how the Giants came back to kick the Pats in the ass.

By midday, they'd sunk a few more beers and were ready to go exploring, to suss out where to set up to look for coyotes or bobcats as it got dark.

"Guns or no guns?" Asked Adam, eying up the rifle.

Jack raised his eyebrow. They'd been hunting before; he knew Adam could handle a firearm. Still, city life meant he wasn't used to carrying a loaded weapon around and he wanted to arrive back on Monday with both feet intact.

"Why don't we leave the girls here, killer?" He suggested tactfully.

Adam shrugged okay, indicating he wasn't bothered either way.

And off they went into the woods.

* * * *

Nose twitching, the creature poked its head out of the mouth of the cave. It detected a scent, something it hadn't caught on the wind for many years. Human.

And not only that, but male.

A sort of grin stretched across its face.

Male, good.

Hehe, very good.

A play-thing ...

* * * *

Whilst they had been arguing over whether Brady or Manning was a better QB, the men hadn't quite noticed how far into the woods they had managed to traipse. Adam had no sense of direction or instinct for survival outside of the 'bad-lands' of Boston. Having met at a sports bar almost 20 years ago, when Adam was pre-law and Jack was majoring in English. They'd bonded over football despite hating each other's favorite teams. Once they'd graduated, Adam had stayed in the city, joining a prestigious law firm and Jack headed back to Connecticut.

They'd remained the best of friends, despite the miles between them. Groomsmen at each other's weddings, Jack God-Father to Adam's kid. This annual weekend away was a highlight for both. Over the last few years, Jack had tried to get a bit more creative, hence, the old cabin in the Maine woodlands belonging to his father's side of the family.

Grinning, he looked over at his oldest friend. Although the telltale signs of a high-power and long-hours job were clear, he was already looking more relaxed despite his bitching about people hating on Brady.

Right at that moment, things were good, things were great! Actually, they were –

"Ouch, god-fuck-damn it!"

Stopping abruptly, his righteous train of thought disrupted, Jack turned to see what on earth had caused the sudden commotion.

Adam was rubbing his ankle, cursing and grimacing as he tried to put his weight onto it.

Rolling his eyes, Jack dared to ask, "what the hell you done, man? Only you could try to follow all the classic horror tropes and end up busting your ankle in the woods."

Scowling, and feeling foolish for over-reacting, Adam replied.

"These stupid woods are testing me. It's ok for you. You're built like a QB, I'm the ex-line-backer who sits on his fat ass all day."

He plopped himself down, resting against a tree, and lit a cigarette.

"I ain't as fit as I was in college, bro."

Sniggering, jack joined him, taking a swig from the hipflask of whisky and then passing it over.

"You weren't that fit 20 years ago, *bro*."

After a few minutes, Jack jumped back up again.

Adam stayed resting on the floor, leaning against the tree for support.

"You gonna be able to walk, man? I mean, I ain't carrying you, that's for sure."

Using the truck as leverage, Adam shakily got to his feet, wincing.

"Well", he began. "The good news is, I don't think it's broken. But," he continued, "it hurts like hell. I'm not gonna be able to walk far."

Sliding back down the tree onto the floor, he continued massaging his ankle.

These were certainly not ideal circumstances. Things were starting to echo The Ritual ever so slightly. Jack was not happy with the situation. He might have been a writer, but he sure as hell didn't want life to start imitating art.

Looking around, he was also loathe to admit that he wasn't one hundred percent sure of their location. And Adam was starting to pale a little, which was in no way a good sign.

Frowning, he stood and stretched, looking around and hoping for some sort of inspiration. Scanning the area in front of him, he noticed what appeared to be the opening of a cave not too far away. If he could support Adam while he hobbled over there, he could hopefully leave him to rest for a bit while he raced back to the cabin and found something they could improvise as a crutch. Once they were both back safe, they were home free. The coyotes would live to see another day.

Sighing, he resigned himself to the fact he was going to have to take a lot of his buddies' weight whilst they stumbled together over to the shelter.

Now or never he thought, and with that, he stuck an arm under Adam and hauled him to his feet.

"There's a cave, or some sort of shelter. I can just about make it out over there." He said, pointing towards the edge of his sightline.

"Let's head there and you can drink some more Jim and take a nap."

It wasn't the fun trip they'd wanted, but things don't always go according to plan. Hobbling towards the cave, Adam chastised Jack for insisting their bro weekend involve the Great Outdoors and not a batting cage and a bar with IPA on draft and 24/7 sports on the big screen.

Plonking Adam unceremoniously on the ground, Jack rolled his eyes and gritted his teeth. Sometimes he needed to remind himself this guy was his oldest friend, and as much as he moaned, it was his release from a high-power job. On more than one occasion, he had helped dig Jack out of a financial hole when he was first starting as a writer and pay-checks were few and far between. How he'd flown back early from an overseas business trip when Jack's mom was sick and had been there with him when she passed.

"Urgh, what the fuck, man? I can't stay here, it fucking stinks like something died in there!"

"Sit there and rest whilst I head back and grab a shovel or something from the cabin. If it doesn't work as a crutch, at least I can use it to bash you over the head and put you out of your misery."

"But that smell!"

"Drink and numb your senses. Shouldn't be too difficult for you."

Flipping Jack the bird, Adam managed a wry smile. He was actually in a fair bit of pain, and guzzled down a very generous intake of the whisky to try to dull the ache in his ankle, which was now travelling up his entire leg.

Resting his head against the crumbly walls, he exhaled deeply. "Well fuck off then, go and make yourself useful for once."

And with a smirk of camaraderie, Jack was gone.

* * * *

She could hear the males now, their pungent masculinity driving her mad. It had been a long time since she had been able to satisfy her carnal urges, and the musky scent emanating from the strangers filled her with a base lust that needed instant fulfilment. Peering from her hiding space, eyes adapted to years of darkness, she saw one of the males head off, leaving the other alone. He was rubbing his leg, a look of anguish on his face. There was a spicy smell coming from something he was drinking, which piqued her interest. But mostly she just wanted to play …

* * * *

Lighting a cigarette, Adam gagged again at the revolting aroma originating from inside the cave. Wishing he'd picked up the gun from back at the cabin, he hoped the rotting stench wouldn't attract any scavengers. The coppery tang of blood was strong enough that he could decipher it even though years of smoking had desensitized his sense of smell.

Gulping back another swig of the good stuff, he closed his eyes and indulged in a little light fantasy. He and Jack might be old college pals, but there were some things they didn't share. Like the fact he had been fucking his intern for the last couple of months. Fresh out of law school, he had no idea why a young attractive girl like Clarice would show even a modicum of interest in him, but she'd made the advances and before long, he was bending her over his desk and giving it to her nice and hard. As he'd exploded inside of her, he'd felt a moment of guilt, thinking of his wife. It would be a one-off. Mustn't happen again. He'd thought the same thing after she'd knelt in front of him and given him the best damn head he'd ever received.

"God damn you, Clarice." He groaned, the mere thought of her causing a stirring in his loins.

Seriously considering jerking himself off whilst waiting for Jack, his hand was just starting to travel to his belt when he heard a noise. It sounded like a branch snapping from inside the cave.

All thought of lust disappeared in an instant. Eyes widening, he wondered what was in there, and if it was coming out.

Or, if it felt as frightened as he did.

"Hurry the fuck up, Jack." Murmuring, he hoped his buddy would be back soon, with that shovel ...

* * * *

Sensing the male's arousal made her careless. Feeling so excited now, she couldn't wait a second longer. This type of opportunity, where her prey was ready and raring to go, was a once in a lifetime opportunity. She knew exactly what she wanted to do to him.

* * * *

Ah yes, that'll do nicely thank you very much. Pleased with himself for remembering ol' Uncle Smokey kept a shovel in one of the make-shift closets, Jack collected it swiftly and grabbed the shotgun too, just in case. If for some unknown reason they ended up not getting back to the cabin before nightfall, no way in hell was he sleeping in the woods without protection.

Grabbing his daypack, he shoved in another bottle of Jim, some more smokes, and a couple of packets of jerky. That'd keep them going if push came to shove. He also threw in his notebook and a battered copy of *Forest of Shadows*.

Chuckling to himself he imagined any hungry beast that came looking for dinner would select Adam for the feast for sure, since he was carrying a whole lot of meat.

* * * *

Whatever was in that cave, was coming out, that much was obvious. Adam began to eek himself gingerly away from the mouth of the cave and back into the woods, as if somehow he could hide from the creature. Running various scenarios through his mind, he tried to remember if there were wolves or cougars in this part of Maine. God damn it, right now he didn't even feel up to a clash with a squirrel.

Heart beating at an alarming rate, he squeezed his eyes shut in an almost childish fashion – the whole if I can't see you, you can't see me protection from the monsters under your bed.

Ew, what the-

Recoiling as his nose was assaulted with a repellent stench, Adam could almost taste the rot in the air. Not that he'd met many bears, but he just didn't equate this horrendous pong to an animal.

Eyes watering, he was hit with the noxious bouquet of shit and piss, sweat, unwashed body parts, and the distinctive overpowering odour of blood.

"Bleugh!"

Gag reflex on over-drive, he vomited breakfast and the sour whisky burnt his throat as it reappeared. The second wave of nausea caused him to double over in pain and once he was done spraying the ground with last night's chili, groaning, he lifted his head back up.

"Ahhhhh!"

* * * *

Neither the smell of the fresh puke nor the ear-piercing scream from the male's mouth bothered her.

She was in heaven. Dancing around him, she paraded her naked form, like a female baboon getting ready for mating season.

As she easily fended off his pathetic attempts at pushing her away, hitting and kicking out, the realization that he was just like the others saddened her.

Oh well. She didn't need him for the nice feeling in between her legs. She did need him for the other fun though.

And it was just beginning.

* * * *

Ambling back through the trees, taking his time and enjoying being off the grid, Jack froze when he heard a very distinctive noise.

A scream.

What the-

Nah, fucker's messing with me.

Haha, almost got me there, man. No way I'm rushing over there like an idiot just to find that ass-hat laughing at me.

I might even just rest here for a while and read some more about Jessica.

Congratulating himself for spotting a practical joke, he nestled down in the leaves, resting against an ancient trunk, and began to read …

* * * *

"No, no, get away you fucking bitch!"

As much as he battered and pummelled at the creature in front of him, she (and regrettably he had no doubt it was a 'she', thanks to the full in his face thrust of what he supposed was her womanly area) seemed to dodge them with ease.

All of a sudden, she reared back from him as if he were the monster.

"What-what do you want?" he cried, trying his best to make himself small by pushing up against the tree and wishing to god his useless ankle didn't hurt so much.

Before his eyes, the creature arched her back in an almost impossible fashion and then leapt at him.

"Uh-ug-uhh."

Trying to scream, but only able to gurgle, he attempted to make some sort of warning call to Jack.

Looking at the creature in utmost horror, he saw why he'd been unable to project his voice.

Hanging out of her maw, was his throat and vocal cords.

Closing his eyes, as the cascades of blood spurted like a cannibal's chocolate fountain, he was just about to feel sharp teeth ripping his body apart before he gratefully lost consciousness and the world faded to black ...

* * * *

Um, yum oh yes, yes. This was so much better than anything he could have done to her with his... thing.

Sinking her teeth into the rolls of skin on his white, hairy belly, she relished in the taste of the flesh, sucking out the yellow pus-like fat, her eyes rolling into the back of her head in sheer ecstasy.

Lapping up the blood like a kitten with a saucer of milk, it would have been hard to tell her apart from Carrie White by the time she had finished burying into his flesh.

Rising from the delicious treat, rubbing her tummy like someone after eating Christmas dinner, she threw back her head and roared.

Ringing the dinner bell ...

* * * *

Jack's feeling of superiority was soon whipped away when he heard the panicked shouting followed by what presented like some sort of a ruckus.

"Okay, Adam," he muttered, putting Jessica back into his bag, "you've got my attention now. Hope it's not a grizzly."

He wasn't too far from where he'd left his buddy, so he quickened his pace to a fast walk.

What the-

Shit!

Upon hearing what he could only describe as a roar, he felt his stomach drop and his balls retract. Something really fucking bad was happening, and his friend needed help.

Gut-instinct told him that he needed to use stealth. Whatever was occurring, it would do no good to rush in, guns blazing. Upon approaching the cave, he dropped to a crouch and crept as quietly as he could.

Urgh, covering his mouth and nose with his hand, he could actually taste the thick, rancid stench drifting in his direction. Recognising it meant trouble; he struggled to find an innocent, innocuous reason for the smell. In his previous experience, it foretold one thing only – death.

Finding a decent vantage point, well hidden in the bush, he allowed himself to take in the scene.

The human mind can trick us and protect us in many ways. It can shut down when we feel pain, it can manipulate what is in front of us if we are too fragile to be able to cope.

Unfortunately for Jack, as a writer of the macabre with real-life experience of horror, his mind had already gone to the bad places. He just never thought for one moment that Hell would be right in front of him.

Using every inch of willpower to stay hidden and not run away as fast as he could, Jack witnessed his oldest friend being dined upon. Two, what he could only presume were female 'creatures' were ripping into him, tearing flesh to gorge on his entrails.

Retching and trying to keep the vomit from spilling out, he attempted to keep the trembling at bay whilst his body fought going into shock.

Gotta stay quiet, gotta stay quiet.

Oh, fu-

One of the creatures, having finished munching on the juicy goodness of Adam's genitalia, was now cavorting around the second female in some kind of messed up naked ball-room dance. She began then grinding against the still feasting figure, whist rubbing more blood and viscera up and down her body.

Oh god, is she, no, god, sick fucking cu-

Oh fuck.

Just as it looked as if the creature was about to get her rocks off, she stopped abruptly, body tensing as if in alarm.

Nose twitching, teeth bared like a wolf, she suddenly whipped around to stare in Jack's direction.

Jack realised in terror that the creature had somehow detected him. That he hadn't needed to be quiet, his only chance of not being noticed would have been if he had masked his scent.

With a roar like a wild banshee, the creature abandoned her companion and raced in Jack's direction.

Sensing there was little point in trying to escape, despite being in decent shape, instinct kicked in like muscle memory.

In a tuck, roll, grab move that a movie stunt-person would have been proud of, Jack grabbed the forgotten shot-gun and aimed it in the bitches face.

"Take that, mother-fucker!" He war-cried, and unloaded the weapon. Time hadn't lessened his accuracy, and the bullet entered and cleanly exited right through her face, blasting most of it up into the air and onto the ground.

Splat.

Quickly followed by.

Bang.

As he popped another round into her, just in case.

Always gotta double-tap.

Although it highly unlikely she was some sort of undead parasite, Jack had absolutely no clue what kind of a humanoid cryptid he was facing. At the very least, they were cannibals who had binged on his best buddy and that was very fucking far from okay.

Pointing the gun at the second thing, which unbelievably was still crouched in a protective stance next to Adam's body, he noticed she didn't appear perturbed by her friend's demise or indeed frightened of him or the weapon.

He'd met perps like this before though, usually coked up or fucked up on PCP. Even met a guy who'd chewed off part of his girlfriend's face.

Wasn't long after that he left homicide and the police entirely and began to write. At first, he found it cathartic—to put the horrors onto paper made them less real in a weird way.

Thankfully, he still had his marksmen accuracy although he hadn't been banking on how fast this bitch could move.

Like something from The Matrix, time seemed to move in slow motion and as the bullet simultaneously left the chamber of the gun, the creature reared up and threw herself at him.

The shot went wide as she landed on top of him, her lithe frame weighing more than it should. As he fell, the back of his head hit the hard ground with such force that his teeth rattled.

Bang.

The gun unloaded another round, this one hitting the rocky wall of the cave and causing stones to cascade towards them.

Having landed awkwardly and now the ricochet from the misfire, the shotgun was tragically just out of Jack's reach.

"Arghhhhh!"

Thinking he might pass out from the stench of this thing screeching right into his face, fighting the vomit that was rising, he thought he saw something far worse than any of the atrocities he had witnessed thus far.

The thing atop of him, grinned and right in between her fangs, was a piece of Adam's skin. From his right arm. And the reason Jack knew this? He could still see part of the ink from his Red Sox tattoo.

This was it.

Allowing his thoughts to wander to better times, he recalled a female detective who had been the love of his life until their divorce, the first time he saw one of his books in Barnes and Noble, the—

Wait, what?

His eyes were still shut tight, but he could no longer feel the tight pressure on his chest. Opening them quickly, he sat up and grabbed the shot-gun.

The back of his head, his ribs, and the hand that had been holding the gun hurt like crazy. But he was alive.

And alone.

Jumping up, he looked all around him, holding the weapon out, finger on the trigger. But there was no sign of her anywhere.

Knowing he couldn't hang around, in case the bitch returned with back-up, he ran as fast as his aching body would allow him back past the cabin to where they'd left their vehicles.

Jumping in his truck, he put it into drive and sped the hell out of there. Once he hit the road and civilisation, he'd dial 911. Call in some favours.

Weeping, the shock of what had happened and the loss of his friend tearing at his heart, he looked in his rear-view mirror, half-expecting to find another one of them hiding in the back seat. But thankfully there was no one there.

Gripping the steering wheel, Jack tried his best to keep his eyes on the road and hands steady.

I'll find you. No matter what it takes. You killed my buddy. Wait 'til you find out what I'm gonna do to you, bitch. You ain't no Final Girl and I ain't no Final Guy. I won't rest 'til you are dead. You won't be the one that got away for long …

JANINE PIPE is a Horror lover and writer who was first introduced to the genre at the tender age of 9 by reading 'Salem's Lot - and she hasn't looked back since. She is inspired by Stephen King and cites Glenn Rolfe and Jonathan Janz as her favourite current writers. She likes to shock with her writing- there is usually a lot of gore and plenty of swearing ... She is very thankful to her biggest cheerleaders, her husband, and daughter and her mentor, Graeme Reynolds. She chews the fat with fellow authors on her blog, Janine's Ghost Stories, and is a guest reviewer for Gingernuts of Horror and Nightworms.

You can find her work at Tales to Terrify, Ghost Stories the Podcast, and The Horror Tree. Coming this year, she has shorts with Iron Faerie Publishing and Black Hare Press. She is also working on a top-secret anthology for the NHS.

Check her blog here –
https://janinesghoststories.wordpress.com/
Follow her on Twitter here –
https://twitter.com/disneynine

ATLA'S JOURNEY
Carmen Baca

The teens, a boy and a girl, lay still on the forest floor. Santa Muerte appeared out of the dark, doing what she had been created to do: to deliver the souls of the deceased to their final destinations based on their life choices. After all, they had a conscience; following it should be easy. Those who closed their consciousness to the voice in their heads and the feelings in their guts went down while the rest flew up. This pair would be entering the gates of hell in single file; though they committed their crimes together, they would face justice alone. The third in their party got away, just barely.

When the two bodies were discovered, so much time had passed they were nothing more than incomplete sets of bleached bones whose identities would remain unknown for another decade at least. Forensic science was in its early stages and DNA testing far in the future. But because the trio had gone missing several years before and because they had last been seen together, it was assumed the remains were at least two of theirs. The third was never found.

There was no way to tell which bones belonged to which teen, but the two incomplete and separated piles were buried by their loved ones in as normal and traditional means as they could. The three mothers' wails at both funerals conveyed not only the despair of the calamity, but also their anguish at burying bones that were most likely a mixture of two of the three best friends. *Las madres* didn't even know which one of them might still have a living child, so the loss was tinged with a bit of hope. That was somehow worse. The town and surrounding communities' shock spread to the entire state of New Mexico and beyond. No cause of death was ever determined, but everyone feared they had been murdered. They were right, but they would be even more shocked to discover the identities of the murderers. The meeting with the odd one revealed the monsters they hid inside themselves.

Cathy, Luke, and Dominic had been good friends since third grade when a bully had cornered Cathy behind the school building and was doing his best to make her cry. Luke and Dominic were walking around the corner when Cathy's knee struck the boy where it counted, and she gave him a two-palm shove away from her that sent him to the ground like a falling plank. When his body curled around his center like a caterpillar, she spat on him, stomped his head, and saw the other boys looking at her.

"You want to try me too?" She glared with fists raised like a boxer.

"Heck no," Luke had responded while Dominic shook his head. "I wanna learn how to fight like you," he added. Their friendship was formed, and now here they were, in their last year of school—eighth grade for the boys, sixth for Cathy—having established themselves as the three *amigos* teachers never seated together. They weren't bad children. Quite the opposite. They were good students, well aware they would be looking for employment soon. They played a daily game of "What will I be when I grow up?" and shared what they knew of each profession. The town library was their favorite place. The woods around the town were their second favorite. There, they experimented with whatever they discovered in the books they chose for the day.

They also based their daily competitions of jobs on what they learned through research. They knew more schooling wasn't in their future, but there was plenty of employment. Ranch hand, blacksmith, crop picker and wood seller, many more in their area. The boys would find employment and live at home while they were apprenticed to someone who would have them. Cathy refused to consider a bleak future of wife and mother. Not her. She'd find something, nanny, seamstress, surely there was something she could do until she saved enough to finish her education at a real city school. She hadn't told the boys, but that was her plan.

They hadn't yet decided what topic they would next tackle, perhaps "evidence of the paranormal," when they exhausted their dream jobs. That had been an idea they had thrown around before. The trio were on the path to good adult lives. So why had two been killed? Was the third a murderer? Everyone wanted to know. Or had it been a freak accident? That still didn't explain the one who got away. Either way, the whole business was a darned shame, *una lastima*, for sure.

The *gente* didn't know the half of it. The three friends hadn't been the good future pillars of the community they displayed outwardly. There was a darkness to them that emerged when they were together, something that was fueled by the dares they proposed to one another because of what they read. So, when the three friends came upon the girl about their age at the town dump, of all places, they huddled for a moment in discussion. They decided to try a new experiment with their decision for the next topic of research. Luke fiddled with something he took from the knapsack Dominic wore on his back and nodded to the rest that the game could begin. They were about to have hands-on experience their consciences warned were forbidden.

* * * *

The day Atlaclamani Ahuatzi met three young people ended in one more turning point of her young life. All because as the descendant of powerful Aztec women, she knew things, she had been tutored in many skills and crafts, and she had done things. Things which, in her mind at the time, had been justified. There were no regrets, no need for apologies then or now. After the death of her mother and grandmother in separate incidents (more pre-ordained than accidents) on the same day, Atlaclamani, age 14, had fled into the woods instead of allowing her future to be decided at the hands of authorities.

She had discovered a stone *casita*, a one-room structure with a dirt floor and no roof. The roofing took forever, but she made the little house habitable and turned it into home. Nearby was a little cemetery where Atlaclamani had a friend, the previous inhabitant. She was the perfect *amiga* Atlaclamani could never harm by accident. She told her deepest secrets to the girl who would never share them with the living. Regina Abigail Padilla, aged 14, had died on June 6, 1922, according to her headstone. Atlaclamani felt a kinship with the girl, having found her diary when she had first discovered her new home. The previous condition of the abode and the little book still held some of the gruesome details that had resulted in her death. But Atlaclamani was content with her new dwelling and her confidant.

Two incidents in her past taught her that until she could control her emotions and her actions, she should not be around people for their sakes. While the two events had occurred with years between them, they were both the results of her experimentation with what others would later refer to as spells. She owned the book her mother and grandmother had handed down to her. The *libro* held herbal recipes, healing practices, and other important information that had originated with their maternal lineage. She had experimented with at least two-thirds of the contents so far and practiced her powers on animals, perfecting her abilities without harming any. Her heart had always accepted los *animalitos*; she would never hurt them. It was humans she didn't trust easily. For good reason.

The first event in her youth which resulted in human death was the result of her innocence. The second was a combination of that with her self-protective nature. Her naïveté made her think her powers could work miracles; that was how poor six-year-old Delbert had died. Atla had gotten miffed at something the boy did, something he should have atoned for but didn't. What happened to him was an accident, justified, but nonetheless, an accident. So she didn't feel responsible. She had only been seven years old. That was how her grandmother and mother knew her life would be guided by the number seven.

She had barely turned fourteen the second time she acted on impulse through misconceived self-preservation. Atla's victim, a young man who had been guided into her orbit, had met with a gory end of his own making. As much of him as could be scraped together was gathered into burlap sacks. The men who dealt with such things tucked the bundles into a plain pine box and nailed the lid shut. No one wanted the mother to see. They debated whether to tell her the whole truth all the way to her doorstep.

No one knew what was said, but the poor woman, well into her eighties, changed that day. Those who knew her said she was a living shell of the doting mother she had been before her son's death; the human part of her on the inside, the soul and the emotions, were already on the other side with her boy. She was proof a person can will themselves to death. The following week, the woman's body followed. Atla felt bad about that, but not about the other two. The powers that governed her life had preordained their ends, not Atla.

Now, here she was on the last stop of an all-day trek, foraging for whatever she could find, and instead, having an unexpected encounter with what she had avoided successfully—until today. She had spent the rest of her fourteenth year as cautiously as she could, knowing this period until her next birthday could be dangerous for her or for any human she encountered. So these three had been put in her path intentionally. If the trio had passed through here a few minutes before or after she had, they would never have met. Atlaclamani's life was governed by fate, which would determine her afterlife, according to her beliefs. So, it was also destiny which designed this meeting. There had to be a reason.

She had ventured close to the edge of the small town, having discovered a deep and long arroyo the residents had taken to using as the town dump. Since it was close to dusk, she didn't think she would run into anyone and was focused on the treasures she had already placed in her cart: an old coffee pot, a few spoons, a pretty good little knife, and even a bag of old clothes. Torn and dirty didn't matter. They could be washed and sewn when she got home.

"Well, well," a female voice spoke, with a loud emphasis on the second "well."

Atlaclamani was bent over a crate, using a stick to move objects apart. She started, then looked up the few feet to the edge of the arroyo where three youths stood. Two boys, one dark and short, the other lanky and red-headed, and a girl, a pretty ivory-complexioned brunette, stood between them. They were all looking down at her, and for a moment Atlaclamani wondered what they must think. She was filthy, she knew. Looking down at her dirty hands, she figured she probably wore smudges of dirt on her face, too. She suddenly became self-conscious about her appearance. She had outgrown her previously large clothes and now the *calzones* reached to her calves like gaucho pants, and the sleeves of all her *camisas* had to be folded up at the cuffs since they didn't reach her wrists. The kids' clothes were pristine, like they had just gotten home from school, even though it was early August and school might not have started yet for all Atlaclamani knew. She had never been enrolled in one.

The three spoke at once, leaving Atlaclamani to decipher their words after as if listening to an echo in her head.

"Are you alright?"

"Where do you live?"

"Do you need something? You don't have to look in the dump. I'll take you to my house and we can get you what we can spare," the girl offered.

"I'm fine," Atlaclamani answered. Never having experienced embarrassment or shame, Atla didn't know what the heat on her face and running down her body was. "I—I don't live far," she added. She took her place between the long handles and then started making her way up the incline, pulling the cart behind her. The three strangers ran down the steep embankment where the trash was barely beginning to accumulate. When she reached the top of her side and turned to look back at them, they were already running up right after her. When they joined her, they circled like coyotes around prey. But Atlaclamani was no scared animal, and so she stood her ground.

"I'm Cathy," the girl said. She pointed to the redhead and said, "Luke," and then

motioned to the short boy, adding, "Dominic."

Head high, back straight, prepared for mockery like the last time she told a stranger her name, she spoke clearly and enunciated her syllables. "Atlacamani."

When the inevitable "Atla what?" emerged from Luke, she added, "Call me Atla."

"Why are you getting supplies from the dump, Atla?" Cathy asked. "I have plenty of clothes I think will fit you." She stepped up to the cart and looked at the contents. "And my mother has an old coffee pot and probably the other things you ha—"

"Thank you," Atla interrupted. "I've found what I need here."

Dominic shrugged, saying, "If it was me, I'd go to the general store rather than use something from here." His nose crinkled up as though a whiff of garbage had assaulted his sense of smell. He even dry heaved and turned aside to spit.

Atla was sure there was a smirk on his face after his action, and it hit a nerve. This mockery was not lighthearted; it seemed mean-spirited to her. She took an immediate dislike of this boy. Atla started moving off. "I must get going now. It will be night soon, and I don't care to travel in the dark." She turned back once and saw them huddled together with something between them. She quickened her pace and moved away from the direction of her rock house just in case.

They let her reach the woods about fifty feet away and then followed. They caught up and in lockstep, the three moved along with her. Then Dominic fell back to walk beside her cart, and the other two remained on each side. She stopped. "What are you doing? You aren't coming with me."

"Why not?" Luke asked.

Cathy turned Dominic around and rifled through his knapsack. "We aren't," she said, handing Atla a pop and taking three more for each of them. "We just thought we'd walk along for a bit, get to know you better."

The coffee-colored liquid gleamed through the glass—a rich tempting brown which glowed almost gold in the sunset—and Atla's mouth watered. She'd had one of these sodas every time she had gone into town on errands with her mother or grandmother, and it was a favorite she hadn't enjoyed in a long time.

"That is, if you don't mind," Luke added, pulling out a pocket knife and opening all their drinks. Then he held his aloft. "Let us toast," he said with a smile.

"Yes, let's," Cathy agreed. "To new friends." They clinked bottles, Atla joining in after seeing what this toasting entailed. The only toast she knew involved a fire, so she was relieved that wasn't what this one needed.

The drink was exactly how she remembered. But it also had a sharp, sour aftertaste that made her jaw twinge like after eating a sweet and sour, a small plant resembling a three-leaf clover. She didn't remember the drink having that before and wondered what this trio of new "friends" was up to.

"Drink up," Dominic urged. "It's better cold than lukewarm." He slapped his knee and punched Luke in the arm. "Lukewarm, get it? Getting hot there, Luke?"

"Shut up," Luke growled. His smile had disappeared and his eyes took on a dark angry look directed at his friend.

"Aww, fellas," Cathy interceded. "No fighting now. We all get a turn. Just like we
discussed."

Atla was seeing double, so instead of three, six people were surrounding her. They came into focus as if right on top of her and then blurred as they backed off, or so it seemed. Her legs grew weak, and she sank to her knees. "I—I don't feel well."

"Oh, whatsa matter?" Luke leaned over her, taking her chin in his hand. "Can't handle a bit of booze?" He pulled a flask from his front pocket and dumped a good dose into his friends' drinks. Before replacing the cap on the bottle Cathy handed to Atla, he had added enough to make a non-drinker intoxicated fast. They never left home without their supplies in case they dared one another to experiment by experience.

Cathy crouched down and ran the back of her hand over Atla's forehead. "You're a bit warm," she announced. "Maybe you're coming down with something. Here, let us help you."

She set her bottle down and moved behind Atla, her hands pulling her gently by the shoulders, back and down to the ground until she lay on the dirt. Cathy held her down while Luke moved to her feet. He took one last drink and launched his bottle toward a large boulder where it broke with a loud crash.

"Here," he said, pulling a ball of string from his pants pocket and tossing it to Dominic.

His hands wrapped around Atla's ankles and held her feet still. Dominic set his bottle on her cart and knelt beside Luke, unwinding the string and smiling at Atla. He opened his mouth to say something, but she didn't give him a chance to speak. Atla's pretense of complacency ended. She didn't have to know human behavior and motives to understand something bad was coming.

Though she had been sheltered all her life, she had accompanied her grandmother or mother into nearby towns, and she had been schooled in reading people's eyes, their intent more obvious there than by any words that came out of their mouths or by any movements they might make, threatening or otherwise. She never left home without drinking her homemade tea, one which gave her clarity of mind so she could protect herself. Like Medusa's snakes reaching in different directions, her directive entered the minds of the three youths simultaneously.

'Kill Cathy and Luke.'

'Kill Dominic and Cathy.'

'Kill Luke and Dominic.'

The light of life and innocence went out in all three pairs of eyes when the intent was understood and humanity left the young people as though they were the undead. Only one thought governed their actions. They rose together and stood staring one another down long enough for Atla to get out of their way. She settled not far off to watch the show.

Cathy turned on Luke first, teeth clenched and fingers curled like claws. As he defended himself, Dominic attacked Cathy. Mindlessly, he dropped the string and wrapped his bare hands around her throat. The trio turned into a monstrous phenomenon of flailing limbs, striking blows where and when they could. It might have been an hour or only twenty minutes. Time ceased to matter when death became the objective. The ripping flesh, howls of pain, the rending of clothing, then the crack of a breaking bone resulting in an ear-piercing scream. The death of all of them would be the only way to end it. Evenly matched in purpose, the girl and the two boys tore at each other, no two-against-one plan here, only the same thought on each mind—self-preservation. Only Atla knew death would satisfy the dictates of the old ways. She stood by and watched as first Cathy weakened, and the two boys attacked as if they'd planned their moves though it was every man for himself. It wasn't so much the clubbing of Cathy's head by Dominic as much as the bite to the jugular by Luke, which did her in after what she probably thought was longer than the 72 seconds it took for her to lose her ability to think. Her lifeblood took longer to finish pumping.

The thick branch in Dominic's fists swung at Luke's head like he was going for the winning home run hit. The glancing blow caught Luke's shoulder before he dodged. Then he swooped in under Dominic's arms and punched him right in the groin—one, two—fast. At the same time, Dominic's club smashed down on Luke's head, a spike in the branch carving a hole in the boy's skull. Luke's body fell forward, just enough to cause Dominic to lose his balance. Luke was dead before he hit the ground. Unable to catch himself, Dominic's backward stumbling succeeded in causing his own fall, his head striking a rock when he landed. He didn't move again.

Atla watched the blood start pooling beneath Dominic's head. Did he twitch? She wasn't sure. There would be search parties. She dragged the bodies into a small arroyo, covered them with brush, rocks, everything she could find to hide them for a while. Then she remembered a particular experiment she had tried on a squirrel once. She had put it into sleep and followed the instructions in her book which made it so camouflaged she couldn't see it at all. She'd had to get on hands and knees to find it and wake it up so it could go on its way. She spoke the words and made the motions until limb by limb, body part by body part, the three kids were invisible to the human eye. She had no way of knowing whether hounds could sniff the bodies out, and she didn't stick around to find out. She picked up her cart by the handles and hurried home. They were far from her little shack, six miles more or less, but she wouldn't be able to remain.

She packed her meager belongings and slept until right before dawn. Then she set her little home on fire, making sure everything was ashes on the inside since the rock walls would remain standing. She cocked her head when she heard a faint cry, like when a predator catches its prey and the realization of absolute terror that it will be torn apart for food results in a death wail. She smiled, knowing the final member of the hunting party which had been directed into her path was gone. Whatever they had planned for her, she knew the one who got away had met his end in a more horrific way than the others.

He would have been the first to do to Atla what he wished. He deserved worse. But the three gave each other bravado, and together they would have succeeded with someone else, a mere human with no powers to stop their brutality. They had to go. Those three had turned to monsters long before they had encountered her; she had merely used their monstrosity against them. She looked one last time at the shell of the casita she had hoped to inhabit till her twenty-first birthday, told it goodbye as though it were an old friend. Then she set off away from the town, going south where her fate awaited.

* * * *

Dominic woke when the first rays of the sun were turning the dark into gradual light. The back of his head pounded with each heartbeat, and he was cold and growing stiff. He rose from under the criss-cross of branches and boughs, shoving them aside as he got to his feet with much stumbling, falling to his knees more than once. Moving out of the small arroyo and deeper into the forest, the one who got away with murder and with his life traveled like a somnambulist, weaving with stops and starts but eventually getting some distance away from the friends turned enemies. The sun had begun to hover just above the eastern horizon, a while ball exuding continuous rays of light. The only dark places that remained were in the deep part of the forest. Dominic fell for the last time due to blood loss and a split skull which had been dribbling brains along the path he forged. He turned over on his back so he would see the sun above him when it rose to its zenith. His last wish was to see the brightest light he could think of and will his soul to reach it. Surely, up to now, he had lived a life still worthy of heaven even with what he did with his friends or what he had done to them.

He saw something approaching and tried to brush blood that was dripping from his hair into his eyes. His arm and hand didn't follow his usual attempts to get them to move, and he wondered why. He didn't hurt. Where was the blood coming from? He blinked. Not far away, a pair of eyes was becoming less blurry and getting closer. A hot breath with the stench of a corpse reached his nose. The huge dark shape took form, and the one who had escaped a quick death looked with horror into the hungry eyes of the bear…

CARMEN BACA taught high school and college English for thirty-six years before retiring in 2014. Her command of English and her regional Spanish dialect contributes to her story-telling style. Her debut novel El Hermano published in April of 2017 and became a finalist in the NM-AZ book awards program in 2018. Her third book, Cuentos del Cañón, received first place for short story fiction anthology in 2020 from the same program. To date, she has published 5 books and 43 short works in online literary magazines and anthologies. She and her husband live a quiet life in the country caring for their animals and any stray cat that happens to come by.

Nightcrawler
Ushasi Sen Basu

Mili and I were insomniacs. She stretched and dug her claws into the blanket while I sat up in bed, at last, exhausted from all the sleepless tossing and turning. We watched the clock go tick-tock for a while, then, as if she knew it had just turned 2 am, Mili turned with a flourish of her tail, squeezed herself through the gap in the window grille, and dropped down into space. I heard a muted thump as she made a perfect landing onto the cornice below, and then a slighter noise as she leaped on to the boundary wall that circled our high rise. My mind followed her as she picked her way through the glass shards planted on the top of the wall, as dainty as a ballerina, and then dropped into the street behind. Her night had just begun.

I was still stuck in my bedroom staring at the clock. I threw the blanket off—it was too hot anyway—and walked in my bare feet to the living room. As I imagined Mili stalking further and further off into the night, I began to pace the length of my small living room, frustrated that social convention dictated I could do nothing when I felt most alive. My pace quickened; I reached one end of the hall, swivelled on my heel, and reached the other wall in a matter of seconds. I had to walk or go mad. I thought wistfully of the long, dark corridor that lay beyond my front door. I could walk all I liked there and in complete peace. Perhaps a good walk would help me soothe my thrumming nerves and the blood that beat relentlessly against my eardrums.

My hand faltered on the handle of my main door. People would call me crazy if they saw me. But who would see me?

I stepped out and felt better immediately. A cool breeze dried my sweat as I paced in the spacious corridor that connected everyone's flats on the first floor. I reached the farthest wall and glanced at the doors that stood on either side of me. Flats 310 and 311. Families I knew in passing — a small smile for the women, a quick sideways glance, and no acknowledgment for the men, as was appropriate. And a toothy grin for the young ones, who would beam back.

They were all blissfully asleep behind those doors. I wish I were too.

I walked another leisurely length of the corridor to the front of my door. 309 and 308. Old Mrs. Dutta lived in 308. Fallen asleep in front of the TV again—I could hear it muttering. I lay my hand on the door handle and turned it, and only realized what I was doing when it met resistance from the lock. She had locked it.

Good, good. Sometimes when Mrs. Dutta fell asleep in front of the TV, she forgot. She must have locked up before sitting down to watch her soaps tonight.

I turned to repeat my walk to the other end again. When I reached it, I turned the other knobs, too. I was bored, and it was a game. Locked! Locked!

I decided to climb higher; there was no dearth of corridors to wander—this building had eleven floors. Perhaps I should see if I could get to the terrace. I could be like Mili under the inky sky. But yet, there was no hurry. I stopped on the next floor and regarded the door of 319 with interest. They had one of those custom-made doors; people, animals, and vegetation writhing in carved profusion out of some expensive looking wood, a garland drooping from the arch. I stood caressing their carved faces for a minute and then touched the cool brass knob. The knob wouldn't turn as easily as the regulation steel handles on the other doors. I put some extra weight on my arm and turned it until it stopped with a click.

Aah, too loud, walk away! Though a perfectly innocent way for an insomniac to pass her time, one never knew what motive suspicious minds could impute to it. I gave the opposite door a fleeting glance and decided to abandon the floor altogether, and then the next.

I was headed for the terrace finally, where I could take a few turns as I looked out at the city, breathe a few draughts of the cold night air before returning home. Since I'm being honest, I rather enjoyed walking along the thick boundary walls of the terrace. It was invigorating. I had no trouble with my balance. Or heights.

On the 4th floor, I paused for breath. I ambled to 341 and leaned on the handle. Locked! What were these people afraid of? I often forgot to bolt my own door and discovered it only in the morning. It hardly mattered in a building like this with guards at the gate, high glass-spiked walls, and even barbed wire in places. Some people were just nervous by nature, I guess.

I climbed another flight of stairs and stopped to get my bearings. Which floor was I on? Let me see, 359 already? Hmm. This was the family with the most adorable little boy, all floppy curls and curling eyelashes. I pushed on the door handle and smiled at the memory of seeing him earlier that day.

Little Rohan had solemnly asked if he could pet Mili, as the latter had wound her way through the gaps of our ankles. He had only bent to stroke her fur after I smiled and said 'of course'. A sweet, well-behaved boy, so rare in today's brash world.

There was no resistance and the door creaked and then swung open under my weight. Surprising! A twist in my little game of Russian Roulette! Now obviously I would have to reach in, quietly get hold of the handle again and pull the door closed as noiselessly as possible. Then I would head to the roof as I had always intended. I reached into the flat without stepping over the threshold; somehow that didn't seem right.

A gust of cold air from behind me, and the door swung further open. Drat these creaky doors! Had people never heard of oiling hinges? I stood and stared at the door for a while, chewing my lip. Perhaps I should leave it open; turn tail and run. But that wouldn't be right. God knows who could wander in?

I put one foot in and then another. Blood roared in my ears, so loud it blocked everything else out. Now the handle was within my reach again. My long nails grazed the cold metal and I grasped it firmly. *You're not getting away again.*

I paused with my hand on the handle and looked into the house. I admit, I was curious. People didn't really invite me to their homes. I was fine with that, of course, but it was always interesting to see how people projected their personalities differently on identical spaces. The flat was in darkness, except for the pool of yellow light that fell in from the corridor behind me. My eyes adjusted in a trice, and I caught a flicker of light that played on the corridor floor and vanished again. Little Rohan's nightlight. I smiled and tiptoed in, remembering to close the main door softly behind me. I padded through the house plunged in darkness, with the nightlight as my guiding light.

I walked barefoot down the cool tiles of the tiny passageway that led to the three bedrooms at the far end of the flat. Different layout than mine... At last, I was at the door of the bedroom. A bedside lamp rotated gently and threw many-hued stars and moons on the ceiling and floor and the sleeping child's face. He looked like an angel.

I hesitated before stepping in. Perhaps look in on the parents first? A few steps in the opposite direction took me into the master bedroom, where Mr. and Mrs. Das slept with their backs to each other. Mr. Das's face looked much younger in repose, denuded of his usual pompous air of being a very busy somebody. Slight snores and deep breathing rose in the air. I turned and walked into the child's room.

Once again, I admired the delicate play of patterns across the room and then moved to the ludicrous racing car bed where Rohan lay.

How beautiful he looked! I could sense the quick beat of his heart mere inches away. I bent forward a little to see him better and started when Rohan's eyes snapped open. For a second, he just looked, then his eyes widened. He squeezed his eyes shut and opened his mouth wide to scream. No! I was at the balcony door in a flash; I had no time to get to the main door. I slid the door open and closed it behind me, hoping the rattle it made was drowned by the piercing sound of the boy's wail. I leaned ramrod straight against the stuccoed outer wall.

I stood still, eyes closed, trying to regulate my breathing. That cramped flat downstairs now seemed very inviting. The boy's scream stopped, or rather sounded smothered, like someone had held him against them. A woman's panic-stricken voice said, "what, Rohan? what happened, Rohan?"

"There was someone in this room, she was standing here!" the child sobbed.

His mother's voice softened, "Oh Rohan! It's just a bad dream, shona."

"No, no I tell you! She was here! Strange hair… she was… I couldn't see her face but I know she was here!"

I risked a look through a gap in the curtains.

Rohan's mother pulled him onto her lap and rocked him, "shhhh, don't cry." Mr. Das stood behind his wife and scratched an arm. His voice rasped with sleep, "Rohan, be a brave boy. Bad dreams can't hurt anyone."

The little boy shook his head so hard all his curls quivered. "It wasn't a dream I tell you." He looked wildly around the room. His gaze fell on the balcony with a dawning expression.

"She's out there, baba," he whispered.

I broke into a sweat. The hair rose on my arms. I licked the length of first one forearm and then the other. It calmed me.

"Ugh, Rohan, I have to get up early tomorrow. I don't really have time for this."

Rohan's voice rose hysterically, "she's out there I'm sure of it!" He didn't know it, but he was pointing straight at me. I had my ways of blending into the darkness.

"Alright, alright!" his father snapped as he headed towards the balcony. "I'll do it just to show you no one's there."

The boy broke out in renewed sobs of terror and Mrs. Das hugged him tighter. I could see she looked a little spooked herself.

I looked around. I was cornered. Flight or fight? I took a deep, deep breath and felt my heartbeat slow. There was nothing like the night air.

In a trice, I had made my decision and sat crouched on the thick iron railing nearest to me, still hidden, I think, by the drawn curtains and the night. I heard the man scrabbling at the lock with a sleepy clumsiness behind me. I launched myself out into the darkness.

* * * *

After what felt like an eternity of fumbling with the door ('Time that could have been better spent in bed' he thought to himself), Mr. Das emerged onto the balcony. He rubbed his eyes again and looked around.

He muttered through gritted teeth to his son who stood inside, "See Rohan? Nobody here, just as I said."

Rohan and Mrs. Das trotted out to join him. The three of them stood still for a moment, a tableau of unusual figures standing under a setting moon.

The woman squeezed her son's shoulders and said, "Come on, you can sleep with us just for tonight!"

Rohan looked around the balcony bug-eyed, and then with the child's unquestioning acceptance of the word of an adult, turned and went back in, holding on tightly to the fabric of his mother's nighty.

The man stood for a second longer. The night air felt good on his skin. There was a slight thud below. Skin prickling, Mr. Das suddenly remembered the warm comfort of his bed and the alarm set at 6 am. He rolled the door closed with a click and double-checked the lock.

* * * *

Six stories below, I landed perfectly, and retracted my claws. There had only been the slightest sound. I, an errant child of Bast, stood in deep shadow, as I watched the now-empty balcony.

It was difficult to have two sides of you constantly at war. A member of both tribes, but belonging to none. I had kept my feral instincts under control for so long, smothered under the baggage of human existence.

But there was something about the quick trip-trip of a young one's heart that brought the feline predator out in me. Things had not turned out the way I would have wished.

This one had got away.

Hunting in the city was frustrating, always fraught with uncertainty. Though Mili, my domesticated cat companion, liked urban areas, I preferred forests where it was easier to pick off prey on the fringes of human settlements. I was done being human for a while.

I turned with a swish and walked away, quick and cat-footed.

USHASI SEN BASU holds a master's degree in English Literature from Jadavpur University, Kolkata, India. She has been a professional writer and editor for a decade and a half. Ushasi's debut novel, Kathputli, a contemporary literary fiction novel, was published in 2017. Her second novel, A Killer Among Us, was published by Readomania in 2020. She is also a contributing author to two other anthologies, the Readomania Book of Horror and The Readomania Book of Crime. She lives in Bangalore, India with her husband and daughter. To know more about her, visit her Instagram account @ushasiwriter or her author page on Facebook (@ushasikathputli).

Little Sally Ann
Shawnna Deresch

"It's stuck." Carl jiggled the handle on the front door of the dilapidated, two-story farmhouse. He pulled the key out of the lock and inspected it. It looked like any other key he had dangling from his keychain. He tried the key again but this time put his shoulder into pushing the door open. Janice walked up to the porch of her new flip watching her husband banging his shoulder against the door. "It won't budge," he called back to her.

"Here, let me. Sometimes things just needed a little prodding," Janice nudged her husband out of the way and kicked in the door to the house while juggling a camera in one hand and a toolbox in the other.

"I loosened it for you," Carl chuckled, rubbing his shoulder and surveying the lock to see why it had been stuck. Pieces of the wooden doorjamb crumbled off in his hand. A huge piece dislodged, hitting the floor with a thud. "That needs to be fixed. Mark that as the number one thing to be fixed on your fix-it list."

"He's all mine, ladies," Janice mocked to the camera she held. She dropped the toolbox next to the door and panned around the room with the camera.

"Whew, what is that smell?" Carl covered his face with his hand as Janice moved around the room, oblivious to the stench.

"Shush, I'm filming." She swiped her free hand at him.

"But can't you smell that? Smells like death." He sniffed louder and made a gagging noise.

She stared hard at her husband from the other side of the room, willing him to quit nitpicking everything. He had been critical of this whole project and wasn't quiet about letting her know how he felt.

"Open a window. It's an old house and no one has lived here in a while." No, she wasn't going to let his shitty attitude get to her. She resumed filming while Carl half-heartedly attempted to open a window.

"It won't open," he whined to her. She turned off her camera, annoyed that she had to help him, but she kept her mouth shut. He had grudgingly agreed to come along on this project with her, miles away from his mistress, to work on their marriage. Their second chance. She reminded herself of that. Not many people get second chances.

"Back up, please."

"Sure." He moved to the side.

She unhinged the lock on the double-hung window. It slid open easily. Dust exploded in the air and Carl sneezed on her shoulder.

"There you go." She didn't want to fight. She was tired and wanted to get an empty house tour filmed in the natural light before it got dark.

"Do you have to film everything?" He asked rubbing his temples with his index fingers. His voice deepened and Janice knew he was losing patience with her.

"You know I do. I have to have B roll and my viewers love before and after videos." She sighed because she knew how much he hated having their entire life filmed. If he cared about a second chance, he wasn't showing it with all his whining and complaining.

"Yes, you're Ms. Fix-It." He air quoted "fix it." You can fix anything. Can't you, Janice? But you can't fix this marriage." That stung. Janice's eyes burned from the tears she was holding back. Don't let him see you cry, she repeated in her head over and over again. She wasn't an overly emotional person, but lately, she cried over the tiniest things. Maybe the therapist was right. The stress was getting to her.

"Are you finished?" She crossed her arms, shielding her chest. She needed to regain her composure before she lost it and became a blubbering baby.

Carl threw up his hands in surrender. "I'm trying here, Janice, I really am. I'm going to get more boxes." He headed back outside.

This second chance wasn't off to a good start. But they would have more time to talk and rekindle their relationship after they got situated in the house. Carl had to understand how she sacrificed everything on this flip—even their last dime. It was for them. For their future. But it would pay off once her Ms. Fix It channel got a contract with the producers of the House and Home network. Then they would be set.

Janice took a few deep breaths to get her head back in the game. Whew, maybe something had died in there. She looked around for the source of the smell. She would have to figure out how to mask that rotting odor if she couldn't find the dead animal. But she needed to get back to work for now. She turned the camera on herself. She was a natural, instantly transformed into Ms. Fix It, handywoman extraordinaire.

"C'mon into the dining room. I need to show ya'll this beautiful wainscotting on the walls."

Bang.

Janice stopped filming and cranked her ear toward the staircase, waiting for the sound again. "Carl?" No answer. She figured he had dropped a box. She knew she should have hired moving people. Carl was neither a handyman nor a mover. She got back to work.

Thud.

This time the noise was louder. "Carl, you okay? What are you doing?" She walked into the living room, calling upstairs.

"Can you give me a hand?" Janice jumped almost dropping her camera. Carl stood behind her cradling two lamps. "What's wrong?"

"I heard noises upstairs. It was nothing. Probably mice." She would need to get an exterminator out here if any critters were roaming around. They would need to be evicted before she could put the house on the market. She made a mental note to call an exterminator first thing in the morning. It would eat into the profit but she didn't want to take the chance of getting sued over an infestation.

"It's an old house. They make noises." Carl reminded her.

Find a happy place and go there, she repeated in her head. Her therapist suggested she do this whenever she wanted to go off on Carl.

"I'll go look." Janice climbed the ornately carved oak staircase. She turned around halfway up to pan the living room with her camera. The house had been remodeled several times with 70's paneling covering one of the walls in the living room, and wall to wall green shag carpet. Janice spied what looked like hardwood floors under a ripped-up corner of the carpet. This house would be her ticket to leveling up in her career, if she could get it rehabbed and on the market in 45 days. She would beat any other contenders for a show on the House and Home network. It was a tight schedule but she was up for the challenge, barring any catastrophe. Older homes always came with their own problems. But she felt this place had good bones.

Janice moved back onto the next step. Crack. Her foot broke through the rotted tread, splintering the wood. She caught herself before her entire foot went through the hole. "Shit."

"Hold on." Carl ran up the stairs, careful to walk lightly on each tread and holding onto the railing for extra support. He reached out to Janice, who grabbed his hand while cradling her camera in the crook of her elbow.

"Are you okay, babe?"

She looked up at him, surprised he had called her babe. He hadn't said anything sweet to her in a long time. Not since Allison, his mistress, came into their lives.

"I'm fine. Just scared me a little." She'd lied to him. It scared her a lot. She brushed his hand away and made her way to the top of the staircase, being extra careful on each step.

"Okay, then I'm going out to the truck to get some plywood to lay across the step temporarily." Janice watched her husband take initiative for once. Maybe he did still care about her and their marriage. It was a nice, comforting feeling.

Carl's phone buzzed and Janice looked down the stairs to see him run outside quickly before answering it. She walked over to the bank of windows overlooking the driveway where they had parked their trucks. She watched Carl waving his hand wildly. She had to shake the feeling that he was talking to *her*. He promised he would give the marriage 100% and never contact her again. The short-lived feeling of comfort dissolved into jealously and bitterness.

* * * *

Little Sally Ann, with her tattered dress and ratty hair, stood at the top of the stairs. She clutched her baby doll as she looked down at the man and woman who had invaded her home. The woman was walking around the room with something in her hand and the man was bringing in boxes. She wasn't sure if she liked these people yet. The last people were nice enough, until the mommy took a knife and stabbed the daddy in the chest. And before that, a mommy smothered the daddy with a pillow. They weren't good mommies at all.

Sally Ann swung her baby doll up in the air, and when it came down, it knocked over a lamp. She tried to pick it up but couldn't. She let it go and it crashed back to the ground. Sally Ann placed her hands over her ears to pretend to disappear so she wouldn't get scolded. She didn't want to get in trouble with the new woman. She might not want to be her new mommy if she did.

"Oh no, she's coming up here." Sally Ann ran to the corner of the room and crouched down behind some curtains.

The new mommy walked over to the windows and looked out. Sally Ann wanted to ask her new mommy what was wrong, but the woman hit the wall with her hand. Sally Ann tugged the curtains tightly around her.

The woman walked down the hall toward Sally Ann's bedroom. Sally Ann followed the woman, staying just far enough behind her so she wouldn't be discovered.

"She's going to my room."

The woman tugged at the doorknob to Sally Ann's room at the end of the hall. It wouldn't open. Sally Ann didn't like anyone going into her room. The woman gave up and walked into the bathroom. What was she doing in there? The woman started singing a song. Sally Ann liked listening to the woman. She sounded like an angel. Sally Ann had found her new mommy.

* * * *

"Oh God, no!" Janice cried, sitting on the toilet with her elbows on her knees and her face in the palms of her hands. "I can't believe this. Why did I let this happen?"

She stood up from the toilet and pulled her underwear and pajamas over her hips. Sure, she had gained some extra pounds and even craved some strange foods, but pregnancy was the furthest thing from her mind. Janice splashed some cold water on her face. She counted back to her last period. She couldn't remember. Was it two or three months ago? She was so preoccupied with competing for a contract for her own show and keeping her marriage together, that she had forgotten when her last period had been.

She grabbed the four pregnancy tests off the counter and wrapped them in toilet paper, pushing them deep into the trash can. She wasn't ready to tell Carl she was pregnant. Their marriage was in shambles and she wasn't the kind of woman to trap a man by getting pregnant.

They had talked about having kids years ago but since she had trouble conceiving, she figured she couldn't get pregnant.

She had to keep it together until she put the house on the market. She could hide it until then.

She dried her face and walked out of the bathroom. She caught a glimpse of herself in the bank of windows in the sitting area. She turned to the side to see her profile. How long before she started to show? And how long before a viewer noticed? She pushed out her stomach to see what she would look like. She wasn't sure how she felt about it. A baby. Her baby. Their baby.

She didn't want to think about it at the moment. She was exhausted. She ran down the hall to her bedroom and climbed into bed next to Carl, who was snoring softly. Thank goodness he was asleep because she didn't think she could face him at the moment. A baby. Their baby. She didn't want him to stay in the marriage out of obligation to her.

She looked down at her feet, her ankles swollen. She opened her phone and looked up pregnancy symptoms. Carl's phone buzzed next to her. It was 2:00 a.m. Who would be texting this late? Allison, his mistress. She rubbed her belly. A baby. A baby? Her baby. Yes, her baby. Carl was too busy playing house with his mistress. She put on her headphones and listened to House and Home's latest episode to help her fall asleep.

A crash down the hall woke her up. She took off her headphones to listen for the noise. Carl was still sound asleep next to her. She was dreaming. All homes make settling noises, she reminded herself. Janice turned over away from Carl and fell back to sleep.

* * * *

Little Sally Ann pulled out the toilet paper from the trash can. She wondered what it was that made her mommy cry. She flung the toilet paper holding the pregnancy tests in the air and they landed in the sink, unraveling from their toilet paper cocoons. She giggled. Just paper. Little Sally Ann kicked over the trashcan. It made a rattling sound. She covered her ears. She didn't want to wake up her mommy.

* * * *

Carl rubbed his eyes. He couldn't believe what he saw in the bathroom sink. Pregnancy tests. And they were all positive. He sat on the toilet and put his face in his hands.

"No, no, no." he gritted his teeth. "This can't be happening."

He could count on one hand how many times they had sex in the past few months. Two or three times, he surmised. She was never in the mood anyway. Always so busy with her career. Her life. Rejection was always the end result.

He had loved her once, but he wasn't sure he did anymore. He also wasn't sure he wanted to work on the marriage. Their second chance, as she called it. The only reason he even agreed to come along was that Allison had gone back to her husband. So dejected from another rejection, he decided to stick it out with Janice—until she decided to move them across the country for this career opportunity.

Janice always put work first. And appearances. And she always worked around guys. Who's to say she wasn't having an affair too? Nah, she wasn't big on sex. She wanted to be the one with the balls in the relationship.

So, the baby could be his. Probably was his. Damn, it was his. How was he going to get out of this marriage now that there was a baby? Coming to this house to revive his marriage wasn't the answer. He didn't want to be there as much as the house didn't want him to be there.

He rubbed the bridge of his nose. The rotting stench was giving him a headache. He had to find out where it was coming from. It was getting worse.

The doorbell chime knocked him back into reality. It was probably another delivery from the lumberyard. In less than 24 hours, the house had boxes of cabinets in every corner, electrical conduit lining the perimeter of every room, and plumbing fixtures sitting in the dining room. Soon Janice would have enough materials to build a new house. So why was she bothering to rehab this one? How much was this costing them?

The doorbell rang again, its chime reverberating until he knocked on the long metal tubes hanging on the wall with his fist. Just another thing that needs fixing.

"I'm coming," he yelled, running down the stairs and hopping over the plywood tread he'd fixed the night before.

"I hope so," a woman belted from the other side of the door.

"Oh, shit." Carl's heart dropped into his stomach. It was Allison. What was she doing here? For a split second, he debated if he should open the door. But his curiosity got the better of him and he opened it to find her standing there with a bottle of champagne in one hand, and a piece of paper in the other. She opened her coat to reveal she had nothing on underneath. Oh, shit, this was going to be harder than he thought.

"What are you doing here?"

"Aren't you going to invite me in? I'm a little cold." He avoided looking down at her body but she moved up closer and his eyes dropped down to her breasts and her erect nipples. He backed away so he could concentrate on something else and bumped into the newel post of the staircase.

"Allison, no, you have to leave. Janice will be back any minute. She just went out to get some more materials."

"I don't want to hear about her. I'm here because I want you back. Look," she shoved the paper in his face. The words Clerk of the Court were stamped in bold letters on the paper. "I've filed for divorce. Now we can be together." She snuggled up next to him, planting a kiss on his neck.

"Not now, Allison." He tried pushing the woman away from him. As much as he wanted her, he had to get her out of the house before Janice returned. Allison was persistent kissing his neck again. He inhaled her perfume. It intoxicated him. A few seconds later, she was on her knees unzipping his pants and pulling his erect cock in her mouth. He wanted to push her away but it had been a while since anyone had touched him like that. Carl let out a moan and Allison bobbed her head up and down faster.

A truck door slammed outside bringing Carl out of his trance.

"You've got to go." He pulled Allison off him. He shuffled her toward the kitchen and to the back door before Janice walked in on them.

"I'm not leaving without you." Allison stopped dead in her tracks at the back door and wouldn't budge. She pouted her lips and folded her arms across her chest like a child.

Carl had to think fast. "I'll meet you at Sully's down the street in a half-hour."

"You promise?" She batted her eyes at him.

"I promise." He would have agreed to anything just to get her out of the house.

Allison puckered up for a kiss and Carl pecked her lips but she pulled him closer. He couldn't resist tasting her.

* * * *

Sally Ann crouched behind the sofa and listened to her daddy and the stranger talking. She didn't like the woman trying to hug and kiss daddy. Her mommy wouldn't like that.

Sally Ann spied the woman's purse on the sofa and grabbed it. She opened it up. She liked to play dress up and this woman had plenty of makeup and perfume in her purse. Sally Ann pulled out a small glass bottle of perfume. She sprayed it on her dress. "Pee-ew," she grimaced. She threw the bottle on the sofa.

That woman needs to leave my daddy alone she thought. Sally Ann wanted to make the woman stop. But daddy wouldn't push her away. She couldn't watch anymore. She didn't understand why daddy kept kissing her. She had tried to kiss her doll once and all she got was a mouthful of dirt and hair.

* * * *

The door swung open and Janice stood there, carrying a box of nails. "Here, let me get that for you." Carl took the box from Janice and laid it on the floor.

"Thanks." He was being extra nice. She hoped it was because he really was trying to work on their marriage and not because he was hiding something like before. Janice sat down on the couch. She sniffed the air. "Do you smell that?"

"The only thing I can smell in this house is that stench. Did you remember to call the exterminator this morning?"

Janice sniffed the air again. No, it wasn't that smell. She remembered that perfume smell from the nights Carl would come home late and shove his clothes into the washer. Or he would come to bed after showering some night, still reeking of her. Her long-lasting scent permeated her bedroom and was now in her living room. It made her want to vomit. Hormones. It had to be her hormones acting up, because he'd promised he wouldn't contact her ever again. She watched Carl wipe the sweat off his forehead and fidget with his collar.

"Do you want anything to eat or drink?" He asked, passing by her to get to his jacket near the front door.

She wanted to scream at him. Call him a bastard for lying to her. He never wanted a second chance.

Instead, she asked, "who texted you at 2:00 in the morning?" He couldn't get out of answering that.

That familiar deer in the headlights look, just like when she had discovered a pair of size 5 panties under their bed and had thrown them at him. She had screamed that she wore a size 7. His face was frozen in shock.

He stuttered. He always stuttered when he was lying. "I, I, it was Andy from work. He wanted to let me know he was in the emergency room last night and wouldn't be available for our Zoom meeting today."

"Really? What happened?" Janice played along. "Are you sure you're not hiding something?"

Carl twisted his jacket in his hand as Janice stood combatively in front of him. She wanted the truth, and she wanted it now.

Like a cornered bear, Carl roared, "I should ask you that, Janice. Are you hiding anything from me?"

Caught off guard, Janice took a step back and sat on the couch. How did he find out?

"I know you're pregnant. So, who's keeping secrets?" Carl turned away before Janice could answer and slammed the front door behind him.

* * * *

Sally Ann stood at the top of the stairs listening to Carl and Janice fighting downstairs. Her lower lip quivered and tears fell from her eyes. "Mommy is going to have a baby? No, she can't. She has me." Sally Ann threw her baby down on the ground. She couldn't let this happen. She sat down on the top step and looked through the spindles watching Janice cry. "It's okay, Mommy. I'll take care of you. I'll take care of everything."

* * * *

Janice cried into a pillow. Nothing was going the way she'd planned. *He'll be back,* she reassured herself. *He wouldn't leave us.* She shifted her weight from side to side. She was sitting on something. She pulled it out from underneath her. A perfume bottle.

It's her's. She knew she wasn't going crazy—she *had* smelled Allison's perfume. Carl lied to her. She held the bottle up to her nose and gagged. The smell made her want to vomit.

"I see you found my perfume. The one Carl bought me." Janice dropped the bottle and looked up to see Allison standing in her living room, her coat slightly opened to reveal she wasn't wearing any clothing. Allison bent over to pick up the bottle and spritzed herself with the perfume. "Carl likes this on me."

"What are you doing in my house? Get out before I call the police," Janice screamed at the woman who didn't move from her spot. She hated this woman for coming back into their lives. Maybe she never left.

"I'm here to see Carl."

"My husband, you mean." Janice corrected her.

"For now."

"Then I'm sure he told you, we're pregnant." Allison sided eyed Janice as if she didn't believe her but instinctively looked down at her belly. Janice pulled her shirt taut against her body to show the tiny bulge of her stomach. With her other hand, she rubbed her belly.

"He told me that you had one too many abortions while in college so he didn't think you'd ever be able to carry a child full-term."

Janice smacked Allison hard across the face. She wondered what else her husband had divulged to his mistress. "Get out of my house!"

Allison rubbed her cheek. She smiled at Janice and walked to the back door.

* * *

Sally Ann stood in front of the back door, blocking Allison from leaving. She didn't like this woman.

"Who or what are you?" Allison's eyes widened in horror as the skin on Sally Ann's face melted off like candle wax, puddling on the floor in front of her. Allison stepped over it to get to the door but the puddle followed her. The basement door flew open and Allison sidestepped the puddle. She stepped on the landing leading to the basement. Little Sally Ann yanked out a handful of her hair and threw it at Allison, causing her to tumble down the stairs. She landed on several other bodies splayed out in all directions on the basement floor.

"Now, stay down there with the other bad mommies." Sally Ann giggled.

* * * *

Janice couldn't believe that woman had the nerve to come into her house. She wrung out the washcloth and placed it on the back of her neck. She was getting a migraine. She had never had a migraine before but she blamed it on her hormones. And Allison's perfume. And that smell. That rotting stench Carl had been complaining about was starting to get to her, too.

Janice walked out of the upstairs bathroom heading for the staircase. She wanted to lay down on the couch and wait for Carl to come back. *If he came back*. They needed to talk.

Janice looked up to see a child near the staircase. She blinked to make sure she was really seeing her. A little girl with black curly hair smiling at her. How did a child get in the house? She called to her, "Honey, who are you? Is your mommy with you?"

Sally Ann reached out to Janice, "You're my mommy."

"No, honey, I'm not. We need to find your mommy." She took Sally Ann's hand and led her to the staircase. She wondered if she was a neighborhood child who had wandered off. Someone had to be looking for her.

Sally Ann pulled Janice back toward her room at the end of the hall. "My room."

"Oh, sweetie, no. This isn't your house. Let's go find your mommy." Janice led her back to the staircase, but Sally Ann wouldn't go.

Sally Ann's lower lip trembled and tears streamed down her face. Janice tried to hug her but Sally Ann pulled away. Janice wondered if she would have the patience to deal with her own child, since she was having trouble wrangling this one to do what she wanted. She needed to let the child know she was the boss. She leaned over to pick the girl up but Sally Ann wiggled free.

"No." Sally Ann turned her back on Janice.

"Honey, we need to find your mommy."

"No, no, no, no." Sally Ann stomped toward her room at the end of the hall and picked up her doll. She turned back to Janice and flung her doll at her, hitting her in the head. Janice lost her footing and fell backward.

* * * *

Janice lay at the bottom of the stairs, not sure what had happened. Her whole body ached. She called for Carl but then remembered he'd left the house. Probably going to meet up with his whore. But she didn't have time to think about him. She needed to save her baby.

Her lower back throbbed and pains were coming in waves in her belly. "Hold on, little one. Please be all right. Please be okay," she repeated over and over. She could see her phone on the couch. If she could get to it and call 911, everything would be okay. Janice dragged herself up onto her side resting on her elbow for a moment. She took a deep breath and scooted herself over to the couch. She felt a gush come out of her and reached down her pants fearing what she already knew. She pulled her hand up out of her pants. Blood smeared on her fingers. Janice wailed.

* * * *

Carl helped Janice to the couch. She had lost so much blood that she was dizzy and light-headed. He put her hospital bag next to her on the floor. "Can I get you anything?" He asked propping the pillows behind her and tucking the blanket around her. He must feel guilty about lying about his mistress. Their second chance was over. And there would be no third one.

"Just some water, please." She rubbed her belly. She had lost the baby and now she was losing her husband.

Carl covered his nose. "We're not staying here. We'll go to a hotel for a few days and you can rest. Isn't the exterminator coming tomorrow? Maybe he can find out where that smell is coming from."

Janice laid back on the pillow. She wanted to forget the last 48 hours.

Carl called out from the kitchen, "Maybe you should call Dr. Thornton. Talking to your therapist might make you feel better."

"I saw a little girl, Carl. I'm sure of it." She knew she sounded crazy. Maybe it was her hormones, the stress of the filming schedule, and Allison's appearance, but she was sure she saw a child on the landing upstairs. And the little girl threw her doll at her, causing her to fall down the stairs. She knew she hadn't tripped.

* * *

Carl sniffed the air. He couldn't believe that the rancid stench was getting worse. Warm bile rose from his stomach and he leaned over to vomit in the sink. He turned on the faucet and cupped some water to rinse out his mouth. He wanted to get away from this house and his marriage and even Allison. Everything was a disaster. He turned the water off and dried his face with a towel. A child's giggle came from behind the basement door. He put the towel down and walked over to it. Locked. He knew he had heard a child's laughter from the other side. Maybe the smell and the house were getting to him.

He had walked back to the sink to get Janice a glass of water when he heard a child's laughter again. No, he wasn't going to let this house get to him, too. He took a crowbar out of one of Janice's toolboxes on the floor next to the cabinets. He was going to open that door and prove to himself that there wasn't anyone down there.

As he got closer to the basement door, it swung open. The stench rushed to him. Bile raised up from his stomach again. He swallowed hard to force it back down. He had found the source of the smell, something down in the basement. Carl squinted, making out a silhouette of a small child with her back to him at the bottom of the stairs.

"Who are you? What are you doing in my house?" His fingers fumbled to find the light switch. Maybe a neighborhood child had gotten into the house. He switched on the light.

A little girl was standing on top of Allison's body, which lay at the bottom of the stairs.

"Allison," Carl called out to her, but she didn't answer back. Something was moving on Allison's body. Maybe she was still alive. He went down the first step to get a better look. He gasped at the sight of maggots feeding on a huge wound in Allison's side. Several other decaying bodies lay next to Allison. He felt that familiar burn of bile rising from his stomach. The child turned to face Carl and opened her mouth, vomiting maggots toward him. He put his hands up to shield his face. "Oh, my God!" Carl screamed. "Oh, my God, oh, my God."

He ran up the step and back into the kitchen slamming the door behind him. He screamed for Janice.

"What's wrong?" Janice sat up on the couch.

"I saw her! I saw a little girl in our basement. I mean, I think it was a girl." Carl ran his fingers through his hair, pacing back and forth in front of Janice. "We have to call 911. We need to get out of here. I saw bodies down there."

"Bodies? What are you talking about?" Janice tugged at her husband's pant leg to get him to sit down next to her but he broke free. "I thought you said you saw the little girl I saw upstairs."

"I did in the basement. But," he hesitated not able to spit out the next words easily, "she was a corpse, decaying, standing on top of Allison's body. Janice, baby, we need to get out of here now."

Carl pulled Janice off the couch and helped her to the door.

"Allison?" She'd seen her walk to the back door. What was she doing in the basement?

"Not now, Janice. We have to leave." He opened the door and helped his wife out slamming the door behind them. Leaving the house, Sally Ann, and death behind.

* * * *

With snot bubbling out of her nose, Sally Ann stood at the front door holding her one-eyed, crusty-haired doll at her side. Tears streamed down her face.

"Where are you going, Mommy? I was good this time. Please don't leave me here alone."

Sally Ann knelt at the door crying, "I'll just sit here by the door and wait for you." She rocked her doll back and forth. "Mommy, come back. Don't leave me, Mommy."

Sally Ann looked her doll in the face and said, "she was the one who got away."

SHAWNNA DERESCH has been crafting scary stories since she could first talk. Her love of horror began when she was a child watching horror movies with her father and now as an adult is obsessed with anything horror-related. She's a lover of paranormal investigations and loves checking out cemeteries and old buildings.

She travels extensively and splits her time between the Chicagoland area and anywhere down south where the temps don't go below 80 degrees. She lives with her three children, two black rescue cats, and one blue-eyed puppy in a condo near the beach of a big city.

She is a member of the Horror Writers Association (HWA) and is the Chairperson of the Chicago Chapter of the Horror Writers Association. You can find her on Twitter: @shawnnaderesch or on the HWA Chicago Chapter on Twitter: @ChicagoHWA

BRAMBLEWOOD
Meg Hafdahl

~~~

I know what you're going to say. And you're right. It was a mistake to leave in a scarlet hot rage, digging the crescents of my nails into the tender flesh of my neck. It was all I could do to walk in those regrettable cork wedges, out the front door of Rowdy's, pinching myself because if I pinched him, well, I might not stop.

I know you'd tell me not to let a man talk to me the way Rowdy does. That's what I'd tell a woman if she was in the same position. He's not worth it, I'd say. He'll never grow up. He'll call you names till the end of time.

I know.

It was a mistake to pass his shitty Dodge pickup and kick the tire. I stubbed my big toe and cracked my teal polish.

And I know the biggest mistake of all was hooking out my thumb at the end of Rowdy's gravel drive.

But tears, sour and stinging my bottom lip, clouded both my sight and my judgment. Music, the godawful retro-punk Rowdy grooved his skinny hips to, thumped behind me. A loud reminder of Rowdy's insistence on disobeying the world. His mom had warned me. And Sylvia, my best friend, had too.

The Ramones vibrated up through my sandals like he'd set his stereo to some sort of earthquake setting.

Summer, cloying and sticky, deepened my frown.

Rowdy's neighbor appeared in the darkened section between their houses. He pressed his thick legs into the scraggly bushes. "Hey! Tell that boy of yours to turn it down or I'm going to knock his head off that scrawny neck!" The man spoke with a thick Okie accent. I'd noticed that drawl before, when he yelled at Rowdy over the dead cranberry bushes nearly every night over the music or trash or for screaming. At me.

"He's not my boy anymore." I held out my arm as straight as could be, making certain my thumb was visible under the sagging streetlamp. "Call the cops." This possibility made me grin. I sucked the last few tears up my nose.

The neighbor was always dressed in a pair of muddy shitkickers. This night was no exception. I watched as he swayed from side to side on the untied boots, thinking about my suggestion with a surprising amount of consideration.

"Yeah, and what'll that solve?" He finally asked.

I shrugged.

The man gestured toward me with his right hand. I caught a glimpse of a highboy in his grip. "You shouldn't hitchhike. It's dangerous."

When he said it, I felt the rise of my anger again. It scorched my skin and made the cuts on my neck as fierce as a grease burn. "Well, I don't have my phone." I lied.

"I'd drive ya but…"

"You're three sheets."

A gurgling sound started in the man's throat. It was a laugh, I realized. A wet and drunken laugh.

"To the wind, my dear! Three sheets to the wind! You call 'em when you see 'em, dontchya?"

I gave another shrug, turning my attention to County Road 92, where Rowdy had lived his whole miserable life.

Someone had to be coming. The light from their headlights would illuminate my slightly crooked thumb and I wouldn't have to talk to the neighbor man.

He hiccuped. "This road gets damn quiet at night. I mean if it weren't for your shithead boyfriend."

"I said he's not my boyfriend anymore." That was a lie, too, I think. Even then, I knew I'd be back.

Rowdy's music shook the ratty window screens of his house.

I looked back at the man in the bushes, wishing he would go away and leave me to my dark and lonely road. At least Rowdy, drunk and pissy, wasn't running out after me. That would be more than I could take.

The neighbor man didn't seem to notice that a sharp bristle had scratched his hairy thigh. Blood traversed his rough skin, winding around a varicose vein before disappearing into the open cavern of his left shitkicker.

I wanted to pinch the vulnerable skin of my neck again, to forget.

Suddenly, the sound of a motor moving west cut through the music. I actually felt the heat of my anger mellow. With a deep inhale I stuck my thumb out as obviously as I could, balancing on one sandal as I leaned forward.

The white sedan, a Toyota, rolled to a stop at the edge of Rowdy's drive. Unless it was Ted Bundy himself, grinning while he sported a fake cast, I was jumping in.

He drove a VW bug, Darcy. A yellow bug.

"And he's dead," I muttered to myself while lowering my arm. It had already begun to ache from the hitchhiking effort.

The driver's window buzzed down. A woman, not Ted Bundy, stuck out her pale elbow first. Next came her moon face, nearly a perfect circle. It was framed by slick, shoulder-length hair that glistened a little too heartily under the streetlamp.

"Don't you have Lyft? Uber?" She wrinkled her pug nose at me. I guessed she was knocking on forty.

"Nah." I moved closer, away from Rowdy, away from the man in the bushes.

"Pointless anyways." The woman gave a high-pitched titter. It reminded me of the squeak, Bucky, my mom's Chihuahua, makes when he wants a slice of bologna.

"The Uber drivers in this town are all meth heads," she continued, eyeing Rowdy's neighbor. "Foster? That you?"

"Evening, Pamela." When he spoke her name it made me all the more eager to get in her car. She was from the neighborhood. She probably even knew Rowdy and what a royal piece of shit he was. I got close enough to touch the hood of her white car. It was oddly clean for a rural Texas vehicle. New, I realized, new and untainted by the desert soil.

"Getting in?" The woman leaned back, setting both hands on the steering wheel.

I nodded, not daring to take a look over my shoulder at my life. The sound of Rowdy's music trickled away as I hopped into the passenger seat. When the woman hit her window button, the synthetic beat was mercifully killed for good.

The new car smell made me happy for a beat. And then my nose was filled with strong, floral perfume. It came out of every crease of Pamela. When she shifted in her seat I could nearly see a plume of it escape the folds of her polka dot blouse.

"Here." She pulled a Kleenex from a little package in the console and dropped it on my denim skirt. "If it's a man you've been crying over, just tell me it's not that old pervert, Foster."

Unaware of the makeup disaster on my face, I swiped at my cheeks with the tissue. "Gross, no!" I looked down at the mix of tears and smeared mascara.

The woman let out a relieved sigh. She put the car in drive, heading toward town. "I'm Pam."

"Darcy." Not sure what to do with the soggy Kleenex, I stuffed it into my purse. "Thank you for picking me up, Pam."

"No problem." Her honey-colored hair looked hard, like she'd dipped it in shellac. I had the strangest urge to reach out and touch it. "I assume you're heading into town? Where do you live?"

Her question was like a blinding wallop to my gut. Until twenty minutes ago I lived with Rowdy Thau, master at pretending to be a decent boyfriend. I had been so desperate to get away, I hadn't remembered there was nowhere to go.

Instinctively, I brought my sharp nails up to my neck and pinched the skin just below my right ear.

"You shouldn't do that."

I pulled my hand back like an embarrassed child.

"Hurting yourself won't help anything. It only makes you feel worse about... everything. Trust me."

Pam spoke with tenderness. I wondered how someone like her, in a brand new car and wearing a blouse with no wrinkles, could know anything about something so shameful.

She directed her eyes back on the dark road. "Where are you heading, then?"

"Uh... well..." There was no way I was going to my mom's. Her knowing smirk, that subtle raise of her top lip at my misery, would wring me dry. My friend Sylvia was more than busy. She had a newborn in the ICU in El Paso, premature, which left my brother. And there was no chance he was home on a Friday night. He'd be at that dive bar, the one with no name where Rowdy brought me when he was feeling rich.

"No place to go?"

I thought about sitting outside my brother's, texting him all night until I fell asleep on his filthy stoop. "Well, I guess-"

"You can stay with me tonight." She glanced over, offering a toothy smile. "We have a guest bedroom."

"Oh no, that's really nice of you, ma'am. Real nice, but I don't think I should."

"Call me Pam, please. And why not?" She clicked on the radio. It was set to Radio Disney, but she quickly turned the dial to WFXD, our local top forty channel. "You can stay just for the night. So you can sort out your problems. A good night's sleep will put everything in perspective."

I noticed a bag of Goldfish crackers in the console, next to a small, sparkly headband. "You have kids, I don't want to bother them."

"Heavens no! If they're still awake by the time we get back, they'll be pleased as punch to have a visitor! My youngest, Dottie, loves to give tours of our house!"

My stomach settled at the thought of smiling, happy Dottie in her sparkly headband. "Okay, I guess. If you really don't mind."

"Oh! Not at all!" She squealed, and again I thought of Bucky the Chihuahua.

"Thank you, really, I... I just can't look at Rowdy's face right now."

"Rowdy!" Pam tightened her manicured nails around the wheel. "You're the poor soul dating Rowdy Thau? No wonder you're crying!"

I tried a little light-hearted laugh. "It all makes sense now, I'm sure."

"Yes! Back, oh ten years ago, I was his Sunday school teacher, Avalon Lutheran," Pam shifted in the seat, stirring up another cloud of stringent perfume. "He was Ryan, not 'Rowdy' then of course, though he got up to spitfire even at that age. I just about quit after he clogged the toilet with crayons."

"I haven't heard that one."

"Pastor... oh who was it then? Pastor Hyman! Oh, he made Rowdy sorry!" Pam laughed. "Made him take over for the janitor the rest of the summer, I bet he can scrub a mean toilet, now, hmm?"

"Not that I know of." A flare of anger ignited tightness in my ribcage. I'm not sure if I was mad at Rowdy, or at Pam for making me think of him as a mischievous ten-year-old prankster. I turned from Pam, taking in a pleasant suburban development lit artfully against the night sky. Bramblewood. A series of taupe and salmon two-stories with well-trimmed cacti, was the place my mom promised we would live just as soon as she got a promotion at Denny's. Spoiler alert: it's been twelve years and she hasn't made manager, yet. Oh, and she spends all her money on Miller Lite and flowy scarves.

There was never any hope of Bramblewood.

"I'll stop talking about Rowdy." Pam thumbed her turn signal. Its rhythmic click told me I was finally going to enter the development. "I'm guessing you'd like to pretend he doesn't exist."

The Toyota turned.

"Sounds good to me." I studied the dramatic rock garden flanking both sides of Bramble Drive. The boulders and raw granite stones were surrounded by solar lights. Through the painted iron gates, always open as far as I knew, we took a slight curve, passing the first gorgeous home. There was a pool party in the back, BBQ smoking.

"Pretty neighborhood." I felt I had to say something. But, truly, I was starting to wonder if she brought me there so I could marvel at a life I never had and would never get.

"We've lived here, oh," she waved her arm, producing another cloud of her potent perfume, "only two years this May. We're considered newbies. I used to be out on Willow, you know? Right behind the Piggly Wiggly."

It was her attempt to remind me that we weren't so different.

"Oh yeah. I know where you mean." I guess that made me more comfortable, knowing she'd spent time staring at the butt end of the Piggly Wiggly, that she hadn't just sprung up from the soil beneath Bramblewood like it seemed all the others had. The women with slick nails and gold, real gold, bracelets that jangled on their impossibly thin wrists.

"Just down here." Pam turned left, down a shallow cul-de-sac. Her house was at the crux of the pavement circle, a traditional beauty with a covered porch and glimmering driveway lights. Three bulbous cacti filled in the space beneath that mailbox post.

"I chose this one because it looks like some sitcom house, doesn't it? The establishing shot before the jokes start." She snorted, hitting the garage door opener with the back of her hand. "That's what I said, but my husband, Gary, he cares about the boring stuff, property taxes, and energy-efficient windows. This house passed his tests, thank the Lord."

We drove into the pristine garage. Shelves lined the far wall, filled with tidy Rubbermaids.

If Rowdy was there he would wonder what was inside them. His mind would be filling with all sorts of ideas.

She kept talking as I followed out of the car and through the door into the house. Something about her realtor and Gary, but I wasn't listening. I was pretending that her house was mine and that it was normal as day for me to take my sandals off at the threshold while I felt a cooling burst of air conditioning through the strands of my sweaty hair.

"...and Gary told her, you better throw in the hot tub. After all those headaches, we want them to leave it! And sure enough, they did!"

At the end of the narrow mudroom was a squeaky clean kitchen that, indeed, looked like the set of a 90's sitcom. I shit you not, there was even a plate of homemade cookies on the granite center island.

As we entered, it became clear that Pam's scent emanated from her home. The counters were peppered with bowls of potpourri, and a caramel latte candle had been left burning on the glass surface of the spotless stove.

"Thank you." That was all I could think to say.

"Oh, honey, don't think twice. I know what it's like to break it off with a boy and have nowhere to go. I kissed a lot of frogs before Gary."

I tried to imagine her behind the Piggly Wiggly, her hair less groomed, smelling like cigarettes, kissing on some loser.

I couldn't do it.

Pam opened a cupboard above the stove and took down a cow-speckled kettle. The spout had been fashioned into a pink snout with a painted bell. "Tea ought to do the trick. Soothes the soul." She filled the kettle with water.

"Got anything stronger?"

She swung her head around, her hair staying in place. "That's not funny."

There was something in her eyes, a purple flash that reminded me of Rowdy when he's drunk or pissy.

"Sorry, yeah, lame joke."

Pam turned her back to me, setting the kettle on the stove. "I suspect you're under twenty-one, Darcy."

An unexpected warmth flushed my raw neck. I felt oddly cared for.

I took a seat at the island, luxuriating in the air conditioning. Pam set an empty mug in front of me, white with black, fancy flowers. "Have a cookie."

The digital clock on the microwave read 9:41.

"It's quiet." I carefully picked up a cookie, afraid to drop a crumb on her polished counter.

"The kids are asleep. They have school. Gary, too, he's so good at giving them their baths and tucking them in. Especially since he has to get up awful early to work at St. Mary's. I'm lucky he's such a hands-on dad."

"Oh, is he a doctor there?" I took a small bite. It was delicious, of course.

"Uh-huh. Trauma surgeon. The best in Texas if you ask pretty much anyone! How about you Darcy? Where do you work?"

I swallowed. "Cinema Six." That made me remember Rowdy was the only one who gave me rides to work. He had been good for something, I guess. "I pop the popcorn and mop up the spilled Coke." How was I going to get there, now? Worry threatened to prickle my improving mood.

"Gary and I go there for date night on Saturdays. I bet we've seen you."

"Probably." I hadn't recalled ever seeing her before. I felt like I'd remember that hard, immovable hair. And her scent, sweet yet bitter at the finish.

Once the cow kettle squealed, Pam placed a green tea bag in my mug and poured in the hot water. She kept on talking about Gary and Dottie and their son, Andrew. I sipped and nodded, marveling at the serene beauty of the kitchen. I hated myself for being such a cliché.

"You look tired." Pam covered the cookies with saran wrap. "Let's go to bed."

"Thank you," I said again, nearly crying. The thought of being in a bed alone, without Rowdy's foul Cheeto breath made me weak with gratitude. I followed her through a formal living room, past a sunken den full of Barbie dolls and Tonka trucks. Even the toys were spotless and displayed in even rows as though they were planted props and not children's playthings.

Pam noticed my interest.

"We keep things tidy here." She stopped with me in the shadow of the den. "I grew up in an unkempt home." I knew from the soft way that she patted me on the shoulder, that Pam knew I had grown up that way, too. Not because she had ever known me, but because there are people who live in Bramblewood, and others. People like me.

Up the carpeted steps, into the darkened upstairs hall, Pam stretched her arms and gave a deep and trembling yawn. "Oh, my! What a night. Sleep in as late as you want."

"Thank you." It was my new mantra.

"The bathroom's there. Towels under the sink." She pointed to a slightly open door with a twinkling night light escaping through the crack. "And here you are." She crossed in front of me, peppering me with more of her treacly scent, and then opened the silver knob of a bedroom. I peered into the darkness, not surprised to smell more potpourri.

"Goodnight, Darcy."

"Goodnight." I felt for the switch on the wall as she left me. I clicked it on as I closed the door, revealing a room for a teenage girl. There was a white desk in the far corner with Nancy Drew hardcovers piled on top. A cozy chair on the opposite wall held a fluffy stuffed cat and a bright pink afghan. A poster of a leaping black stallion had been framed and hung above the bed, which was drowning in throw pillows. Like the kitchen, it felt like the set of a television show. I had the strangest belief that the drawers of the painted dresser would be empty, or perhaps stuffed with cardboard.

I shivered, promising myself I wouldn't peek.

Had Pam mentioned an older daughter? I sat on the end of the lavender duvet, wondering what it would be like to grow up in such a tidy house. Ceramic horse figurines stared blankly at me from the bedside table. One wore an unnerving human grin.

Through the wall at the head of the bed, I heard the low hum of voices. Pam must be warning Gary that there was a nineteen-year-old trailer harpy mussing up their beloved daughter's sheets. Hopefully, he wasn't the type of man who would tip-toe down the hall and check up on me. See if I really was a harpy after all.

I lay back onto the heap of pillows, wondering how I got myself into such a peculiar position.

Rowdy would laugh.

Another thought occurred to me. It was an unwelcome sort of idea that rolled in my head like a loose marble.

Why would Pam be driving around on the outskirts of town? On a Friday night? There was nothing back there but Rowdy and more of those "meth heads" she spoke of. Her car was so nice and new. So clean on those back roads.

Scratch scratch scratch

I sat up, holding my breath.

Scratch scratch scratch scratch

The horse figure on the table kept grinning, not owning up to any mischief.

Tap, Tap, TAP!

It was behind me, through the wooden headboard, coming from what I assumed was the master bedroom. I flipped over on my knees, pushing a few pillows out of my way to listen.

Scratch tap scratch tap scratch.

I pressed my hand against the cold wall, alarmed by the purposeful and measured communication. Images of fanged and menacing horror movie creatures came and went, leaving behind the heavy truth.

My fingers curled into a fist. I gave one solid knock above the headboard.

TAP!

It was little Dottie, I told myself. Or silly Andrew, nine years old, Pam had said, and looking to play.

Yet, the saliva in my throat had thickened making it harder to swallow. And both my hands instinctively found the tender skin of my neck. I pinched on both sides, struggling to understand the fear.

The room, which had felt spacious, now squeezed at my sides. I was hot and anxious and I tingled all over. Questions and worries poised on the corner of my consciousness, whipping me into a froth. I kicked the remaining pillows off the bed and sprung up, uncertain what to do with all my strange, vibrating energy. My bare feet were vulnerable in the thick carpet. I felt every fiber. A voice within me urged that I stay quiet, if not calm.

Something was off.

Scratch Scratch Scratch

I pushed my thumbnail deep into the flesh at my jaw, concentrating on the glorious burn rather than the whir in my brain.

My free hand reached for the doorknob, and that was when I knew I would rather be on my brother's stoop, my mom's trailer, or God, even back at Rowdy's, than this pungent museum to suburbia.

I snuck out into the dark hall. The pain in my neck made it easier for me to breathe. Illuminated by the bathroom's night light, the door next to my room nearly called to me. When I think about it now, questioning why I ever opened it, I have to consider what my mom says about me is true. That's why I fell in with Rowdy in the first place. I like to disobey the world. That's what I say about him, but I guess I have to accept it about myself, too.

So, just like when I stuck my thumb out to hitchhike, I stuck my hand out and I opened that door.

Fragrance, the most stifling yet, burned my nostrils. I buried my nose in my elbow, braving a look-see. It was the master bedroom, decorated with fresh flowers in glass vases and mounds of potpourri. The bed was a four-post monstrosity beneath a lit chandelier. To my right was another closed door, a light coming from underneath. I could hear water running and Pam humming some Disney-esque ditty.

I bent in a bit further, keeping my feet in the hall.

A lump shifted beneath the pastel yellow comforter.

"Gary?" I whispered.

There was a hitching, snotty moan.

"Gary, hey, you okay? Were you tapping on the wall?"

I held onto the doorframe, freeing my nose in order to keep my balance. In the interminable silence, I heard Pam start up an electric toothbrush.

"Help…" it was an inhuman croak. "Help me please."

Fear bled into disbelief. If Gary the orthopedic surgeon needed *my* help, he was far gone. I ignored the screaming voice in my chest and scuttled into the bedroom.

"Help."

The pale craven face on the pillow reminded me of my grandpa's open casket. Except Gary's lips were frayed and gnawed as if he'd been chewing on them for lunch. A dribble of dried vomit stained the comforter at his chin.

"You're bleeding." He said through his tattered mouth.

I absently rubbed at the cut at my neck.

"What's wrong with you?" What a pointless thing to ask. Everything, Darcy, clearly everything was wrong.

His skinny arm ending in long, yellow nails was raised above his head. I tried not to think about him scratching the wall with those claws, but the remembered *scratch* filled my head with dizzy clouds like too many shots of vodka.

"Get me..." His eyelids fluttered. "Out. Call 911."

I nodded as though I knew what the hell was going on.

He looked as if he was part of the bed, sunken into the sheets, his chest concave and his eyeballs stiff in their sockets.

It seemed to take every ounce of his energy to shake a metal band on his wrist. What I thought for a moment was a watch, was actually a shackle chained to the cherry-stained bedpost.

Behind me, Pam's toothbrush ended. The faucet shut off. Gary's filmy eyes doubled in size at the sound of her shifting in the bathroom. I knew then, as I had probably known somewhere deep within me, that Pam was the one to fear. I gave the poor creature in bed an awkward thumbs up and turned to slip out. My bare foot caught in something wet and crinkly. Hurrying out of the bedroom, it wasn't until I safely shut the door that I realized an adult diaper, extra soaked, was clinging to my ankle. The bitter scent of piss mixed so improperly with dried flowers made me retch into the back of my mouth.

I kicked the thing off, desperate to jumpstart my brain.

My phone my phone my phone

It was downstairs in my purse, hanging beside the door leading to the garage. Right where that crazy bitch had told me to put it.

My body swayed in the hall, which was feeling narrower with every second. I caught sight of a door across from my room with a pink wooden sign. It read DOTTIE in playful letters.

Oh, fuck.

That sparkly headband in the car stuck to my mind with more vigor than the soiled diaper. If there was a little girl chained up in there, I couldn't just leave her. I had to try to grab her on my way out.

"Fuuuuuuck." I turned the handle with one hand while rubbing my throbbing neck with the other. Neon green stars swirled on the dark ceiling, projected by some humming, electric cube on the dresser.

"Hey... pssst... hey!" I stared at the figure under the Peppa Pig sheets, half expecting to see Gary's haunting sallow eyes.

Fast asleep, Dottie didn't move.

Low voices came from Pam's bedroom. A knot pulsed in the bottom of my belly, urging me into the dark, little girl's bedroom to hide. Frankly, I was surprised my instincts were bothering, as I'd made it pretty clear I wasn't going to listen. If I was smart at all I would already be downstairs, phone in hand.

Over my shoulder, I made out a shadow by the door, and in slow deliberate motion, I watched as the master bedroom knob turned. My brain, a dusty useless wasteland, allowed my belly to take a turn. I swiftly shut myself into Dottie's room, leaving a sliver of door open in order to peek.

Pam, barely visible in a robe and twisted towel on her head, walked to the closed door where she believed I was sleeping.

She's going to see I'm gone. She's going to find me in here, crouched in a pile of stuffed animals.

But instead of knocking, Pam affixed something to the wooden panel of the door. I squinted, unable to make it out. When she turned on her heel, Pam stopped so suddenly both slippers squelched in the carpet. She crouched, her eyes wild in the jagged light. The towel fell from her hard hair, slipping down her shoulder. She did not notice. Her attention was on the heavy, misplaced diaper.

Terrified, I backed away, nearly toppling over a beanbag chair.

My mouth opened, yet only a hiss of air, like a deflating balloon, came out. I righted myself in the hell of dancing, green stars, and grabbed for the poor child in the bed.

Dottie's arm was hard and cold. I ran the back of my hand onto her forehead, like my mom did when I had a fever, and it, too, was remarkably stiff.

Dead dead dead.

No.

Green light swept across the little girl's face. It was paler than Gary's, though her eyes were a bright, pleasant blue. It was the eyelashes, painted on and much too long that tipped me over the edge.

"You're a doll," I told the staring, lifeless thing in the bed. Its placid expression remained in agreement.

A trembling fear awoke, not to just my own mortality, but to the inner workings of a tormented brain. I could only think of Pam stretching a pajama top over a nude mannequin while she cooed as though it were a girl named Dottie. A girl who liked sparkly headbands. Again and again, that image revolved until a scream, like a pained caterwaul shook the upstairs hall.

"DARCY?"

I hunkered down next to the bed, dizzy from terror and swirling stars.

"DARCY! Come to your room, you need rest, dear!"

I scratched into the side of my neck, concentrating on the pain. Blood, warm and comforting, trickled between my first finger and thumb.

A door down the hall, where Andrew, pretend or real, might sleep, swung open with a thud. "DARCY! WHERE ARE YOU?"

The desperation in Pam's voice rose like an ocean wave. "YOU WOKE YOUR DAD UP, DARCY!"

She was moving closer down the hall, banging on the wall with her fists, and maybe kicking with her slippers.

I considered a classic slip under Dottie's bed, or even an ankle-breaking fall from the window above the desk. I imagined myself dragging my legs behind me into the driveway of another suburban house. Begging for help as desperately as the grey thing that once had been Gary. Although, at this point, I had to assume the neighbors were cannibals or vampires, monsters who made Ted Bundy and Pam look sane.

But, I'm too much of a coward. It's why I stayed with Rowdy as long as I did. So, instead, I curled into a ball just as Pam threw open the bedroom door.

When the light flicked on I buried my eyes into my knees and I suppose, if I'm being honest, I felt like I deserved what was coming next.

"There you are!" She sounded relieved. "Bothering your sister, I see."

My eyes screwed shut even tighter. I couldn't look at all that crazy. It might take me with it, down into a vortex of insanity.

"Your dad is trying to get some sleep before a big surgery, and here you are scurrying all over the house."

The star projector buzzed in the silence.

"I'm sorry." I couldn't stop shaking. It was as though I was cold, a bitter frigid air swirled inside me. "I'm sorry, Mo... Mom?"

That last word caused Pam to take in a sharp, surprised inhale. Without looking, I could tell I had made her happy. Happier than I'd probably ever be, especially considering how short my life was looking to be.

I hoped she'd consider that and take it easy on me.

Pam stepped toward me, crouching so close I could smell her sweet, minty breath. "Come on, let's get you back to your room." She spoke with more tenderness than my own, real mom had ever used.

With weak limbs, I allowed her to help me up, my eyes still shut. Her hand was hot and sweaty.

"Apologize to Dottie." She whispered into the crease of my throbbing neck.

I turned, allowing one eyelid to slide open. The doll's blonde hair pooled on the pillow in the stark light, her red lips pursed in an eternal pout.

"Sorry for waking you." It came out easier than I thought it would. Play-acting.

Pam led me out of the room. She stopped to shut off the light and carefully close Dottie the doll's door.

My legs felt numb and my cheeks burned like ice.

When she hooked my arm and turned me toward the opposite side of the hall, I saw it. The glimmer from the bathroom perfectly captured what Pam had hung on the door of the room I had escaped.

A wooden sign with whimsical magnetic letters.

DARCY.

Something broke inside of me. It was an internal snap like the brittle crunch of dead leaves beneath the feet. Rowdy had made me feel like this. Like if I didn't fight and scratch my way out, I'd sink and finally suffocate.

"...you can apologize to your father at breakfast." Pam led me closer to those letters on the door. More audible cracks ran jagged across my brain.

I began to flicker to what breakfast would be like. It was a nightmare tableau of Dottie, propped up at the table, oatmeal dripping from her plastic lips. And pale Gary and I, sharing an ankle chain and in matching diapers as we choked down whatever Pam served.

The final, reverberating snap came when Pam leaned in close, whispering, "no more naughty stuff, Darcy. Be your best."

My body reacted before I could make sense of what I was doing. I whipped my arm away from her, hitting her in the cartilage of her nose with my elbow.

Pam shrieked, scrabbling to grab me with one hand while she held her nose with the other. I stumbled backward, my hip banging into the wall.

"HELLLLP!" Gary's ghoulish moan rattled my resolve. "GET HELP!" he hollered from the open bedroom.

I held onto the banister, watching blood fall from Pam's nostrils onto her terry cloth robe.

"Darcy!" Pam moved toward me. Her wide eyes swam with pain and disappointment.

I turned my back to her, jumping down to the carpeted landing of the stairs. I ignored a snap, this one real, emanating up from my left ankle.

The monster breathed fire behind me. As I rushed down the last stairs in the dark, Pam's frustrated screams and Gary's moans entwined in a sickening harmony. She followed in big, thundering steps.

Lost in the shadows, I slid on the kitchen linoleum. I could think only of Dottie upstairs staring at the ceiling, twinkling stars playing across her dead eyes. I needed something sharp.

"DARCY! IT'S BEDTIME!"

A slice of moonlight cut across the kitchen island. I grabbed at the counter, desperately opening the first drawer.

The light overhead turned on.

Panting, Pam stood at the threshold of the kitchen, her helmet hair finally showing signs of distress. She had smeared blood on the light switch, an eerie sight in such a pristine room.

I tore myself away from the nightmare waiting for me, in order to rip open another drawer. I gripped the handle of a steak knife, raising it in front of my face.

She took in a long, shaky inhale and blew it out through a snotty bubble of blood in her nose.

"I know you're a teenager," she spoke much too calmly. "So you feel this need to rebel. I get it, dear, I do." Pam extended a bare foot, her slippers obviously tossed in the chase.

"DON'T!" I waved the knife. "I'll fucking stab you!"

Her eyes narrowed. They were complicated orbs of anger, compassion, even pain.

"Do not come in here." My voice trembled on every word.

Pam nodded. "I can make more tea, or hot chocolate. You love hot chocolate."

"No. I don't. I never have. It tastes like shit."

I have to admit I enjoyed how her cheeks slid into a frown.

"I'm leaving. If you follow me, I'll kill you." I stepped around the island, keeping the knife trained on her face.

From the corner of my vision, I made out a glass door beyond the breakfast nook. It looked like it led to what rich people called a sunroom.

"Darcy…" My name was spoken saccharine sweet.

I ignored her, winding between the chairs and feeling the doorknob with my shaking fingers.

"Stay." She swayed back and forth on her heels, accidentally exposing the top of the tan bra beneath her robe. "Stay and we'll be happy. Me and you, Dad, Dottie, and Andrew. We're a family."

I had the urge to say something clever or mean. But I felt sorry for her, at that moment, before I pushed through that sunroom door. I even wanted her to get better.

In one motion, I used my backside, pressing against the glass as I twisted the knob. My awkward momentum caused me to lose my balance. I fell over a darkened lump on the slatted, porch floor.

The smell enveloped me in a hot, putrid embrace. It was more cloying than the house full of potpourri. It was death, vicious and oddly sweet.

Bile tunneled up my throat, gagging me. I kicked and vomited, forgetting the knife.

She was on me in the darkness, amidst the rotting lumps wrapped in sheets. Her minty breath stung my eyes.

"QUIT!" Her clawed nails found the vulnerable skin on my neck. The pain made more vomit come. I felt the hot stink on my chest and was glad it helped cover the smell of death. I fought her in the unstable moonlight, kicking at her belly and tearing at her crunchy hair.

She yelped and dug her nails deeper, her weight pinning me to the floor.

I felt the knife flat against my back.

"Come home." She wept. Tears, hers or mine, I'll never know, soaked my cheeks. "This is home."

I stopped fighting. It was the hardest thing I've ever done. Letting her cry on top of me in that room full of death.

"Home." I nodded. "This is our home." I'm not sure if I was play-acting for her benefit or my own.

"Yes, yes, we're happy, Darcy. Happy. We belong here." Pam raised herself on a knee between my legs. As she gazed down at me, smeared in sick and blood, her hair frazzled, I could see the woman she had been. The woman who had lived behind the Piggly Wiggly and wanted more.

My hand shook as I lowered it to the floor. I stared into Pam's eyes as I slid the knife from underneath me.

You know, looking back on it now, I think she knew. I think there was a small, or maybe even a big part of her, that needed me to do it.

I am a coward. But I didn't hesitate.

As soon as my hand found the blade, I rocked on to my side and then forward, finding purchase on the handle. I thrust the knife into the exposed skin of her chest. I'll always remember that feeling, of the serrated edge sawing into her ribcage.

The sensation comes to me on long nights, along with the smell.

Pam tried to scream. It was more of a hoarse wheeze. She sprayed blood from her mouth as she pinwheeled backward. I removed the knife and stabbed again, at some point standing above her in the dizzying horror.

I know I kept stabbing until she was as lifeless as the rotting corpses around us. And until the tears dried on my face.

It was as though I was in a coma after that. A waking nightmare. I crumbled to the slippery floor, trying to make sense of the shapes around me. Of the stained sheets with hands and feet poking out. Of the gaping wound in Pam's chest, a ragged, red, confusing maw.

Gary moaned upstairs. It was the tortured cry of someone who would never be the same.

The knife was on the floor and I stared at that, too. It made me think of Rowdy. I'm not sure why.

The moon called to me. It was round and hearty.

I stepped over them all. The big lumps, the little ones. Pam.

My slippery hands struggled to open the porch door.

Finally, I was out, stumbling down a few steps on my numb ankle. A pleasant desert breeze rippled the water of the backyard pool. Outside smelled like the dying embers of a barbeque grill.

I followed the lights of Bramblewood; tall, wrought-iron street lamps with swinging pots of chrysanthemums. I passed a shining, red Corvette in one driveway. There was a koi pond at the entrance of the cul-de-sac, where I stopped to watch the orange fish leap over each other in a coiled arch. As I walked, my fingers found the screaming hiss of pain on my neck.

By the time I reached the gates of the development, I knew where I was headed.

"I'm coming, Rowdy," I told the darkness. There was no other place.

Bramblewood was not for me.

Or for Pam. She knew it when she cried hot tears over me. She knew it when the first tip of the knife entered her chest.

This time I didn't stick out my thumb. I walked alone, barefoot and covered in my blood and hers, back to where I know.

Back to where I deserve.

Back home.

MEG HAFDAHL - Horror and suspense author Meg Hafdahl is the creator of numerous stories and books. Her fiction has appeared in anthologies such as Eve's Requiem: Tales of Women, Mystery and Horror and Eclectically Criminal. Her work has been produced for audio by The Wicked Library and The Lift, and she is the author of two popular short story collections including Twisted Reveries: Thirteen Tales of the Macabre. Meg is also the author of a trilogy of novels; The Darkest Hunger, Daughters of Darkness and Her Dark Inheritance called "an intricate tale of betrayal, murder, and small town intrigue" by Horror Addicts and "every bit as page turning as any King novel" by RW Magazine. Meg, also the co-host of the podcast Horror Rewind and co-author of The Science of Monsters, The Science of Women in Horror, The Science of Stephen King published by Skyhorse Publishing and distributed by Simon and Schuster, lives in the snowy bluffs of Minnesota.

@MegHafdahl

www.meghafdahl.com

https://www.facebook.com/meghafdahlhorrorauthor

Cold Comfort
Amy Grech

Jack Masoch woke with a start and flinched when he felt someone resting next to him on the spacious bed in a strange bedroom—everything here had a place, including him. He waited anxiously for his eyes to adjust to the darkness while he tried to make sense of it all. Jack looked around and groaned when he realized where he was—another strange woman's apartment, much larger and neater than his cramped studio. Waking up in strange places, next to women he hardly knew had become a kinky rut—purely spontaneous—especially if he'd been drinking.

He thought for a minute, struggling to recall the woman's name—lately they'd become a random jumble of desire, fueled by his insatiable libido—a moment later it came to him: Sadie O'Grady. It fit her perfectly given her bright red hair and *wild* temperament. Such an unusual combination of remarkable beauty and unbridled passion fascinated him and left him helpless against her charms.

* * * *

They met at Mango's; a tropical bar nearby. Hazy smoke lingered, dense and brooding, creating a hypnotic ambiance. Lou Reed crooned sweetly in the background. Lust filled the tight, dark space, oozing across the bar like precious liquid gold, yearning to be tasted.

Jack drank in the crowd, admiring the bevy of beauties ripe for the picking—dressed in alluring outfits that clung in *all* the right places—accentuating choice cleavage and other valuable assets. That's when he caught a glint of metal out of the corner of his eye and snapped out of his daze long enough to remember his wedding ring—a simple, silver band on his right ring finger—weighing him down. He slipped it off discreetly. Jack held it tightly in his palm for a minute, and felt it grow warm before slipping it into his pants pocket. He should have stopped wearing it by now, with Mary gone six months, but her hasty departure still gnawed at him, a bone of contention.

He had been drinking Apricot Sours, numbing the pain, staring at his third glass trying to decide if it was half empty or half full, when *she* appeared—an unanswered prayer—and sauntered over to the only empty barstool left in the place like she owned it.

Her perfume, sweet and light like lilacs, captivated his senses, reminding him of happier days. The girl wore an emerald green, sleeveless dress that left little to the imagination. One look at her and he knew he wouldn't be going home to his lonely studio apartment, chock-full of bad memories.

"You look thirsty." Jack rested his foot on the lower rung of the barstool and lost himself in her intense green eyes. "What are ya drinkin'?" he asked, slurring his words.

"Nothing, yet. I just got here." She rubbed his leg with the tip of her shoe and watched him shudder.

"I have a girlfriend." He shoved her away and frowned, apologetically.

"Then why isn't she here? Lover's quarrel?"

"No, Amy had to work tonight, so I decided to go out; I need to clear my head; I've got too much on my mind lately." He stared at his half-empty glass—almost time for a refill.

"I'm glad you came." She ran her fingers across the bar. "Make yourself useful. Buy me a drink."

"If you insist." Jack smiled, looked her over, and forgot about Amy for a while. "Pick your poison."

"A Zombie," she whispered, her breath hot, quick in his ear. "I could just eat you up!" The girl licked her pink lips slowly while he watched.

"Is that a threat or a promise?" He rested his hand on his chin.

"You'll soon find out." She twirled a lock of curly, red hair. "What's your name, sweet thing?"

Jack gasped, polished off his drink—for courage—and slammed his empty glass down on the bar. "Jack Masoch." He leaned forward and extended a large, bony hand. "And who might you be?"

"Sadie O'Grady." She shook it; her grip was firm, warm. "The pleasure's all mine." Sadie gave his hand a sudden, bone-crushing squeeze. He winced and felt his knuckles pop under the strain.

"Wow! That's quite a grip you've got there! You caught me by surprise." Jack bit his lip, stifling a scream.

"Thanks. I work out. A single girl's got to protect herself. This is a tough town—it will swallow you whole if you aren't careful." Sadie released his hand, and let her eyes wander slowly up and down his slender physique. "What's a cute, young guy like you doing alone in a dive like this?"

There's a first, he thought, amused by her daring overture.

"It's Ladies' Night." Jack chuckled. "I'm here to buy drinks for lovely ladies like you."

She shook her finger at him. "I doubt your girlfriend would approve."

"I promise not to tell."

Sadie folded her arms. "Have you bought anyone drinks yet?"

"You're the first girl to pique my interest." He waved the burly bartender over and ordered a Zombie for her and another Apricot Sour for himself. "Amy would have a fit if she found out I was here." Jack winked.

"You've got spunk and you're brutally honest. You're a rare find. Amy is a *very* lucky girl." Sadie grinned.

"She takes me for granted." Jack blushed and took a final swig of his Apricot Sour.

"Where do you live? You're not East Side material, I can tell—you're too rough around the edges."

He examined his throbbing hand and found no harm done. "I'm from the West Side. I haven't figured out how to blend in. Maybe you can teach me. I'm a *fast* learner."

"I'd be glad to show you the ropes, for a price." Her foot inched higher, grazing his thigh.

Jack shivered in anticipation. "Name it."

"Your pride. Can you handle that, Jack?" Sadie shrugged.

He snickered, relieved. "Sure. I've got plenty to spare."

"Consider yourself lucky, I'm feeling generous tonight—it's a rare occurrence." She ran her fingers across the bar. "What brings you to this side of town? Looking for someone new?"

He felt the crotch of his jeans tighten instantly. "Maybe, if the right girl comes along."

"Am *I* the right girl?" She placed her hand between her plump breasts and watched his dark, blue eyes settle there.

"Absolutely." Jack smirked, raised his glass, and polished off his drink. "This half of the city seems less crazed."

Sadie nodded. "It is and that makes it really dull if you ask me. A girl has to search *hard* for excitement."

"Isn't it worth the extra effort?" He raised his eyebrows.

She shrugged. "Sometimes."

Jack looked her up and down. "You look luscious."

Sadie licked her lips again. "Are you hungry?"

"I'm ravenous!" He nodded, thrilled by dumb luck. "God, you're *gorgeous*."

She laughed, long and hard. "God had nothing to do with it."

"Fair enough." Jack smiled expectantly.

The bartender set their drinks on the bar; Jack handed him a twenty and a ten from his tattered wallet.

Sadie hoisted her enormous glass "Here's to chance encounters."

"I'll drink to that!" He raised his drink, spilling some on the bar.

She plucked the cherry from the Zombie and lowered it into her mouth slowly. Intrigued, Jack looked on.

"What ya up to later tonight?" He gulped down the rest of his Apricot Sour and dabbed his mouth with a cocktail napkin.

She drank her Zombie. "That depends."

"On what?" Jack stared at her intently.

"What you have to offer." Sadie winked.

* * * *

The sumptuous shape beside him stirred in the darkness and his cock betrayed him once more.

Mary.

No, it couldn't be!

Groggy, Jack opened his eyes and studied the woman lying beside him disappointed to discover she wasn't his wife, Mary. No, it was only Sadie, his latest conquest, another momentary lapse of reason.

"Glad to see you're finally up. I wondered when you were going to come around." Sadie wrapped her arms around him and squeezed. "You passed out. I guess I got carried away. I get lost in the moment. Sometimes I don't know my own strength."

He draped an arm across her shoulder. "Yeah, you really wore me out. You're *amazing*."

"You bring out the best in me." She nuzzled his neck.

Jack felt his soft skin bruise under the strain. Tomorrow he'd look like someone who'd gone six rounds in a prizefight and lost.

"Hey, Jack, know what I love about you?" Sadie wrapped her arms around him and held him tight.

"Let me guess. Is it my boyish charm? It's my best feature." Jack squirmed, trying to get comfortable, but failing miserably. The more he moved, the harder she squeezed, just to remind him that, ready or not, he belonged to her now.

Her nimble fingers tousled his thick blond hair, caressed his soft face, his long neck, his hairy chest, his huge hard-on, his firm ass. "No, everything. You're the perfect fit."

"I can't decide what I love more: Your angelic face, your stunning eyes, your luscious lips, your perky breasts, or your long legs." With trembling fingers, he traced her sculpted figure, relishing each moment, every fantastic sensation.

Sadie clasped his hands in hers and positioned him underneath her. He gasped and braced himself for another round. She pressed her lips against his eager ones, practically smothering him. Panting, he came up for air.

"Are you OK?" She released his hands.

"Yeah. Just try to go easy on me, I bruise easily, like a peach." Jack ran his fingers through his hair and rubbed his eyes.

"Your skin *is* soft." Sadie kissed his damp forehead. "I'll *try* to be gentle, but I make no guarantees."

"You don't want to break me, do you?" He sank deeper into the bed.

"I promise to handle you with care," She laughed, crossing her heart. "I wouldn't want you to end up in the hospital just because I'm kinky in bed."

Slowly, Sadie slipped out of her peach teddy and matching panties. Then she pulled down his dark blue boxers and tossed them in the corner. She mounted him and wrapped her arms around him. Sadie's sensuality surged through him, delivering a powerful jolt that shocked him to the core.

Jack ran his fingers across her muscular shoulders and squeezed her breasts. He trembled, scarcely able to keep up with her intense pelvic thrusts. Jack fought to stay conscious in the thick of it all, but it wasn't easy, and he faded fast.

* * * *

When he came to the next morning, dazed and aching, his bony wrists were tied tightly to the bedposts; coarse ropes dug into his tender flesh, leaving vicious mementos. Sadie loomed above him, naked and menacing. "Oh, good. You're awake. For a while there I didn't think you were going to make it."

Eyes wide, Jack stared at her when he tried to move his arms and found them frozen in place. "Why did you tie me to the bed, Sadie? It's a bit drastic don't you think? Were you afraid I'd leave in the middle of the night? I wouldn't *dream* of it."

"Let's just say you were fit to be tied." She laughed. "Do you have a death wish?"

"Should I?" he taunted.

Sadie pouted. "You already know the answer."

"You've done this before. It's an elaborate scheme to humiliate me." Jack struggled against his restraints. Every touch, every sensation Sadie delivered set him off, like a live wire. The bed creaked under his weight, demanding a brief reprieve.

"Don't take it personally. After the workout I gave you, I knew you'd sleep soundly. I wanted to stress the *binding* nature of last night's get-together." She came closer; he steeled himself for her wrath.

"What are you talking about? We just fucked. I wouldn't mind another turn. It was purely physical, really intense, but there wasn't an emotional connection, at least not for me. You're definitely a bit more extreme than I'm used to. Hey, I'm not complaining—you really know how to rock my world, but I'm already in a *relationship*—I told you that last night at the bar. I saw an opportunity to have some fun and I took it. You know, a harmless fling. Since when is that a crime?" Jack ogled her breasts, wanting desperately to taste her plump nipples; in his haste, he bit his tongue, tasting his own coppery blood instead.

"Flings are *never* harmless; believe me, I know. They can get messy, especially if someone gets careless. I think I'll introduce myself to Amy. I'll make it a happy coincidence. Would you like that, Jack?"

"You wouldn't *dare*." He shook his head. "Don't threaten me, Sadie, or Amy will make you regret the day you met me."

"Really? I find that *hard* to believe. What could Amy possibly do that would be so terrible?" She rolled her eyes.

"You have no idea." Jack writhed on the bed, trying desperately to break the ties that bound him. "For your sake, I hope you never find out. Consider yourself warned."

"Thanks, but in case you haven't noticed I'm not easily intimidated." Sadie sat next to him on the bed, slipped her hand inside his boxers and caressed his stiff cock. "We took an emotional journey and formed a tight bond that won't be easily broken, just like the ties that bind you now."

"You're absolutely right." He took a deep breath, closed his eyes. "It was the best night of my life. I'm sorry. I've been very selfish. Let me make it up to you."

"She tickled his ribs and watched him squirm, struggling to break free. "Do you think you can earn my trust? It won't be easy, but it *will* be worth your while." Sadie released his throbbing dick when he came.

"I'm up to the challenge. What did you have in mind?" Jack sat up. "I'll do anything, just name it—I'm eager to please."

"Promise you'll come back real soon. I insist." She winked. "I'm not a very patient person. I hate to wait."

"With pleasure." He grinned. "See you soon."

Sadie committed his body to memory before releasing him. Amused, she watched while he struggled to regain his composure. His bruised body bore the burden of Sadie's desire. She admired her handiwork while he picked up the pieces.

Jack stretched—his joints snapped in protest—and rubbed his raw wrists. He got dressed in the rumpled white T-shirt and black jeans he wore last night and kissed her intensely to prove his devotion.

"Remember, if we don't get together next week, I'll wrap a rope around your scrawny neck when you least expect it. Do you understand? And that's not a threat, it's a promise." Sadie held him tight. "I spend a lot of time in Central Park—it's one of my favorite spots. Chances are pretty good you'll find me there."

Jack rubbed his throbbing neck, nodded, and left quickly without saying a word.

* * * *

After another exhausting day at the office, he reluctantly returned to his crowded studio, haunted by memories of his beloved Mary, meek and mild, the polar opposite of the wickedly wild Sadie who'd made him her plaything.

Jack approached the answering machine. Its bright, red light blinked, demanding his attention. He took a deep breath, pressed PLAY, and listened to the message. He expected it to be from Sadie, even though he didn't remember giving her his number; she might have looked him up. Jack blushed when he recalled his night of unbridled passion.

The message turned out to be from Amy; she called to see how he spent his night while she was stuck at work. She didn't sound annoyed, just sorry she couldn't be with him.

He picked up the phone, sat down on the couch, and called her at work.

"Hello, this is Officer Amy Kiernan. What can I do for you?"

"Hey there, Officer Kiernan. It's Jack. I just got your message." He cleared his throat. "Sorry I missed your call last night. I had to work late and when I got home, I just peeled off my clothes and tumbled naked into bed. Have you ever had one of those days?"

"Yeah, I'm having one right now… I'd give anything be naked in bed with you right now," she whispered. "Uh-oh, Sergeant Travis is coming, I've got to go. See you tonight?"

"I can hardly wait. Don't work too hard. Save some of your legendary stamina for me."

"I've got plenty to spare," Amy purred into his ear.

Jack hung up and grabbed a framed picture of Mary sitting on the polished teak coffee table she found at a quaint antique shop in Chelsea; he stared at it for a long time, trying to conjure up her likeness in his troubled mind. He touched the smooth, cold glass that preserved her likeness in a silver frame. Radiant and beautiful with long, black hair and soft brown eyes, his soul mate. He missed her terribly; it pained him to look at her picture, but he wanted to remember Mary in her prime.

Mary…

She left him against her will late one sultry Saturday night in July while they wandered around Times Square, mesmerized by the bizarre mixture of sleaze and glamour that dazzled tourists and locals alike. When they crossed the street at Broadway and 42nd Street, a cab sped around the curb and struck Mary, who had been walking on the edge of the sidewalk, closer to the street. The instant the cab hit her; Mary's neck snapped. Jack knelt on the slick sidewalk clutching her limp body, weeping while he waited anxiously for the ambulance to arrive. A doctor pronounced her dead on arrival at Saint Clare's

Hospital. He slid the diamond wedding ring off Mary's finger and took it with him, a memento.

Justice prevailed. The cabby's license was permanently revoked for manslaughter and he got slammed with 24 months of jail time. The judge, a stern woman with a grudge, forced the cab company to pay Jack $500,000.00, compensation for his loss; more than enough to give Mary a proper burial, with plenty to spare. But the money didn't matter, it couldn't bring her back, nothing could.

He refused to accept that cruel fact—denial became bliss—he chose to drink himself into oblivion instead, where he found comfort in the arms of eccentric women, who demanded little of him in return for their affection. Sadie wanted him *all* to herself and she didn't want to share. She made that painfully clear. Jack wasn't used to being a kept man; it made him *very* uncomfortable. If he refused, Sadie promised to give him something none of the other women he confided in since Mary's death could offer—salvation.

* * * *

Amy arrived at eight 'o clock, prompt, as always. Jack pulled her close and kissed her passionately.

She kissed him until he ran out of breath and slipped out of her navy blue New York City Police Officer's uniform in two seconds flat. Amy tossed her handcuffs on the nightstand and led him over to the bed. Jack sat down on the edge and spread his legs, his enormous cock straining against tight denim. Amy lifted his white T-shirt over his head and ran her hungry hands across his hairy chest. She worked her way down to his faded jeans and unzipped them slowly, freeing his bulging erection.

"I've missed you terribly, Amy." He brushed her cheek with the back of his hand.

Her infectious smile illuminated his dingy apartment, making her simply irresistible. "It's a long, hard week. Seeing you is the perfect way to unwind. I've got plenty of pent up tension to unleash." She stepped out of her arrest navy blue uniform and walked towards him.

"I don't deserve it." Jack sighed. "I've done a bad, bad thing."

"What did you do this time? You naughty boy." Amy pinned him down. "It's a good thing I'm a cop—somebody's got to save you—you're too reckless. It's bound to be your downfall if you aren't careful."

"Guilty as charged." Jack smirked. "Aren't you going to arrest me?"

"I'm off duty, so I guess I'll have to punish you instead." She lunged for the handcuffs. "You need a good dose of discipline."

"I seem to attract trouble the way honey draws bees." Wide-eyed, Jack watched her spring into action, his body rigid to soften the blow. "I didn't work late last night—I went to a bar instead—I needed a change of pace… I met someone. It was an accident—we just sort of collided. Her name is Sadie O'Grady. She told me she'd come find me and kill me if I don't come back and see her in a week."

"Ugh, Jack. You've gotten yourself into a sticky mess." Amy muttered. "Let me guess you were drinking Apricot Sours and Sadie O'Grady sat next to you at the bar and chatted you up."

"Guilty as charged. I should've left the second she sat down, but she drew me in before I could get away." In apology, he kissed Amy's breasts, licked her sweet nipples. "You know how I get after a few drinks." Jack flashed a smile.

"Do I ever! You let your dick lead you around without considering the consequences. That's a really nasty habit, in case you haven't noticed." Amy grazed his throbbing cock with the handcuffs.

The cold metal made him flinch. "I know. Sadie scared me into submission."

"Now there's a surprise." She traced the contours of his sinewy frame with the cuffs, working her way slowly up to his wrists. "You're much too submissive, Jack. You need to learn how to resist temptation."

"Show me the way." He closed his eyes, kissed Amy, eager to set things right. "You're my saving grace—I'm lucky to have you. Sadie meant nothing to me—she was a terrible mistake. You're my girl, Amy. I want to be your guy, if you'll still have me."

She brushed the stubble on his chin with the back of her hand. "You're weak and helpless as a kitten. I think I'll keep you, but you've got to learn how to behave."

"I promise to be good, if you'll help me out of this bind. Let's have some fun and put Sadie in her place. You won't regret it."

Too weak to protest, he held his arms out in surrender.

She studied the bruises on his bony wrists. "Who did this to you?"

His voice trembled when he spoke. "Sadie did. She dragged me back to her apartment and tied me to her bed. She overpowered me and took advantage of me, even though I told her I have a girlfriend. She wouldn't take no for answer."

Amy kissed his wounded wrists. "Did you tell her I'm a cop?"

Jack shook his head. "No, I figured she'd find out soon enough."

"I'll bail you out, but you're going to owe me big time, Jack." She winked.

Jack closed his eyes. "I'll do anything, just name it."

"Promise you'll stop being a victim."

"I'll do whatever it takes to set things right."

"What's in store for Sadie?" Amy grabbed Jack's lanky arms and handcuffed him to the bedposts. The smooth wood already bore evidence of their kinky encounters.

"I'll take a walk in Central Park on Saturday night—Sadie told me she spends a lot of time there—when you're out on patrol. Just follow my lead and let the mayhem begin. Sadie won't know which way to run!" He wrapped his legs around hers.

"Consider it done. This is going to be fun!" She kissed him again, madly, deeply, while she straddled him, driving Jack to the brink of ecstasy.

Jack matched Amy's passionate fury with equal fervor, synchronizing his movements with hers, expressing his gratitude for her unrelenting love.

* * * *

Whether drawn to Central Park in the dead of night—on a bitter cold Saturday no less—by Sadie's lethal threat or his diabolical plan to settle the score he couldn't say. Perhaps a combination of the two lured him: An overwhelming desire to be surrounded by trees and open spaces, instead of blocks of angry asphalt and endless gridlock; the park provided a soothing pocket of calm in a whirlwind of chaos.

Being there reminded him of the long walks he used to take with Mary, holding hands while they laughed and talked. Snow fell slowly, silently around him; he walked along the dimly lit path while his feet crunched under a pristine blanket of white, his hands buried in the warm, deep pockets of his black leather jacket with only his shadow for company. Sleeping homeless men occupied the benches where he and Mary used to sit. Jack shivered and moved on.

Retribution came swiftly, like the wintry wind.

He heard the staccato click of a woman's high heels hit the pavement behind him, closing in.

Sadie.

He broke into a run—steady and deliberate—sprinting through the park's winding paths, blinded by blowing snow, his breath escaping in short, quick bursts ahead of him. Sadie ran after him, undeterred by her high heels—*click, clack, click, clack, click, clack*—smacking the hard asphalt, gaining momentum. Jack recalled her impressive strength and cursed himself for being so foolish. That's when he felt a coarse rope around his neck, dragging him down. Jack landed on all fours. The frosty grass pricked his bare hands, like a thousand tiny icy needles. He gagged and struggled to his feet.

"Looks like you've got some explaining to do, Jack. You'd better hurry up— time's up." Holding the rope taut like a leash, Sadie made her presence known. She'd dressed from head to toe in black for the occasion; she left nothing to chance. "Did you forget about our little agreement? You're not very good at keeping promises, are you? Now you've got to suffer the consequences."

He shook his head; the rope constricted around his neck instantly, like a vicious viper. Jack winced. "Sorry, I've been distracted lately, but if I remember correctly, today is my last day to see you, and here I am."

"Cutting it kind of close; don't you think?" She gave the rope a good tug, drawing him closer.

He grinned. "I work best under pressure. Stress can be a powerful motivator."

"You've been avoiding me. I want to know why." Sadie balled her large hands into fists. "You better have a damn good reason."

"I already *told* you I have a girlfriend. Does that *mean* anything to you?" Jack clutched at the rope, desperately trying to loosen it.

"Then why did you go home with me? You stupid fuck!" She slapped his face, already raw from the harsh winter wind. "You're some piece of work."

"She reminds me of you. The resemblance is uncanny—piercing green eyes; she's a regular vixen in bed." He grinned, feeling smug.

"Where's your girlfriend now? You're in deep trouble, Jack. Is she going to save your sorry ass? I doubt it." She kicked him in the balls.

Jack curled up in a ball; his hands covered his aching groin. "Amy had to work tonight. She's a cop. Lucky for me Central Park is her beat." He stared at her; his eyes radiated hatred. "You wouldn't *believe* the things she does with handcuffs!"

Sadie gave the rope a good tug, pulling him closer. "What do you mean 'Central Park is her beat'?"

Jack snickered. "Amy is a cop. She patrols the park every night on horseback, looking for delinquents like you to arrest."

Sadie's jaw dropped. "Fuck!" She dropped the rope and turned to run.

"Going somewhere, Sadie?" he asked, casually. "You won't get far! Amy will see to that!"

On cue, Amy emerged from the snowy night. Her fiery red hair whipped in the wind. Her enormous steed, a black stallion, blocked Sadie's passage.

"You're just in time, Amy! Sadie tried to *kill* me!" Jack worked the knot loose and tossed the rope on the ground. He rubbed his raw neck.

Sadie backed away. "Jack defied me! Now he must accept the consequences!"

"He needs discipline—no doubt—a trait you're obviously lacking." Amy dismounted and tackled the woman clad in black. She landed on top of her. Stunned, Jack watched them obliterate the pristine powder. Amy pinned Sadie down quickly and cuff her.

"Hey, these cuffs are too tight!" Sadie winced.

"You're in no position to complain, Sadie. I'm arresting you." Amy pulled her roughly to her feet.

"Why? I haven't *done* anything wrong!" Sadie spat in Amy's face. The cop wiped her cheek with the back of her hand.

Sadie shivered. Amused, Jack wondered if fear or the chill in the air finally got to her.

"How do you explain that rope you had tied around his neck?" She placed her hands on her hips. "I'm charging you with attempted murder."

Jack nodded. "I can't *wait* to hear this!"

"This is kind of embarrassing, but sometimes Jack likes to be led around on a leash." Sadie raised her eyebrows. "Does that surprise you?"

He buried his face in his hands.

"Not really. I handcuff him to a different piece of furniture every night while we fuck." Amy nudged Jack. There's just one problem. As far as I can tell, you didn't have him on a leash, you deliberately tied a rope, complete with a noose around his neck so tightly Jack has rope burn. That's weapon and motive."

"You're very clever." Sadie clapped; her manacled hands clinked rhythmically. "Congratulations! You win the grand prize! How does it feel?"

"I'm bringing you down to the station. I'm sure Jack wants to press charges. I know *I* would." Amy started to lead Sadie away.

"Hold on. I've got a better idea. Let the punishment fit the crime." Jack shook his head. "Let's settle this right here. Right now."

Amy turned around. "What did you have in mind, Jack?"

Sadie tried to wriggle out of the cuffs.

He rubbed his hands together, anxious to get down to business.

"You'll see soon enough. Follow me." Jack tugged on her muscular arm. "Come on, Sadie, I've got a surprise for you."

She shot him a dirty look. "Where are you taking me?"

"Someplace safe." Jack and Amy brought Sadie—he held one arm; she held the other—over to a secluded section of the park where they wouldn't be disturbed. He leaned in close to whisper in her ear: "What's the matter, don't you *trust* me, Sadie?"

Sadie gave him the finger.

Jack leered at her.

Amy became Sadie's shadow, ready to pounce—billy club in hand—in case she decided to bolt.

He paused in front of a ladder resting against a lamppost—a lucky find—and grabbed it. "Amy, give me a hand," Jack grunted; Amy kept a firm grip on Sadie.

"Sure. Why don't you take the ladder and I'll keep Sadie out of harm's way?" She winked.

Sadie glowered at Amy.

"Sounds like a plan!" Jack scooped the rope Sadie wrapped around his neck out of the snow. It felt damp and rigid between his fingers—his dried blood caked the noose. He slung it over his shoulder and closed in on Sadie. She backed right into Amy, who whacked her shoulder with the club. Sadie threw a punch at Amy but came up short.

"Now it's time for *you* to bear the burden of guilt. Try *this* on for size!" He slipped the rope around Sadie's long neck and cinched it tight. Her hands flew up and yanked, trying desperately to loosen it. Sadie's breath became a series of frantic gasps and her cheeks turned bright red. Jack gave the rope a good tug and led her over to the nearest tree.

"You're a dangerous woman, Sadie, but something tells me no one will miss you when you're gone."

"You have no idea," she muttered, her voice raspy. As she continued to wheeze, a steady stream of white breath appeared in front of her.

Jack watched her carefully while he positioned the ladder against the mighty Oak. "Up you go."

Sadie regarded him with pleading eyes. "Do I have a choice?"

Amy drew her pistol and cocked it. "You can climb that ladder, or I can shoot you right where you stand. Pick your poison."

Slowly, silently, Sadie climbed the ladder. The metal rungs made her chapped hands numb, and the handcuffs restricted her movements. She struggled to keep her grip. Jack waited until she reached the top and stood above the lowest branch. Then he did something Sadie never expected. He pulled another ladder out from behind the tree and set it up next to the first one. He scaled it quickly, like a cat, and tied the other end of the rope in a hangman's noose around the branch. "This branch should do the job quite nicely." He grinned.

Amy nodded approvingly.

"Well, it's been real. I'd love to *hang* around, but this is supposed to look like a suicide." Jack tested the knot to make sure it would hold. Sadie's weight "Do you have any last words?"

Sadie balled her hands up into fists. Yeah, fuck off!"

Amy kicked the ladder out from under Sadie and shoved her. Jack watched in morbid fascination as Sadie's body twitched while she dangled in midair, until her face turned the perfect shade of green.

AMY GRECH has sold over 100 stories to various anthologies and magazines including: A New York State of Fright, Apex Magazine, Beat to a Pulp: Hardboiled, Dead Harvest, Deadman's Tome Campfire Tales Book Two, Expiration Date, Flashes of Hope, Fright Mare, Hell's Heart, Hell's Highway, Hell's Mall, Needle Magazine, Psycho Holiday, Real American Horror, Tales from the Canyons of the Damned, Tales from The Lake Vol. 3, Thriller Magazine, and many others. New Pulp Press published her book of noir stories, Rage and Redemption in Alphabet City.

She is an Active Member of the Horror Writers Association and the International Thriller Writers who lives in New York. You can connect with Amy on Twitter: https://twitter.com/amy_grech or visit her website: https://www.crimsonscreams.com.

KISS

R.A. Busby

"My most terrifying patient?" The doctor chuckled, a grim little sound. "Of course. I have often thought of it. Of her." He paused as the butler refilled the glasses. "And tonight—yes, after all this time, the hour has come round to tell it. That is why this ragtag band of miscreants meets, after all. For the tales."

"And Alister's brandy," remarked a voice from within one of the deep leather armchairs clustered around the fire.

"To be sure," the doctor said, raising his glass. "So. My patient." He gave a reflective sip and began in earnest.

* * * *

"It happened in the waning years of the last century. A young man then, I was new to the taste of disillusion. Having failed to achieve the heights of Byron or Shelley in Paris, I returned in disgrace to my father's home in New Bedford. There, I pursued his ambition for me and became a doctor, though my practice primarily consisted of dispensing laudanum to the wealthy and the bored.

"One autumn evening as the chill of the winter drew near, I found myself in an alley by the harbor—well, everything in New Bedford is by the harbor—and that is when I heard her. She had followed me, you understand.

"I was quite intoxicated, and for that reason had embarked on the bracing walk back home, to which I did not wish to go. My wife Alice was a harridan, stern and unyielding; our son Charles, a miserable bully. More and more, I'd found myself drawn to—well, a certain club whose name is notorious even in these licentious times."

The doctor glanced at the company about the room. "I can tell what you think," he said with an ironic smile. "I shall not deny a word. Indeed, I have tales from that place that would make the most jaded of us blush like virgins—even you, Montague." At their ripple of laughter, Dr. Eliot signaled for more brandy and cigars.

"This club was, I knew, a mere exchange of one vice for another. Dissolution for disillusion, that is all, boredom and failure obliterated by absinthe and laudanum and flesh. Still, it was a delight in its own way. The most notorious event of the season was, of course, our masquerade ball. That year, a certain Mrs. S. dressed—I use that word loosely—as Aphrodite, and save for a coat of marbleized paint, as nude as the goddess herself. Another gentleman came as a map of New Bedford."

There was a strangled cough from one of the members, a mariner of long-standing. "Oh, my," he said, and cleared his throat again.

"Indeed," the doctor agreed. "Given the peninsular shape of the city—coupled with his own physique—the man resembled a rather chubby uncircumcised penis. Still, although the night was a whirl of lights and laughter, I recall little of the other guests. Except, of course, for one."

"The love of your life?" An elegant woman smiled, leg draped over the arm of a chair.

"Ah, Eliza." The doctor nodded. "I did not see you there in the shadow. The love of my life, you ask? Perhaps."

"And how was she dressed?" asked one of the others, a junior member with a face flushed red as the dying coals. "Like Salome? Lilith? Madame de Pompadour?"

"Well," said the doctor, "though she had dressed in an elaborate black gown of a French aristocrat, it was her mask I saw first." A shadow came over his face then. "It was... memorable. It consisted of a veil of fine white satin drawn down over her head and tied below with a broad scarlet bow at the neck. The effect was... distinctive. Unsettling. It was the blankness of the veil, I suppose, the red shock of ribbon about the throat intended to represent the fatal kiss of La Guillotine. In that," he chuckled, "I know now I was not altogether wrong. Still, by the time I grew weary of the masque, the woman had vanished. Without giving the matter further thought, I drew my coat about me and departed.

"The evening air smelled of salt and sea, the tang of open flesh. I stumbled down the street—Acushnet, I think, or Johnny Cake Hill, my toes catching the uneven setts as I meandered home. The weathered buildings stared at me in stern reproach, drawing themselves up in the shreds of their New England rectitude and returning only silence.

"Just then, the rasp of a shoe on the choppy sidewalk made me whirl about, fearing a robber. Beneath the streetlamp, I saw her, the woman from the masque. I recognized her at once, not only from the wide French skirts, but from that shrouded face. In the uncertain light, her head seemed to float above her inky dress like the blank face of a scarecrow. Through the whiteness of that veil, I could—I could feel her eyes looking at me, blank and sightless, and I felt a chill then, more than the cold New Bedford night.

"I turned then and walked faster, but she kept apace with me, though always a half-block behind. When we came to my street, my heart hammering and all vestiges of intoxication flown, I stood at my door and fumbled with the keys like a fool, praying I could enter without waking the servants or Alice. Even as I did, the woman called me by name."

"Whatever did she say, old friend?" Alister leaned forward, his cigar half-forgotten between his fingers.

"She cried, 'Dr. Eliot—please, do not go.' My hand was on the door, and I swear that for a second, I almost pretended I did not hear her." The doctor's lips turned up in a grim smile. "And how the rest of my life would have been changed had I simply stepped inside. Why, I might still be in New Bedford, an old and bitter man salted by the sea like a cod."

"What did the woman want?" asked Eliza.

"An appointment," he answered simply. "'Dr. Eliot,' the woman said, 'do forgive me, but I am in great need of you.' Well, I am sure I do not need to explain what I thought. When a young and healthy-seeming woman insists on seeing a doctor without delay, the reasons are almost always those one might expect. It was, let us say, the other part of my practice.

"'Are you in any pain?' I asked. 'Any fever? Vomiting? Hardness of the abdomen? Are you bleeding?' Beneath that odd white veil, her head swung back and forth in clear denial.

"'I cannot explain here,' the woman whispered. 'May I please come tomorrow after dark?'

"To this, I agreed, and with that, the woman vanished up the street until the shadows swallowed her.

"The next evening, I waited for her. My office, you know, took up the first floor of our house, a solid and respectable dwelling. I lit a lamp and placed it in the window, the warm glow awakening in me that desire for the laudanum I had grown more and more of late to crave, the aching need that growled and scratched from somewhere in my very veins, a hunger to feel that golden haze obliterating all present, past, and self. Alice had left that morning for a visit to her mother, taking Charles with her, and though I promised to follow them the following day, I realized it was of little importance if I stayed. In any case, I would not be disturbed.

"Not long after sunset came a short, soft knock on my door. As the woman entered, lowering the umbrella and cloak that had hitherto concealed her face, I noticed with surprise she wore the same white mask she had worn at the ball."

"How odd," a clubgoer remarked.

"Indeed. I then began to suspect some cruel disease had deformed her. Syphilis does that, as you are aware, and the results can be horrifying. Noses caved away. Holes in the scalp as deep as to the bone. Lesions treated with chloride of mercury. I steeled myself, determined to maintain a mask of stolid professionalism and banish from my face all signs of horror. I assumed an aspect of studied neutrality, as if regarding something unremarkable—a rock, a fish, a shoe—and prepared for the worst."

"Was it truly terrible?" asked one, his youthful expression troubled.

The doctor glanced at him over his glass of brandy. "Yes," he replied. For a moment, the room fell utterly silent.

"When the woman spoke," said the doctor at last, "her voice was low and cultured as I remembered, but her tone bore an edge of desperation. 'Please,' she insisted. 'You must help me.'

"I showed my patient to a chair and drew the curtains. I almost retreated behind my desk then—always the cowardly defense of the professional—but thought better and sat beside her instead. '"How can I assist you, miss?' I asked. For a long moment, the woman did not reply, her hand creeping to the luxuriant red ribbon still wound about her neck.

"'Is it your face?' I inquired. 'May I?' I moved my hand upward, and she turned to me. Only then did I perceive that there were no eye-holes cut in the white fabric at all. Nothing. The surface of the white fabric was smooth and unbroken save for two shadowed dips on either side of her nose, and yet—" He broke off, staring at the fire. "And yet, she saw me. What's more, despite the unimaginable horrors I knew she would soon reveal, I could tell that she was beautiful. Or had been. I raised my hand and almost touched the ribbon.

"'No,' the woman replied. 'I shall do it.' As she drew a breath, I watched her chest move with the rise and fall of normal respiration, but the fabric about her mouth and nose did not stir. I shivered again, as if a cold and questing finger tapped the back of my neck and slid slowly down to my spine.

"I came within a half-second of grasping the wrist of the delicate hand that reached for the ribbon, holding it back from that ghastly revelation, but I did not. Without a word, she drew the cloth aside."

"And what did—was it as you'd feared? What did you see?" Eliza frowned.

The doctor stared into the fire. "I saw nothing," he said at last. "I saw nothing."

"Whatever do you mean?"

"I mean I saw nothing. She undid the ribbon and smoothed it on her lap, a slash of scarlet as if she bled between her legs. For a heartbeat, the woman stood before me like a virgin bride beneath her veil and then, then with a sudden gesture of resolution, pulled it off." He took a sip of the brandy, steadying the glass with both hands. "There was nothing there," he declared at last. "Where you would expect to find a face—or a head—there existed only vast and formless blackness."

"You mean," asked Alister with a frown, "her skin was somehow... painted?"

"No. Even in the dim light, I could determine that at once. It was not lamp-black, ink, nor any kind of cosmetic paste. Where her head should have been was—how can I put this? It was a mass of living darkness."

The doctor struggled for words. "We have all seen those silhouette pictures from the previous century, have we not? Those outlined forms of solid black, as if the artist drew a picture of your shadow? Her head looked like that."

"But how are you sure it was not paint?" asked Eliza. "You did not touch her face."

"Not at that moment. But I know it was not."

"How?"

"She had no eyes. Only darkness. And..." he added, "the darkness was alive."

When they had fallen silent for a moment, the doctor continued. "As she moved, my brain could perceive the fleeting images of shapes—the sweep of a cheekbone, the dip of an eyebrow, the straight prominence of her nose—but those were only impressions, for the black substance of her head appeared to swallow the light around her. There was a flatness there. No shadows. No ridges. Even the beams from the lamp I had lit in the window seem to bend as they approached the dark depths and disappeared within."

"My God," whispered Alister.

"And mine," said the doctor. "It had an irresistible pull, this darkness, as if it could swallow not only light, but souls. I found I could not look away, but was drawn in, mesmerized by that swirling and evocative darkness, the abyss of her eyes and her face.

"I heard her voice as she explained. A chance encounter, she said. An intimate embrace. Days later, she had started to change. First a paleness, then translucence, then the shadow. She had long since lost the need to eat or drink. The woman—she did not know if she was human anymore.

"But as she spoke, I sensed something else. She was leaning forward, moving closer to me by nearly imperceptible degrees with every word. Her face—the devouring mass that would have been her face—filled my vision, and to my astonishment, I perceived it was not black at all, but a radiant world of swirling colors, shapes, and forms that did not exist, could not exist. Vines, canyons, petals of orange and violet fire. Then, from the shimmering expanse above her neck, I saw a nest of dark loose tendrils slip away and hover in the air like smoke or hair in wind sprung free of a confining veil."

The doctor cleared his throat. "Her voice went on, but I lost her words in the pound and rush of the blood in my ears as her face eased closer to my own, her hands now on my knees, my legs, my hips. And though with some exceptions, my affections did not naturally tend that way—a fact I could not admit then—I found myself half-wild with desire. One touch, one breath on straining skin, would end me, and I would explode like a blossoming flower. My sole wish was to bury myself within her, feel my flesh torn wide, dissolve into the darkness of that face.

"I looked up, and in that moment caught a glint of light. From within the darkness, I saw light. Two silver pinpricks stared out from inside, and I knew the dark somehow… beheld me. There was an intelligence there. Something old. Something alien. Whatever this woman—whatever she had been—the darkness had absorbed her. It saw me, what I was. It wanted me."

Alister let out a breath. "Good lord, Eliot. What did you do?"

The doctor gave a rueful smile and glanced up from the floor. "Why, I ran, old friend. Without a second thought, I retreated in terror from my own offices, dashing off into the night with as little care for my possessions, records, or instruments of my office as if Hell itself were empty and all the devils there.

"I flew to the harbor, and at last in a place known only to a few devotees, I found obliteration. In that den, I sought to erase the memory of darkness by drowning it in golden draughts of laudanum. Despite these efforts, I was haunted by the visions of that night—the black and questing tendrils, my mindless rank desire, those two tiny silver pinpricks.

"I returned a day or so later, before Alice and Charles came back, certain I would find my office nothing but a looted shell. In this, thank God, I was mistaken. My consultation-room was quite as I had left it. Only the wick of the lamp revealed it had been no dream. When I'd lit it, I'd drawn the wick far up to lend illumination. I found it now turned down, as if in leaving, the woman had thoughtfully lowered it and then put out the light."

"And afterward?" asked someone. "What happened?"

The doctor regarded the dying coals. "Why, from that day forth... I saw her everywhere. In the shadows of a doorway. Among the faces of a crowd. Beneath a wet, black umbrella in the rain. Lingering at the bottom of Johnny Cake Hill. Framed by the upper window of a sea captain's mansion. Pacing in the small upper room they call a widow's walk."

"Was it a delusion?" Alister asked quietly.

"A delusion?" The doctor considered. "Perhaps. Or not." He thought some more. "I began to awake each night in blank and unreasoning terror. This proved, of course, a deep disruption to my marriage. First, Alice moved out of our chamber, and then out of our house altogether, taking Charles with her to her mother's. I did not blame the woman in the least. As for myself, I left New Bedford before three months had passed, never to return."

He sighed. "From there, I departed to the globe's four corners. To Alaska. Paris. Istanbul. Nepal. And in my journeys, gazing on the sea, the peaks, the ice, I faced the truth about the man I wished to be. The man I was. And finally, the man I came to love.

"Over that time," said Dr. Eliot, "I spied the woman less each passing year. The last occasion—well, almost the last—occurred in the city of Malaga, in southern Spain. At the end of a busy market street redolent with spices, I caught a flash of white. She paused for me at the top of the hill, her face concealed in that veil, red ribbon still wrapped round her neck, and raised a single hand as if in greeting."

The doctor's face grew reflective. "Does it seem odd to say this? I sensed an odd sort of kinship with her then. In that market of spices, I understood that I had come to miss her. Now she appeared. Tears came to my eyes, and I wept as you might weep in seeing your first love after decades, years melting away like insubstantial clouds. I suppose in a way that is what she'd been. The first love of my life," he said, nodding at Eliza. "But not the last. No, though I still cannot bring myself to speak his name, not the last. But he is gone. Gone from me this year, after all this time."

The doctor paused. "You realize, I have often reflected upon that moment before I fled my office, thinking of that moment when the tendrils of that swirling darkness reached for me. I understood in that moment that the darkness would peel my face from my skull like an orange. And worse yet," he admitted with a shuddering breath, "beneath it all, what would there really be? Below this unassuming face," he said, gesturing at his receding chin and patchy beard, "I feared that I was hollow. No," he amended. "I *knew* it."

The company around the fire looked at him in silence. Alister stared down at his brandy, Eliza at the man's shoes she wore with such élan.

"It was this fear that woke me from my sleep. Not the memory of her face, but the fear that I myself had none… and never had. Just a mask of flesh above a hollow void. I have spent a lifetime," the doctor said at last, "in facing myself."

With a slight groan, he put aside his glass, then leaned upon his cane and rose. At this, the footman brought a heavy wool coat and draped it over Dr. Eliot's shoulders. Around his neck, the man wrapped a long silk scarf of white, and those who had heard the tale shuddered, thinking of the veil.

"But where will you go now, Eliot?" Alister asked, rising from his chair. "Surely you shall return soon?"

The doctor sighed. "No, my friend. I think this is the last." Straightening his hat upon his head, he said, "I have seen her again, you see. Tonight. She waits for me beyond the hill, and I will walk with her. And if she turns to kiss me—well." He touched Alister's shoulders with a warm and steady hand. "Goodbye, old man. By now, I do not fear the dark. After all, it is… so very beautiful."

R.A. BUSBY : An award-winning literature teacher and die-hard horror fan, R. A. Busby is also the author of "Bits" (Short Sharp Shocks #45), "Street View" (Collective Realms #2), "Not the Man I Married" (Black Petals #93), "Holes" (Graveyard Smash, Women of Horror Anthology, Vol. 2), "Cactusland" (34 Orchard #2), and "Kiss" (Kandisha Press). "I was always instructed to write about what I know," she states, "and I know what scares me." In her spare time, R.A. Busby watches cheesy Gothic movies and goes running in the desert with her dog.

The Last Thread
Paula R.C. Readman

"Hold on, old girl! You've brought me this far," the sole occupant of the ailing spacecraft pleaded with its onboard computer. "You've got me out of so many scrapes befor, please don't let me down this time!" Fulton studied a chart as it flicked off and on. He slammed his fist down as the chart vanished from the screen again. The sound echoed around him as the lights danced, threatening to plunge the control deck into darkness.

"No, girl, you can't do this to me."

On another screen, a speck raced towards him. He shuddered at the thought of the space pirates keeping their promise. Why hadn't he kept his mouth shut and just accepted the loss of his money?

His money. Fulton chuckled. It wasn't his to lose. Of course, gambling had always been his weakness. Pride, that's all it was. The pirates weren't known for compassion. Bruised pride caused a lot of unnecessary bloodshed. He for one didn't want to see his spilt. He banged the control panel again. As the screen lit up, he sideswiped it as fast as he could and held his breath.

The sudden change of direction caused his surroundings to shudder and creak as the craft answered his demands. "Well, Girl, you can't outrun them, but maybe there's a better option."

On another screen, Fulton saw a swirling mass of debris orbiting a small, uncharted planet. "Hold tight," he muttered and swerved between the two carcasses of wrecked cargo carriers. With care, he steered his much smaller craft through a gaping hole in the side of the ghost ship. "Let's hope they lose our signal. To them, I'll be just part of the detritus."

Fulton turned on searchlights and began to manoeuvre between the structural frameworks of the wreck. He had just cleared it and was heading into deeper space when a bright red light flashed on his screen followed by a series of bleeps.

"Hello. Someone needs help?" The screen began to flicker again. "Don't do that."

Fulton scanned the charts trying to locate the area the distress signal came from. "We're in luck, it's reachable."

The screen flickered as he altered course. "Hang on, girl," Fulton cursed as the ship shuddered. His gambling had robbed him of everything, apart from this loveable old rust bucket. His laughter echoed around him. For a moment, he wondered if the onboard computer was laughing with him, or at his stupidity.

The distress signal flashed across the screen again. "Maybe this is my chance to get you fixed by helping another."

The *Complex Six* space station, in the outer belt, had once belonged to an old mining company, long since disbanded. Fulton's choice to join the pirates on their own turf had been ridiculous. Their laughter and free-flowing drinks hadn't convinced him of their camaraderie, even as he joined them at the card table. The odds were stacked against him, his refusal to join their band seen as an insult. With the few hundred josses, he'd pick-pocketed off their leader, Captain Zander, he felt he might be able to bluff his way out of the awkward situation.

He should've left as soon as the purse was in his pocket, but the strong arm of Zander's second in command, Bellamy, had blocked his way. A flash of tombstone decaying teeth and the graveyard stench in his face left him no choice but to remain.

As he turned the cards, the pirates' women, valued for their sweetness and beauty, watched on. Kept in an artificial perfumed garden where piped music and alcohol flowed, the women lured in the tired men. Wise to their game, Fulton watched his drink carefully.

As the men slept in an alcoholic stupor, they were robbed of more than just their money. Fulton had heard from unfortunate men whose lives were spared only to find out important body parts were missing. It wasn't as though you could track down your missing lung or kidney on the black market and have it replaced. Fulton was fond of his internal parts and shuddered at the thought of covering his debt with the sale of them so some rich old guy could live past his sell-by-date.

Unsure whether he had been quick enough when side-swiping the controls, he glanced at the other screen. The telltale flickering blip told him the pirates' ship was still tracking him.

"Come on, old girl. You've got it in you." He checked the speed of his ship. A burst of light erupted on the screen, grabbing his attention. Fulton's fingers danced across his touchpad as he punched in the location manually. Old technology it may be, but if it saved his arse, he didn't care. He held his breath and waited for the spacecraft to react to the new coordinates. It shuddered, forcing him to grab the arms of his seat. "No, don't die on me now! Damn you!"

Finally, the pull of the planet took control. The descent became quicker once they slipped into the planet's orbit. Fulton strapped himself into his seat just as the emergency oxygen mask dropped into place. He hoped there was enough power to supply him with what he needed.

"I shouldn't have wasted my last josses on gambling, but on servicing you, old girl," He fitted the mask into place, closed his eyes, and breathed in deeply. The control deck darkened as the ship raced towards the planet's surface.

* * * *

On the planet, an elderly woman moved unsteadily. The corridors echoed to the sound of her shuffling feet, while all around an alarm boomed. She leant heavily against the metal walls for support. The iciness of the unheated corridor bit into her bare paper-thin arms. Her white matted hair hung down her back and brushed against the dusty floor. Fearing she would trip in her haste, she scooped up the hem of the ragged skirt that hung off her slight body.

On reaching the end of the corridor, she climbed some steps and opened a door. With thin, gnarled fingers, she tore at the gossamer covering that blocked her way and took her seat in front of the control panel. She leant forward and squinted at the flashing screens until she located the one she wanted. She swiped and a burst of static white noise filled the room as the main screen opened. An image of an old spacecraft appeared. As it entered the atmosphere, it flashed silver against the darkness of space.

The old woman placed two fingers on the side of her neck. She rubbed a raw patch on her throat, her nails gouging out the dry flesh. After a second, she opened and closed her mouth rapidly, gulping in stale air before croaking out, "Hello…" The word echoed around her, seeming alien to her ears. She coughed and tried again, swallowing a couple of times. "Hello. This is Skylar Harrap of Ganymede." She pronounced the words carefully.

"How can I help you, Skylar?" A distant voice filled the void.

She touched her neck again. A stinging pain shot through her fingers. On lowering her hand, she glanced down as she swiped the control panel to answer. A trickle of bright blood ran down her finger and dripped onto the panel. As the blood pooled, specks of silver light gathered around them. In a shimmering dance, the lights turned from silver to a pulsating red as the blood disappeared. Skylar fondled her neck more, pushing her long fingernails into the blistering skin causing it to rupture. She lifted her head and twisted it side to side as her dry skin rippled and parted. She shed the remainder of her clothes along with her old skin. The dancing lights brushed against her fresh new flesh and once again, she was reborn.

"Skylar?" The distant voice crackled as though edged with fear, or was it panic she wondered not able to recall the last time she had spoken to another human.

"Skylar?" Fulton banged the screen. Had he really heard a woman's voice? The connection crackled as he tapped another screen. Suddenly there was visual contact as the horizon opened up to him. "My Moons, it's a bloody graveyard."

The onboard cameras captured a swirling hell's twister that obscured every type of spacecraft that littered the planet's surface. From what Fulton could make out, there were small scouting crafts, as well as larger explorational crafts of every make. He manoeuvred his scout craft between the old ships, eyeing them as he went. One of the ships alone would contain enough precious metals to set him up in a new venture. Perhaps Skylar would reward his help by granting him permission to strip those abandoned crafts.

"Don't worry old girl; I'll always be loyal to you." Fulton tapped the control panel as he cleared two large container ships.

"My Moons, what in hell's name is that!" Before him, a huge sparkling dome rose out of the parched landscape, clouds of swirling dust rippling and churning beyond it. Occasionally, they parted to reveal more ships, and what appeared to be ruined buildings. "It makes you wonder why there's so many abandoned crafts."

Skylar watched as the scout ship travelled towards her, reminding her of the crafts that had answered her call on previous occasions. No longer did she expect to escape her fate, an endless cycle of death and rebirth.

Once the craft had docked, a lifting mechanism moved it aside to make room for the next vehicle to enter. An oxygen dome covered the craft allowing its occupants to enter a maze of well-lit corridors that encircled the main tower of Agrona.

Skylar waited until the dome had sealed the craft before leaving the control room. From experience, she knew the occupants would check the quality of the air before leaving the spacecraft. This allowed her plenty of time to prepare herself for their endless questions. She stretched her back and flexed her long, straight fingers. With dancing fingertips, Skylar set the automated air cleansing equipment into action, ready to receive her new guest. Gathering up her tatty gown, she disposed of it, before heading to her quarters to refresh herself and slip on a new dress.

"Oh, my stars, what's happening, girl?" Fulton asked, knowing that no one would answer him. On touchdown in the empty bay, he switched on an external camera as a clear dome engulfed the length of his vehicle. He checked the oxygen level, and found it was breathable, but decided not to take any chances. He slipped a portable mask and canister into the deep side pocket on the leg of his trousers.

As the door closed behind him, Fulton inhaled. The air, though a little stale, was breathable, but he could also detect an unfamiliar odour. "Now let's see where this takes us, girl." He addressed his onboard computer, even though it had been months since she was last able to communicate with him. He looked longingly at the other ships stacked around him. Like the graveyard outside, there were plenty of spare parts available, if only he had time to search for what he needed. He set off down the corridor as a door slid shut behind him. His footsteps echoed along the seemingly endless corridor. As the unfamiliar smell became almost overwhelming, Fulton rounded a corner.

"By the stars, how's this possible?"

From a viewing platform, he stood looking across a lush green valley, filled with trees, running water, birds chattering, butterflies, humming insects, and bees. Among the lush vegetation, animals grazed, all under an artificial sun.

"It does seem amazing, doesn't it?" A softly spoken voice answered him.

"Skylar?" Fulton wasn't sure what he was expecting, but an angel wasn't on the top of his list. The light behind her head created a halo out of her white hair. As she stepped towards him with her hand outstretched, her floor-length gown shimmered. The skin about her temples was delicately smooth as a child's skin, but something in her mannerism showed she was much older. "Thank you for coming… to my rescue…"

Fulton nodded, smiled, but didn't reach for her hand. Too many years roaming the galaxies had taught him to be cautious. "I'm Josh Fulton. Most call me Fulton. How can I help?"

"It's difficult to explain, but first let me show you around. Afterwards, you might have a better understanding of my situation." She let her smile widen just a little.

"You live here alone?"

"Yes, I'm the last one left." She lowered her eyes.

"It's a real ship's graveyard." Fulton gestured over his shoulder. "Surely you haven't always been alone. What of the crafts gathering dust?"

Skylar nibbled at her bottom lip and her gaze shifted. She placed a hand on the window. Fulton studied it. The paleness of her skin showed a lack of sunlight as her veins pulsated beneath. His mother had nagged him constantly about the importance of visiting the sunrooms whenever he had the opportunity. Lack of sunshine causes all sorts of health issues, so why didn't she enjoy the sunlight she had, he wondered. The blue of her sad eyes matched the colour of her dress. Its high collar hid the softness of her neck. Fulton focused on her slightly parted lips and waited.

"My parents were born here…" The sound of her voice jarred him out of his thoughts.

"Were they… How long have you been on your own?"

"I'm not sure. As you can see most of the building is empty. Come, let me show you my quarters. This way."

Fulton followed her down an adjacent corridor. The perfumed air bothered him, reminding him too much of the pirates. He ignored the thoughts racing through his head at the sight of Skylar's swaying hips. Her hair, with the quality of spun silk, brushed the floor, clearing the dust away.

"Dust," Fulton whispered the word. *Dust. No footprints. They were the only ones to walk this way in some time.*

The corridor opened out onto an enclosed bridge. On one side, a vast wasteland stretched on forever. Dust swirling around skeletons of ships, their doors gaping like open mouths in silent screams. On the other side, under a glass dome with an artificial sun, a surreal lush green landscape seemed endless. Fulton pressed his hand against the glass and found it felt warm. He tried to imagine walking on the grass, smelling the flowers and the feeling of sunlight on his skin. After years spent in the cold brutality of space, spending time walking among plants and flowers would be heavenly.

Skylar swung round. "It's very beautiful, isn't it?"

"Is it real?"

"Very much so." She smiled, but her face quickly grew cold. "Once the planet supported a wide variety of life, but this is all that remains now. I'm a sort of custodian."

There was an ageless beauty to her, Fulton thought, with her high cheekbones and thin lips. Her eyes windowless, devoid of any genuine emotion or life, reminding him of the soulless eyes of the women the pirates valued. Perhaps loneliness had robbed her of her spirit.

"Later, I'll take you out there…" She muttered, not really addressing him.

"I've only ever seen grass and trees in pictures. I bet you're out there all the time." Fulton turned and found Skylar heading down a corridor.

"Is it like a giant greenhouse?" He asked, hurrying to catch her up.

"Yes, in a way. Those who designed it programmed in daytime and night along with the season and weather cycles too."

A door hissed opened in front of them and they stepped into a large open-plan space. Fulton had expected to see Skylar's personal belongings but instead, it was as cold and as impersonal as space itself. His sleeping compartment was cluttered on board his craft, full of things to remind him where he came from. Skylar glided across the room and tapped on a screen. A panel opened.

"Would you like a drink?" she asked.

"Hmm… yes, water if you have it." Fulton kept a half-eye on her. There wasn't anywhere to prepare food, no propagators to grow fresh produce. This was something his mother had taught him to do onboard the starship where he was born.

"Just water," she repeated while tapping the screen.

Fulton's reflection smiled back at him as he watched the birds flittering among the branches of a massive tree, just beyond the window. He wondered what type of fruit hung from it. Too large to be apples, he decided, as the tree dominated the dome. He tried to remember the last time he'd tasted one. His mother talked about orchards, full of apple trees on a green and blue planet, but no one knew what had become of it or whether this mythological place had even existed. Fulton dropped into a seat facing a window. A thin layer of dust lifted causing him to cough.

"Here you are. This might help." Skylar held out a glass.

"Oh, thank you." He cradled the glass in his hands. His mind raced. If Skylar was having supplies brought in, why send out a distress signal? "What's the problem you need my help with?"

"The sealant here," she pointed to the window frame. "It's disintegrating. The dust is getting in. If the glass doesn't hold the raging storms out everything within the dome will die."

Fulton studied the shimmering sealant. It showed no signs that it was disintegrating. He reached to touch it, but drew back as it rippled and undulated, lifting towards his fingertips as though alive. "Well, I might just have something on board my craft that you could use as a temporary repair." He sprang to his feet.

"Okay, we'll give it a go." Skylar pointed to his drink, "Your water, you haven't touched it."

"What did your parents use?" Fulton glanced at the sealant. "Do you have any left?"

"I'm not sure." A look of puzzlement crossed her brow. He smiled, unsure whether she was trying to read his mind, or his facial expressions.

"Is there a storeroom, or a workshop they used?"

"Yes, an old storeroom." She looked towards the glass of water. "I've never thought about checking in there."

"Let's have a look." Fulton headed to the door. "I'm sure the builders of this vast complex must have foreseen this situation."

On leaving Skylar's apartment, they descended into the heart of the building. Their footfalls echoed back at them. After passing numerous unmarked doors, Skylar finally opened one.

"I think this is a storeroom." She stepped back to allow Fulton to peer into the room. Rows of shelving filled the space. Overhead lights flickered, creating ghostly shadows among a maze of freestanding units.

"This looks promising even with the bad lighting." He pulled out a torch from his breast pocket. Its beam lit up the darkness as he stepped into the vast space. "Are you coming in too?"

Skylar shook her head. "I'll wait here. You know what to look for better than I."

"Okay. Haven't you been here before?"

"No. My father saw to everything. I'm sure you'll find what you need." Skylar stepped back from the doorway.

Fulton shivered. He cast the torchlight about as the lights overhead flickered. Plastic containers lined shelves from floor to ceiling. Everything was clearly labelled. Some containers held plumbing parts, others electrical equipment, some a few parts for outdated computers.

"Hello, what do we have here?" Fulton pulled a container down. A cloud of dust lifted, causing another coughing fit. He wiped at his face.

"Are you okay?" Skylar's concerned voice echoed from the doorway

"Yes, I'm fine," he called while wiping some sticky cobwebs from his fingers. Finally, he ran his hands down his trousers. "I might've found something."

Within the container, the torch beam picked out several tiny boxes. Fulton read the numbers off them. "What a great find, just the component I wanted." He slipped three of them into his trouser pocket. Then he hesitated and added one into his breast pocket.

After replacing the container, he moved further into the darkness. At the far end of the room, his torch beam passed over some tools that hung from hooks. Alongside these was a collection of old space suits, covered in a fine mesh.

Fulton stepped closer to check to see if the suits had their owner's names across the front of them. His mind tried to process the image before him. *Surely it can't be*? Something flashed silver in the shadows as the lights overhead flickered. He jumped back, finally processing what he was looking at. Hollow sockets met his stare, while gaping mouths held sets of white teeth highlighted in the flashing lights.

Fulton turned away only to find himself caught by a pair of withered arms. He twisted, trying to free himself, and fell forwards. Crashing towards the floor, he put out his hands to save himself. They made contact with something hard that buckled and cracked under his weight. As his hand disappeared into the chest cavity of a dead man, Fulton found he was staring nose-close into a shrunken face and a pair of sightless eyes. He pulled himself free and crawled to where the torch had rolled. As he snatched up the torch, its beam up-lighted that what he'd thought to be spacesuits were actually a row of mummified bodies hanging on silver threads.

"What in the name of Jupiter caused their deaths?" Fulton was wondering when a wailing alarm shattered his thoughts. He dashed for the door, thanking the moons that Skylar hadn't entered. Bursting out into the corridor, he caught sight of her rushing up the stairs, her blue dress billowing out behind her. "What is it?" he called.

"Another incoming craft," she said.

"What! You mean you didn't turn the distress beacon off?" Fulton asked as he caught up with her on the final landing and followed her into the control room. On the screen, the pirate's ship was docking. "Holy Moons!"

"You know who they are?" She eyed him carefully.

"Unfortunately, yes. They are hunting me."

"Who are they?"

"Pirates, and scavengers, together, with the gypsies, they scour the galaxies looking for abandoned space crafts and space stations to strip anything of value from them. These spaceships you have here are full of precious metals. I'm so… "

"I must welcome my guests as I welcomed you," Skylar cut him off.

He hung back. On the screen, he watched as Skylar hurried along the corridors to the viewing platform where he had met her. He flicked the screen to the next camera and watched as six pirates disembarked. Their excitement was unmistakable as they took in their surroundings. Fulton tapped his trouser pocket. He could just leave. The part he had stolen would make his ship faster and far more reliable. He turned towards the door, deciding once the pirates were busy with Skylar he could slip around them, and be gone. He looked back at the screen one last time. Skylar stood in the shadows, watching them, waiting for the right moment to make her presence known.

Had she done the same with him? Fulton guessed. "Oh, my moons! She's so unprepared for what they will do to her." Fulton slammed his fist down. He couldn't just leave her to whatever fate they dished out.

He dashed along the corridors, the sound of his boots echoing. Images of the pirates towering over Skylar while her thin bones snapped under their weight filled his mind. Her beautiful pale face bruised and battered while they robbed the dome. Too many tales of murder followed in their wake as the scavengers crossed the galaxies. *Death Walking,* Fulton always thought of them. As he burst around the corner, he froze. Skylar was on her knees, her arm forced up her back as Zander stood over her, his nails digging into her pale skin.

"You're a lively one," he said as the other pirates stood laughing.

"Let her go!" Fulton stepped out of the shadows and held his hands out to show he carried no weapons.

"Well, look what the moons have brought us, lads. So, the coward wants to be a hero now. Where's my money?"

"Let her go. I'll show you."

Zander threw his head back, his laughter echoed around them. "Chasing you was worth it, Fulton. The old hell of a graveyard out there? Plenty of rich pickings and fresh food. What more could we want?" Zander yanked Skylar's arm further up her back. "Open it!"

"Please leave…" A sob escaped her thin lips.

"Let her go!" Fulton charged the pirate captain and threw a punch, but Zander was quicker. A stinging backhand sent Fulton flying. He slid across the floor. The oxygen canister dug into his leg until he came to a neck-breaking halt crashing into the glass wall. On lifting his head, he wiped blood from his lips, smearing his cheek.

Skylar's eyes widened as tears gathered in her hollow eyes. She pulled a metal card from the folds of her skirt. "Here, you'll want this."

Zander let her arm go, and pointed to the glass wall. "Open it!"

She rose, crossed to the wall, and pushed the card into a narrow slit. A panel slid back and suddenly the corridor was full with an array of birdsongs and sweetly perfumed air. Fulton pulled himself up and saw Skylar nod in his direction, as if to let him know she was okay. He noticed her face seemed more lined, her eyes sunken.

Zander pushed Skylar aside. "Watch them, Bellamy."

"Aye, Captain," Bellamy grabbed Fulton's arm, while another pirate grabbed Skylar's, and together they were frog-marched into the dome. The pirates slashed at the vegetation with their swords, scattering flower heads and butterflies about them. Soon, they forgot about Skylar and Fulton. Like possessed demons, they dashed around, swords in hand chasing rabbits and sheep.

"We've got to stop them," Fulton said reaching for a fallen branch.

"Leave. Go now." She blocked his way.

"I can't just leave you."

"Go!"

"Get these fuckers off me," Zander cried. He stood under the massive tree, his sword arm caught by thin threads that shone in the artificial sunlight. Bellamy and the other pirates rushed to his aid. They slashed at the threads that bound his sword arm. Zander's sword dropped with his hand still attached as the thread sliced through his wrist. As fast as the pirates cut the threads, others replaced it. Fulton narrowed his eyes, but he couldn't see where the threads were coming from. An icy cold touch on his arm shocked him into life. He turned.

"You must leave now before it is too late." Her voice, thin and breathy

"Come with me."

"I cannot." She clawed at her collar, tearing into her skin. She lifted her eyes to meet his. Silver tears edged her red eyes. "Go now." Her voice cracked.

A blood-curdling scream made Fulton turn again. A rainbow of colourful birds took flight as thousands of fine silk threads spiralled down from the branches and wrapped themselves around the pirates. With high-speed jerks, their clothes were torn from their bodies until they hung like naked marionettes. Their blood-soaked clothes and weapons, with their hands still attached, lay scattered at their feet.

"Captain," Bellamy croaked as his pallid body hung bleeding. "What's happening?"

Zander lifted his bloody head; his thick hair lay at his feet, ripped clear off his scalp. Fixing his black eyes on Fulton, he snarled through gritted teeth, "I will kill you slowly." He pulled at his bindings, the silks cutting into his wrists and ankles as he struggled to free himself.

Fulton retreated towards the door. The pirates twisted in their restraints, all eyes on him. They grunted as they tried to free themselves. Blood trickled down their arms, over their bodies, and down their legs, pooling at their feet. A low hum caught Fulton's attention and he looked up.

Between the branches of the tree, a silvery light flickered. He realised what he had thought was fruit was actually hundreds of cocoons hanging in the tree. The light descended. It hovered over the pirates' heads. They stopped struggling and looked up.

"What is it, Captain? Bellamy asked.

"Help us, Fulton," Zander shouted. "I'll spare your life, Lad."

Then without a sound, the light fractured, bursting into thousands of tiny lights that floated down onto the pirates. The dancing lights swarmed over them like flies feeding on a rotting corpse. They started screaming while their bodies twitched and jerked. The tiny pin-pricks of silver pulsated red as they crisscrossed the pirate's bodies at great speed. One by one, the pirate's faces became nothing more than empty eye sockets and gaping mouths in shrunken faces. In seconds, the lights had cocooned them in silk and with a jerk, they disappeared one by one up into the branches of the huge tree.

"Skylar, come with me." Fulton turned to the woman. Her face held no expression as her forehead cracked and crumbled, releasing silver dancing lights. He moved backwards without taking his eyes off her. A silver light burst from her neck as her body twisted. She flung her arms out as silver threads burst out of her wrists. "I'm the thread…" Skylar's voice cracked as her face crumbled to dust. "…that holds this world together."

Fulton didn't need asking again as he dashed on board his craft. As the door closed, he reached into his pocket. "No!" Two of the boxes were crushed. The third was repairable, but there was no time. He patted his breast pocket. The last one. He tore off the wrapper and pushed the component home. The spacecraft shook as the panel lit up.

"Where to Josh?" A light, positive voice filled the control deck.

"Welcome back, Girl!"

"Have I been away?"

"I'll explain later, but we need to leave now."

"I do detect a strange phenomenon on the planet once known as Earth."

"Earth!" Fulton leant back in his seat and watched as strands of silver encased the dome. As Girl took them out of the planet's orbit, he realised where all the crews from the abandoned ships had gone. They had become the silk that bound the dome together in a last-ditch attempt to save the planet.

PAULA R.C. READMAN is married, has a son, and lives in Essex, England, with two cats. After leaving school with no qualifications, she spent her working life mainly in low-paying jobs. In 1998, with no understanding of English grammar, she decided to beat her dyslexia, by setting herself a challenge to become a published author.

She taught herself 'How to Write' from books her husband purchased from eBay. After making the 250th purchase, Russell told her 'just to get on with the writing'. Since 2010 she has mainly been published in anthologies in Britain, Australia, and America and won several writing competitions. In 2020 she had her first crime novella **The Funeral Birds** published by Demain Publishing, a single collection of short stories **Days Pass Like A Shadow** published by Bridge House Publishing. Her first crime novel **Stone Angels** was published by Darkstroke.

Blog: https://paularcreadmanauthor.blog

THE LETTER
Lydia Prime

~~~

Emily couldn't have been more thrilled; she was thirty-seven weeks into her pregnancy and her excitement oozed from every pore. She daydreamed about motherhood with a permanent smile plastered across her face, delightfully imagining who her son might someday become. She stood in his lime-green nursery struggling to get the elephant mobile to play its gentle lullaby. Aggravated by the fuzzy pastel pachyderms and their stubborn unworkable mechanisms, she tossed the mobile to the far side of the crib. Her husband could figure it out when he got home. She'd had enough.

Scanning the room, Emily inspected every nook and cranny. Everything had to be spotless—immaculate for her little man's arrival. She kept a mental inventory of each stuffed animal and starter book she'd purchased. Daily, she would count and recount all the perfectly-folded baby clothes stacked up near the assorted wipes, powders, and diapers. She sighed happily at the framed sonogram photo on the wall, flooded with love for her tiny peanut. Her eyes traveled to the sponge-painted wood blocks strategically staggered beneath to spell out 'Jacob.' Satisfied by the arrangement, Emily strode to the rocking chair and carefully lowered herself in.

"You better start getting ready." She gently rubbed her belly. The baby kicked against her palm and she giggled and rocked back and forth, humming a little song. He kicked again, somewhat harder this time. Emily winced— maybe he could tell she was tone-deaf. Emily moved her hand up and down, lightly pressing on her tummy. Her touch seemed to settle the baby; her organs were thankful for the break.

"How about a story, a snack, and a nap? What do you think, Jacob?" She stretched her arm down the side of the chair into the overstuffed wicker basket, withdrawing one of the recommended books from her online mommy group.

"No monsters, or spiders, or slippery snakes! No hamsters, no geese, no giraffes in this place!" Emphasizing each rhyme as if her life depended on it, she continued, "none of those *weird* little things in my town! If you don't like it you can-"

The melodic tones of the doorbell cut off their story. Emily jumped. She closed the book and drummed her fingers against the arm of the chair. "I wasn't expecting anyone today, how about you, Jacob?" She asked, looking down at her bump. The baby was still, but Emily snickered at her joke anyhow. The bell chimed again, and she hoisted herself up, groaning all the while. Her balance not being what it used to be, she placed one hand on the crib, and the other on the small of her back. Once Emily felt steady, she began her long waddle to the front door. Several more dings sounded for the third time. "I'm coming!" She shouted, hoping that would deter whoever it was from ringing again.

The door was heavy mahogany that her husband had painted brick red when they moved in. She popped up on her tippy-toes, closed one eye, and tried to get a look at who was on the other side through the frosted half-moon window. Oddly, there was no one to be seen.

Maybe I took too long? She waddled to the living room window, moved the blinds, and tried to look out over the porch. Confused by the abandonment of someone so persistent, she wrinkled her nose and shrugged *Must've been some missionaries or maybe a couple of particularly impatient girl scouts. Cookies would be nice though.* Her mouth watered at the thought. *There's some pickles and sugar cookies in the kitchen* She toyed with possible food combinations as she turned toward the goodies. She took two steps away and the bell rang again. Annoyed, she craned her neck to look over her shoulder, muscles and tendons stretched to their limits.

Emily narrowed her eyes at the door as the bell chimed twice more. Tiptoeing to the window, she peered out, but was stunned to find no one was there. *The world's fastest Ding-Dong-Ditch players need to cut it out,* she thought as she walked to the door and unlocked the deadbolt. Leaving the chain in its cradle, Emily twisted the brass doorknob, opening the door just a crack.

SLINK.

Unable to see anything, she heard the sound of thick paper slide down the length of the doorjamb, clumsily landing on the welcome mat. It'd been months since she was able to see her own feet, so there was no chance she'd be seeing what it was without opening the door further. Taking into account the bizarreness of the invisible delivery person, she huffed and dismissed it as nothing more than some local take out menu, or perhaps a pamphlet for whomever the lord and savior was this week. Emily quickly shut the door and replaced the locks.

The bell's deep tones sounded rapidly. Her heart pounded in her chest. Emily undid the locks again. This time she included the chain and wrenched the door open. Her anger dissolved upon seeing a hefty black envelope. The size of a greeting card, it obscured the image on her carefully-chosen welcome mat. Emily picked it up and looked around—no mail trucks or delivery vans were visible on the street. Knees creaking, she forced herself upright, mesmerized by the peculiar parcel. She bit the corner of her mouth, inspecting the piece as she gently closed the door.

Lower back pain shot down her legs. Instinctively she tensed up, causing her to bite through her inner cheek. Copper liquid pooled around her tongue before dribbling past her lips, down her chin, and onto the item she'd retrieved. "Shit!" She stopped in her tracks, cupped her aching cheek. Additional splashes of blood smeared across the back of the envelope; Emily failed to notice as the paper absorbed each droplet with a barely audible '*suuuck!*' The twinge in her back fought to overrule the sensation in her mouth. Mounting discomfort made the corner loveseat in the living room seem mighty inviting. She sucked on the cut in her mouth as she staggered through the room.

Emily made herself comfortable in the oversized chair and continued examining the envelope. It was much denser than typical junk mail and had an abnormally opulent aspect to it. She tapped the lamp that sat on the end table.

Rough fissures coalesced on the covering while a low scratching permeated her ears. Emily watched in disbelief as her unborn son's name materialized in a silver script from out of nowhere. Not sure what to make of this odd delivery, she presumed it to be some novelty item a friend sent their way. She got her phone from her pocket and shot several photos. Hastily, she forwarded the images to the group chat she had with some friends, as well as one with her family. The returned messages pinged back in no time. Each bubble contained more questions; not one person admitted to sending the strange little thing or even knowing anything about it.

Emily's older sister was first to notice the writing on the back of the cardstock. She zoomed in and sent a screenshot of the blurry words. Emily's focus quickly returned to the ever-changing item in her hands. She breathed deeply, shaking as she flipped it over. Tiny compact script—similar to what was on the front—emerged. She brought the envelope close to her face. The writing explicitly stated that the contents were for Jacob, and Jacob only. Emily scrunched her nose. *Why would some random person send my baby a letter?*

More words formed beneath the surface of the paper. Eyes wide, she watched as thick powder-blue instructions popped up. They rather bluntly elaborated that Jacob's parents were not to look until it was *'time.'*

What the actual fuck? Emily's frustration level matched that of the envelope's cryptic evasive notes. She tried to take more pictures, but one after the other, they came out blurry. *Am I losing my mind?* She dropped the letter on the table, rubbed her eyes, and let out an exasperated sigh. She massaged her temples with minimal pressure and tried to think.

"I must be going crazy," she mumbled, still eying the freaky piece of mail. *Someone I know had to have done this. Why would they lie, or not tell me the truth? Maybe it's just a prank.*

Emily tongued the cut in her mouth, the sting reminding her that this *was* real. She drummed her fingers against the newly-embossed paper. "Do you mind if we take a peek a bit early, Jacob?" She took the kidney shot as his way of saying, 'Do it.'

"Alrighty then." She began to peel the flap but found it more challenging than she'd anticipated. Emily ripped off the left side with her teeth after deciding she wasn't going to get in through the top. She held it eye level, squeezing the sides to open up a dimly-lit glimpse. Frowning, she couldn't make out anything that way; she was going to have to pull out whatever was in there.

As she turned the covering over, slime oozed onto the table. Emily gasped. The smell the strange violet goo gave off was enough to make her gag. Almost immediately, the odor dissipated, or maybe she went nose-blind to it. Either way, she was determined to follow through. She slid her index finger and thumb inside and felt a tacky squish as she removed the contents. Emily's blood ran cold—already uneasy about whatever this was—touching it made it so much worse. Her face contorted with a mix of disgust and anxiety.

It was an aluminum sheet, covered by a gunky licorice-colored substance. Moist soot was caked on anywhere the grotesque sludge wasn't clumped over. That familiar putrid stench wafted through the air. Emily kept going. She questioned why someone would send something so horrible to a baby. Trying to brush off the filth with her sleeve appeared to be a fruitless effort. The coated metal swirled; Emily's eyes glazed over.

Shrill cacophonous shrieks erupted from the document in her hand. Time was unfolding in her mind. She heard and saw butchery that would make even the most seasoned veteran cry. The child in her tummy wriggled while his mommy's heart raced.

The grisly cries and brutal scenes she envisioned came to a grinding halt. Suddenly Emily was back in her calm, quiet living room, in her enormous squishy chair. She struggled to grasp what had just happened. Her baby seemed to be trying to rearrange her organs, as if he was trying to barricade himself inside her womb. Her vision was blurry and her heart felt like it could give a hummingbird a run for its money. Her right hand released the arm of the chair, her tendons sore and her knuckles cracked. She wiped away the sadness as it trailed down her face. Her left hand still firmly clutched the strange sheet of warping metal. Emily eyed it skeptically. The metallic sheath revealed a hidden letter:

Choices build the future, yes?
Then all must have a consequence.
Bearer of an evil mind—
Mother's punishment for child's crime.

"What is that supposed to mean?" Her mind felt fuzzy for a moment. She placed the letter and envelope on top of the table, "Whatever. Let's have some lunch, shall we?" Jacob's tiny foot (or fist!) thrust against her belly. "Guess you're hungry too, huh?" She smiled, and then wiggled up and out of the loveseat.

As she made her way to the kitchen, the lamp on the end table strobed, brightening with each flicker. Electric humming and clicking from the bulb grew ferociously before finally popping from the pressure. Shattered glass sprinkled the tabletop, the cream-colored lampshade resting lopsided around the floral accented base.

Tendrils of onyx and ruby smoke spiraled from beneath the thick paperboard. They moved wildly, twirling as they extended around the room. Burgundy light flashed brightly between the cracks of each window and door. The openings suddenly bubbled with amber putty. Several picture frames shattered, bursting a surplus of jagged shards around the floor of the living room. The television flashed on, and a man in a white cowboy hat chased after a man in black. He shouted something unintelligible and began firing his six-shooter.

All the commotion brought Emily charging into the living room. Her sudden panic led her to step directly onto the glassy mess. The bottoms of her socks tore into blood-soaked scraps of cotton. She fell to her knees and attempted to inspect the damage. Her stomach turned at the sight of tiny shards poking through her skin. "Ughhh!" She groaned, and used her ruined socks to force some broken bits away. The scent of burning wood pulled her attention towards the corner of the room; the end table by the loveseat was smoking. Emily gasped, scrambling to make her way toward the table. She rocked back and forth, then pushed herself up with help from the coffee table. On her feet, she could see the open envelope, its contents strewn about haphazardly. She had vague memories of checking it out, but couldn't quite grasp them.

Emily tried to back away. Glass crunched under every step; a high-pitched yelp escaped in tandem. Finally, at the doorway to the kitchen, she crashed into an invisible barrier. She howled and banged her fists against the unseen wall, each blow reverberating with a muted thud.

The inky slime that bathed the metalwork bubbled. Remnants left in the envelope gurgled. Seemingly self-aware, the syrupy mixture melted through the porous wood. Four scarlet clouds rose above blotches of ash, twisting together while yellow dust spewed from beneath the boiling varnish. The metal message shook violently, radiating a blistering cherry glow as it drifted towards the spinning smoke screen.

Already destroyed picture frames dropped from the walls, creating a thunderous crash that drew Emily's eyes away from the smoky swirl and sputtering ebon slime. She screamed and tears raced down her cheeks. The veiled barrier that stopped her escape continued to hold. Emily touched her stomach, her feet aching, her heart pounding. She could barely get a full breath. "What is happening?" she shouted, and leaned against the ghostly wall behind her.

Sand-speckled mud wormed away from the nearly liquified end table, collecting sparkling shards of glass in its wake. The foul blob appeared to be growing—pulsing. Thick veiny threads stretched up through the opaque haze. Her unborn baby was more active than ever; Emily's adrenaline spikes caused little Jacob to shift. His tiny body thrashed, jabbing her organs as he did. Both hands on her stomach, she tried to comfort him, his fists and feet visibly moving beneath her skin. Her whole body trembled as she slid down the hidden wall and hoped desperately for this to be the product of some bizarre pregnancy nightmare.

Brass instruments blared an upbeat tune, the repetitive western pounding through the speakers. Emily cupped her ears, blood trickling through her fingers. Credits rolled on the television as the cowboys and horses corralled jovially in the background.

The esoteric vortex situated in the center of her living room started to ossify. An enormous man-shaped silhouette began to form. Her baby's relentless flailing added to her indescribable dread. Emily tried to push herself through the barrier, but the action continually proved futile. Glassy splinters sliced her palms, her fingers—any exposed flesh was punctured by sparkling slivers. Pain pushed her over the edge; she wept as her body fought against the need to dry heave. The floor seemed to be spinning; jagged chips of transparent detritus shined from every surface. She focused back on the semi-formed being; its bright white eyes breaching through its unfathomably black guise.

Ripples of recall washed over her. Explosive bellows of people in pain, of those in fear—all flooded her brain at once. She shook her head, eyes shut tight. Jacob was tiring himself out, his movements calmer, less forceful. Emily hugged her belly lovingly. *This can't be real, this can't be real!*

"Oh, it's real alright. An actual bonafide warlord is presently growing in your rotten womb." Appalling words barked in an unfamiliar scratchy voice. "You despicable creature. Your innate failure to heed a basic warning has brought the judgment before its intended time." Hideous screeching erupted from the being in the center of the room. Emily inhaled sharply; she knew she had to look at it. She didn't possess the mental faculties needed to process who or *what* stood in her decimated living room.

Veritably inhuman, of that much she was certain. A teal-tinted aura traced the creature's jet-black complexion, its features seeming to fade in and out. Emily tried, but staring too long made her head throb. Needle-tipped fingers squirted lime green and bright orange acid. The venomous liquids scorched anything they landed on. Its hideous screeching sounded again. Emily realized that was its *laugh*. Her flight reflex instinctually devolved into a freeze.

Emily rubbed her stomach compulsively. Her shirt absorbed some of the blood from her still gushing palms. She felt cold; the room felt the way it often did outside the house just before a massive snowstorm. A boisterous slam came from her left. Her body jolted as if she'd been falling in a dream. Emily kept her head down, her breath misting in front of her. Every bone felt as if it was made of ice, and her tears abruptly hardened on her cheeks.

The beast growled, its serrated maw grinding as it snapped shut. Gnarled fangs protruded from top and bottom jaws, all coated with shiny brown mucus. Two additional sets of ascending eyes broke through its obsidian skin. Neon teal coloring filled the entirety of the six orbs, each partly obstructed by thin pastel stitching that laced meticulously through the lids. As more of its body stabilized, Emily shivered, still too frightened to raise her head. She stammered as she whispered, "P-please don't h-hurt my ba-b-by."

Again, echoed shrieking burst from the center of the room. It was laughing *at* her; it was laughing at her terror. The creature took a step towards her. She listened as the glass crunched beneath its weight. Her body stiffened; the fact that it hadn't acknowledged any discomfort caused Emily's heart to drop. Her breathing sped up. Larger puffs of frozen mist escaped.

"Stupid girl." Its voice was rough and booming. "I'm not *just* going to hurt your *baby*." It kicked the coffee table. "I'm going to obliterate you both."

It let out an ominous shriek. Emily was resigning herself to the unthinkable, but first, she needed to know why. She needed to know how this could be happening.

"How is it you *know* my son will grow to be such a terror for the world? *Why* would your message direct us to wait so long?"

The entity snarled; its finely tapered digits scraped the floor. On all fours, it leveled to meet her gaze. Emily's pulse thrummed rapidly. It pounded most noticeably through her hands and feet. The insurmountable tiny slashes stung and the frigid atmosphere of the room weren't doing her any favors either. She kept her eyes open, staring into the now cobalt hue that glowed between the cross-stitching. It smiled, or she thought it did—there was a peculiar curl in the corners of its serrated mouth.

"I know," the warmth of its breath thawed the icicles she'd cried, "because it was written. This was not his first cycle, but it will be his last."

Licking the side of her face with its pasty tongue, pus-filled sores burst against Emily's cheek, exploding into her eye. The caustic substance foamed over; heated pressure forced her inflamed eyeball to seep out of the socket and fuse with her steaming flesh. She tried to grab at the afflicted area. The creature kept her still. Surges of adrenaline caused Jacob to start moving within her abdomen. Emily wailed, salty tears burning her raw wound. Pleased with her reaction and the sight of her wiggling stomach, the monster's face split, displaying several rows of decayed teeth.

"Patience," its voice, hoarse and unnerving, spoke again, "*is* a virtue after all." Squeals of laughter slithered around the room. The monster's body jiggled and vibrated from the glee it was experiencing. Its aura illuminated the shadows as it shifted. The color had become a gradient of several shades spanning from navy to silver. Needlelike fingers plunged deep through the outer side of Emily's thighs. They clung to the muscle as it shredded the length of her legs. Her flayed limbs blistered and cracked; her throat was sore from continuously screaming. Blood flowed wildly from her gashes—so much blood loss. She took comfort knowing she'd pass out soon.

Bile dripped as the monster flicked its tongue. The droplets seared through the floor, exposing the basement. It grasped Emily by her bulging stomach, razor-sharp tips sliced her meat with ease.

It dug its face into her abdomen, chomping through the sinew, and devoured her intestines. It slurped and lapped up her finely-chilled blood. When she thought she couldn't take anymore, the creature stopped her from slipping into sweet unconsciousness—she would remain alert until the end.

Jacob's tiny legs wriggled against her exposed womb. The monster cackled in shrill somber notes, and then pressed its talons slowly through her exposed organs. It removed the premature child as if he was nothing more than a rabbit from a hat. Frost began to cover the blood-coated babe. Jacob wailed; his first breath rattling through his tiny lungs.

The demonic being examined the boy. Emily's son was delivered, and that thing slurped the blood from his limbs. Broken, bloodied, burning, all she could think about was her baby, and how empty she was.

Emily whimpered, unable to move but feeling everything. The monster snuggly squished its face back into her open thoracic cavity; its acidic saliva scorched her from the inside out. It plucked hunks of flesh from her torso, allowing the pieces to dangle while crimson juice splashed the walls. It prided itself while it snapped her bones, grating the joints together before yanking them apart. She could see her limbs, fingers, and toes; she marveled at the bits of skin; skeletal fragments mixed with shimmering glass. She turned her head toward the door, cursing herself for opening it that morning.

The doorknob began to turn, keys jingling behind the door. The entity's neck cracked as it turned toward the unexpected noise. It slinked away from the feast. Spindly fingers waved and glowed a brilliant violet. Emily's pleas for mercy went silent. The door's hinges creaked; their abysmal squeal the solitary noise in the home.

A man in a pinstripe suit was on the other side; he'd juggled his hat and briefcase to return the key to his pocket. Just as he stepped past the threshold, a flash of gold caught the demon's aquamarine eyes.

"Ems? Emmy?" he called as he placed his things in the closet. The man in the suit did a double-take as he turned to see the mess. His wife was in pieces around the room. He dropped to his knees, cursing all of creation, blubbering uncontrollably for his family: "EMILY!"

"Roger…" Emily gasped. The creature stared.

"WHAT IS YOUR NAME?" It demanded, as it skulked in the background.

Emily's husband cowered as the beastly visage eclipsed his own six-foot-seven-inch frame.

"NAME, NOW!" It pressed with a guttural howl.

"R-Ro-Roger…" He stuttered.

"FULL. NAME. LAST CHANCE, OR YOU CAN JOIN THAT FESTERING INCUBATOR!" The monstrosity gestured toward the carnage. This time, its lips did not curl.

"Roger Parker…" The trembling man spat as if a bug had flown into his mouth.

"Ah, well, this…. This is embarrassing," the creature crouched, eye to eye with the grieving soon-to-be widower. "Seems, there's been a mix-up."

"W-what?" He looked up, trying to stop himself from sobbing. "I don't understand." Emily was still inaudibly calling out to Roger from the floor. The creature still clasped the baby in its clawed hand. "Jacob?".

The intruder turned the child upright, placing it gingerly in front of Roger. The newborn screamed, its crying echoed through the tension-filled air. "Yeah, you see, it's a bit of a funny story actually... I was supposed to be sent to Parker Rogers... and so... Uh-humm." It cleared its throat. Its voice became nasally and went up an octave. "Totally funny mix-up." It lifted its hands as if shrugging, trying to assuage all liability.

"You—my wife, MY son?" Roger was fuming, albeit incredibly terrified. His fists were balled up, the white of his knuckles threatened to force bone through.

"Super sorry man. Uhm. Good- uh... Good luck!" The fierce monster shrunk down and shifted form to that of a small green spider. It swiftly skittered past the newly single father, through the doorway, and shimmered away in the sunlight.

Roger stayed on his knees, eyes wide, staring at the bloodbath before him. His wife, in perpetual silence, frost coating her face, her eyes oozing an orange and black slime. So many of her parts were splayed out on the floor—internal pieces now external. He watched her still-beating heart pump blood. Roger's eyes flickered to tiny Jacob, his body drenched in his mother's debris. He stared at his tiny form, watching as Jacob reached out to be held. The baby appeared unscathed. Roger swallowed hard, his eyes returning to Emily. Char marks peppered her exposed flesh, skinny streams of bright red slowed from multiple lacerations.

* * * *

The tiny green spider crept into headquarters, its legs shakily carrying it on autopilot. A window reflected the small arachnid, and realizing it hadn't returned to normal, it tapped the window several times with each leg. The vile entity sprang up as its regularly fearsome self and stomped all the way to the Information and Assignment Unit Controller.

"Hey Kenny, wrong family…" Its head shook from side to side. "What the home, man?" Stretching a bit, it slid a timecard across the chrome countertop to Kenny.

"Hey Vic, yeah… we saw! What a total shit show—sorry about that big guy." Kenny snatched the timecard with his tentacle, his mucusy trail sliding back down his side. "You did some amazing work today though, we watched most of it."

"Thanks, I always wonder if my technique is a little dated." Vic brushed off his shoulders, "Any word on the kid I was actually supposed to work with?"

Kenny checked the system, typing furiously. He sighed, "Sorry Vic, the mother terminated 'em last week. Must be why the system mixed up."

"Of cooourse! Son of a bitch!"

Both creatures exchanged looks, tension hanging heavily in the air.

"Too soon Vic, too soon." Kenny's engorged eye rolled and he huffed, returning to his work in the system. "You'll get 'em next time, buddy."

LYDIA PRIME is that friendly monster under your bed waiting for you to stick a limb out from beneath the covers. She tends to frequent the nightmares others dare not tread. When she's not trying to shred scraps of humanity from the unsuspecting, she writes stories and poems of the horror and dark fiction variety. Her work can be found on Pen of the Damned (penofthedamned.com), as well as within The Ladies of Horror Picture-prompt Challenge, on Spreading the Writers Word (spreadingthewritersword.com).

Additionally, she has had several pieces published in issues of The Sirens Call eZine. She's been fortunate enough to have edited for Sirens Call Publications, making her no stranger to the publishing and writing world.

Lydia has also had short stories published in both: Under Her Black Wings: A 2020 Women of Horror Anthology, and

Graveyard Smash: Women of Horror Anthology Volume 2, from Kandisha Press.

Her story, Sadie, won the Critters Annual 23rd Readers Poll for Best Horror Short Story of the Year (2020).

Keep up with all things Lydia on your preferred platform:

Facebook: https://www.facebook.com/AuthorLydiaPrime/

Twitter: https://twitter.com/lydiaprime

Instagram: https://www.instagram.com/helminthophobia/

Blog: https://lydiaprime.wordpress.com/

Piano Keys And Sugar
Hadassah Shiradski

~~~~~~

Molly was singing again. Not out loud, but in her head, where Mother couldn't hear her and tell her off for interrupting her brother's playing. Mother didn't like her very much and tended to talk to her brother more, but Molly supposed that was fair, since her brother was the one who could write the best and play the best and help with cooking dinner – when they had enough food, that was. Just as she reached her favourite part of the song, her brother whispered to her to be quiet and let him concentrate so he could get the notes right this time. So, she stopped singing and instead watched Mother's face go all pinched like that time when Molly had asked very politely if she could try playing the piano instead of Jacob. That had been three months ago – Molly had counted! Mother hadn't spoken to or acknowledged her since.

Mother frowned at them and brought her hand down onto the old, battered piano to stop her brother's hands mid-motion. "Alright, that's enough practice for today. Go to your room and get ready to go for a walk." Without the music of the piano covering it up, the crashing storm outside seemed even louder than before – Molly could hear the trees creaking under the onslaught and the tips of the branches closest to the house scraping against the roof-tiles with a horribly unpleasant screech, reminding her of nails against stone. It would be madness to go for a walk in this weather! Molly had done that last year, so she would know.

"Where are we going?" Molly asked, scowling in suspicion. Mother ignored her as usual but Jacob ignored her too, which was odd and maybe slightly mean. Molly didn't understand why; was he angry with her for talking to Mother? That wasn't very fair; Mother was the one who ignored her, Mother was mean to her first, so it wasn't Molly's fault if she started speaking out of turn, right? Sometimes she hated Mother so, so much. So much that she'd once called her a witch when Mother had sent them to bed without any food on a rare day when they had gathered enough to last for a whole week.

As she brooded, Jacob nodded and lifted his hands from the chipped piano keys, standing up to walk out of the main room of their house and clamber up the rickety ladder into their bedroom, which had also been where the family had stored all their food until Mother started thinking that Molly was sneaking more than her share. There wasn't much there besides a single bed, a small cupboard where Molly's bed used to be, and three shelves, all made of wood. Bare.

Molly came with him, of course. She was always with Jacob, from when they woke up until they went to bed. Sometimes, they used their dreams to play with each other and eat houses made of sweets that they couldn't afford when they were awake. Jacob always wanted to make the roof from chocolate, but Molly always told him that *'it would melt like candle wax and stop being a roof, and boiled sweets work better to keep off rain'*. Jacob would always laugh at her for saying that, since *'Why does it matter? Rain can't get you wet in a dream, Molly!'* That was normally when Molly would wake them up and glare at the leaky ceiling above them whilst her brother muttered that having a chocolate roof would keep the howling storm away if only they melted the edges first so that no raindrops could get through.

"What should we bring?" Jacob asked her as he opened the cupboard and dragged his threadbare coat out, pulling it onto their thin body.

"I'm not sure. It's too cold to go on a walk now, but Mother won't let us stay, will she?" Molly's coat was better than his, but Mother had sold it last year after the particularly cold winter, saying that Molly had gone somewhere she didn't need a coat. *'But Mother, I'm right here!'* Molly had said, but Mother had only rolled her eyes and told Jacob to *'stop playing pretend, honestly!'*... Molly had liked her even less since then.

Mother's voice floated down from the main room, harsh with impatience. "We're going! *Now*, Jacob." He jumped at the call and hurried to the ladder, brushing a spider off his sleeve as he went. Reaching the bottom, they stood up straight and went to where Mother was waiting impatiently at the door, but not before Molly swung their arm out and grabbed the tiny stale roll of bread from the table to hold it hidden in Jacob's sleeve so Mother wouldn't notice. Mother lit a lantern with a flick of her wrist and opened the door into the howling wind, looking down the path into the dark forest, and together they set off into the night.

They hadn't even reached the proper start of the trees before Mother grabbed their wrist and started pulling them along, forcing them to run a bit just so they didn't fall over. Molly didn't want to trip and fall and be dragged along like before so instead of following Jacob like she usually did, she hurried to keep up with Mother. Just like the last time when Molly had been taken into the woods like this, Mother didn't look back at them, not even once. Did... Did Mother not like her brother now? Was it something they'd said, something they'd done?

"That can't be right," Jacob replied. *"Mother likes me when I play piano for her, right? A-And when I cut the apples just how she told me to, she —"*

"Agh!" His foot caught on a root and they pitched forwards to hit the ground, ripping away from Mother's iron grip as they fell. Not even stopping to think, Molly held on to him tight and *twisted*, yanking their body around so that they caught a glimpse of the gnarled web above them — bare branches and abandoned bird nests all tangled up together and creaking as one in the wind. They slammed into the frozen dirt. Pain lanced up their side, jarring through their shoulder and crushing all the breath from their lungs as if someone had stamped on it so hard that all their bones snapped like firewood. She coughed, blinked crumbs of soil out of their eyes, and stared at the sideways world as Jacob struggled to draw some air back into his body so he could push them back up before Mother lost patience with his clumsiness and helped him. Neither of them liked it when Mother helped.

As Jacob dragged them back to their feet with the help of the closest tree, she made sure to grab the bread and hold it tighter than before so it wouldn't fall again and get even dirtier than it already was. They would still eat it if it was dirty, of course, but neither of them liked it when the dirt made their stomach hurt afterwards. If they put some sugar on it, would it hide the taste?

"Come on, stop being a cry-baby, and hurry up!" They were crying? Oh. That's odd. Jacob nodded and hastily swiped his hand across his face to scrub away the tears that neither of them had noticed, and they set off again.

Whilst they trailed behind Mother, Molly gently rolled their shoulder to try to lessen the jolts of pain until it faded to a dull – if constant – throb, not even realising that her resentment for Mother had grown ever deeper, as it tended to do. It was a few minutes more before either of them noticed the stinging pain emanating from Jacob's wrist; Mother's nails had torn a path in his skin, criss-crossing like fallen twigs and leaking rivulets of cherry-red blood. Jacob swallowed against the pain and let his sleeve fall back over the cuts, and on they walked for what felt like hours as the winter wind blew, and the trees creaked, and Mother still didn't look back at them, not even once.

The blood began to run down their hand and drip from their fingertips, speckling the frosty ground and dry leaves with blots of red that glistened in the moonlight.

"Mother, where are we going?" Jacob asked at long last, and the witch finally turned her head to glare at them and spit out words like shards of ice that hit Molly harsher than the thin branches that whipped back against their body.

"We're going to a very special place, and you are going to stay there until I come for you. It's for your own good." Mother was lying. She was always lying, and she was especially lying about this. How dare she? How dare she do to her brother what she did to Molly a year ago, what she never thought she would do ever again? She thought Jacob was the perfect child… Or at least, Mother liked him more than she liked Molly. But not enough. Not enough to spare him from what she did to Molly. Not enough to let him keep his sister's coat when she didn't need it anymore. She told Jacob what Mother wanted to do, was trying to do, was going to do, but her brother didn't seem to care as much as she thought he should.

"*Not now, Molly,*" he told her, "*we have to wait until she goes before we do anything- she'll know, otherwise.*" What did he mean? Did he not understand how little time they had left? Jacob sighed and pulled his coat tighter around them.

"*We just have to wait,*" he said. Molly rolled her eyes but nodded in reluctant, stubborn agreement. It was fine, right? It was fine. She knew the way back, so they'd be fine.

At long last, Mother stopped next to a huge, familiar tree that seemed to Molly like it scraped the sky, even though it creaked and wavered just like all the other trees in the forest. Mother grabbed their arm near their bad shoulder and hauled them behind it, shoving them back against the rough trunk.

"Stay. Here." And then she was gone, vanished back through the trees towards the house that Molly knew was somewhere behind them. They wasted no time in running after her, chasing after a spectre back around the ancient tree and through the forest, hurtling over fallen branches and roots that reached up to trip them as they pursued Mother, the one who'd tried to abandon Jacob like she'd left her daughter so many months ago. But Mother didn't know, Mother didn't know that Molly hadn't forgotten the path, because how could she ever forget? And Mother didn't know that Molly was leading her brother back through the maze of skeletal trees because Molly couldn't allow this. She couldn't allow Mother to trick her brother as she'd tricked her, and she would *make her pay*. Jacob nodded in fierce agreement and they charged through the patch of earth that passed as their garden and burst into the house and looked around for Mother.

Jacob spotted her first and Molly flung their hand forwards to hurl the roll of bread at Mother, who turned too slow as they ran forwards and Jacob grabbed her arm, right where Mother liked to hold him too tight, and Molly *pushed* as hard as she could. And the witch stumbled back; one step, two, three. And Molly *thought*, and the smouldering logs burst into bright flames, and Mother tried to get away, but Molly dragged her back in and held her down with a thought and a flick of her transparent hand. And the flames leapt up from the burning logs and licked at her clothes like it was a boiled sweet and Mother let out a terrible scream as her children watched her burn and did nothing to help.

And Jacob's eyes darted up to stare at Mother's agonised face and Molly's followed, she always followed, and– and it was melting, melting down like someone had lit a furnace underneath and … wait – someone had, hadn't they? She had, and Mother was melting, melting, boiling down like sugar cane and maybe they could make a pie? Make a pie out of Mother-sugar and then they'd never be hungry again, never ever ever ever! But wait, was that sound bubbling up through Jacob's – no, *her* throat laughter?

"*Yes, yes it was!*" Jacob screamed the answer back at her through their minds so that she could still hear him over his screaming-crying-laughing-horror and her relieved-amused-laughing-pain because the witch, the witch, the witch was finally burning like she'd burnt Molly's frozen body and it was funny in a terrible sort of way.

It was funny!

And Mother reached out for them with spindly, blackened fingers and a mouth gaping open and choking on ash and they scrambled backwards before she could touch them, and Jacob lashed out with his foot in her general direction as Molly dragged them up and away from the shrieking fire-fuel in the fireplace.

Still laughing, the two of them half-ran, half-stumbled to Jacob's attic bedroom and nearly threw themselves up the ladder, not even pausing to make sure that the blood dripping from his wrist didn't get on the wooden slats as they clambered over Jacob's bed and curled up in the corner, crumpling themselves up like a sheet of music notes. And Mother – Mother was still shrieking as the flames consumed her and took her for their own and would it stop, it wouldn't stop, would it ever stop? Molly didn't know, and Jacob didn't know, and neither of them wanted to listen to such an awful cacophony so one of them slammed their hands over their ears and one of them screwed their eyes tight shut, and then there was only blackness.

And they hid deep, deep down, and did not make a sound.

Silence.

Molly didn't know how long they stayed like that, but eventually, she cracked open their eyes and lowered their hands from their ears. Cautiously, cautiously, they crept back over Jacob's bed and went to the ladder.

"When did it break?" Molly wondered. Jacob told her, only a little shaky, that it must've broken when they'd come in, and that she'd been a bit too distracted to notice.

He dropped down into the living room and they stared for forever and a day at the twig-like heap that had partially spilled out onto the floor and stained it black with sugar-ash. The air smelled acrid, but Molly didn't mind.

Jacob's lips twitched into a hint of a smile and he turned his back on the fireplace in order to walk to the old piano that stood solitary by the wall. She followed him, of course. She always followed her brother when he went to play the piano. But since there was no Mother to tell him off and berate him for acknowledging Molly, his sister didn't stay silent behind him or next to him or in him like she usually did. Instead, she opened her mouth and asked him something she'd wanted to for months.

"Jacob, can I play the piano?"

"Want me to teach you?" Huh? What? "You can't play if you don't know how, Molly!" Oh.

"…Then, could you, please?" A smile, returned. It had been so long since she'd done anything but frown… Molly quite liked this forgotten feeling. Maybe… Maybe they could keep it? Jacob nodded in response to both questions and placed their hands carefully on the ivory keys, and together they played until dawn came and his fingers ached along with his stomach. They had a lot of sugar in the fireplace now, so perhaps they would make a pie with it later, and everything would be just fine.

Right?

HADASSAH SHIRADSKI is a horror writer from Hertfordshire, UK, who graduated with a BA (Hons) in

Philosophy and Creative Writing. Since then, she's been spending her time falling down the rabbit hole of gothic fantasy and quiet horror, where she's been making her home. Twitter: @DassaWrites

Dear Meat

J Snow

Hunting: the least honorable form of war on the weak.
~Paul Richard

I. Winter is A Beast

The cold stretches thin the skin of her face like cracked leather. The wind twists around her, licks her core, her bones. She prefers the darkness of the shadow-cloaked woodlands over dayshine, even when sheathed in ice. Tonight it might save her life.

She runs.

Droves of bloodwood trees crowd the forest. They shouldn't survive here but do — a semblance of hope. When the limbs are cut, sap bleeds bright red as if from an amputated arm, a stark reminder of the massive loss of life she's witnessed in her lifetime. It has become a local religion — these trees are believed to carry and protect the souls of the lost. What began years ago as a memorial, one planted for each death, now outstrips the native oaks, maples, pines. Their bases are decorated with crystalized, crimson stains, striking and distinct, a menacing omen, but it doesn't slow her pace.

She darts through a snow-dusted maze of broken, wind-splintered branches and snarled underbrush, snatches frantic glances behind her. She doesn't keep her focus to her wake, however, but on the faint moonlight parting the trees ahead, just beyond the natural stone wall.

Heartbeats like thunder pound her eardrums, smother the crackling of dead leaves, the snapping twigs beneath her well-blacked hobnail boots as they hammer down on the unyielding earth. Teeth clenched, eyeballs reddened and raw, she pushes herself forward into the clearing, into the white wilderness beyond the camouflage of the wooded realm and its debris.

All is bleak, winter-waxen nothingness.

Just before night settled, the first snowfall of the season. It stretches out before her. Untouched and moonlit, it is a blank sheet, a soft field of glistening powder.

Disoriented, she is unsure of her direction and halts. She turns herself around in slow circles, seeks some familiarity. Strands of sweat-slicked hair cling to her face, sting her flushed cheeks. Utter silence hovers until the decaying leaves, still holding fast to the crown, utter a harsh whisper in the breath of a gale.

An orange glow of flame reflects off the walls of an enormous cave visible in the distance, and hope slides across her with the promise of warmth. She is desperate for shelter from the ice-wrapped, lifeless fingers of the slumbering trees, the creeping fog slipping rings down around the surrounding snow-capped peaks.

I can reach that cave before dawn.

An illusion of safety embraces her, washes away her awareness of vulnerability. She lets out a wavering, nervous giggle, then inhales deep the cold of night to fill her aching lungs. Lifting her right heel to remove the boot, the one with laces too short to tighten around her calf, she dumps the collected snow from its yawning gape. Then, as she sets it down to replant her foot within its dampened interior, she remembers the many tales of wildland traps set by old and wise hunters.

She hesitates. Her despair and desire for a reprieve cascade over logic, and she considers the risks of the cave once more. Her delay is long enough for the quiet to prove itself cunning.

Breaking the stillness, footfalls echo behind her. She whips her head around to its direction, her stare unblinking and panicked. She becomes rigid, listens. He is closing the distance, death a certainty if she doesn't strengthen her lead.

Reason returns, and she bolts back to the treeline, follows her own boot prints in reverse, but banks a sharp left behind the stone wall. She runs its length, puffs heavy breaths like plumes of blooming-white smoke.

His dedication to the chase will never end, and she dares not shorten her stride. She must reach the sanctuary beyond that which her village is named: *Bloodtooth*.

II. Proem to a Solution

"Gentlemen, we must begin eliminating huge sectors of the population. We will first concentrate on the unproductive and poverty-stricken."

The words were impassive, as was the expression of the man speaking them, a malignantly elephantine politician dressed in a pressed, black suit and thin, pale yellow tie, the same pale yellow of the boardroom walls. All members owned a tie of identical color, worn when presiding over a meeting. Soft colors subdued aggressive personalities, made for easier negotiations. Nothing was done without purpose in the capital.

"There are far too many people breathing our air, eating our food, drinking our water, reducing our chances, and they still hold their hands out. It's never enough, will never be enough, and they now threaten our very existence."

Yellow Tie paused, his breath ragged from the physical exertion of standing. He crossed his arms, rested them atop the high back of his chair to ease the strain. "I will not offer up my own flesh to help some ignorant, inbred beggar with an empty belly."

He shook his head in disgust but kept his attention on his audience. Voice like honey, he added, "Never forget: the strong will overtake the weak, but the wise will feast on the strong."

Yellow Tie pressed the circular implant beneath the skin behind his right ear. His six-man assembly, all in similar suites with tight, military haircuts, narrowed their focus to the table's center where an array of images was displayed. None could see what any other saw, each subjected to preprogrammed scenes based on individual variables to achieve maximum impact.

In the muteness of the boardroom, alarmed expressions on every face, each sat upright in response to their tailored scenes of depravity.

Satisfied, the speaker continued. "As you can see, moral corruption is the obvious byproduct of hunger. People turn on each other, become monsters, all for one tiny morsel. Using this to our advantage will prove invaluable."

Yellow Tie clicked off the monitors and cleared his throat. The men turned their attention to him like well-oiled machinery.

"Recall the introduction of HIV in the late 19070s. That virus was our first real attempt to thin the herd. It didn't pan out as predicted, but do not misunderstand," he tapped his index finger on the table for emphasis. "It trickled through the population and took out a huge percentage of other undesirables — drug addicts, prostitutes, prisoners. Every death was a small victory, a step closer to our goal. Even the innocents helped our cause, so we moved forward. Now, many years after implementation, over forty thousand lives a day are lost to AIDS alone."

He stalled to look at each, solemn, stern. "It is not enough."

Yellow Tie took a sip of coffee, again triggered his implant to reopen the holographic exhibits. He eyed the men with scrutiny, looking for any sign of weakness as they watched an era of debauchery dance before them. The effect was the same for all though the grimaces and winces occurred at varying intervals. This pleased Yellow Tie. His team had been well-chosen.

"It takes years to devise a setting for such a successful venture. I point this out because the same concept must be utilized if we are to have any hope of success with our newest endeavour."

Yellow Tie took another sip of coffee, slow and deliberate, allowing time for the suits to absorb the information. He then set his cup on the boardroom table with a brief clink, pulled out his oversized chair, and pushed his girth into a comfortable position on its leather seat.

"Preparations for the project we now undertake began at the turn of the century. In the first quarter of 2000, we began distributions of tainted vaccines, sterilizing one of every five newborns. The effects wouldn't, and didn't, show until proving contamination was an impossibility. Few people knew of this project. It was kept tight-lipped, had to be for success. No doctor knew they were pawns. We couldn't afford to trigger moral righteousness in even one individual.

"Today twenty percent of all people of childbearing years are sterile. We then created impotent men unable to bear fruit through genetically modified foods and contaminated water supplies.

"Still, it's not enough.

"Independent studies show the population growth last year was sixty-two percent higher than projections. Last year, the US alone brought to life over twenty million babies. Twenty million.

"We dropped hints, we asked politely, we begged, all to no avail. We now have to force the hands of the public to achieve any success at all. We no longer have a. choice. We must set *Project Dear Meat* into action."

Yellow Tie paused. He enjoyed melodramatic flare.

"Of course, we won't know if licensing by demographics will turn out a success story or be the very thing to bring us to our knees, not until long after execution, but such is the way of these things. All we do know for certain is we *must* eradicate huge numbers, more than two-thirds of the population as a whole, or we face inevitable extinction. It is just that simple."

III. Prelude to Inquietude

The bell sounded as the door of the shop opened. The butcher looked up. Wiping blood from his hands with a rag, he smiled at his childhood friend. "Hey there, Brady. How's it going?"

Brady didn't smile back. The white-blue flecks of his eyes were muted, his stare vacant and dull. "Not so good."

"What's the trouble?"

"It's Ash. She's going ahead with it. One day left." He dead-eyed the butcher. "One day."

The man behind the counter stopped rubbing his hands with the cloth. "I'm so sorry."

"Yeah. Me too."

"I know it's hard, but it's better for Kira. Little girls are a hot commodity in this wicked world."

"I don't need to hear this shit right now." Brady, eyes like silver lightning, shot the butcher a level stare.

The man held his hands up, palms outward in surrender. "Bad choice of words, wasn't thinking."

Brady relaxed his stance. "It's just…" he sighed and dropped his eyes in defeat. "It's just been a rough couple of weeks."

The butcher went back to rubbing his hands with the cloth. A moment of awkward silence passed before he inquired: "So what can I get you?"

"The usual," Brady muttered, his voice like gravel. "I have a ticket here left for 'family'."

IV. Revelations

Yellow Tie swiveled his chair, turned from his audience before speaking again as if pondering his words. "We are quickly depleting an already scarce food supply. Laws created for the sole purpose of deleting population numbers and retarding growth allowed medications to be distributed that were fatal to certain sectors of the populace. Decriminalization of heroin and other hard drugs led to even more death. It wasn't enough."

None of the attendees looked in his direction as he pressed the button on the small patch behind his ear once again, changing images on their virtual screens to those enslaved by the relentless agony of sluggish death. Frail, gaunt creatures with shame painted on the sallow skin of their haunted faces reflected off the strained eyes of the men. Lifeless eyes stared back at them through an ancient lens. Desperation was etched onto the limp spirits of the grief-stricken public. Not one of the men viewing the scenes appeared empathetic. Yellow Tie's mouth twisted to a sideways grin.

He clicked the button again. "Free tubal ligations and vasectomies for all those of childbearing years, regardless of family objections, free abortions regardless gestation, and, *and*, elimination of any child under two months of age, no questions asked, and still, it's not enough. The population continues to grow. Sustaining it is an impossibility." Another click and the images disappeared.

"If we are not successful, it will be us, our families, *our* lives," Yellow Tie concluded, then peered at each man as they sat back in their own plush chair. Their individual expressions mimicked those on the faces of the others — pinched brows, lips pressed tight and thin. The presentations had been effective in their targeting.

Yellow Tie nodded his appreciation to the men and stood to leave the meeting.

V. Rations

The line was longer than usual this month. Brady hung his head and sighed. It would take at least another hour to get home. The meat from the butcher would spoil soon.

"Adult. Male. Diabetic," the girl called out. Behind her, two assistants grabbed hard squares of plastic from the third shelf down marked *D200* and loaded them into the box at the counter. The prepackaged meals were vacuum-sealed like those of the military during the oil wars, each requiring one tablespoon of water to prepare.

The man standing in front of him reeked of stale, soured whiskey. His clothes engulfed the frail figure. A malodorous mixture of mildew, feces, and the sharp tang of engine grease assaulted Brady's nostrils, left a film of sticky residue on his tongue. He took a step back to lessen the pungent aroma but couldn't help wonder why the old man carried the stench of both homelessness and a garage. Vehicles were obsolete, skeletons that littered roads and yards.

At the counter, the *D200* customer lifted his box and headed to the exit. The old man ahead shuffled forward, the torn soles of his shoes slapping the squares of linoleum. Brady hesitated, relieved to catch a breath of air not wrapped in the ripe stink of a rotting soul. Too many like him roamed the town, and he wondered how they survived on so little.

Brady stood beneath a dim bulb hanging from the ceiling by a thin wire and watched it sway back and forth. It cast oblong shadows across the walls. Caught in the rhythmic movement of light, he turned his thoughts inward, searching for a solution to the horrors he would soon face, to his dilemma, but if one existed, it eluded him.

Every household was allotted precise rations of dehydrated foodstuffs and bottles of distilled water, both distributed using a predefined algorithm for exact calculations by body weight, age, health. In total, every documented citizen living in the United States was provided eight months of life-sustaining provisions yearly. No more. No less.

To supplement the other four months, citizens had to hunt their food. Those unable or unwilling to hunt hid inside their homes until hauled away and slaughtered for failing to 'contribute to the common cause'.

Farming the land was no longer an option. Years of overconsumption had all but eliminated the planet's natural resources — deforestation, urbanization, pesticides, and fertilizers, and countless chemical mishaps stripped the soil of the nutrients necessary for the production of edible vegetation.

Livestock could not survive without either food or water, both of which were far too precious a commodity to share. No vegetation or water meant no livestock. No livestock meant no manure to replenish the exhausted soil. No soil meant no possible option for growing food and maintaining herds.

Government representatives dared not compromise the staggering profits of the wealthy, so shortcuts were made in their favor. Politicians and corporate conglomerates disregarded regulations to control and counter the effects of pollution, in all its forms, and instead reassured voters with winks and smiles and false promises.

"Sir?" The young clerk pulled Brady from his reverie. "Your ticket, please?"

VI. Kill Tags

"Morning, gentlemen," Yellow Tie muttered through a forced smile as he entered the boardroom. It was to be the final meeting before executing *Project Dear Meat*.

"Time is not on our side, so let's get right to it, shall we?" He squeezed himself into the chair at the head of the table, took a swig from his coffee mug. With a hefty sigh only old, fat men can manage, he began the briefing.

"We have divided the population by demographics. Tags will be distributed to all citizens of legal hunting age just as we once did for deer, turkey, and other live game. Compatible weapons, specific for tag use, will also be distributed.."

A suit interrupted. "Guns were outlawed years ago to reduce crime rates. Why would we go backwards on progress?"

"Because guns are necessary for *Project Dear Meat* to work, and because you'll wish yourself on the receiving end of a one if the public doesn't do enough of the killing for us."

"Our expected success rate?" asked another suit.

"If we rely on statistics of the past, when hunting was more for sport than necessity, and consider all other factors involved, such as the steady and rapid decline of resources and an almost detectable slowing of the birth rate (thanks to government interventions), our calculations show a thirty to forty percent decrease in the populace as a whole within the next five years. Being there is a negative correlation between natural resources and people, the numbers should continue climbing until we are able to sustain those within the US borders."

Yellow Tie tapped behind his ear and the image of a graph materialized at the far end of the table. Unlike before, all could see the same. The title read 'Religion'.

He allowed them to study it a few seconds before continuing.

"We need to keep things as simple as possible. Religion has a ridiculous number of categories and subcategories, but as you can see here, we minimized it to include the major three: Christianity, Muslim, and Judaism. The remaining subcategories have been placed under the heading 'Others'.

The suit closest looked to him, confusion pinching his eyes to strained slits. "Why does Christianity have the highest number of members but fewer tags and a shorter season?" he questioned.

Yellow Tie surveyed the room. "This serves multiple purposes. Yes, logic does indeed dictate this category should have a much larger tag number and longer hunting season; however, those in office are Christians. Politicians are exempt, so that point is moot, but the powers that be want their constituents to be of the Christian majority, and we must make the powers that be happy lest we find ourselves removed from the exemption list. The formula for religion tags was created specifically to eliminate more of the minority religions while increasing the Christian percentage. The conversion rate will be staggering as non-Christians are given damn good incentives for swapping faiths. The most devout and loyal to their unholy belief systems will choose martyrdom, but martyrs *want* to die for their religious beliefs. It's a win-win."

"But, sir," a suit with a wide jaw said, "won't this eventually bring us right back to the position we're currently in?"

"We'll make adjustments to tag numbers and seasons and such as needed once we see the actual impact. Then we should be able to project numbers with a fair amount of accuracy and will adjust yearly based on our needs at those times."

Yellow Tie took a sip of his coffee, now cool, and invited more questions before continuing. There were none.

"Notice that 'open season' under the heading of 'others' means at any time any person on this list, regardless of what other exemptions they may hold, are legal to kill. Be glad you are all Christian," he finished with a smirk.

"Sir—" the suit closest to him began.

Yellow Tie, eyebrows hiked, interjected, "I would like to remind everyone all boardroom meetings are recorded. So again, be glad you are all, in fact, faithful Christians."

The suit fell silent.

Yellow Tie cleared his throat. "This is just the beginning, gentlemen. We have yet to cover socioeconomic status, intelligence, profession, and the like, and we have a hectic schedule before us these next few weeks." He paused to take a final swig from his mug.

"One last thing: the standard deviation, there on the last line of the chart," he pointed, and their eyes followed, "reflects the impact hunting will have on refugees and illegal immigrants. We no longer think a heavy influx of wall-jumpers will be a problem once tags are distributed."

The men laughed in unison.

VII. *The Sacred*

Her obviousness is disquieting. She's certain her lead in this chase is temporary. Stricken with the reality he might find she is beyond the gray stones of the wall, she quickens her pace.

Straight ahead, maybe the length of a city block, a single bloodwood stands, majestic and monstrous in stature. The first of its kind here, a headstone planted for the first slain, it is a common gathering place, known by the locals as *The Sacred*. Today it looms in its solitude and beckons her with an illusion of safe refuge.

She is weary, desultory, her momentum waning as she nears the beast of a tree. She's lost count the hours since fleeing her home in wild panic, lost count the minutes since discovering her trail was picked up by the hunter in the wooded darkness.

Determined to reach the towering, silent observer, she pushes herself toward the shelter of its haven.

In her haste, she loses her rhythm, fumbles a double step, and tumbles forward. She flings her hands outward to catch herself but fails and drives herself into the ground chin-first, sliding to the trunk. Snow packs itself up the sleeves of her outstretched arms, into the narrow opening around her neck.

She jumps to her feet and scurries into the shadow cast by the bulky layers of foliage overhead. The branches should be bare, the ground covered with its quietus, but *The Sacred* does not die — it mourns the fallen with sunset colors yearlong.

She presses her back to the tree, shrouded by the eclipse of its elongated canopy. Her fingertips slip into the deep crevices of its fibrous bark to grip the gaps in its massive, gnarled trunk, as wide as three huddled men. She feels tiny beneath its structure but far too visible.

The girth of this sleeping giant separates her from his line of sight if he followed her path. She shivers, not from the biting cold but from fear his icy glare is boring into her backbone. She is too afraid to turn and see if he's gained ground, afraid it will become her truth.

Her desire to survive wraps her in a state of hyper-awareness. The bitter air, as if alive, vibrates around her, but all is quiet save the liquid surge of her own blood. It thrusts fierce through her veins, throbs deep inside her ears like war drums. She is convinced the sound of her pulse reverberates through the still night like yelps of screeching coyotes, but the world around her is soundless. Not a single whisper of breeze disturbs the darkness. Uncanny. Eerie.

Faster, stronger, more stealthy, the hunter should be drawing near. Her boot prints will surely give away her location. Anxiety tightens her ribcage. Not knowing where he is, or how close, proves more frightening than the chase.

A scream builds within the walls of her unraveling mind. She keeps it buried. Her face feels blistered; inside her skull, stabbing knives. She tries to calm her panting, raspy and cracked, swallows hard to ease her stinging lungs, but saliva is chalk in her mouth. She bends for a handful of untouched snow to coat her scratched throat and her stomach rolls over itself. Before she can turn her head, vomit scorches her esophagus and hurls from her mouth with such violence she chokes. Chunks of undigested stew meat spatter the snow at her feet. She wipes the bile clinging to her lips with the back of a gloved hand.

She is struck by the beauty around her in an unexpected instance of sudden clarity. She hadn't noticed, in her frenzied state, the fog had settled across the frost-kissed wild like layered wisps of ghost-white smoke. The actuality of her dilemma does not dissolve into the winterland scenery, but it does seem less dire for the brief period she considers its peaceful allure.

A fat droplet of red slaps her sleeve and startles her bag to alertness. She winces at the contrast: strawberry-red against the white of her coat. She looks upward for its source in the bloodwood crown. Just above, a branch dangles, its sap dripping like sacrificial blood to remind her of her inevitable demise if she holds her position much longer.

She must reach the small village beyond *Bloodtooth*. It holds her only chance for survival. The hunters are unwelcome there.

They will forgive me, she promises herself, takes a deep breath, peels away from the protection of the bloodwood, and heads westbound for the bridge.

VIII. Unholy Vow

Exiting the shop with his box of provisions, Brady heard a familiar voice call out to him. He turned to see the butcher jogging in his direction, still wearing the blood-stained apron, and nodded a greeting.

"Doing alright?" the butcher asked, winded, once the two were standing together. Sincere concern laced his question.

"She has just one day. What do you think?" Brady returned with a resigning shrug.

The butcher shook his head. "Rigged system. I'm telling you. All these years, not one wealthy man or trophy wife or meaty politician on my slab."

"Not one butcher either," Brady added.

"Nope. Not one," he admitted, "but I'll tell you this: if I knew what I'd be doing, I'd never have signed up for this bullshit. Exemption was meant to be a reward. I've lost my family, my friends, my faith, everything. The only reward is death. I was a fool to believe anything else."

The butcher ran a hand through his greasy, black hair. "Children, man. Infants. Babies. So goddamn many. Sleep does not come easy, my friend."

Guilt stabbed Brady in the gut. He hung his head, blinked away his anger. "I guess God hasn't been kind to any of us."

"God?" the butcher scoffed. "What God would bring such nightmares to the innocent? God is an illusion, a creation by the administration to keep all us sheep in check. Nah, I do my work by order of the devils who rule, and if I don't? It's my head on the chopping block."

"Look. I didn't mean—"

"Don't you dare apologize," the butcher interrupted and clasped Brady's shoulder. "I wouldn't trade my hell for yours, not for anything." He let out a sharp exhale and stared with intensity into the eyes of his long-time friend.

Sudden realization stiffened Brady. "I can't ask you to take that risk. I can't live with—"

The butcher held a palm up in protest and shook his head. "I have no one else to lose but me. I welcome that consequence."

Brady's eyes welled with tears. "Don't..." was all he could manage to utter.

"Listen, bud. This probably won't offer much relief," the butcher inventoried their surroundings — left, right, behind and around — before continuing, "but I want you to know she won't feel a thing. Your wife will *not* suffer. Your God can't promise you that," a slow, steady breath, "but I can."

IX. *Escape*

Brady entered the kitchen of their small apartment. His daughter didn't look up from the table or offer a greeting. Auburn spirals hung limp around her pouting face, halfway down her back.

"What's wrong, sweets?"

"Dinner sucks. Same old thing." Kira stabbed at the chunks of meat in her bowl and scowled. "*Stew.*"

He leaned over and kissed the top of her head, then replied: "Chow down. Gotta keep your strength up."

Her tiny frame slumped. She rolled her eyes. "Whatever."

He tilted his head to study her. She was beyond her eight years in many ways. He wondered how much she knew already.

"Where's Mom?"

"In bed," she mumbled, pushed meat around in her bowl like dead goldfish. "Been in bed all day."

His heart froze. He left his daughter to finish her meal, headed down the narrow, unlit hallway with slow but heavy steps. He reached the bedroom door and swallowed his reluctance. His arms hung like boulders at his sides.

Kira fixed on him through her straggling bangs. He shot her a reassuring grin before grasping the knob. Locked, it wouldn't turn.

"Ash?" he murmured.

She didn't respond. Apprehension lay like a bowling ball in his stomach. He rapped on the door with his knuckles. "Ashlyn, honey."

Several seconds passed. Fear washed over him. Then her voice, tiny and hollow, flitted through the wooden barrier.

"I thought I was strong," she moaned. "I thought I could do this. At least for her," a quivering sob disrupted her words, "but I can't. I just can't do it. I'm scared to die."

Brady stood with his hand on the doorknob, his expression blank. Half a minute passed. Tears stung the winter-blue of his eyes. Two minutes. He squeezed them shut, pinched the bridge of his nose.

Can't let her see me like this. Neither of them. Can't turn coward now.

He let out a quavering breath, one he'd held clenched in his chest, then pushed his shoulder into the cheap particleboard. The door popped open.

Ashlyn was gone. The bedroom curtains fluttered in the wintry breeze.

X. *Bloodtooth*

Browline knitted into a frown, the hunter anchors her attention with his hawkish glare.

"*You?*" she gasped.

He lifts his weapon and trains it on her. He responds with a simple nod.

He'd stepped from behind the shrubs lining the bank opposite her just as she'd reached the small deck of the hand-woven rope bridge. He blocks her access to liberation, traps her at the farthest edge of the *Bloodtooth* hunting grounds.

Her defeat is evident in the slight but visible tremors coursing through her petite figure. She is weak from the chase; her hope, deflated. Weighted with physical and mental exhaustion, her prize for reaching her destination is the business end of her husband's rifle.

The two stand staring at each other across the void which divides them. It is but a brief period, though it feels long, drawn-out, endless.

The quiet threatens to devour her sanity, but bone-tired himself, Brady heaves a heavy sigh and breaks the silence.

"Why did you do this, Ash?" he calls out from the landing across the pit. "We agreed euthanasia was best, saving Kira was best. She'd be exempt, but you took that from her." His guttural voice betrays his despair. "I have to give it back."

He places a foot onto the fragile bridge.

She glowered at him with contempt, her eyes like daggers. "I couldn't abort her. I couldn't go through the pain of losing another one."

"Ancient history, Ash. The point is, you broke the agreement."

"I didn't break it. We did."

"Rationalize it all you want, but you know the law: a life must be taken if one is given." His voice shakes. "You *knew* if we had Kira, we'd have to sacrifice a blood relative, a loved one, but you couldn't—"

"*We* couldn't."

"We didn't," he corrects and begins to cross the tethered planks with determined caution. He does not look away but focuses on her trembling lips to steady his rapid heartbeat.

"You left me no choice!" he shouts. He hopes his amped volume will seal his mind to his task. "You chose to give yourself. *You* made that choice, Ash. Not me."

"What other choice did I have? There is no family to sacrifice. Who else is left but us?" Her response is soft and sad.

She places a gloved hand on her tummy. "And who would we give for this one?"

Brady's mouth drops open. He stares at her belly, still flat, hidden beneath the coat.

"No bump yet," she admits, one eyebrow raised, her smile brief, apologetic.

His stunned expression is as if carved in granite. She lets out an almost soundless giggle. "Just nine weeks along,"

Brady doesn't speak.

Her lashes sweep up as she lingers on the hypnotic blue of his eyes. His inability to respond causes her to lose her composure.

"Just let me cross the bridge," she pleads ."I'm safe if I'm not in *Bloodtooth*. The laws don't touch me that side of the world."

"You know that's not true." His words are like snowfall. "You're now on the open season list. No matter where you go, you'll never be safe. The implant was triggered when you crossed the forest boundary, out of tower range." He nods to indicate the wrist resting on her stomach. "Look."

Her dark eyes widen with horror as a green glow flickers against her coat. She jerks her sleeve back to see the blinking light emanating from just below her pale flesh. A shudder cascades down her spine.

"You think I want to do this? You think I want Kira to grow up without a mother?" Tears slide down his face. He ignores them.

"Don't do this to her —" she begins.

His voice rises in pitch. "*You* are doing this to her? It was *your* choice. Remember?"

Ashlyn doesn't respond.

He continues: "We had a plan, but you ran. You *ran*. What choice do I have now?"

"Just let me leave *Bloodtooth*," she begs.

"And go where? You would leave Kira? You'd risk her knowing… everything?"

His eyes reflect the melting moonlight as dawn begins to wake. She weakens beneath the grief in his gaze. Her posture wilts, and guilt twists her mouth into a strained grimace as she weeps.

"It has to be me, Ash. Another will hurt you in ways you can't even imagine, long before pulling a trigger. People are not what you think. They're vile. They're not hungry for human meat. I'm not doing this to her. I'm doing this for you."

"Please don't tell Kira," she squeaks. "Please never tell her what a selfish mother I was."

Brady lowers his weapon. He considers her a moment then blurts, "Come to me. Let's do this like we planned. No one has to know you ran. The butcher will cover your... our mistake."

She tries to speak but can't, shakes her head, her body once again rigid with fear.

"It'll be okay, babe. I promise. You'll fall asleep. That's all. And I'll be there. I'll hold your hand," His words quaver, expose his own despair. "You'll never again have to worry about protecting Kira from the cruelty in this world. It'll be my burden to carry."

She holds her position, mulls over the decision. Brady reaches a hand out in her direction. He takes another step forward on the suspended rafters. Weak, they jerk with his movement. He grabs for the rope-sewn rails with his free hand and steadies himself.

"*Bloodtooth* is not a safe place. The hunters will be out for you soon if they aren't already. I have no idea how long it's been since your implant rang their alarms."

She steps from the snow onto the rotting timber, suspended high above giant, jagged stones like row upon row of shark teeth. They reach skyward from an ice sculpted ravine. Arctic blasts thrash the knotted wood beneath her boots, buckling the warped and distorted rope woven structure. The frayed ropes of the bridge snap.

She grasps the hanging rope railing tight, her body dangling. Her eyes move downward in terror as dawn crests the horizon to illuminate the gulf of blood-covered stones, ominous and hostile.

Bloodtooth, the natural wonder for which her village is named, is a place for suicides. Both the hunters and the hunted come here to end the agonies of cannibal culture. The irony is not lost on her as she prays to live just one more day.

Her shriek echos off the massive rocks below as the resounding *pop* of a gunshot rings out from across the chasm.

All turns to black nothingness.

XI. A Bounty Paid

The butcher had cut and packaged every edible slice, his eyes deep with grief when he'd handed over the bundle.

"Prime cuts, abdominals, and pecs, save for last," was his habitual mantra of sorts when Brady would come to collect his processed kills. That day, the man hadn't spoken a single word.

Sacrifices weren't to be counted toward the kill requirement. They were bonuses, meant as incentives to eliminate what *Project Dear Meat* deemed undesirables.

Ashlyn had not gone to the butcher to give herself as a sacrifice as planned, but the butcher took pity on the family and recorded it as if she had all the same. The alternative meant a tagged kill would be filed.

Beaten and bloodied deaths didn't bother the man; his morality did.

With the sacrifice on the books, he'd ensured the two of them, parent and child, were placed on the exemption list until Kira reached the legal hunting age. The butcher had bought them both eight years of protection.

A documented sacrifice was considered a bounty paid and presented them one more thing: an unused kill tag. Intended as a gift, it came as a burden instead — another human to hunt.

XI. The Last Supper

Stew was prepared from the long, smooth tissue of the heart. Left to simmer as a roast until the meat fell apart, the aroma was mouthwatering, the broth thick and hearty.

She set a bowl on the table for Kira, one for herself.

"Anything new?" Kira asked, scowling at the meal.

"Nope. Same old thing — dear meat."

Kira afforded her an exaggerated eye roll. Then, "When is Daddy coming home? It's been two days." as she stabbed a cube of meat with her fork.

"I don't know."

"Where is he?" she raised the gravy-covered chunk to her mouth.

"Probably stuck at the shop in town because of the blizzard," Ashlyn offered and watched her daughter chew the mouthful, cringed at the sound of swallowing.

"It'll probably never stop snowing." she moaned and peered at her mother.

Ashlyn forced down a bite from her own dish. It proved far tastier than she cared to admit, yet she found it difficult to keep down.

She stole glances at her child. The girl was mature for her eight years but too young to understand the necessity of consuming human flesh for sustenance, too young to know she was a practicing cannibal. Kira would one day be required to hunt her fellow man, would one day herself be hunted like a wild animal.

She wasn't sure the girl would ever be old enough to learn the means of her father's death and thought it best to avoid the topic altogether. The truth was unbearable even for her; guilt threatened to crack her mask.

Kira lifted another bite of meat to her mouth. They should never have let their child lick a human soul.

Ashlyn rubbed the swelling lump of her tummy, eyebrows crinkled, lips pressed tight. Right then she decided Kira would never learn she'd feasted on her own father, brought down with a single shot to the face.

In his wild panic, Brady had dropped his gun, and when the butt slammed onto the crimson-stained rocks, it had activated the firing pin and discharged the weapon. The expelled bullet rocketed upward to meet his horrified expression — a bullet meant for her.

Only she and the butcher would ever know the truth of the first accidental suicide at *Bloodtooth*.

J SNOW is a poet and author who pens psychological thrillers and tales of terror. Her work has been described as disturbing, visceral, haunting, evocative.

Pulling inspiration from personal traumas, she delves deep into the darkness haunting the psyches of both predator and prey. Snow's unique insight into the psychopathic mind allows her to breathe life into harrowing yet multifaceted characters that have both horrified and fascinated those of conventional morality for generations.

Creator of the *Scribblers Chamber* online writing community and founder/editor-in-chief of the literary journal, *Blood Puddles: Night Terrors she Daymares*, Snow holds memberships with P&W, WPN, and NWU.

Her published works include two in a best selling series of *Hellbound Books*, one in an award-winning *Author's Tales* collection, others through *Horrified Press, Zombie Pirate Publishing, Nothing Books, The Horror Zine, Sirens Call, Soft Cartel Magazine, Ariel Chart...*

J Snow is currently working on a memoir series and debut novel.

The One That Got Away
Rebecca Rowland

I'm the one that got away.

Not the one you wanted to marry who said *no*, not the one who smiled coyly at you during third period English but you never rousted up the nerve to ask out. No, I'm that other one: the one you took to the movies freshman year of college, who kissed you wet and long in your dorm room after but never returned your calls in the weeks following. I'm the coworker who flirted with you all fall but didn't attend the Christmas party, then quit the second January appeared. I'm your best friend's fiancé, your boss's daughter, your son's older, wiser *American Beauty*. And I'm back to give you another chance.

When I say *you*, I mean men; preferably, married or otherwise attached men. Men with families, steady jobs, reliable cars, Christmas photos on annual greeting cards, and Disney timeshare vacations. You are so easy to spot, even when your wedding ring is muffled by woolen gloves, or surreptitiously hidden in a pocket. Your look of resignation as you wait patiently in line at the bank in front of me (*Excuse me, but may I borrow your pen? Mine just ran out of ink.*) Your nervous energy hovering along the edge of pained restraint as you walk purposefully through the parking lot (*Gosh, I'm so embarrassed, but my door lock appears to be frozen: would you lend me a hand?*) Your barely hidden exasperation at having to buy a whole case of baby formula, a bright green box of super-strength Tampax, or an industrial-sized can of Metamucil for your prenatal vitamin-chugging wife at the pharmacy at ten o'clock at night (*You are too kind—I am such a klutz, tripping over nothing!*).

As they say in poker, everyone has a tell. Yours are just easier to recognize.

You are so quick to accept appreciation (*You've been so nice: please, let me make this up to you*) and just as quick to acknowledge that my thanks will be in a currency best-kept secret from your significant other (*Do you know that place on Worthington Street? They make great martinis, I hear*). Once you've walked through the door, you've sealed your fate.

We both know where this is leading. Don't play coy with me.

You like to talk. You're lonely. Unappreciated. The little missus? She never has time for you anymore. You tell her a story, an instant replay of that work confrontation, a summary of the playful row with the guy in the next cubicle or the misunderstanding between you and the Millennial barista, again and again and again, but—*What was that, dear? Of course I was listening; you do plan to mow the lawn this weekend, don't you?*—she's no longer your captive audience, your ready defender, your biggest fan. She has tuned out, dropped out, phoned in. I understand, and I'm here for you with a sympathetic ear and a razor-sharp memory.

Of course, that makes it easy as pie to find out everything I need to know about you. In this age of social-media-cum-perpetual-narcissism, I know that if you don't have an active Instagram or Twitter account that provides regular updates on your job, Saturday barbecues, and closet obsessions (why are you following a Facebook group on bizarre taxidermy nightmares, exactly?) it's a sure bet you have a spouse who does. It's the rule of overcompensation: the more of a straying dog you've been, the happier Stepford-family posts your wife will display for the world to view. A desperate ploy to convince everyone, including herself, that everything is just fine, that your increased irritation with her, lack of interest in the bedroom, and well, sudden regular gym attendance is *definitely not* because you have a pussycat girl on the down-low. No, you're just distracted from work, and after working all of those late hours, isn't it selfless of you to make certain you're taking the best care of your health so that you can be there for her and the kids?

So, I sift through your Thanksgiving snapshots, trying not to judge your goofy selfies at the Cape Cod waterpark, ignoring the halfhearted *Like* emojis you slap under each of the Mrs.'s pics of her latest casserole, your daughter's dance recital, and the whole brood wearing matching pajamas, crowded around the television to watch Green Bay finally secure that Super Bowl trophy. Within a fortnight, you're thankful for my coming into your life. You can't remember being this happy before I did. Finally: a woman who anticipates your every desire, who seems to know what you need before you ever vocalize it to her. A girl Friday, aide-de-camp, abettor, and attendant, not for your paperwork but for your personal pleasure.

I've been a partner in crime to so many of you.

First, there was the city planner. Three kids, a dog, and a mousy wife with stringy hair and a pained expression in every family photo op. His fiscal year budget granted a surplus of new iPhones for the whole staff: surely they wouldn't miss one? And wouldn't you know it—I left my beaten-up Android on the subway last night. I'd never want to be out of touch. I am always appreciative of your generosity, and of a phone that allows me to switch numbers as easily as flipping a SIM card.

Then there was the redheaded HVAC mechanic with the stretched lobes, arm sleeve tattoos, and pregnant wife bedridden with twins on the way. My condo fees were becoming exorbitant, and wouldn't you know it? They don't cover heating repair. How toasty and warm I was that winter with the installation of a new furnace. And to think it was a manufacturer return that was lost in the mail? My luck could not have been better.

The childless beat cop who raised Weimaraners and complained about his wife's dismissal of his Cross-Fit discovery didn't last long, but it was his name I dropped when I was caught making out in a parked car in the back of the movie parking lot. Yeah, that's right: I'm a friend of Jerry's. We were gym partners—you know, he threw the big tire as I air-jogged to nowhere on the elliptical. *Of course* I'll give his poor widow your condolences at the memorial this weekend. The body shop mechanic with the four-year-old son and ten-year-old marriage was more than happy to come to my aid when a hit-and-run damaged my front fender—one late night at the shop is worth it for your special girl—and the short-statured locksmith with the guitar-playing girlfriend helped me out in a caper or two until he got a little too clingy.

It always happens. You think you're getting the best of both worlds: cake and eating, fork and spoon, a family and a fantasy, and I am around just often enough to leave you satisfied but elusive enough to make you crave me for days following. When you call on a Tuesday and it goes straight to voicemail, you assume I am with my mother, I am shopping with friends, I am working late. I must be driving and don't want to endanger other commuters. I must be on the train, outside of service range. But it's an hour later, and I still do not pick up. Am I with someone else? Have you been replaced? Your mind races, panic sets in. Maybe you should set me up with an apartment. That way, you'd know I was safe and sound. The hotel charges are adding up to a monthly rental anyhow.

Oh, there will be no evidence tying me to you, your family, or your circle of friends. We're strangers, and we'll stay strangers, long after you've booked and paid for king bed suites while I wait patiently in my own car until it's safe to make my way up the elevator to meet you inside. We'll never go to my house (*I have a cranky roommate, a sick dog, an active neighborhood watch: it's just too risky!*), never discuss my day job (*I'd put you to sleep, it's so boring! Besides, I'm much more interested in hearing how YOUR day was, darling*), and never quite commit to which high school I attended or what year I graduated: those pesky Classmates pages and Facebook alumni groups can be so informational.

Your wife will cry fat tears for the media. If only you hadn't been so stressed at work: maybe you wouldn't have mixed those Xanax and martinis. She didn't even know you had a prescription: no one did! You must have secretly procured the pills from a friend out of desperation.

Your wife will wear her best navy pantsuit to your wake. Poor thing: you ran yourself ragged, between your job, your family, and your workouts—it's no wonder your reflexes were too weak to prevent that terrible fall from the fourth-floor balcony at your company's flat. You were such a trooper, dropping off a last-minute welcome basket for the visiting client who was due to check in the following morning.

Your wife will file her claim on your life insurance within two weeks after she's mailed her last thank you for the condolence cards. You were a provider right up until the end, and even afterward: it's so tragic that the jack spontaneously collapsed on your Nissan while you were stranded on the side of the road with an inopportune flat. Just one swift kick and down it went. They should really make those zippy sports coupes higher off the ground.

And me? Oh, I'll be simply devastated to learn of your passing. You were so kind to help a stranger in need, and so personable once we met... and of course, the fringe benefits were lovely as well. But I'm off to the bank: I want to make a quick transaction before the sun sets and it gets really chilly. I never know how my car locks will perform once the wind starts blowing.

Look for me, and you'll glance right past me. I hide in plain sight.

I'm the one that got away... over and over again.

REBECCA ROWLAND is the author of the short story collection The Horrors Hiding in Plain Sight, co-author of the novel Pieces, and curator of the horror anthologies Ghosts, Goblins, Murder, and Madness; Shadowy Natures, and the upcoming The Half That You See and Unburied: A Collection of Queer Dark Fiction. Despite her love of the ocean and unwavering distaste for cold temperatures, she resides in a landlocked and often icy corner of New England. For links to the cutting-edge and kick-ass publications where her short fiction has appeared most recently (or just to surreptitiously stalk her), visit RowlandBooks.com. To take a peek at what she's fixating on these days, follow her on Instagram @Rebecca_Rowland_books.

ABOUT THE EDITOR: Jill Girardi is the author of Hantu Macabre, the internationally best-selling novel featuring punk rock paranormal detective Suzanna Sim and Tokek the toyol. The book shortlisted for the 2019 Popular/The Star Readers' Choice Awards. Suzanna and Tokek will also be taken to the big screen, as a full-length film based on the characters is set to start shooting in 2021, with former MMA Fighter Ann Osman starring as Suzanna. Jill currently lives in New York where she is the editor of the Kandisha Press Women of Horror Anthology books. Please find her on Instagram/Twitter @jill_girardi

LIKE WHAT YOU READ HERE?

PLEASE CONSIDER SUPPORTING KANDISHA PRESS AND OUR AUTHORS BY GIVING US A REVIEW ON AMAZON, GOOD READS OR BOOK BUB!

ATTENTION ALL WOMEN HORROR AUTHORS:

If you are interested in submitting your work for consideration for a future Kandisha Press Women of Horror Anthology, please get in touch with us for submission guidelines and upcoming deadlines!

WOMEN OF HORROR VOLUME 4 COMING JULY 2021

FACEBOOK: @KANDISHAPRESS
TWITTER: @KANDISHAPRESS
INSTAGRAM: @KANDISHAPRESS

WWW.KANDISHAPRESS.COM

Made in the USA
Middletown, DE
06 February 2021